Dangerously Forbidden Love

Copyright

Paperback ISBN: 978-1-961966-32-1

Published by: Carxander Publishing
Minnesota

Opening Quote

Now the door is open. The world I knew is broken. There's no return. Now my heart is not scared just knowing that you're out there watching me. So, believe I'll be here waiting, hoping, praying that this light will guide you home. When you're feeling lost, I'll leave my love hidden in the sun for when the darkness comes.

When the Darkness Comes by Colbie Caillat

Chapter One

⚔ Ryan ⚔

It's been one hell of a fucking week. I've had just about enough. Of every-fucking-one. Sitting on the couch in my penthouse suite in Chicago with my eyes closed is the only way to keep myself from tearing the world apart piece by fucking piece.

I love my family. More than anything. I'd do anything for them. They all know that. The issue, is they wait too fucking long to pull me in. I solve problems. It's what I do. But solving problems is a lot easier when the problem doesn't explode into a fucking supernova. And I typically don't get the fucking call until that happens.

"I need a fucking break." I lean my head against the back of the couch and force myself to breathe. I close my eyes and rub my temples.

It's been one thing after another for me for the past two years. First, my sister-in-law and having to save her from the Lucinio mafia. We were able to take Matthew Lucinio, the leader, down, with the help of Alex and Josh, Matthew's twin sons. Josh took his rightful place as leader. Alex, who's like my brother, is helping him out.

Then, a piddly ass gang tried to move into my area in Miami. Didn't end too well for them. Then, a few people in Paris were getting a little out of line. Also didn't end well for them. My faction in L.A. nearly fell to shit with epic spectacularity. A mafia I thought I had eliminated came back from the fucking grave. I lost a couple good men, even though I teamed up with Josh and Alex. The other mafia was decimated.

Then, I get a call from my brother, Taylor. Well, I adopted him as one anyway. His brother's girlfriend and her sister ended up inadvertently involved with the fucking cartel. I took the cartel out and cleaned up the town they were from in Minnesota. And the three cartel dickwads who were fucking with their lives lost theirs.

As if all that wasn't enough, last week, I get a call from Taylor that is wife was in the fucking hospital. A small-time gang was trying to shake her down. I could almost believe that. Almost. Small-time gangs pop up all the time. They think they can grow and run the town by doing stupid shit, like shake down small-businesses.

The problem? The small-time gang was after my territory. Not small businesses. They were targeting my area. They took over a few small areas in Chicago, but they were all my areas. They went after Nicole and her bakery last, after they'd had her entire block. Which was located in my territory. Put my little sister in the hospital.

When will they ever fucking learn? People don't fuck with me. It never ends well. Ever. I always win. I'm not one of the most powerful men in the world by fucking chance.

I've never believed in chance. I got where I am with hard work. I expanded this mafia to a level beyond even my wildest dreams. I don't believe in chance or coincidence. Everything happens for a reason.

And because of that deeply rooted belief, I'm starting to feel like all of the shit over the past few months is connected.

There are so many things that don't make sense to me. I could almost believe that everything that happened in Minnesota with the cartel was just some fucked up thing Breetana and Nicole got caught up in. It wasn't their fault their exes and their uncle just wanted to ruin their lives. But throwing in the cartel is convenient. Too fucking convenient.

Above and beyond all of that, I found out that my girlfriend's dad is trying to marry her off to another mafia to combine them. Finding out that they wanted to combine to take me out? Arianna's father knows how big my mafia is. There's no way he could take me on and win the battle. Even if he did combine with another mafia.

I know all of the mafias in New York. I have to. It's part of my job. An important part. I know there's no mafia in the entire state that he could combine with to take me out. He could combine with all of them and still not be big enough. Unless he allied with the Lucinio mafia. They're the only ones big enough. Since they're allied with me, I know that ain't fucking happening.

It's all too convenient. Too much of a coincidence that all of these events are occurring. I don't like it, and it pisses me off that I can't figure it out. Something about all of this isn't right. I know I have a huge problem. And I fucking hate that I don't know what it is.

"Ryan?" The sweet voice behind me makes me smile. She's always been able to do that. No matter how pissed off I am. No matter how much I'm brooding.

"Aria?" I don't open my eyes.

"I know you told me to go to bed, but I just wanted to check on you. I know you've had a hard week, and I'm not helping." Her voice is so incredibly soft and sad, it nearly breaks me.

I sigh and drop my hands from my head to my side. I keep my eyes closed for fear my head will explode if I don't. "I'm fine. Just need a bit of time to center myself again."

"O-okay. I-I'm sorry. I know you've been busy. I'm sorry this happened, and I couldn't leave you to deal with this Chicago... mess."

I take a deep breath and hold it a second, willing my head to behave as I open my eyes to look at her. She's biting her lower lip and wiping away a tear. Fuck me. The biting of her lip turns me the hell on. I can't help it. My girlfriend is incredibly beautiful. But seeing her cry…

"Aria. Come here, baby." I can't stand to see her cry. I don't give a damn about any other woman. But my mother, my three sister-in-law's, and her start crying, I'm done for. I'd give anything to make them stop.

Arianna walks towards me, still chewing her bottom lip. She sits next to me, and her scent immediately overpowers me. Jasmine. It's my fucking kryptonite. She's my kryptonite. And she knows that. Better than anyone.

I pull her close because I need to feel her. Touch her. She closes her eyes and cuddles into me as I run my fingers through her hair. She knows what she does to me. She's felt me against her, though I've never done anything but hug her or kiss her. I've held her close. I refused to do

6

more with her because a romantic relationship with her had been so forbidden. She just turned eighteen today.

"Don't ever think that you can't call me. That I'm too busy for you. I don't care what I'm doing. I'd drop everything for you, sweetheart."

"It's just that..." She trails off and buries her head in my shoulder. I play with her hair, gently tugging it because I know she loves it when I do that. She puts her arm across my lower stomach, just above the waistband of my jeans. "I'm so scared."

"I know you are. But I'm not going to let anything happen to you."

"I hate him."

"I know, baby."

Our plan to get her away from her dad hadn't gone the way we wanted. This morning, the plan was she would walk up early and leave. She'd walk out the door and call me. Taylor and I had a plan. We had someone meeting her. She was going to be driven to my brother's, Jason's, office, and Nick, my other brother, was going to escort her by private plane from Manhattan to here. Chicago.

The problem was that her father surprised her. He was awake and sitting on the couch with the fucker he wanted her to marry. She still hasn't told me who he is, and I've been way too far in my head to figure it out on my own. He told her she would be marrying him. That their mafias would combine, and they would take me down. She tried to run. They chased her. She fought them off.

She hasn't told me everything, but the fact that it was her eighteenth birthday, and I was not only not there, but also not there for her when something happened, is slowly killing me. She was in a panic. Which threw me into a panic when she called me. I never panic, but I had to give my phone to Taylor so I didn't cause her to panic more. When he finally got her to calm down enough to tell us what happened, my blood turned venomous.

Combining.

To take me out.

I still can't fucking believe it. I could call in people from everywhere and cause all of Manhattan to shut down because of the hell I'm capable of raining down on them. The police would just sit there and fucking watch. But an all out war isn't my style. I prefer direct attacks.

Stealthy. My enemies never know when I'm coming until it's too late for them.

"The guy he wants me to marry? He's more mean than my father. He scares me even more. When I told him I'd never be with him, he threw me on the stairs and straddled me. And then he pulled my hair really, really hard and made me look at him while he told me that I'm already his."

My grip on her hair inadvertently tightens. She's been telling more and more of what happened as the night goes on. It's another reason I haven't pressed her too much about it. She's processing things and tells me more and more as she's able to find the words.

I let out a low and dangerously possessive growl. "I swear to God, Aria, he won't touch you. I told you before. No one touches you but me. You're mine, baby. Not his. No one else's. Mine. And it's different now that you're eighteen."

"It made me feel like I'm just property to both him and my father."

"Fuck, Ari. Come on." Those words hurt, though, I know how fucking true they are.

"I do. My father has never treated me as more than that. And, honestly, neither has the guy my father is forcing on me."

"I know. But you know better. I've never treated you like property. I never will, Aria, and I'm the only one that matters."

She's quiet for a moment before she takes a deep breath. "What did you mean? When you said it's different now that I'm eighteen? How is it any different than before? Other than that we don't have to hide and can be together? I mean, I know all of that. We can just be. But I know that's not what you meant."

I smile into her hair and kiss her head. My girl is smart. "I couldn't go after him before. I could only tell you to run to me if you needed to get out. Or call. I couldn't do anything about him because you could get caught in the crossfire. You being promised to that other guy could have caused a lot more chaos that put you in more and more danger with every move I made. Now? I can tell everyone you're officially and finally mine. I have the claim on you. And you know that's not what it is for me, but you also know how different mafias run. Claims on women by powerful leaders means everything. Which means I can keep you the fuck away from him and do what I wish I could've long ago."

"When he killed my mom?" The words are barely above a whisper. My heart breaks for the fiftieth time today. She fists my shirt in her hand like she's using it to anchor herself. That day was hard for me, but it was far, far more difficult for Arianna.

"Yeah."

A few years ago, I met Arianna's mom at a bar. She was celebrating her newfound freedom after her divorce was finalized. I'm not typically one for second dates, but that girl was sweet. Fun. Interesting to talk to. First girl I picked up in a bar and didn't sleep with. When I picked her up for our third date, she had to cancel. Her daughter, fourteen-year-old Arianna, was having a pretty shitty day. Her teacher gave her an "F" on a paper because her resources, while cited, were not cited properly.

Arianna was really upset and didn't know what to do. She'd never failed a class. She was a straight A student. I knew she was hiding something. So the next day, I met her at her school for lunch. She was surprised to see me, but within seconds, the entire story came rushing out. She turned down this teacher's unwanted advances, and he was retaliating.

It was her last class of the day, so I told her I'd be back to pick her up. I texted her for the classroom number so I could be outside the door waiting for her. I had every intention of having a civilized conversation with the motherfucker. Right before I got him removed from his position as a teacher and crushed his career hopes under my size twelve boot.

Sure as shit, he kept her after class, as I suspected he would. He asked if she was willing to give in or if she wanted to fail. The fucker was touching her. A fourteen-fucking-year-old girl. I casually walked into the classroom. He was surprised as hell when I shoved him down on his desk and wrenched his arm behind his back enough to hear a nice, audible pop. I told him if he touched her and used her grades as leverage to make her fuck him, the next thing I break will be his other arm, both legs, and then his dick.

He never touched her again and no longer has a job teaching anywhere.

After her mother was killed, the very next night after my encounter with the teacher, Arianna was forced to live with her dad. I made sure she knew that she could always turn to me for anything. She started doing just that over the years, mostly when her father was treating her like shit. I was

9

able to get her out of dodge for a little while with dinner and a movie, or a walk. Whatever she wanted.

"Thank you, Ryan. I... don't know what I'd do without you."

"You know I'd do anything for you, Aria. Anything."

"I know."

"You aren't going to have to marry this guy. I won't let it happen. Even if we weren't together, baby, I wouldn't let it happen. Like I said before. I didn't want you caught in the middle of a war with him. Now that you're with me, and we're officially together, I don't have to worry."

"Thank you for always protecting me."

"Always, Aria. Always."

I rub my fingers soothingly up and down her arm. She burrows into my side, draping a leg over mine and dropping her arm lower so that her hand is directly on my cock. I suck in a breath and take her hand.

A couple of years ago, I started having serious feelings for her. More than just friends. I refused to acknowledge them. I did all I could to ignore them. Until one day I found out she had the same feelings for me. We talked. I said we needed to take things slow, and I meant it. I wouldn't touch her while she was under the age of eighteen. I still won't touch her until she's ready for me to. She's not ready for that aspect of our relationship yet.

Not that I don't want it. I know she does, too, but not like this.

"Aria. Bed. Now," I groan.

She jumps up, realizing where her hand had been, and puts a hand over her mouth. Her eyes go wide as fucking saucers. She can't take them away from my large, very on display cock. She's fucking sexy as hell. I chuckle. While she's felt me against her, she's never touched me. I've never let her.

"I... I'm so... I..." She looks at me quickly before quickly standing. She turns and flees from the room. I don't move until I hear the door to the second bedroom in the suite close.

I don't know how in the hell I fell for her, but I did. Fucking hard. I sort of feel like a dirty old man since she is so much younger. I absolutely hate myself sometimes because I fell for her before she was even of age.

I need a cold fucking shower to get rid of the raging hard on I have right now. It's not the first time I've ended up in a cold shower after being near her. Not only did my morals refuse to allow me to take things further with her even though the law said I could've, Arianna is also a virgin. While she's dated, she's never let anyone else touch her.

Despite everything that happened, we were both happy she turned eighteen yesterday. It meant we didn't have to fight just being together as couples would be. I can freely kiss her and touch her without the feeling of being a pedophile.

Still, I refuse to ruin our very new relationship by pushing her into something she isn't ready for. And if she had kept her hand where it was, even though she didn't know it was there, I'm not sure I could've resisted letting her explore, considering how badly I want her.

No. Letting her continue to touch me for my own pleasure isn't fair to her, and I love her far too much for that. She needs to come down from everything that happened. That's the priority.

Sexual release for me, though, might take the edge off and get me out of my own fucking head for a little while.

The more I think about everything that's happened, the more I'm convinced there's something far bigger going on.

And I won't rest until I figure it out.

XXX

After my cold shower and intense session of jacking off, more than once, I step out of the shower and dry off. I wrap a towel around my waist and head out of the bathroom.

I inhale sharply when I see Arianna sitting on my bed. It makes me inwardly groan. Her on my bed is sexy as hell. "Good fucking thing I decided to wear a towel. How much of that did you hear?"

"U-um... A lot?"

She looks down at her hands, and I grin. Part of me wants to get her the hell away from me to save her from how badly I want to touch her. But that's not the part that is in control anymore. She's the one in control. There's no way I'd be able to resist her anymore if she touched me.

"I thought I told you to go to bed?"

"I tried."

I sit down next to her. My cock is immediately hard. Even after getting off four times in the damn shower. "Try harder."

11

She bites her lip. Fucking adorable. It's killing me. My eyes fall immediately to her lips. All I can think about is kissing her. Tasting that vanilla bean lip gloss.

"I don't have anything to sleep in. I didn't think to really take anything other than me here. I just wanted to get away."

I smirk. Despite the gravity of those words, it's too easy to tease her. It may become my new favorite thing to do. "Sleep naked."

"Ryan!" Her cheeks flush. She playfully shoves me.

I laugh. "Alright! Alright. Do you want a t-shirt? We can go shopping and get you whatever you need tomorrow."

She nods. I decide to be serious and get back to ignoring my reaction to her because it's best for everyone. I'm really trying to be good and let her do this at her pace. Not when she's as upset as she is. I get up to find a t-shirt and hand it to her. She stands and walks into my bathroom. I raise an eyebrow, but don't question her as I quickly pull a pair of boxers on. I crawl into the bed just as she comes out. She isn't carrying her clothes.

"Aria? Where's your clothes?" I freeze in place. She doesn't answer me as she crawls into my bed with me. Uh oh. I swallow. Hard. "What the fuck do you think you're doing?"

"Please don't make me sleep alone, Ryan. You know how scared I am right now."

"I also know that no one is going to get to you on the hundred and second floor."

"Please?"

I sigh as I look at her. In my t-shirt.

In my bed.

I'm going to end up on the couch. "Honey. You felt me on the couch. I know you didn't mean to touch my dick, but you did. You felt how hard I was. You've felt me against you before. You heard me in the shower. I have no idea why you stayed in this room after hearing me in there. Especially knowing what you do to me and how hard it's been for me to resist you. Do you have any idea what you being in my bed is going to do to me?"

She looks at me with the saddest eyes I've ever seen. I know this conversation just ended. "I just don't want to be alone. I'll sleep on the chair in the corner if you want me to, but I feel safe with you near me. And

I really am scared. I trust you. I know you won't do anything unless I say it's okay. I'm just scared, Ryan. Please let me stay in here with you. It's nothing different than laying together on your couch watching movies together."

I watch her for a few moments before closing my eyes and letting out a breath. I can't say no to her. Never have been able to. "The difference is you're in my bed. It makes it harder not to finally feel you underneath me. You can sleep in the bed as long as you understand you're fucking killing me right now. I'm trying to let you take this at your pace, Aria. You're not making it easy on me."

"I know. I'm really sorry. I'll stay over here. I-if it makes it easier for you to take things slow with me. Like you have been."

She succeeds in making me feel like an asshole. I groan low and finish getting into bed. "Baby, I'm not going to be a dick and make you sleep on the edge of the bed. It may be hard for me, but if you're scared and you need me to feel safe, I'll be here for you. Just sleep with your back to me and watch your hands." I give her a teasing grin and wink that makes her blush.

She nods, not acknowledging my teasing. It makes me sigh because I was hoping I could lighten things for her a little.

The reality, though, is I need to protect her. I can't do that if she runs away from me because I gave in before she was ready for me to. Not like I would dream of doing anything she didn't want me to anyway.

I reach over to shut the light off. She curls up next to me with her back to me as I told her to. I put my arms around her. A few moments later, wrapped in my arms, she falls asleep, and I'm truly happy I have that effect on my girl.

Quite a while later, I finally drift off only to be woken up by Arianna screaming. "No! No! Please, stop!"

"What the hell?" My arms are still around her, but she fights me.

She elbows me in the chest, knocking the wind out of me.

I'm forced to flip her so I can hold her arms over her head.

She starts kicking.

"Holy shit." My heart skips a beat as she fights me with all of her strength. "What the hell is happening?" I straddle her and pin her to the bed, her arms still over her head. "Aria! Hey! Wake up, sweetheart. Wake up, baby. Come on." I gently caress her cheek with my free hand as she starts calming down and coming to.

She's so small, I can hold both of her wrists with one of my hands. I'm six feet five and built of solid muscle. She's maybe five feet. I tower over her and easily control her movements, which I realize all at once is fine when it comes to me, but she needs to be taught what to do in situations like this to protect herself if someone is trying to hurt her.

"Ryan?" Her cheeks are wet. I don't know what she dreamt, but whoever instilled that much fear into her is fucking dead.

"What the hell was that about?"

"J-just a bad dream."

I let her arms go and roll off her. She immediately curls into my side.

I let out a breath as I lay on my back and put an arm around her. "So? You gonna tell me?"

Her arm snakes across my lower stomach just above my waistband again. The feel of her bare skin against mine is breathtaking. It always makes my heart feel like it stops beating.

"I just dreamt that Chad, the guy my father is forcing on me, caught me. He took me somewhere private. Where no one could hear me scream."

"Baby. I won't let him touch you. I won't, Aria."

"He tied me up and cut my clothes off. And then he started cutting me." She chokes back a sob. I hug her as tightly as I can. I have no idea who this guy is, but I'm going to. And he's about to wish I never found out.

"I will *not* let him near you. That shit is over now. You aren't going back there. You're mine now, baby. No one will dare fuck with you now." She presses her lips against my chest. I look down at her. I fucking love when she kisses me so sweetly like that. I kiss the top of her head.

She shifts slightly so that she's as close as she can be to me. After a few minutes of silence, I fall asleep to her even breathing with her safe in my arms.

I stand over the stove in my suite with my arms folded over my chest glaring at the pan in front of me.

It really isn't the bacon's fault I'm in this mood. It's the fault of the person who texted me an hour ago threatening my life. I'm really not afraid. I don't believe for a second he could take me out.

No.

I'm pissed off. I'm pissed off that Arianna's douchefuck of a father thinks he can intimidate me into turning her over to him. He obviously has no idea who I am.

I growl irritably and flip the bacon. The fact that this is all over territory really gets under my skin. Selling his own daughter to amass enough support to attempt taking down someone more powerful than he is seems like a huge stretch.

And stupid as fuck

I take the bacon out of the pan and put the slices on a paper towel to drain excess grease. I feel a pair of silky arms snake around my waist. Just like that, the tension releases.

I smile. "Always know how to make me feel better when I'm brooding."

She presses herself against my back and squeezes. "I saw the text. You left your phone on the bed. I didn't mean to look, but when I rolled over, I expected you and found your phone. It opened when I touched it."

"Aria, I don't care if you look at my phone, baby. I have nothing to hide from you."

"I'm just saying I wasn't trying to, though."

I take her hands in mine, mine engulf hers, and turn to her, taking in the sight of her in one of my dress shirts. I clear my throat. "What... uh... happened to the t-shirt?"

"Oh... I was kind of cold. I can put something else on. If you want."

I smile down at her and take her face gently in my hands. "Trust me when I say you make my clothes look better than I do." I give her a sweet kiss. I love that I get to kiss her now without a war waging inside me about if I should or shouldn't do it even if I told her I would.

"You don't look so bad yourself, you know. There's something so sexy about a man in jeans. Especially when he's mine." Her eyes roam appreciatively over my shirtless physique.

I laugh. "Lucky for you, I own a lot of jeans."

"Very lucky."

I kiss her again before turning back to breakfast. She sits on a stool at the kitchen bar and watches me.

"Did you turn your GPS off like I told you to?"

"Oh. Um. Yes. Actually, Jason made me leave my phone with him. To make sure," she tells me. I smile. My brother may have walked away from this life to start his own life, but he still has my instincts when it comes to protecting loved ones. "I'm sorry my dad is after you."

"I'm not worried about him. He seems to think he can intimidate me because that's what he does to everyone, but I don't scare off easily. And he has no chance in hell against me anyway." I finish breakfast and put it on a plate.

Arianna's eyes light up. "Quesadillas?"

"Yes."

"My favorite."

"I'm well aware."

"Nothing gets by you. Does it?"

"Wouldn't be where I am otherwise." We both eat in silence for a few minutes.

"This suite is really nice. It's like a two bedroom apartment."

"It cost a lot more."

She laughs. "Not afraid to flaunt that, are you?"

"Very few things I'm ashamed of, baby girl." I smile as she laughs again and starts to get up to put her plate away. I hold her back with a hand on her bare thigh. I relish the feeling of her silky skin. "There's a couple things we need to go over."

I don't know how she's going to take any of them, but I do know that I won't allow her to feel like she isn't safe with me. Like there's anything she needs to worry about. Specifically being dragged back into the clutches of her father, and forced to marry anyone she doesn't want.

Not like I'd ever let that happen anyway. Arianna has been mine ever since I let myself admit my feelings for her. Maybe even before that. My only hope right now is that she'll go for the plan I've come up with and not think it's too soon to say yes.

Chapter Two

☒ Arianna ☒

Ryan's hand on my bare thigh is both comforting to me and warm. I don't know what it is about him, but even when he looks like he's upset about something, like he does right now, he's always been able to soothe me.

I swallow as he starts rubbing his thumb lightly back and forth across my skin. "Oh?" I finally manage to squeak out.

He nods and squeeze's my thigh. I bite back a moan and question why his touch consistently lights me on fire.

"We can get you a phone today. Don't give your number to anyone unless you talk to me first. I don't mean to sound like a controlling asshat, but it's for your own safety. You need some clothes. So, we can go shopping, but you don't leave my side. I mean that."

"Do you think he's here? My father?" Fear immediately rises.

"No. But I won't negotiate on your safety. Also, I own this building. It's one of the most secure buildings in the world. Nick does security for all of my buildings and all of Jason's, Alex's, and Josh's. The glass on the windows is bulletproof. It's thick. It won't break unless you fly a helicopter through it. And even then, I'm not so sure. But that being said, you need to get your picture taken for the security system."

I blink, slightly confused. "Why? Are we staying in Chicago?" I silently beg him to say yes.

"Because without it, you won't have access to this floor. I need to get you a key card. You also need to know that when I give it to you, it becomes a part of you. You'll have the same access as me, and it'll be for all of my buildings. Which means you'll become one of a select few people in the world who have this access. It's the highest security clearance. You can access any part of any of my buildings."

"A great responsibility."

"A great sense of trust. I don't give that out lightly, Ari. The only people who have access to my buildings are my family."

"I know." I reach up and graze his cheek. I know what he's saying to me. The sense of trust he's instilling in me. It means the world.

"I'm completely letting you in. More than just telling you everything that's happening. I couldn't do that until now, even though I wanted to, baby."

"I know." It makes me feel even more for him than ever before. Not because I'm getting the access, but because of the level of trust it entails. I know what this means for both of us and our relationship. He turns and kisses my palm.

"You do understand what I'm saying to you right now."

I smile softly. "You're saying that this is about to be very real, very quickly." I've never spoken truer words.

He smiles and takes my hand in his. "Always thought you were smart." He kisses the back of my hand. "There's no turning back."

"I know. I don't want anything else. I just want you. And a life with you."

"Being with me also comes with other... consequences?" He's a little hesitant with those words. I draw my eyebrows together in confusion. Ryan lets out a heavy breath and gives me a pained expression. "I'm a very powerful man, Aria. My life interests people."

I nod and tilt my head. "You mean the reporters that follow you around trying to photograph you with all of the women you're with?"

"Kind of. I mean. Yes. But they only photograph me when I give them tips on where I'll be. They don't follow me around."

"Oh." I try to follow.

"You're still confused."

I bite my lip. "Kind of." Mainly because I don't know where he's going with this. I already know he feeds them gossip and pays them to leave him alone.

He smiles. "People are obsessed with rich people. I'm just as dangerous as I am popular, so the reporters don't bother me because we have a mutual understanding."

"I know, Ry. You've told me that… You feed them gossip and pay them off. They leave you alone."

"Exactly. And I only feed them gossip when it benefits me."

Still all things I know, but I mull it over. He wouldn't tell me this again without a reason. I just don't understand why he's beating around the bush. Unless… I nod. "I... think I see what you're getting at."

"And?" There's a slight tremor in his voice. He's nervous. He has no reason to be, but it warms my heart that he is.

I take a deep breath hoping that I'm right and that my heart isn't about to make a fool of me. "You want to feed them an engagement. So, the media covers that you claimed me. It gets out to everyone quickly. Including my father and... and Chad." I hug myself as I stand. I don't want to be wrong about that. It's all I want.

I walk over to the floor to ceiling window and watch the sunrise over the skyscrapers of the Chicago skyline.

After a few moments, he stands and walks to me. He wraps his arms around me and kisses me on the back of the head.

"What are you thinking?"

Having the few seconds to myself has allowed the small voice in the back of my head to become louder. I know it's wrong, but I guess I need to hear it from him in order to quiet the niggling and doubt.

"That you just want to flaunt the engagement and claim to protect me. That it's not real." It's stupid to think that. I know Ryan loves me. We've discussed marriage. "I'm thinking that I thought we'd have more time. And that it isn't that I don't want to marry you. I do. But I'm scared that doing it now will make it not real."

"I hate that I can't give you more time, but you know how this works with mafias. I have to put a claim on you to send the message we want to send. If I'm going to go to war with your dad and this other small-

19

time crew in order to protect you and get you out of this, then it has to happen quickly." He nuzzles his lips against my ear. "But all of that aside, you know as well as I do it's real. I'm not one to fake anything, Aria. Especially when it comes to you. I want to marry you."

My heart feels a little lighter. I relax against him as he starts swaying gently with me. "I know."

"I won't rush you, Aria. Into anything. How long ago was it that I told you that? Nothing has changed. This is all still at your pace. The only difference is you'll have a ring on your finger showing everyone you belong to me. To your dad and this Chad asshole, that'll mean I claimed their property. And they'll come after me. But to us, nothing changes except a piece of paper. Everything else between us remains exactly the same."

I turn in his arms and wrap my arms around his waist. I know Ryan. He'd do anything for me and not give it a second thought. As long as it means I'm safe. Even if we weren't actually in love, he'd marry me and put a claim on me just to keep me away from my father and his twisted plans for me. It's who he is.

But we are in love. I just needed the words to shut the nagging voice up.

"I know you won't rush me." I lean my head against his chest and hug him tightly. "Honestly, I really would like to tell everyone I'm yours. As crazy as that sounds. It's going faster than I thought it would, but I know I want to be with you. Just because we're feeding an engagement doesn't mean you're going to force me to do... things I'm not ready for."

Ryan has always been able to read me like no other. It's like a superpower. I don't need to tell him I'm talking about sex. He knows I've never been touched by anyone other than him.

My eyes widen when he leans down and cups my ass, lifting me. I blush as I look into his deep brown eyes and wrap my legs around him. He carries me to the couch and sits with me straddling him.

"I'll never ever force you into things you aren't ready for. But the fact that you want me... Do you know how happy that makes me?"

I blush darker. His hands haven't left my butt. I love when he touches me like this.

Intimately.

20

The words come out softly. "I hope it makes you as happy as it makes me."

"I have no idea how I got so lucky."

I smile and lean down to kiss him. His hands lightly caress over my panties. I arch into them, for some reason hating the idea that he might let go. "Can we just stay like this forever?"

"For a little while. We have things that need to be taken care of." He wraps me in his arms and holds me close to him.

I shift slightly, burying my head in his neck as I wrap myself around him. I press down against his length, enjoying feeling him in ways like this without wondering if things are going too far for him or me. I inhale sharply, quietly, and get slightly dizzy when he twitches against me.

I've dated before, but I've never felt ready for anything more than hand holding with them. I never wanted to kiss them. I didn't want any of them to touch me.

Not like this.

Feeling him between my legs, even though he's covered in jeans, is a feeling I've only wanted with Ryan. The zipper of his jeans pressed against the thin satin of my panties... His hard cock against my thigh... I want to feel things with him I've never felt before.

I want everything with him.

XXX

I haven't been able to stop smiling all day. For the past two years, all I have wanted was Ryan, but given our age difference and the fact that until yesterday I was underage, I had been suffering just as much as him. I could see it every time he touched me.

Over the past few months, since we admitted our feelings to each other, Ryan and I had fallen harder and harder for each other. When we were alone, he'd allow himself to hold my hand. I loved that. He'd hug me a lot. Which I loved even more. He'd even kiss me, which made me weak.

But that wasn't all. He started picking me up from school almost every day. I had met his brothers, Jason and Nick, and Jason's wife, Jessa, but I got to go with him every time he had dinner with them. His family quickly started to become mine. They accepted me as one of their own.

21

This morning when he talked about the engagement and putting a claim on me, I knew it was everything I wanted. I don't want anyone else. I may be young, but I've always known what I wanted. I've always been driven and worked hard to reach my goals. Ryan is like the other part of me. I hate the idea of not being with him.

Our morning after getting dressed was spent getting me identification and access to his buildings. I love that he trusts me enough with that responsibility. I take it very seriously. The level of respect that he shows me by doing it is enough to stop my heart every time I think of it.

After that, Ryan let me decide where to shop. We were walking down the street hand in hand, finally not having to hide, when a gorgeous dress caught my eye. I don't wear very many dresses, but I had to at least try it on.

Unfortunately, I hated the dress on me. It looked terrible. But the store has tons of other cute stuff I'm excited to try. Some things are strapless, which is a huge stretch out of my comfort level, but I really want to at least try them on.

The issue now is my stupid bra. Somehow, in my excitement to take it off and try on the dress Ryan saw and wanted to see me in, it got severely tangled, and I'm now stuck. No matter what I do, it won't untangle. I'm stuck in it. I give up and try to lift it over my head but it gets caught in my hair successfully making me even more trapped.

Damn.

"Um... Ryan?" I call softly.

I'm in the dressing room hoping like hell he's outside the door. I really don't want to show myself off to a strange person.

Especially since the only clerk in the store is a guy.

I don't care that he's as gay as gay can be. Nicest guy in the world, but I still don't want him to see my boobs in all their naked glory. I don't care that Ryan hasn't yet. I trust him more than anyone else.

"Ryan?" I call again, a little louder.

"Yeah, gorgeous?" his deep voice answers.

"I can't explain what happened, but will you come in here?"

"Sure."

I hear the door handle jiggle and sigh. "Sorry. Hang on. I forgot it locks." I manage to bend enough to open the door a crack, but the evil bra pulls my hair. "Ow," I whimper.

22

Ryan closes the door to the dressing room behind him and chuckles. "What in the hell happened to you, beautiful?"

I blush at the fact that he can see me in a way no one ever has before, but I shake my head, banishing any thoughts that creep in. "Don't you dare laugh. Just help me. It's pulling my hair, and I don't want to rip it out."

He bites his lip, choking down the laugh as his eyes zero in on my tits. He clears his throat, but I can see the heat in his eyes. I shiver. "Turn around so I can see what I'm working with."

I do, and Ryan gasps. My eyes widen, and my heart leaps into my chest. "What? Is it that bad? Please tell me it isn't that bad."

"Aria."

I turn to him, my naked tits completely forgotten. "What?" The expression on his face is horror stricken, and I nearly start crying. "Am I going to have to cut my hair?" My hair is one of the things about myself that I'm so incredibly proud of. I've worked hard on growing it and keeping it healthy. It's around the middle of my back, maybe a little further. There's a mixture of pain and complete rage waging a war in his eyes. "Ok. Now you're scaring me. What's going on?" My heart feels like it might pound out of my chest.

He closes his eyes and takes a deep breath. "I'm... going to have to cut the bra off."

I look at him as he opens his eyes. "Please talk to me." It's a nearly whispered plea, but he's scaring me. My lip quivers.

He bends down to kiss me softly. "Just let me get this off." I take one last look before turning around.

He takes a pocket knife out of his pocket and starts gently cutting the fabric. After a few moments, I'm free, and he's untangling my hair. He says nothing until all of the fabric from my bra is out of my hair and laying on the ground. With a shaky hand he lifts my hair. Like he's looking for something.

"Ryan?"

"You have bruises. All over." He nearly chokes on the words.

I close my eyes. "I... I'm sorry." The words are a whisper. I slowly turn to him, crossing my arms over my breasts, and looking down at the ground, terrified he's going to not want me anymore for keeping this from him.

"Why didn't you tell me it had gotten that bad?"

"It happened yesterday… before I left." They are the result of what Chad and my father did to me. He reaches out to cup my cheek. I lean into his touch. I take a deep, shaky breath. "Please don't leave me." I hesitantly look up at him.

He steps closer and wraps his arms around me, crushing me to him. "I won't. I don't know how you think I could, Aria."

"Because... I d-didn't tell you everything."

He keeps me in his arms a few moments longer but says nothing more. I'm uncertain what to think, and for the first time since I've known him, I can't quite tell what's going through his head.

"Let's finish your shopping. I'll take you out to dinner. When we get home, you're telling me everything, Arianna. I mean it. I'm tired of you keeping things from me, beautiful. You never told me the fight was this bad." He runs his fingers through my hair.

I squeeze my eyes shut and nod. "I promise. No more secrets." I hug him as tightly as I can.

He kisses me on top of the head. "Finish up and get dressed so we can get out of here. Please."

He turns and leaves the room. I see the shadow of his feet under the door a moment as he briefly leans against it, like he's regaining his composure, before they disappear.

"I really hope you don't leave me," I whisper to the empty room before I finish trying on clothes and picking what I want.

After everything I've been through, him leaving me would be more than I could take. My heart says he won't. That he never would. But sometimes, my heart and my head fight. Him walking away... It's not something I could ever come back from.

✗✗✗

Hours after my dressing room incident, Ryan and I are entering his penthouse carrying more bags than I anticipated ending up with.

Ryan has been quiet, and I feel horrible about it. I should've told him from the beginning. I shouldn't have kept it from him. I shouldn't have kept anything from him.

He follows me down the hall to the bedrooms. I hesitate outside the one he told me I could use. I bite my lip to stop from crying as I glance at him. He's watching me intently, but the pain hasn't left his eyes.

"I d-don't know where you want me to stay. Or if y-you want me to l-leave."

Ryan closes his eyes, like he's trying to reign in his temper. When he opens them, he shakes his head and takes my bags he's carrying into his room. I lean my head against the wall and try not to cry.

After a few moments, Ryan walks out and takes the rest of my bags to his room. When he's done, he takes my hand on his way out to the living room. I follow, trying to subtly wipe my eyes.

"You and I have a lot to discuss." He sits and pulls me into his lap. "First and foremost, I'm not kicking you out. I don't know why you'd think I would, but I won't. I love you. Second. I won't leave you. I think I've proven to you that I'm not going anywhere. Third. No more keeping shit from me. Starting right now." He reaches up and wipes my tears away with the pad of his thumb and pulls me into his chest.

I shift and melt into him, all of the tension and fear of him not wanting me anymore immediately leaving my body. I rest my head on his shoulder.

"I told you about school."

"You told me part of what was going on at school. Not everything. I know there's more. If we're doing this, baby, we're doing it the right way."

I take a deep breath and nod. He's right. "The person at school. He really was my dad's friend's son. My dad really did want me to go out with him. I didn't want to. And the more I denied him, the angrier he got. He started out just slamming the door to my locker. And then he would slam the door to my locker and shove me against it. He tried to choke me once, but Renza was meeting me after school. We were supposed to go have coffee and catch up. She saw him and shoved him off me. He got so pissed. He threw her against me."

I wrap my arms around his waist and shiver. Ryan reaches around to the back of the couch and grabs a fleece throw blanket. He wraps it around me and wraps his arms around me again.

"Robby showed up just in time. He almost hit both of us, but Robby stopped him. He told him to stay away from us both. Robby made

25

sure to meet me at my locker every day after that. But he still found ways to get to me. He shoved me down a couple of stairs. I nearly broke my ankle. The day you picked me up when you hired the production crew? Renza and Robby got held up after class. I was hurrying, but he caught up to me. He teased me about my stutter, which only happens when I'm scared or nervous."

"I know, beautiful," Ryan whispers. He has started rubbing his hands up and down my arms because the shivering is uncontrollable. I don't even know if it's because I'm cold or scared. "I got you, baby." He kisses my cheek, then the side of my neck.

I sniffle. "He called me retarded. He said he was going to have me one way or another. Robby showed up and shoved him off me. And he made sure he met me after my last class every day. One morning, the guy met me before classes started. I was walking to class, and he shoved me from behind. Hard. A teacher stepped in, but he just said he tripped. I told Robby. He started meeting me in the morning and escorting me to every class."

"You promised if it got bad, you'd tell me," he says quietly into my hair.

"Please let me finish," I whisper.

He sighs and holds me closer to him but says nothing. I silently thank him.

"When we graduated, I thought that was it. He'd been the one who started all of the rumors. He was the reason all of the bullying started. I honestly thought when I graduated, I'd never have to see him again. But... I was wrong." I look up at him. "The reason I didn't tell you who he was is because I know you. I know you would've taken care of it. Just like you came in and took care of the football player that day Renza texted you and told you I needed you; to come to the school. But if you did the same thing with him, you would've been throwing yourself into a war with another mafia. I know what you deal with. I didn't want that. So I didn't tell you."

"You didn't tell me because you wanted to protect me." He half smiles. I shrug. "You know who I am and what I do for a living, don't you?"

I smile and curl back into his arms. "I didn't know at the time that the reason my dad was pushing him on me was because of you. Because he wants to combine their mafias to take you out. But that's what he wanted.

26

That's what his intention was. Last week, when I was constantly texting you and calling you, and I was crying and so upset? It was because my dad had pretty much invited him to move in. I was trying to just stay in my room and bide my time the week between graduation and my birthday when I could leave."

"So, this Chad kid that he was forcing on you was the same kid from school."

"Yes."

"You should've told me, Aria."

"I'm really sorry, but I care so much about you, Ryan. You've been dealing with so much. I didn't want you to deal with yet another mafia. I didn't know that you were already going to have to. I really didn't. I thought I was doing the right thing."

"Aria. You really don't need to worry about me. I've taken out mafias and gangs that are far bigger than your dad's."

I narrow my eyes a little. "I don't care if you've taken down entire countries. I care about you, Ryan. I love you. I didn't want you to be more stressed out."

He strokes his hand across my cheek and through my hair. "Well, thank you for caring that much about me. I get where you're coming from, but you can't keep things from me. Especially not things like this. How did you get the bruises? They're on your back. Your neck. I didn't notice them yesterday because it was dark. Was it from the stairs he shoved you on?"

I nod. "I was getting ready to leave yesterday morning. Like we planned. I had nothing with me since I have clothes and necessities at your house. Our house. Just my phone and keys. I shut off my GPS. When I got down the stairs, Chad was there. With my father." I take a deep breath and kiss his neck softly. "My father... told me that I would be marrying Chad. That night. Last night. I said no. I was really mad. I screamed at him and asked how he could do that to me. My... f-father... said I would be marrying him. I had been promised to Chad since I was a baby."

The tears I had been holding back fall. I can't stop them anymore.

Ryan kisses my forehead and runs his fingers through my hair. He holds me tightly against him.

"I s-said n-no again. And I tr-tried to leave. Chad g-grabbed m-me. He s-said I was his a-already. I br-broke fr-free and ran. Chad c-caught me

27

b-by my h-hair. He gr-grabbed me b-by the b-back of the neck a-and h-hair and th-threw me on the s-stairs. I f-fought."

"Baby. Shh... Take a breath. I got you. I'm right here." He rocks me in his arms as I start sobbing uncontrollably into his neck. His shirt is soaked quickly.

"I-I'm s-so s-sorry."

"Aria. Baby, listen to me," he whispers soothingly. "I don't know why you think I blame you for anything. But please stop. You're breaking my heart right now, beautiful."

He stands with me in his arms and carries me to his bedroom while I try to catch my breath. He sets me down, but keeps me close to him as he pulls the blankets back on the bed. He lets me go long enough to get one of his t-shirts out of a drawer. He hands it to me. We both get ready for bed. Ryan pulls me in next to him and covers us both with the blanket.

"I don't know what I'd do without you," I whisper against his chest as he wraps me in his arms.

"You'll never have to find out, baby."

I take another deep breath. I have to finish. "When he had me on the stairs he shoved me hard back onto them."

"You don't have to continue, Ari. I get the picture."

"Yes, I do. I said no more secrets." I sniffle but continue. "He threw me onto the stairs and pinned me. I kicked him, and he shoved me down again. I bit his neck. Hard. I drew blood. My dad caught me when I ran. I turned and stabbed him in the neck with my keys. In the chaos, I ran. I didn't have anything but my phone and keys that I ripped out of his neck. Nothing else. I ran as far as I could."

"And then called me."

"Yes."

"I'm so fucking proud of you, baby. So proud of you for fighting."

He kisses me sweetly as he holds me close to him. I've never felt so loved than I do in his arms.

He is my safe place.

Chapter Three

✗ Ryan ✗

It takes me a minute to figure out what's going on when I wake up. My senses are assaulted by both bacon and... something burning?

The second thing I notice is that Arianna is not in bed next to me. I sniff the air and force myself up out of the bed. I grab a pair of gray sweats and very cautiously make my way out of the bedroom.

The burning becomes slightly more metallic, and the smell of bacon burning becomes overpowering. I quicken my pace thinking Arianna hurt herself or something.

When I reach my kitchen, I'm completely shocked. The bacon is on the floor. The toaster is in the sink. There's a pan upside down on the stove. Something that looks remotely like burnt toast is on the counter. What I'm guessing is waffle mix drips down the wall. And in the middle of the chaos is my beautiful girlfriend staring in absolute horror, and maybe a little confusion, at the mess.

I clear my throat. "Uh. Baby? What happened?"

Arianna looks at me like she has absolutely no idea how to answer. "Um... I was trying to make breakfast."

"I see that."

"And something happened to the toaster. It started smoking. And then it flung the toast at me. I was making a piece because my stomach was upset. I was mixing a mix for waffles. When the toast flew at me, I flung the bowl and mixer. I unplugged the toaster, and it sparked at me because I pulled the cord so hard. The toaster flew into the sink."

I'm having a very difficult time not laughing. I lean against the counter and cross my arms over my chest as I bite my tongue. Arianna is slowly looking from each mess as she explains everything with a more and more dazed expression on her face.

"And then the bacon was burned to a crisp. I grabbed the pan to move it off the burner and accidentally touched the pan itself. It burned me. When I took my hand away as quickly as I did, the pan flipped, and the bacon went on the floor." She puts her finger in her mouth and frowns at her mess. I walk the last few steps to her and gently grab her wrist, removing her finger. I bring it to my mouth and kiss her fingers, then lean down to kiss her. "I'm sorry about the mess."

I smile and kiss her again. "It's fine. Messes can be cleaned up."

"I know. I just wanted to do something nice for you."

"How about we be petulant children and leave this to the housekeeper while we go get dressed? I'll leave her extra money and a sweet note of apology for being a rich asshole who can't clean up his own messes." I grin as she giggles a little. "I have a surprise for you."

"A surprise?" She runs her hands up my stomach and muscles. I smile and catch her hands as she starts trailing her fingers back down.

"A surprise." I kiss her hands and take one of them in mine. I make sure all the burners are off and lead her back to our bedroom.

"What kind of surprise?"

"One that involves you getting dressed. I'm not saying anything else." I look at my watch. "You have two hours. With Chicago traffic, we have to leave here at eleven."

She glances at the shower, then the bed as she bites her lip. She smiles shyly. She's adorable. Truly adorable. I know she's been wanting to start taking things a little further. I could tell by the way she pressed against me yesterday. All of the shy touches. Like she's exploring how far I'll let her go while trying to figure out what she's comfortable with.

"I was kind of hoping we wouldn't have to do anything today," she says shyly.

I give her a soft, knowing smile. "I know there are things you want to try, and I know you want a day to relax, but I think you'll like what I have planned. I promise it'll just be you and me tomorrow, and we won't leave the penthouse. Deal?"

She smiles as she blushes. "Deal."

I pull her against me and grip her ass. She looks up at me and bites her lip as she brushes her fingertips up my abs. "I think your ass is one of my favorite things in the world."

She giggles. "You do seem to have an obsession with it." Her arms encircle my waist, and she rests her head comfortably on my chest. I kiss her on the top of the head, then spank her ass.

"Oh!" She looks up at me in surprise.

I grin. "Go take a shower, and get dressed."

She's still in a sexy state of shock as she turns for the shower. She looks over her shoulder. "I can't believe you spanked me."

"And if you don't get that incredibly beautiful ass of yours in that shower, I'll spank you again."

She laughs as she closes the door to the bathroom. I grin to myself as I find an outfit for the day. I'm going to have a lot of fun with her. I'm honored that I get to be her first and only experience with everything. I don't want anyone but her. Lucky for me, my girl feels the same way.

XXX

I'm sitting in the living room waiting for Arianna kind of impatiently. We're supposed to be at Taylor's house by noon, and it's currently ten-forty-eight. We have to leave by eleven if we intend to get there in time.

I'm just about to head to our room when I hear her walking out of it.

I let out a breath and stand. "Thank God, Aria. I thought you were going -" I stop mid-sentence as soon as I turn and see her. My mouth goes dry.

Standing in front of me is the most beautiful woman I've ever seen. Arianna is wearing jeans that hug every curve and a red tank top that clings to her body perfectly. It's not too tight that it would make her uncomfortable, but it's not so loose that she looks like she's trying to hide something behind it. It covers her chest and ties around her neck. Her beautiful, long, dark brown locks cascade down her back, some falling over her shoulders.

"Um... Y-you didn't say where we were going. I-is this okay?"

I clear my throat. I can't help but reach out and touch her hair. I run my hand down her collarbone, her chest, and stomach. When I reach her waist, I pull her close. The soft smile on her lips and the love that shines from her eyes at me gives me butterflies.

I kiss her, and the butterflies take flight. I haven't felt butterflies like that in... ever. She's the only one who has made me feel like this.

I force myself to pull away, but I keep her close. "You're beautiful, Aria. You look beautiful."

"It's not too much? Or too revealing?"

"No, baby. You're beautiful."

She smiles and smoothes down my black button up dress shirt. Her eyes roam further as she takes a small step back to take my tailored jeans in. Her eyes darken slightly with unmistakable lust. I love the way she looks at me. Like I'm the last drop of water in a burning desert, and she has to drink me to survive.

"You look really nice."

"Thank you, baby." I give her hip a squeeze. "You ready to go?"

"You still aren't telling me where we're going?"

"Nope. It's a surprise."

She sighs, but I can tell by the sparkle in her eyes that she's excited. "I'm ready."

✗✗✗

It's nearly noon when we finally get to Taylor's house. Arianna's mouth falls open. "This house is gorgeous. Whose is it? Yours?"

I laugh. "No, baby girl. I don't own a house in Chicago. I own my Manhattan house and a house in Hawaii."

"You own a house in Hawaii?" She looks at me with wide eyes. "I love Hawaii."

32

"So does your sister-in-law. Well, soon to be. Bree loves Hawaii. She's been trying to get Chase to buy a house near mine ever since their wedding." She blushes and pushes her hair behind her ear, ducking her head and going suddenly shy. "What?" I ask with a grin.

She looks up at me, her beautiful golden eyes glittering. "I just really like the idea of being married to you. Is that stupid?"

"Not in the slightest." I lean over and kiss her. I rest my hand on her thigh as I pull back. "Is that what you really want? To be my wife?" I don't know why I feel the need to ask her. Maybe it's because I need to hear the words, even though I know her heart.

She smiles and puts her hand on top of mine on her thigh. She gives it a light squeeze. "More than anything."

"Then, I'm a very lucky man." I give her a quick kiss before we get out of the car. I meet her in front of it and take her hand. She entwines her fingers with mine as we walk together to the door.

She glances around nervously. "Are you sure I look okay?"

"You look great, Aria. I promise you." She takes a deep breath as I open the door. "Baby, relax. You'll like the surprise. Trust me."

"I trust you." I lead her into the house and close the door behind me. When I look back at her, she's turning around in a circle taking it all in. The house is pristine. Marble. Hardwood. A gorgeous staircase. It's spacious. Taylor did well when he had it designed. "This place is so gorgeous."

"Thank you," a deep voice rumbles. I grin as Taylor appears at my side.

Arianna startles and turns around. "Taylor!" She jumps into his arms. I smile wider as Taylor staggers backwards slightly as he catches her and balances himself.

"Oof. Missed you, too, sweetheart." He kisses her cheek and lets her down.

"This is really your house?"

"It is."

"It's so pretty!"

Taylor laughs. "Thank you. And happy birthday. I didn't get a chance to say it the other day."

"Things were a bit chaotic," I say as I watch the two of them.

"But that's over. You're safe now, right?" Taylor gives her a dazzling smile.

"Yes! I'm so glad to be out of there. Thank you for helping me."

Taylor hugs her again. "Anytime, sweetheart. That's what family does."

Her smile could light up the room. I give in to my insatiable need to touch her. I reach out and tug her hair lightly. "Baby, why don't you go find Nikki? She's really excited to see you."

"Okay!" She gives me a quick kiss and hurries off to explore and find Nicole.

I take a deep breath and turn to Taylor. "Thank you for this. She needs it."

"Mmhmm. I think you do, too."

I give him a half smile. "Probably."

"You going to take her away from all of this?"

"Soon as we're married. Which is going to have to be quick. I can't just claim her and give her a long engagement until she's ready. I want to. That's just not how the mafia works."

Taylor is one of the few people who knows my plans. Being part of my family has huge perks, but also serious downfalls. One of them is the inner, complex-as-fuck, workings of the mafia life.

"Did you talk to her about what she thinks? How does she feel about it?"

"She says she understands. That she wants to be with me. She knows I love her. But I can see how hard this is for her. She wants everything to just be normal for once."

"Can't blame her for that."

"I think she was hoping that as soon as she moved in with me, everything would be fine. She'd have a normal life. Be with me. Go to college. Get her degree. Start her career. But her life just got tipped upside down. Even with a claim, they won't stop coming after her. I can protect her from other mafias with my claim. No one dares fuck with me. But her father and his fucked up plan?" I shake my head.

"Ry. I don't think you give that girl enough credit. She bit a guy on the neck and stabbed her father with keys just to get away before they hurt her. Or worse. She survived a year of bullying. Fuck. More than that. Kept her straight A's. She got into a school that's hard as fuck to get into. And she managed to tame you. That girl's a fighter."

I can't help but smile. "Tame me?"

"Yeah. Tame you. You have a reputation for being a lady's man. In case you didn't know."

"I know. Believe me."

"How many girls have you fucked in the last two years?"

I look at him and shake my head. "What?"

"Since you realized she was the one."

I laugh. "Okay. Yeah. You got me. None. There's only been her. For two years."

He raises an eyebrow. "She tamed you. Her greatest accomplishment." The fucker has the balls to smirk at me.

"Alright. Enough. Did you learn anything about Luke Ambrosio?"

He laughs. "Yeah. I learned he's a fucking ghost."

Luke Ambrosio is a newer guard who works for Arianna's father. What threw me is that she was always incredibly uncomfortable around his guards. Except him. He had actually helped her a few times. I don't know what to make of him, and I don't like not knowing things.

"I found such structured records on him. Like they were planted. Anyone looking would see he has a rap sheet as long as my arm. He's been in and out of juvie. Jail. But to a cop? I've planted records for my guys. When I threw Jesse undercover into Nicole's bakery, I created his entire life. Squeaky clean. Married. Gay. College transcripts."

"You think he's a plant?"

"I honestly don't know. I have contacts in the NYPD. They have no idea who this guy is. He isn't one of theirs. But if I had to guess? He's law enforcement. No one has a record that easy to find."

"I can contact my FBI contact."

"I don't think he's FBI. The FBI doesn't fuck with small time crews. They would go after someone like you. Factions everywhere."

"So what are your instincts?"

"It's just a guess, but I think he's ATF."

I look at him a second, a little in disbelief, but I've always trusted him. "Okay. Why?"

"There's a whole big push on weapons being transported into the United States. The ATF is leading the takedown efforts. They're even guiding and working with smaller departments along the transport routes in takedowns."

"Why go after them? They're small time transporters."

"Exactly why. Take out the small time transporters. They lead to the major players. That's who we ultimately want as cops, right?"

"That actually makes sense."

"I'm still digging. I'm looking into law enforcement records now. I'll need Arianna to give me some kind of a description to go off of, though. I have ways of digging deeper into law enforcement files and records than a gang or crew or mafia does. Cops aren't erased. They're just very deeply hidden."

"She'll give you whatever you need. But not today. Today she just needs to be surrounded by those of us that love her. She needs to feel that support because she's never had that. Besides me. And her mother."

"You got it. Are you guys sticking around Chicago for a little while?"

"A few days at least. I promised her tomorrow would just be us. We need to talk about a wedding. Where she wants to get married."

"Bring her by the precinct Monday. And by the way? You need a very public proposal if you want it to spread quickly."

"Yeah. Another thing we'll need to talk about."

"And media coverage on the wedding."

"I know. I don't know how she'll feel about any of that."

"It's necessary if you want them to see you claimed her. Made her your own. Took what's theirs. It has to be more than a leaked story. You have to let them follow this. It's big news, but it's also advantageous for you."

"I know. I feel bad about it, though. Rushing this. Not being able to give her the wedding of her dreams."

He scoffs. "You're a fucking billionaire. You can pull it off."

He pats me on the back, and I smile. He's right. I could give her whatever she wanted. What I need to do is take my own advice that I give to everyone else.

Stop thinking and let myself enjoy this moment being around those who love and support us.

Chapter Four

⚔ Arianna ⚔

After saying hi to Nicole, I decided to give her a break and play with her gorgeous, nearly one year old son, Tait. I hadn't seen him, or really anyone in Chicago, since Taylor and Nicole's wedding. I pretty much fell in love with Tait. He is such a happy baby. And he absolutely loves playing with my hair. Tait bangs a rattle on my thigh.

I laugh at how excited he is. "You really like that rattle, don't you?"

Tait coos happily. His attention becomes fixated behind me, and he screams in excitement as he reaches out his arms. A warm laugh I would recognize anywhere wraps around my soul.

"What's up, little man?" Ryan bends down, scoops Tait up, and kisses him. He smiles down at me as he tucks Tait into his arm. He holds out a hand as he stands. I take it. He easily pulls me up with one arm, and I find myself amazed at his effortless strength. "Ready for the surprise?"

I cock an eyebrow. "I thought the visit was the surprise." He grins and leans down to kiss me. Tait gets a hold of my hair, and I laugh as he tugs at it. "He really likes long hair."

"You're really good with him."

The look of love on Ryan's face makes me smile wider and blush at the same time. I've never thought of having kids. I've always wanted to go to Juilliard, graduate, and then teach piano to little kids. A couple years ago, I started thinking of Ryan in my future. Being his wife. Teaching piano. Still, kids had never been in the plans. But today, being with Tait and playing with him, the thought crept into my mind. Seeing Ryan with him, though. That sealed the deal.

"You'd make an amazing father."

He smiles and caresses my cheek. I lean into his touch. "I've never wanted kids."

My heart sinks. I can feel my face visibly fall. I focus on Tait and reach out, letting him take hold of my finger. Ryan gently takes my chin in his hand and turns my face to him. His lips meet mine in one of the sweetest kisses he's given me.

"Until I met you, baby girl."

I feel the love I have for him shine from my eyes. I'm sure it's bright enough to light the entire world. My heart swells with a feeling I've never felt for anyone but him. A feeling of love that grows exponentially every single day.

"Ryan... I love you." I stand on my tip toes and kiss his chin.

"I love you..." He grins. "Your presence is being requested. So, we need to get you downstairs."

"Okay." Still carrying Tait, Ryan takes my hand and leads me down the stairs.

Taylor is waiting at the bottom. "Ready?"

"He won't tell me what's happening. I have no idea if I'm ready or not," I say. Ryan and Taylor both laugh at my teasing tone.

"She's relentless. I don't know how I've kept this secret for so long." Ryan winks at me. I giggle.

"Give me my kid, Crane, so you can cover her eyes."

Ryan hands Tait to Taylor and covers my eyes with his hand. He puts his other hand on my waist and guides me wherever I'm supposed to be.

"What's going on?" I ask impatiently.

"You'll see." After what seems like an eternity, he stops. "Ready?"

"More than you can possibly know." I smile excitedly. He slowly removes his hand from my eyes.

"Surprise!"

Everyone in the room screams in unison.

My eyes widen. "Oh my God!"

Ryan's hands are on my hips. My hands fly to my mouth. Ryan's parents are here. Jason and Jessa. Breetana and Chase. There's a woman I've never met. Tears fill my eyes as I realize what's going on.

I turn to Ryan. He's smiling widely. "You did all of this for me?"

"I had a little help."

I shake my head in disbelief, love filling all of my being. "I don't know what to say."

He softly kisses me. "You deserve this. Sorry it couldn't have been on your actual birthday, but happy birthday, baby."

"Thank you."

"Come on! Come see your cake!" Nicole takes my hand and pulls me away from Ryan.

"Hey, now. Hang on there, Nikki. Cake is exciting, but not as exciting as everyone who hasn't seen her in so long actually getting to see her." Chase pulls me away from Nicole as she pouts. He hugs me. "How are you holding up, sweetheart? Ryan treating you well?"

"Amazingly. Really. I've never been happier."

"Good. Because if he doesn't, I'll beat him up!" Breetana hugs me.

I laugh. "I've missed you guys! Thanks for keeping in touch with me via phone and text, though. I've gotten through some tough days thanks to you and Nikki," I say to her.

"Anytime, sweetie. That's what family is for!"

I didn't think my heart could swell with love anymore than it already has, but the more everyone calls and treats me like family, the more overwhelmed with affection I feel.

"Hey, sweetheart." Jason enfolds me in his strong embrace.

"How are you after what happened?" Jessa asks me.

"I'm doing okay. Ryan has really been helping me and talking me through it."

"I'm so happy you're away from all of that. Our family will keep you safe." Jessa hugs me. She smiles and turns away to join another conversation as Nick takes his turn.

He wraps me in his arms and kisses the top of my head. "My asshole brother keeping you warm at night?" Nick teases.

I laugh as I return his hug. "He made me sleep on the edge of the bed after I got here that first night."

Nick gently pushes me back and looks down at me incredulously. "He fucking what?"

I nod and bite my lip to keep from laughing. I give him my best sad face, but it's too much. I crack up instead. "I'm kidding!"

He crushes me to his chest again. "Fuck me. I was about to go kick his ass, then steal you away."

I squeeze him as he lets me go with a chuckle while his and Jason's and Ryan's parents walk up to us. They each take turns hugging me.

"Happy birthday, honey," Ethan says.

"We're so sorry it's a couple of days late," Jenny says as she kisses my cheek.

"It's okay. Really. I'm so happy you guys are here." I hug them both again. Ethan kisses me on the top of my head.

Jenny kisses me on the cheek once more. "We're so happy to be here celebrating with you!"

Ryan comes up behind me and leans in to kiss his mom on the cheek. His dad hugs him. "Can I steal her away for a minute? There's one person here she hasn't met yet."

"Of course, sweetheart." Jenny smiles at both of us. Ryan's parents join in another conversation near them.

Everyone around me is talking, laughing, and having a good time. Ryan takes my hand and leads me over to Chase and Taylor.

"Arianna. I want you to meet Eve Shaw. This is Chase's and Taylor's mother."

I politely stick out my hand for Eve to shake. She smiles, her eyes shining with tears, and pulls me into a warm embrace instead. "I'm so happy my Ryan finally found someone who makes him happy. It's the final piece to the puzzle of all my boys."

"Oh... Thank you, Mrs. Shaw."

"Please. It's Eve, Arianna."

"I still can't believe you've known Ryan for years, and I only just met him last year." Chase kisses his mother on top of the head.

Taylor laughs. "I told you. They were renovating Ryan's penthouse. He stayed here, and she surprised me when she dropped by unexpectedly."

"It would've been rude to jump out the window in order to keep my identity a secret," Ryan teases.

"And I didn't care who he was. He helped Taylor understand that his partner's death wasn't his fault and convinced him to talk to you and me so he didn't drink himself to death."

"Which I will always be grateful for." Nicole appears at Taylor's side and kisses him on the cheek. Then she turns to Ryan with a brilliantly beautiful smile on her face. I smile softly to myself as Ryan slips his arm around my waist. I wish I had a smile like hers. She's so pretty. "Can it be cake and present time yet?" She's nearly jumping up and down with excitement.

"Aren't we supposed to eat something of substance before dessert?" Ryan teases her. We all laugh.

"You banned me from cooking for large gatherings. Remember?" I love how she teases him right back. The family dynamic is amazing.

"Because you nearly poisoned my entire team and Taylor's with whatever the hell you attempted to cook!" Ryan says wide-eyed. I have no idea what any of them are talking about, but I laugh anyway.

"What is all that about?" I ask looking up at Ryan.

He smiles and kisses me. "Last week, when we were planning to take down the gang harassing her, she thought it would be fun to cook for everyone. Problem is, she can't cook."

Nicole's mouth drops. "I can cook! I have a bakery, you know!"

Ryan laughs. "You can bake! Huge difference! Anyway. My team starts arriving. I start smelling this... atrocious smell."

"It was not atrocious!" She looks at me dumbfounded. "I was cooking eggs for everyone. Like he does in the oven!"

"No. You were burning eggs in the oven and turning it into some bizarre quiche. She had tomatoes in there. And spinach. She put peppers and onions in there. Then I think a cream or something instead of milk. It was runny and smelled like ass."

I laugh as Nicole hits Ryan in the arm. "You're such an asshole! There was nothing wrong with what I was cooking."

"And ham. And bacon. I think sausage. Pepper." Ryan sadly shakes his head, but I can see the half smile he's trying to hide as he looks down at me. "I had no choice. I had to save everyone and ban her from doing anything other than baking. It was for the good of people everywhere."

Taylor laughs. "Thank God I can cook."

Nicole teasingly glares at him as she shoves him. "You both are such assholes."

Ryan grins widely. "Fine. It can be time for cake and presents."

"Yay!" Nicole claps her hands.

I laugh at how excited she is as she leads me to the dining room. On the table is the most amazing birthday cake I have ever seen. It has a light pink frosting and is lined with fresh, white-chocolate covered strawberries.

"Oh my God!" My eyes widen as I take in the spread in front of me.

The dining room and open kitchen next to a sitting area are just as beautiful as the rest of the house. Large and spacious. Simple, yet somehow so elegant.

The table the cake is sitting on is covered in pink and white carnations. There are chocolate covered strawberries, both pink and white, on platters on each side of the cake. At the end of the table, there's a beautiful silver fountain that's cascading white chocolate. Next to it are giant, plump red strawberries.

Part of me wants to dive for everything and try it all immediately. But I refrain from turning into a white chocolate and strawberry crazed animal.

"I can't believe how pretty this house is, but that cake! Did you make it?" I look at Nicole, tears stinging my eyes. I really hope she says yes.

"Yes. Ryan said you liked vanilla, strawberries, and white chocolate. So the cake is vanilla. There's a vanilla bean filling between the layers. And all of the strawberries are white chocolate. The pink covered ones are white chocolate, but they both have a coloring in them to make them the pink color."

I fling my arms around her. "No one has ever made me a cake before!"

42

"Really?" Ryan asks incredulously.

"Not even my mom. They've always been store bought." I look back at the cake and admire it, another well of emotion threatening to overwhelm me. I take a deep breath and turn to everyone. "Thank you guys. So much. For coming. For all of this. And for making me feel so welcome." I can't finish everything I want to say.

Taylor smiles and gives me a quick peck on the cheek as he heads to the kitchen. "Let's get this cake cut. I've been dying to try it!"

Ryan puts his arms around me and pulls me off to the side of the room. I look up and notice all of the balloons. Pink and white. I bite my lip. Even the banner that says 'Happy Birthday, Arianna!' is pink and white with silver sparkly glitter over the letters.

The streamers are pink and white. There's silver streamers thrown in to pop the colors. On the wall near the kitchen is a table filled with presents. I reach up and wipe my suddenly wet eyes.

Ryan smiles as he leans down to kiss me. "You okay?"

"Better than okay."

He hugs me. "Are you sure? I hope this isn't overwhelming to you."

I shake my head. "I've had parties before. But… it just didn't mean anything. You know? I knew that all of the presents would be things I wanted. Like the newest Barbie. Or the latest CD by Pink or Halsey or Selena Gomez. But it was all just… things. Things that I guess I was never truly happy about because I knew they were coming from some place of…" I trail off and look up at him, unsure what it is I'm trying to say.

"Obligation?"

I nod. "Obligation. And also from some place of needing to keep up appearances of a happy family. I knew that none of it meant anything." I gesture to the room. "But this… this is all real. Genuine. It's such a different feeling."

Ryan smiles. "It's all different, baby. You're part of a real family now. It's all going to feel strange to you for a while." He leans down and kisses me again before leading me back to the table.

Taylor comes back with a knife and starts cutting the cake. The rest of the day is spent talking and getting to know everyone.

By the time we're ready to leave, I feel so comfortable around everyone. Like I really belong to Ryan's family. Like I have a family. A real one.

Finally.

Chapter Five

✗ Ryan ✗

I close the door to my penthouse behind me. My mother and father are standing in the middle of my living room, and Arianna is standing nervously near me. I glance at my parents before turning to my girl. I gently take her face in my hands and tilt her chin up so she's looking at me.

"What's going on behind those beautiful eyes of yours?" I say it quietly, blocking her from my parents' view.

She smiles softly and sweetly. "I'm a little nervous. I've been around your parents, but never just you and me and them. And not since we..." She shrugs and tries to tilt her head down. I don't let her.

I tenderly kiss her. "They love you. You have nothing to worry about." She gives me a weak smile. I glance at my parents again before looking back at her. "Is that all this is?"

She shakes her head. "I just feel overwhelmed with all of the love your family shows me. It's so different from what I'm used to."

"Baby…" I hug her close for a few moments as I kiss her hair. I feel her shudder a few times as I sway with her in my arms. "I know it's different. You'll get used to it."

"I'm getting used to it. Slowly," she whispers into my chest as she hugs me a little tighter. "It's just so… different. I've never really been able to rely on family before. Honestly, I've never really had it. Besides Robby and Renza. I know I've said that before, but…" she shakes her head and buries her face in my chest as she takes a few deep breaths.

"I understand, baby." I kiss the top of her head again. "But I do promise that you'll get used to it." I look down at her and push her back slightly so she looks up at me. "Okay?"

She smiles and nods. "Okay."

I lean down and kiss her. "Good girl." I smile and wipe away a tear, knowing there's still something on her mind. I battle with the need to take her back to the bedroom and talk it all out with her now, but I know my parents need a little time with us themselves.

"Ry? Sweetheart, where will your father and I be sleeping? I'm getting a headache, and I'd like to turn in for the night."

Arianna gives me a quick hug before I have any time to say anything, and pulls away. "I can take you, Mrs. Crane."

"Oh, my dear. No need for formalities. We've talked about this," my dad says to her with a soft smile.

"You don't need to call us Mr. and Mrs. Crane, honey. It's Ethan and Jenny. Or mom and dad. You're family, after all." Mom walks quietly towards her.

I watch Arianna. She nods and turns away. I see her reach up and wipe away a tear, and I fight myself to chase after her. My father, who is just as observant as I am, notices and raises an eyebrow. Thankfully, he waits until both my mother and my girl are safely behind closed doors.

"So? What the hell was that about, son?"

I glance at him as I blow out a breath and sink into my couch. He sits next to me. "She's never had this. This… sense of family. People who care so much about her that they'd do whatever it took to protect her. Fuck, I can't even have her talk to the girls because they've all had this before. At least until their parents died. She's never had this. Her mom loved her, but it was never like this."

"She's never felt this level of love. I understand. It can be incredibly overwhelming. Your mother was the same way. It took a long time for her to understand that her life was valued. That she wasn't just some piece of property."

46

"That's what Arianna thought when she found out her dad's plans. Exactly her words. It fucking cut me that she felt like that." My chest constricts. It's so hard for me to understand how someone could be so callous and cruel to another human being. Why would they want to treat anyone like nothing more than property?

"Your mother went through a lot of these emotions as well. Maybe it would be beneficial to Arianna to have a chat with her."

I smile. I agree with him. My mother came from another mafia family. Her dad, much like Arianna's, married her to the leader of another mafia so that the two mafias became one. The hope was that the alliance would be enough to take down my father. At that time, he was, like me, one of the most powerful men in the world. The mafia was one of the largest.

The man my mother was married off to was vicious. He treated her like trash. He raped her every single night, then left her in the basement for the entire day. She was only allowed dinner. Which she had to eat in the basement. She had to eat quickly before they took it away. They didn't give her anything to eat with. She was forced to use her hands. She was laughed at. She was called a pig. She lived like that for months.

One day, my father, who had gotten information that this mafia had intended to take him down, raided the house. He went through the basement just before dawn. My mother was sitting on the cold cement floor. The asshole she was married to had the decency to put a pretty thick comforter underneath her. Not like it did a lot of good. He kept her naked and shackled. If she was cold and wanted to wrap the blanket around herself, she had to also wrap it around the wooden column she was shackled to.

My father immediately released her. He says he cut the chains. I've never believed that. My father instilled a great level of respect into all of us. Respect for women. Respect for family. Respect for each other. Seeing something like that would infuriate me. I have a temper. But nothing like that of my father. I've always been convinced he snapped those chains with his bare hands. I know I damn well would have.

All that matters is he released her. He wrapped her in his coat and had one of his men take her to one of the vehicles so she'd be safe. Then he took out her father and husband as well as their entire mafia. It took two missions to decimate them. His intel had them all in the house he raided. He took out the leaders and probably could have left it at that.

But he's not that type of man. Neither am I. He didn't just take out the main players. He made sure to take out every single person involved with that mafia. He did it completely out of revenge and anger, but I can't say I blame him. He's been with my mother ever since.

A lot of people think I'm ruthless. I know my reputation, and I know it well. People believe I kill without a second thought. That I got where I am because of my body count. I *am* ruthless.

But I got where I am because I'm a ruthless businessman. My money comes from my businesses around the world. My body count isn't anywhere near what people think. Most of the time, law enforcement is taking out my rivals.

Not to say I haven't taken anyone out. I have. I have no regrets. I'm just as ruthless when it comes to that side of this, too. However, I usually only get truly involved in only two situations. The first is if I have no other option. The problem is too big for the cops to handle, and one of my contacts calls me in.

The second is if anyone in my family is being threatened or has gotten hurt. Then, all bets are off. When it comes to family, I have no boundaries. I'll do whatever it takes to make sure they're safe. I don't care how far I have to go. I don't care who I have to go through.

It's one of the things my father ingrained in me. Never get involved unless it involves family or there are no other options. I've lived by that my entire life.

"I never want her to feel unloved. I'll never let her go through what mom did."

My father nods and claps my shoulder. "I raised you well. I know you'll keep her safe. Just remember one thing."

"What's that?"

"Remember your team. Remember you're not alone in this." He looks at me. I let out a breath and lean back against the couch. "I know you, son. You're just like me. You think you can handle everything on your own. You need to learn from me, though. You need your team. Your family. It's the only way to keep her truly safe, Ryan."

"I know, dad."

"There's a difference between knowing and actually taking the advice to heart. What you've told me about what's happening with her... I just think you need to listen to your old man on this."

I glance at him before sighing. "There's just so much shit I don't understand about what's going on. You've always said to trust my instincts. Well, my instincts are on a fucking rollercoaster ride right now."

"Well, talk it out with me. That always seems to give you a clearer mind."

I rub my temples. "It's just so fucking confusing. Things over the last couple of years have just been so... convenient. There's no other word. Ever since we took down Lucinio."

"Like what, Ry? Tell me your thought process. Let's work it out."

"After Jessa things have just blown up. I'm always in some kind of turf war. But it seems like all of the ones I've been in lately are..." I shake my head. "Almost like they're decoys for something larger. Something I'm not seeing."

My dad leans back on the couch. "You think you're being set up?"

I shake my head. "No. Not that." I don't know how to explain what I'm about to without sounding paranoid. But this is my father. If I can't talk to him about it, then I can't talk to anyone. "I just think there's something bigger going on. I don't know what. I don't like that."

"I don't know if I'm following, Ry. But I know better than to discount your instincts. They've saved all of our lives more than once."

"The problem is everything that's been going on just doesn't seem like the normal thing I deal with. Before Jessa, how often has anyone actually gone after anyone in our family?"

"Not very often. Actually not at all since our battle with the Lucinio mafia."

I nod. "And the next time we end up with someone going after one of our own, I'm talking Jess and Jason, it's the same person behind it who went after us before?"

My dad leans forward and puts his elbows on his knees. "The biggest battle I think we've ever been in was with the Lucinio mafia when I got shot. But we called a truce. Left each other alone for years. Had it not been for Jessa, we may not have been up against them again. Not that I regret for a second her coming into this family. I don't."

"Had it not been for her, we probably wouldn't have taken out Matthew. He might still be running the Lucinio mafia. But it's been since then, dad. Since we took him out once and for all that this whole thing started. The mundane turf wars. Then Chase and Breetana. The cartel. Nicole and Taylor. That small fucking gang going after our turf, and going through Nicole to get to me. And now Massena is trying to combine with some bullshit smaller mafia to take me out. It just seems fucking odd that all of this shit somehow comes back to me. Chase is Taylor's brother. Taylor is like mine. Taylor would obviously call me in."

"Okay. I can see where you're going with this. Do you think Alex or Josh are behind it?"

"God no. I trust them. I know they aren't behind it. We've been through too fucking much together. I don't know if anyone is behind it. Maybe I'm reading too much into it. But there's just this nagging fucking feeling that something isn't right. That this is all connected somehow. That I'm totally missing something."

"Like I said, I've learned over the years that your instincts are nothing to fuck around with or ignore. If you're thinking there's a larger picture, then there's a larger picture."

"Thanks, dad."

"You're welcome. The question now is figuring out what that something is."

I sigh. "It's just this nagging… thing. Something in the back of my mind that's been there ever since I flew to L.A. to deal with the Berlusconi's."

"I will admit… Them coming back after we dealt with them years ago was something that's been bothering me."

I nod. "It shouldn't have happened. We took out that entire mafia."

"Not his wife or son." My dad looks back at me.

I shake my head. "His wife was grateful to us for getting her and her son out. Why would she suddenly turn on us like that? She would have had to have been the one to turn the son against us. He was only a baby."

My dad is quiet for a few moments as he thinks. "I think you're onto something, Ryan. But I'm with you. I don't know what. It's something that we're going to have to take time and figure out, though."

"You're telling me," I grumble.

My dad pats my knee. "Now. Let's talk about something else. How about that beautiful woman? Are you happy you don't have to hide anymore?"

I smile and close my eyes. He knows how to get me out of my head. "I love that girl. I plan on taking her away from here for a little while before she starts school in the fall."

"I think that's a good idea. But running away isn't going to make it go away, son. You know that."

I'm quiet for a few moments before opening my eyes. My dad is watching me, waiting for me to continue talking. He knows me better than I know myself. "Do you approve of her? Of our relationship?"

"Would it really matter if I did?" he asks. I shrug and look at the wall. My dad reaches into his pocket and takes something out. I cock an eyebrow. "Do you love her?"

"Yes. Crazy as that sounds. With the age difference."

"And she very obviously loves you. Can you see yourself spending your life with her? Beyond marrying her to claim her for the purpose of pushing her dad to form that alliance so you can take them all down at once."

"I don't want anyone else, dad. I haven't been with anyone in two years. Since I realized she's the only one I want."

"I thought so." He holds out his hand.

I feel an actual tear sting my eye. "Grandma's rings?"

"You always knew they belonged to you. Even though you said you'd never marry."

I take the rings and admire them, imagining how they'd look on Arianna's pretty little finger.

My dad pats my back and stands. He doesn't say another word as he walks to the guest room. I turn the rings in my hand a few moments and then stand myself. I put them in a drawer under the TV.

I smile to myself as I walk to mine and Arianna's room. I don't care that she already knows the need for us to get married. I don't care that she understands it needs to happen quickly; that it's necessary. I love her. With everything in me. Marrying her isn't just out of necessity in my book. I want to be with her. Share my life with her. Be her protector. Her life partner. Be the one who wipes away her tears. Who laughs with her. The one who starts a family with her.

51

I truly want to marry her. She's the air that I breathe. She's the other half of me that I didn't know I was missing. The other part of my heart that I didn't know I needed.

Which is why I hid the ring. I'm not going to just put a ring on her finger and call it good. I'm going to give her the proposal of her dreams. And even though we'll be getting married in a couple of weeks, I'm also giving her the wedding of her dreams. She deserves the best of everything. The best I can give her and more.

She deserves the world.

Chapter Six

⚔ Arianna ⚔

I'm laying on my stomach on Ryan's bed wearing one of his t-shirts and talking on my phone to my best friend, Renza. Given the danger I'm in, Ryan had given me a very strict list of people I can talk to. Thankfully, Renza is one of them. I hadn't had the chance to talk to her about what happened until now. Since she hadn't been able to get in touch with me, she was really worried.

"So, your dad actually thought he could just shove you into an arranged marriage? With a guy who actually physically abused you right in front of him?"

"Yep. And I had no idea until Friday when I was leaving to go home, to Ryan's. Ryan was still in Chicago. The plan was that I would pack a bag for the weekend and Jason was going to take me to the airport where I would board his private plane and fly to Chicago."

"Obviously, that didn't happen."

I sniffle. "No. Chad caught me. Luke wasn't there yet. My dad did nothing to stop him. After I bit Chad and stabbed my dad, I ran. I called Ryan. Taylor had one of his cop contacts get me to Jason's office. Then Nick escorted me here."

"Oh God, Air. Thank God. I'm so happy Ryan got you out. I'm so sorry I wasn't there!" Renza chokes out a sob.

It forces me to cry again, too. "It's okay, Renz. I'm safe. I have Ryan and his whole family now. I've never felt so safe or so... so loved." A fresh sob breaks free. Renza and I both turn into messes all over again.

"I'm so glad he's there. That he saved you!"

"Me, too!" It takes us a few minutes to regain our composure. I'm just wiping my eyes when Ryan walks in. He sees I'm on the phone, so he says nothing. Just looks at me concerned as he sits next to me. I smile softly. "Renz, Ryan just walked in. I'll talk with you tomorrow?"

"Of course. Promise I'll see you soon?"

I glance at Ryan and blush. I hadn't told Renza that I am marrying Ryan. Yet. I want more than anything for her to be a part of it, but I don't know if I have that option.

"I promise." We say our goodbyes, and I hang up. I draw myself up to my knees and look at Ryan.

"You plan on telling me what I just walked in on, or am I supposed to guess?" He gives me a sexy smirk.

I smile as I shrug slightly. "I was just telling Renza what happened."

"That's not everything. I know you, Arianna. I know it's been an emotional day for you. I know you've never felt the level of love from so many people that you did today. And I know telling Renza what happened was probably difficult. But I also know you. I know something else is going on, and whatever it is has been nagging at you all day, baby. Just tell me. I can help you. You promised no more secrets."

He's right. I have been thinking all day.

Of us.

Our future.

Our wedding.

I take a deep breath and crawl up to the top of the bed. When I settle in and look back at him, he's watching me. Ryan stands up and strips his shirt. My eyes trail down his chest and perfectly sculpted abs to the bulge already forming in his pants. I bite my lip and look back up at him with hooded eyes. He starts to unbutton his pants as he stalks around the bed to me.

I've also been thinking of how much I want to take things further with Ryan. I've never wanted to explore anything sexual with anyone but him. Not to say I haven't had urges. I've curiously explored myself thinking of Ryan on more than one occasion. It's something I've never admitted to anyone, though.

When he reaches me, his pants are unbuttoned and unzipped. I can't take my eyes away as I unconsciously reach for him. He usually sleeps in his boxers. It's nothing new. Today, though. Today I just feel ready. I need more of him. I just need him.

Reading me, like he's so incredible at doing, he grabs my hand and shakes his head. With his other hand, he slowly runs his fingers up my leg while never taking his eyes off mine. He stops just at my pantyline. I whimper.

"I promised I'd take things slow with you, Aria."

I look up at him shyly. "I know…"

"Is this your way of telling me you're ready for more?"

My heart pounds in my chest. Being with him… He's all I've ever wanted. "Please," I whisper.

He smiles as he kisses my wrist. "You get nothing until you tell me what I want to know. No touching. No kissing. Nothing."

"Ryan..." I close my eyes and swallow. He trails a finger along the outside of my panties, pressing down on my tiny bundle of nerves just enough to make me gasp and want more as he does it. He runs his finger up to my stomach and pulls away. I whimper. "Noooo..." I whine and pout. I've never been one to give up when I decide on a goal. Now that I've made the decision to take this step, him touching me is all I can think about.

"You can whine all you want. I have far more resolve than you."

"You're being mean."

He grins as he takes his pants off. His black boxer briefs do nothing to hide his hard and rather large cock. He crawls into bed. "That's not mean, sweetheart. Mean would be bringing you to your brink but keeping your fall just out of your reach. Again and again…"

I feel my eyes widen as my mouth goes dry. "Oh my God."

He lays on his side and props himself up on his elbow. He crooks a finger at me. I immediately move to his side. He rests his arm across my stomach and looks down at me. Just his touch makes me nearly come

55

undone. I try to turn onto my side, but he holds me still with one arm and grabs my hand with the other so I can't touch him. How he knew that's what I wanted is something I'll never understand.

"What did I just say?"

I bite my lip and take a deep breath. "I promise to tell you, but please don't make me wait, Ryan. Now that I can actually have you and made the decision to, I just… These past few days. The teasing. Touching…" I look down shyly. I crave him. I need him more than I need to breathe. I feel silly and needy all at the same time.

"I'll give you everything you want and more, but not until after you give me what I want."

I let out a frustrated groan and sit up, knowing I'm not winning this battle. "Okay… I'll tell you." He grabs the back of the t-shirt and pulls me down again. He wraps his arms tightly around me and kisses me on the forehead. I let out a sigh of contentment. I love being just like this with him. "I've been thinking about marrying you." I keep my attention focused on the ceiling and feel him tense.

After a moment, he clears his throat. "And?"

"And... I guess I just wanted to know what you were planning." My voice is quiet, and I can't help the sadness that creeps in. "Are you planning on just going to a courthouse?"

He relaxes and laughs. I glare, though very unintentionally. He immediately stops. He runs his thumb along my lower lip and smiles as he rests his hand in my collarbone and neck.

"Aria. What the hell do you take me for? Do you honestly think I'm not going to give you everything you want?"

I can feel my eyes light up as a smile creeps onto the corner of my lips. "Really?"

"Baby. Come on. I had planned to sit here tomorrow with you and ask what you wanted to do. Where you wanted it to be. Everything." I smile at him, then look away again as I chew on the inside of my cheek. "Aria." He takes my face in his hand and gently turns me so I'm looking at him again. He says nothing as he stares deeply in my eyes.

I take a deep breath. "What about guests?"

"Baby. You realize I know exactly what you're getting at, right? Renza and her boyfriend are welcome to come. You can invite whoever you want to." He smiles. I smile so widely that my face hurts. I fling myself into his arms. "Oof." He tightens his grip around me as he hugs me.

"Thank you."

"Honey, my job is to make you happy. If you ever want anything, I don't care if it's your own island, tell me. Okay?"

I laugh. "You'd buy me an island?"

"I'd buy you the universe." He kisses my forehead. I kiss his chest. "That's what this whole day has been about?" He kisses the top of my head.

"I'm sorry. I've just been kind of obsessing about it. I've known Renza since we were kids and Robby since middle school. I can't imagine getting married without them. I just didn't know if it was an option."

He trails a hand down my back to my butt and squeezes. "I'm not going to keep you from two of the most important people in your life." His hand slowly creeps across my hip to the top of my pantyline. "I'm not like that." I suck in a breath as he hooks two fingers in the waistband of my panties. "Family. Most important thing in the world. Only people you can truly count on." He gives my waistband a tug and pulls them up. I gasp as the crotch of the panties hits my most sensitive places. "Promise to be quiet? I would love to hear you scream my name and moan, but I don't want my parents waking up."

"I promise," I whisper.

"Good girl." He leans in to kiss me as he tightens the grip on my panties. He rubs them back and forth against my wanting center. I let out another gasp into his mouth. It's like a magic I've never felt before. So much better than when I've done things to myself.

His tongue plunges into my mouth and finds mine, beginning a sexy dance as his finger runs down my panties. He pushes into me, finding my sensitive bud. He's still using the panties to torture me and doing everything he's doing on top of them. I moan again. My moans are muffled by his kiss. Feeling an overwhelming need to feel him in my hands, I reach down and rub him over his boxer briefs. It's his turn to let out a moan.

I shiver and giggle because I can't help it. "You're really big," I whisper shyly against his lips. I squeeze him, enjoying every second of the new experience. I've never really been this bold before, but I've been waiting a long time for him.

"Fuck, Aria."

I can tell he's fighting to stay quiet himself as I take his length out of his boxer briefs and start stroking him. He pushes my panties aside and slowly thrusts one finger deeply inside me. Before I have a chance to scream, he plunges his tongue back into my mouth, like he knew exactly what the feel of his finger would do to me.

"Mmm..." I tighten my grip on his dick and start moving my hand to match the pace he's set with his finger inside me. Everything about touching him feels natural to me. Like it's meant to be. Like my whole life was lived just for this moment with him.

As if my body is in tune with his, I begin rotating my wrist as I stroke him. The movement has him twitching underneath me. My heart soars with the knowledge that I'm doing it right. He pulls back from my mouth as his breath quickens and starts kissing my neck.

"God..." He pulls his finger out of me, and I nearly cry, but he very quickly lifts the t-shirt I'm wearing off of me. He tosses it and pulls my panties off. He throws them before he strips his own off and tosses them wherever mine landed.

I watch him with curiosity, missing his touch. Missing all of him. Very gently, he thrusts one of his fingers back into me, and his mouth crashes down on mine again. I find his hard, wanting cock once more and start stroking him as he sinks his finger into me again.

And again.

And again.

He bends his head and takes one of my nipples in his mouth and lightly bites it.

"Ah!" I arch off the bed into his mouth. His finger sinks deeper, making me cry out again as my hips start moving on their own. He feels like silk encased steel in my hand as I grip him while he sends me spiraling towards complete loss of control.

"Shh!" Ryan puts his other hand over my mouth as he continues his masterful thrusts. I start rotating my wrist on his cock again as he takes my other nipple in his mouth.

"Mmm...!" My stomach begins to tighten. I feel myself clench around his fingers. I stroke him faster, gripping him a little bit tighter.

"Oh, shit... That feels so good." He lightly bites my nipple and sets his thumb against my clit as he thrusts into my hand. He starts rubbing in small circles as I feel a wetness coming from him. I try to look down, but he gently coaxes another finger inside me.

My eyes widen. "Oh my God..." He thrusts as deeply as he can inside me and crooks his fingers as he rubs circles around my clit. His other hand is still over my mouth muffling my cries as I arch off the bed.

"Come for me, baby," Ryan whispers as he keeps up his masterful strokes.

My entire body feels like it's coming apart around him. I shake and shiver as I clench around his fingers. My pussy pulses erratically, and my hips jerk hard against him. He doesn't stop thrusting as I ride through the most intense orgasm I've ever had.

I continue to stroke him as he sits up on his knees. He slowly pulls his fingers out of me and takes himself in his hands. A couple strokes later, his warm release finds its way onto my stomach and chest.

I pant and look up at him, oddly pleased that he's, in a way, marking me. Like I'm his. I know I'm his, but this new level of intimacy is everything to me. It's everything I want. Everything I need. A way for him to show he belongs to me just as I belong to him.

A few minutes later, after we're both cleaned up, we lie back down in the bed, still naked. He pulls me close to him, my back to his chest, and nuzzles me. He kisses the back of my neck as he pulls up the blanket around us and wraps me in his arms

I bite my lip, unsure what to really say, so I burrow into him."I… thank you..."

"For what, beautiful?"

"Making that, all of that, really… nice for me." I can feel my cheeks heat up. I cuddle into him and the blankets.

He chuckles, but it sounds more like a hum. "You don't need to thank me for that. I know you've been wanting to do more and more things with me." He smiles against my neck. "I don't mind being the one you're testing things out with."

I blush darker. "I don't want to do any of this with anyone. I never have. I won't ever want anyone but you."

"Good. Because I'm possessive as fuck." He growls low against my neck.

I shiver. Belonging to him. I don't want anything else. "I love you."

"I love you, too."

I cuddle myself as closely to him as I can. He wraps his arms tightly around me. I sigh in contentment.

Crazily enough, I feel… different. More complete. Whole. I don't know if it's normal. Maybe I'm just riding the high of the first orgasm I've ever had. I've never been able to give them to myself. I feel more womanly. I feel more like an adult. Like I'm his.

No. Not like his. I am his.

Moments later, feeling like the most important thing in the world to him, I fall asleep in the comfort and safety of his arms. He wraps even more possessively around me, and I feel satisfied and secure.

Chapter Seven

☒ Ryan ☒

Waking up the next morning with Arianna naked next to me may be the hottest thing I've ever woken up to. I have no idea what stirred me from my slumber, but I smile and bury my head in her hair. Just as I'm about to kiss her neck, my phone starts going off. I groan. Arianna stirs, but doesn't wake up, so I quickly and gently disentangle myself from her and grab my phone as I sit on the edge of my bed.

Three in the morning. Taylor. I remember he wanted a description from Arianna for that guard who was helping her, but I can't wrap my head around him calling at three in the morning.

I glance at Arianna to make sure she's still sleeping before I quietly answer my phone. "Hey. Why so early?"

"I know. I'm not happy either. But I got a lead."

"Oh?" I feel Arianna stir again. I glance at her once more and decide to let her sleep. "Hang on a sec." I put my phone on the bed, quietly grabbing a pair of sweats from the dresser and quickly putting them on. I grab my phone and, as silently as I can, leave the room and walk to my living room. "Alright. Sorry. I didn't want to wake Arianna up."

"I hate to say it man, but you might need to."

I sigh. "What, Taylor?"

"One of my contacts in New York gave me a little information that you and I both missed."

"I don't miss anything."

"Neither do I. But we missed this. Luke Ambrosio. Same last name as a very small-time mafia boss in New Jersey. One who is very deeply involved in the Massena mafia."

"I know that."

"Arianna told you the name of the guy her dad is forcing on her, right?"

"Chad."

"Stephen Ambrosio has one son. Chad Ambrosio. Age eighteen. Went to the same school as her."

"I also know that."

"I got word that he's trying to form an alliance with Massena."

"I know that, too. Massena is trying to combine with them to take me out. It's why he was forcing Arianna into this arranged marriage with the Ambrosio Mafia kid. Did I not tell you that?"

"I know you know all of that. And you did tell me. This is my confirmation of all your suspicions."

"Tell me something I don't know. I know you ain't calling at three in the morning to confirm my fucking suspicions. Back to Luke. You said Ambrosio has one son."

"He does. No record of a second. And believe me. I've checked into everything but his bank records. There are no signs of a double life, second family, secret son. Nothing."

I rub my temple. "You still think he's a cop?"

"Gut feeling. But I need to dig more into this trumped up background. I still think he was placed. The problem is I don't know who did it."

"What do you mean? I thought you said he was new to Massena's band of misfits. Which is fucking ironic if his last name is Ambrosio."

"Agreed. And that's how it looked. I'm still not sure if he is or isn't a cop. But I've dug a little deeper. His record shows dealings attached to Ambrosio. Either whoever planted these records is stupid or really fucking smart. And I have a picture. I'll send it to you now. You'll have to have

Arianna identify him for me. Make sure I'm not barking up the wrong tree with what I'm thinking."

"So what are you thinking?"

"Well. It's what I think we're missing. The link to him. Where he fits. I think he was planted in Ambrosio's mafia a year, maybe two years ago. I think he's managed to get close to him. Get Ambrosio to trust him. Maybe because of his last name. Playing a long lost son. I don't know. But I think when Ambrosio and Massena decided to align against you, Ambrosio put one of his trusted confidants in place as a spy."

I nod and lean back against the couch and nod. "Makes sense. I've done it. Make sure there isn't any treachery or betrayal going on, and that the alignment is on the up and up."

"Exactly."

"Still doesn't explain who he really is, though. I want more information on this guy. Arianna trusts him, so there has to be more to this."

"It's a theory. I have more research to do so I can have a more concrete answer for you. In the meantime, we need confirmation on who we're up against. I need Arianna to identify Luke Ambrosio."

"Where did you find that picture?"

"In his criminal jacket. But I found one matching it in the deep pits of files with the NYPD. I don't know how the two are connected though. It's not with staff files or criminal files. All I know right now, is we need to figure it out. We need to find out his connection and what department he's from. I really think he's with some agency."

I can't help but smile and shake my head as I stand up and walk back to my room. "You keep saying we. You know I have thousands of people at my disposal. An entire fucking army. You don't need to be involved."

Taylor chuckles. "Do you consider Chase and I brothers? Our wives, your sisters? Tait your nephew?"

"You know the answer to that. All of that."

"Then yes, Ryan. We. Like it or not, Chase and I are with you. All of us are. Arianna doesn't deserve this shit. Neither do you. We *all* are going to do whatever we need to do to help. She's family. Just like you are. You bend over backwards for us all the time. It's our turn to return the favor."

My heart actually swells a little at his words. Fuck. Who am I kidding? It swells a lot. Knowing my family is at my side is one thing. Hearing their proclamation is quite another.

I quietly open the door to my room. Arianna is laying on her stomach spread eagle and butt naked across my bed. I groan as I sit on the edge of the bed. My dick is instantly hard for her, but I force myself to behave, given Taylor is on the phone.

I hear Taylor laugh. He really knows me too well. "I promise I'll leave you alone as soon as I get what I need."

"Tell me again why you need this so fucking early in the morning?"

"Do you want this to be over?"

"Yes. God yes."

"Then wake her up. Give her the phone so I can talk to her, and show her the picture."

"You're an asshole."

"I know. But the quicker you do this, the quicker I'm out of your hair, and you can sink your tongue back into her."

I growl low but chuckle and shake my head. "Fuck you. If you were here, I'd punch you. I still might."

"No you won't. Because you know I'm right. Come on. Hurry up. I want to go home."

"Newsflash. She's only had my fingers. And my come all over her stomach. You aren't home? Why?"

Taylor laughs. "I didn't need to know that. And no. Had a warrant to deliver." I hear the amusement and pure, raw enjoyment in his voice as I reach over to Arianna. I put my hand on the globe of her perfect round ass and squeeze.

"You enjoy your job far too much, Reddick."

"So do you."

Arianna stirs and pushes her ass into my hand as I start rubbing it. "Wake up, baby." She whimpers and turns her head towards me. She opens her eyes, giving me adorable doe eyes, and blinks in confusion. "It's early. I'm sorry. Taylor wants to talk to you. He has questions."

She sleepily holds out her tiny hand. I give her my phone. "Hello?" I lean down and press my lips to her ass, leaving a trail down her cheek to her upper thigh. Maybe I won't behave. "Mmm…" I smile against her leg

64

and drop a kiss to her other one, this time dragging my tongue along her upper thigh to her ass, then kissing along the same trail. "Okay."

She takes the phone away from her ear and taps a few buttons to get into my texts from Taylor. I run a finger along her sexy little pussy. She gasps. She tries to move away, but I hold her down by her hips. She looks back at me wide-eyed. I grin devilishly as I straddle her.

She takes a deep breath and goes back to the picture. She brings the phone up to her ear again. "Yes. That's the guard. Luke." I keep my hands tightly on her hips to keep her still as I lean down and bite her ass. "Yes..." Her voice is breathy. I bite the other cheek. She buries her head in the pillow to stop her scream. She's taken the phone away from her ear. I reach over to take it from her hand.

"We're done, Taylor. I'll call you later." I don't wait for him to answer. I hang up and throw my phone to the other side of the bed.

I run my hands up her hips and sides until I reach the back of her neck. I put my hands on each side of her head on the bed and lean down over her. I move her hair aside and kiss her neck.

"Mmmm... Ryan..."

I let her feel my hard cock against her ass and she arches into me. Now that she's let me touch her; now that she's had her perfect little fingers wrapped around my dick, I can't get enough of her. I sit up, still straddling her. She pushes herself up until she's sitting on her knees in front of me, her back to me, as I tug her up by her hair. I don't do it hard enough to hurt her, but I do it hard enough so that she knows exactly what I want her to do.

"Be quiet, Aria. Or I'll stop."

She nods, shivering against me. "I promise. I'll be quiet."

"Good girl." I slowly run my hands down her arms to her hips and pull her roughly back to me so her back hits my chest. Hard.

"Oh..."

I grab her wrists and lift her arms until they're reaching behind her and wrapped around my shoulders. She locks her fingers around the back of my neck. I slowly run my fingertips down her arms until they're grazing her neck. One hand continues down to her incredible breasts while the other turns her head to meet my lips. I kiss her and drop my other hand down. I take one of her tits in each of my hands. I pinch, twist, and massage each of her nipples as she grinds her ass into my cock.

"Fuck, baby…," I breathe against her lips. I bite her lip, hard enough to make her whimper while still being gentle. My tongue twines with hers as I run my hands tantalizingly down to her very smooth, incredibly pretty, and extremely wet pussy. I kiss along her jaw to her ear and nibble on it before whispering to her. "What do you want?" My hand is just above where I know she wants me to be. My other arm is across her stomach, holding her tightly against me while she tries to arch herself into my fingers.

"Your fingers…," she whispers.

"Where?" I let my hand fall lower and run my finger from her clit to her pussy, then take it away as she quietly moans.

She melts against me, trembling. "Right there."

I run my finger from her clit to her pussy again, then take it away again just as she moans.

"There?"

"Yes... Yes… Ryan..." Her voice is barely a whisper. It's more breathy moans; soft whimpers.

I lean down and kiss her neck and shoulder again. "What do you say? What's the magic word?" I cup her core but do nothing else.

She grinds against my hand and pushes back into my dick. "Please. Please..."

I kiss her jaw and then the back of her head as I move to the other side of her neck and start kissing her again. Still holding her tightly against me and cupping her core, I drop my middle finger onto her clit and drag it to her center. I slowly circle her entrance as she struggles to arch into me.

I gradually give her the finger she wants so badly until it's buried deeply inside her. "You're so wet," I whisper in her ear. "So fucking tight."

"Mmm..." I remove my finger, then enter again, harder and deeper as I bite her neck and suck. "Oh!"

I smile as I remove my finger and my hand. I push her forward so she's on her hands and knees. I take her hair with one hand and run the flat of my palm down her back to her ass. I pull her hair so her back is arched.

"What did I say about being quiet?" I drop my voice an octave lower so it's more of a growl. The dominant tone gives my girl chills. She shivers beneath my touch.

"To stay quiet," she whispers submissively as her body arches into every touch.

66

"And what did you just do?"

"I was loud," she whispers apologetically. I bring my hand down on her ass. Hard. "Oh! Mmm..." She buries her face in her pillow. I spank the other cheek. She screams into the pillow. I tug her hair again until she's flush against my chest once more.

"What's the rule?"

"To stay quiet."

"Good girl." I put her arms back around my neck and pull her ass flush against my cock. I cup her again and gently slide two fingers into her this time. Inch by fucking inch.

Her fingers dig into my hair as she moans. "Yes..."

As I give her deep thrusts with my fingers and go back to kissing her neck and shoulders, she lets one of her arms fall. She rests it on my hand that I am using to finger her with.

I smile. One of the things I'm starting to love more than I care to admit is how enjoyable it is for me to teach her.

And I like my control.

"Did I tell you that you could move your arm?"

"No..."

"Then why did you?"

"I... I don't know."

"Then you better put it back before I punish you again for not listening and stop finger fucking you." She quickly puts her arm back around my neck. "Good girl." I lick her neck and then kiss it as I set my thumb against her clit while continuing to thrust inside her.

"Mmmm... Ryan... Please..."

"Please, what? What do you want me to do?" I feel her legs start to shake and her stomach quiver as she tightens around me. I'm loving watching my girl come into her own sexuality and start learning what she likes.

"Make me... Mmm..." Her breathing quickens. Her pussy starts to pulse.

"Make you what, baby? What do you want me to do?" I want her to say it. I never want her to be shy around me. I want her to always feel comfortable in telling me exactly what she wants.

"Make me come." Her voice is barely above a whisper. Shy as hell. I'm enjoying every fucking second.

I chuckle and kiss her ear as I rub circles around her clit with my thumb while I thrust inside her. I whisper in her ear. "What do you say?"

"Please. Please, Ryan." She rubs her ass against my cock harder. I let her as I give her the pressure she needs against her clit.

"Good girl. Come for me."

Seconds later, she collapses against me. She tightens and clenches around me as her hips jerk against me. I slow my thrusts until her orgasm subsides.

She physically can't stay upright without me to steady her, so I help her to lay down. I head for the bathroom and grab a washcloth. I dampen it with warm water and walk back to the bed. I gently clean her up as she smiles softly and sleepily at me

When I finish, I walk back to the bathroom and rinse the cloth out before hanging it to dry. I strip my sweats on the way back out and crawl back into the bed. I pull her down into my arms as I lay on the bed. I pull the blankets up over both of us as she goes limp in my arms.

"What was that? It was so... intense." She buries her head in my chest and wraps herself around me.

I chuckle again at how truly fucking sexy she is. "Are you okay?"

"So much. I'm more than okay."

"Get some sleep. I'm sorry I had to wake you up, honey."

"Why couldn't Taylor wait?" she mumbles into my side as she cuddles into me.

"He's like a dog with a bone. He gets a tip or a lead, and he becomes relentless about it. But in this case, it was a good thing. The sooner he gets what he needs, the sooner we know what we're up against and can take care of it so we can move on."

She yawns. "I understand." She yawns again, and I kiss the top of her head as I run my fingers through her hair. Her breathing evens quickly, and she's almost instantly asleep. I tighten my grip around her and follow quickly behind her refusing to think of what's to come.

Instinctively, I know something about this entire thing with her father and Ambrosio is off. It just doesn't make sense.

Chapter Eight

✗ Arianna ✗

(Two Days Later)

A couple of nights later, Ryan and I are sitting in Boka, one of Chicago's most exclusive restaurants, waiting for the rest of our family to arrive. He rented out the entire restaurant for us.

"Have you heard from Renza?" he asks.

I nod. "I have. They should be here soon. She texted me when they got in the car you sent for them."

Ryan has been really secretive all day long. He took me to lunch earlier, then out shopping for a dress. He sent his plane for Renza and Robby and told me he wanted them here because I hadn't seen them. He said he thought it would be a good thing for me.

I love how sweet he's being, but I also know him. He has an ulterior motive, and he refuses to tell me. The longer the day has gone on, though, the more nervous I've become. I'm pretty sure I know what's happening. Even though we're already planning our wedding, he hasn't given me a ring.

"You look beautiful, Aria. Stunning in that dress. I'm glad you trusted me when I told you how perfectly it accentuates every part of you."

I look down at the light rose colored dress and nervously tug it over my exposed leg. There's a slit that runs from the floor to my upper thigh. The straps are thin spaghetti straps. It dips down my chest, though not enough to really show anything. The soft chiffon hugs my body. I've never worn anything like it.

Ryan reaches over and takes my hand. He brings it to his lips and kisses it.

I look at him shyly. "You really don't think it's too much?"

"No. I don't. You're beautiful, honey. And don't think I didn't see that look on your face after you put it on. You love it. And you love the way you feel in it."

I smile and look away as I blush. I really do love it. As soon as I saw it, I fell in love with it. After I put it on, I fell in love even further with it.

But I'm terrified of wearing clothing that shows this much. Clothing this revealing. I've never been comfortable showing off my body because I've never felt pretty enough. I've always felt embarrassed about it.

I look down at the dress again and run my fingers along the soft chiffon fabric. "I do really like the dress." I turn and smile at him as I reach over to adjust his rose colored tie that perfectly matches my dress. His black suit is tailored to fit him. All of his clothes are. They almost have to be. Being a man as tall and muscular as him… It's difficult to find clothes that fit right. "You look pretty damn good yourself, you know."

He smiles and takes both of my hands in his once more. He kisses them and leans over to kiss me. "Thank you."

I glance towards the door of the restaurant as Ryan's parents walk in. They're hand in hand and looking at each adoringly as they laugh with each other.

That. That's the kind of relationship I want. Being together for so long and still being so in love with each other.

Ryan and I both stand as his parents reach us. His mother immediately kisses me on the cheek and hugs me before she even acknowledges Ryan.

Ryan laughs. "Wow. I can see I've been replaced as the favorite already."

His mother laughs. "You know I've always wanted a daughter."

"You got one, mom! Two years ago. And look. There she is now!" Ryan gestures to the door as Jessa and Jason come in. They're also holding hands and looking more in love than ever.

"Oh my Gosh! Arianna, that dress is gorgeous!" Jessa looks me over. I blush once more under the attention as Chase and Nicole show up.

I look at them, confused, as Nicole kisses my cheek. "Um... Where's Breetana? And Taylor?"

"They're coming," Nicole says.

"Breetana had some kind of crisis with her shoe and Taylor is fixing it. Why are there so many paparazzi?" Chase asks. "I'm not used to that chaotic bullshit around you."

"I know. But I need them. Taylor is fixing a shoe?" Ryan asks incredulously.

"Don't ask me, bro. I got nothing." Chase shrugs.

Breetana and Taylor walk in. She hugs me. "Such a pretty dress."

"That dress is more than gorgeous, sweetheart." Taylor hugs me. I take a deep breath, tightening my grip. He keeps me in his arms as Ryan talks to everyone. "You okay?"

"Overwhelmed. Everyone is complimenting me and this dress. It's just so different."

"You aren't used to the attention. And it's sexier than the stuff you're used to wearing."

I nod. "But I really like it. And I really like the way it looks on me."

"I see. Well, do you want a piece of advice? From your big brother?" He smiles into my hair. I nod again. "It's not the dress that's sexy or beautiful, Arianna. It's you." He pulls back just a little. I look up at him, bewildered. "You make the clothes. The clothes don't make you. I can tell you love this dress. The way you feel about it and about how you look in it is why everyone is complimenting you and the dress, sweetheart." Taylor kisses me on top of the head before he turns to the rest of the group. I smile and look away. "Ry, did you get a car for mom? I have to get hers fixed. I keep forgetting."

Ryan nods. "She should be here soon. I also sent a tow truck to tow her piece of shit car out of there. Honestly, Taylor. Hell, and Chase for that matter. You two need to take better care of that woman. Get her a different car."

"It's not my fault she won't accept one!" Chase says with a grin as he helps Breetana into a chair.

"She's a stubborn old woman. That's for sure," Taylor says.

"Hey, now. I'm not that old, young man."

I turn and see Eve walking in with Renza and Robby. Tears of happiness at seeing them instantly sting my eyes.

I run to them. "Oh my God, you guys! I'm so happy you're here!" I launch myself at both of them. Robby catches me and lifts me up as he hugs me tightly like he hasn't seen me in years.

"Miss me?" Robby teases.

"So much!" I'm not teasing at all. I genuinely missed him.

I bury my head in his shoulder as Renza stands next to him, an expression I can't quite recognize on her face.

"We missed you, too," she says. But there doesn't seem to be much emotion. I would question it, but I'm sure it's just because she's tired.

Robby puts me down after a few moments. I take in their outfits for the first time. I'm speechless. "Oh, wow, you guys. You guys look amazing."

Renza is wearing a simple black dress, but since she never wears dresses, I'm in awe of how pretty she looks. Robby, for the first time ever, is wearing a charcoal gray suit.

"They were under strict orders." Ryan slips his arms around my waist and bends to kiss my neck. I smile as he straightens and moves to my side. "Hey, guys. I know we've seen each other, but never been introduced. I'm Ryan Crane."

"Robby Earnhardt, sir." The two shake hands.

"No need to call me sir, Robby." Ryan turns to Renza and shakes her hand.

"Renza Gregorson, Mr. Crane."

"Not Mr. Crane either. You guys can just call me Ryan." I smile as Ryan kisses the top of my head and looks up at the door. He smiles widely. "Alex! Josh! You didn't say if you were going to make it or not!" He hugs them both excitedly.

Ryan has gotten so close to Josh over the past couple of years. Just as close to him as he is to Alex and the rest of his family. It's heartwarming to me, considering everything everyone has been through with him.

"Oh my God! Josh!" Jessa jumps up from the table and leaps in Josh's arms, nearly knocking Ryan over.

"Holy fuck, honey," Josh says as he catches her.

"I don't think I've ever gotten that reaction out of her. And I dated her for four years," Alex teases as he laughs.

"I'm married to her. She's never greeted me like that!" Jason grins like an idiot as Jessa hugs Josh.

"I lost my place as mom's favorite and my sister's favorite all in one night," Ryan mock pouts as he looks down at me. "Am I going to lose being your favorite, too?"

"You already have!" Taylor says from his place at the table. "I became her favorite the day we met!"

"Fucking asshole." Ryan shakes his head and winks at me as I laugh. Josh puts Jessa down. Alex takes his turn hugging her. I hover shyly behind Ryan as he launches into a conversation I don't understand with Josh. Alex talks quietly with Jessa. I find myself hiding further and further behind Ryan.

After a few moments, Josh's intense blue eyes fall on me. I shiver as he looks back at Ryan. "This the girl you won't shut up about?"

Ryan turns to me and smiles as he reaches for me and tucks me into his side. "This… is Arianna."

I blush and cross my arms over my chest. "Hi," I say quietly, trying to mold myself to Ryan. Not that I'm scared. But being around so many people, even though they're all family, is slightly overwhelming.

"Arianna. I'm Josh." His voice is deep and smooth. Commanding. Just like Ryan's. I can see why they get along so well just with that trait. Lucky for me, I know their backstory. I know how much Josh has helped Ryan since he took over the Lucinio mafia. And I know how much Ryan has helped Josh to go legit, like he's done with Crane mafia.

I take a deep breath and extend my hand for him to shake. "It's nice to meet you." I smile softly. "I've heard a lot about you."

"All good things, I hope." He gives me a sweet smile that drips with sex appeal.

73

My eyes widen slightly. I was wrong. His voice is deeper. Far more commanding. Ten times more intimidating. I didn't think it was possible for anyone to top Ryan in those qualities. He gently lets my hand go.

"Mostly good things," I say quietly. I would usually be terrified of people like him. But I'm not. He may project all things dominating and scary, but I can tell he's just as protective as Ryan. Just as kind.

Alex extends his hand as Jessa steps away and heads back to her seat. "Hey, Arianna. I'm Alex. Ryan has told me so much about you."

"He's told me a lot about you, too. I'm glad to meet you," I say. Ryan hugs me a little tighter to his side as Alex squeezes my hand gently before letting it go.

"I think it's time for everyone to have a seat so we can eat, huh? I'm starving," Ryan says.

"Hear! Hear! Definitely time to eat!" Ethan Crane exclaims.

I take my place at the head of the table next to Ryan, where he told me to sit. His father and mother sit across from me, and Jason sits next to me. I glance at Jason, expecting he would let Renza and Robby sit next to me.

He smiles and leans into me, keeping his voice low. "I'm guessing your dad never had formal dinners," he whispers. I shake my head. "In most formal mafias, formal dinners are different from regular ones. The head of the table is reserved for the boss, the leader. The head of the family. That's Ryan. To his right is always supposed to be his significant other. In Ryan's case, until you, it had always been me at his side because he didn't have a significant other. To his left is always our father. The one who stepped down and handed him the reins. In the mafia, it's a sign of respect to the former Head of the Household. When our father passes, it will be whoever Ryan intends to leave the mafia to. His son or daughter. Right now, that person is Nick." He nods to the empty seat next to his mother.

I bite my lip, trying to follow. "So…, is this where I am supposed to always sit?"

"During formal dinners like this one, yes. If we're just having family dinners like we do at our parents every Sunday, then no. It doesn't matter where you sit as long as it's next to him. Sitting next to anyone else would be a sign of disrespect to him as the leader and him as your significant other. I'm not exactly in anymore. Not to the extent that I was. I have no command over anyone, but when it comes to us being together, as a family, formally or otherwise, Jessa is expected to adhere to the same rules." Jason gives me a quick side hug as I nod. "Don't worry about it. We're all here to help you."

"Thank you."

"Anytime, sweetheart."

"Hey, everyone. I'm sorry I'm late."

I look up as Nick walks into the room. I smile, feeling some strange sense of relief that he's here. Safer. Not because of his large, hulking, over six foot, muscular frame. It's because without him, the family felt incomplete. And I know Ryan well enough to know that, though I trust him and would never question his abilities, his strength comes from his family. One missing link is a chink in Ryan's armor. A weakness he would never admit is there. Now that Nick is here, I feel like Ryan's army is whole.

I watch as Nick walks directly to Ryan with a manilla envelope. He leans down and whispers in his ear. I can't quite hear, but I see Ryan's eyes flash dangerously, and I'm instantly on edge. When Nick stands, he squeezes my shoulder and leans down to hug me. I take a deep breath as I hug him back.

"We'll talk about the envelope later. I don't want to ruin your night." He starts to stand, but I grip his arm slightly. He raises an eyebrow.

If I'm expected to be the wife of a mafia king, I need to start showing I'm strong enough and confident enough to do it. Even though I'm quivering like a three-year-old who just saw a monster.

I shake my head. "No. I want to know what's happening," I say softly. "I feel like it would just be hanging over my head all night and cause worry."

He grins and glances at Ryan before he looks back at me. "There's information in that envelope dealing with Luke Ambrosio and his family. We don't know exactly who he is yet, but we do know a little more about him. We found his mother. So, tracking him is going to be a little easier."

"I... thought he belonged to the Ambrosio mafia."

"So did we. But now? Well, we question. Things don't add up. The information we found is mostly about his mom. I thought I'd let Ryan look and see what he thinks, but to me? It looks like Luke is undercover. Taylor agrees. Ryan agrees, but you know him. Ryan needs all of our theories backed up and proven with facts and evidence and documentation."

I glance at Ryan. He's grinning from ear to ear at my moment of assertiveness. No one else at the table seems to be paying any attention to our whispered conversation except Jason, who is giving my hand a comforting squeeze.

I smile softly and release my light grip on his arm. "Sorry. Ryan has always told me everything… And I… just really didn't want to have that be the only thing I'm thinking about."

Nick straightens with an even wider smile. "Don't apologize. You needed to know for your own piece of mind." He winks as he walks to his seat. I look down at my hands, more to steady myself than anything else.

Throughout the dinner, everyone talks and laughs, and I can't get over how easy it is to fall into such a comfortable rhythm with them.

Other than my mother, I've never felt like anyone in my life really loved me or cared about me. I don't have siblings. Other than Renza and Robby, I've never felt that camaraderie. That sense that no matter what, at least I have my family. My siblings. I suppose Renza and Robby are the closest I've ever gotten. I love them like family. But I've still never been a part of anything like this.

Everyone at this table would do anything to protect anyone else sitting at this table with no hesitation and no questions asked. I can't believe how lucky I am to be a part of it. To be a part of this... this amazing family.

I smile up at Ryan as he stands. He doesn't need to speak or use a fork on a glass to get anyone's attention. His presence and action is commanding enough. Everyone silences immediately. All attention is on him.

"Thank you all for coming. I realize this past week has been crazy. We've solved one problem only to face another. I'm used to people trying to take me out on a daily basis, but not family. I don't take well to that, as you all know. I'd do whatever it took to protect you. Each and every one of you." He visibly takes a deep breath. "Which is why having you all come together for me and the woman I love is so humbling."

Ryan makes eye contact with a server standing at the side of the room. The server nods and then leaves the room. Ryan waits and I'm, once again, confused.

After a few moments, swarms of paparazzi enter the restaurant and Ryan offers me a hand. I take it. He helps me up.

"What are you doing?" I ask so only he can hear as I glance over my shoulder. Everyone's eyes are on us. He leans forward so his lips are against my ear. Cameras flash behind us and in front of us. We're surrounded. My heart quickens as he cups my cheek.

"I told you this had to be public, and I know we're already getting married, but I want to make this as special for you as I can." Ryan slowly sinks to one knee, his hands sweetly and gently running down my sides to my hips.

"Ryan..." Tears sting my eyes. I smile down at him.

"I know we've already discussed everything, but I'm not going to just put a ring on your finger. You mean everything to me. Ever since I met you, all I've wanted is to be a part of your life in some way. The more we got to know each other, the more open with you I became. I couldn't keep anything from you no matter how much I tried. And then over the last couple of years, I realized I had fallen head over heels for you. It was crazy. Irrational. But you're the only one I've ever truly loved, sweetheart."

He takes my left hand in his and slips the most beautiful ring I've ever seen on my finger. The band has to be eighteen-karat white-gold. The diamond in the middle is a princess cut halo diamond surrounded by two tapered baguette cut diamonds. There are several diamonds surrounding both the halo diamond, and the baguette cut diamonds, as well as several diamonds throughout the handcrafted design of the ring. It's so brilliantly stunning that when the light hits it, the ring itself becomes the center of all attention.

But to me? Everything centers around Ryan. I don't notice anyone else in the room. The cameras flashing, our family, the servers. No one. Just Ryan.

"This ring belonged to my grandmother. And now it belongs to you." He kisses my hand, and the ring. "What do you say? Ready to do this thing? To marry me?"

I let out a sob and nod. "Yes! Yes! Yes!"

He smiles more brightly than the ring shines and stands. He picks me up and spins me in a circle. He holds me so close and tightly as he kisses me that any fear or apprehension that I had ever felt about anything, ever, melts away.

When he finally pulls away and lowers me slowly to the floor, I'm dizzy on the taste of him. His touch. It takes me a minute to come back to myself and realize others are watching.

He bends and leaves one more sweet kiss on my lips. "I love you. I'm sorry I had to make it be so staged."

"I don't feel like it was staged. I think it was incredibly sweet that you wanted to make this as special for me as you could. And it will be nicely documented for the world to see." I gesture to the paparazzi.

Ryan laughs. "Right you are." He helps me back into my seat and turns to the paparazzi. "I trust you all got what you needed. You know my terms. Plaster the engagement everywhere. One false word, you don't want to know what happens." He looks around the room. "Where's Dave Jennings with People and Marianne Embers with New York Times?"

One of the young men raises his hand. He's average height. Average looking. His wavy brown hair is styled and neat. "Here, sir. Dave Jennings. People Magazine."

"Marianne Embers. New York Times, sir," an eager, very petite, blond woman says. They both step forward.

"You two stay. Everyone else, you're dismissed. Thank you for your time. Have a great evening." Ryan waits until everyone else has exited the room. He reaches down a hand to me. I take it. He pulls me up to his side. "Arianna, meet Dave and Marianne. I've done an extensive background check on them. They'll be the photographers for our wedding."

"Oh. O-okay." I politely put out my hand to each of them to shake. "Nice to meet you."

"We're here for whatever you need, Ms. Massena," Dave says professionally and politely.

"We'll be photographing the wedding, but we also want to make sure you get the photographs that you want." Marianne's smile is as sweet as she looks.

"They have exclusive rights to the wedding. They'll be the only photographers allowed there," Ryan says next to me.

Dave nods. "We'd like to have a meeting with the two of you when you have time. Just to discuss the type of photographs you'd like."

I look at Ryan. I'm starting to become overwhelmed again. I know he can see it in my pleading eyes. I want to go home. I just want him. Selfish as that may make me, I need his strength to make me strong again. This entire day, all of it, has sapped my energy. I'm not used to so much activity.

He gives me a soft smile and hugs me closer, protectively, to his side. "We'll get it done, guys. Thanks for your help tonight." They both nod and say their goodbyes as they leave. I let out the nervous breath I had been holding. Ryan bends down to my ear as a server brings out wine and desserts. "Are you okay? We'll leave right now if that's what you want. Just say the word."

I look around the table. I want to leave. But I also feel the need to spend time with our family. I squeeze his hand to give myself the comfort I need. He guides me to my seat and helps me in it. Knowing me so well, he scoots his own chair closer to me so I can feel his leg against mine. He rests our hands on his thigh. Somehow, though I'll never understand it, just that one small thing gives me everything I need to keep going.

"No. We can stay. I'm okay. The photographers and questions. The entire day. I'm tired, and it was a lot. I'm okay now."

He leans over and cups my cheek in his hand once more. He looks deeply into my eyes and leans in to kiss me. "I love you."

"I love you." I smile up at him.

At that moment, Josh and Alex stand. I startle as everyone watches them. Josh hurries from the room with his phone to his ear. Alex looks after him for a moment before taking a breath and turning apologetically and tormented to us.

"We gotta go. I'm sorry to you both, but something pretty bad just happened to Josh's girl." He quickly grabs the jacket Josh left on the back of his chair. "I'll call you later, Ry." He runs after his brother.

Ryan's eyes look stormy as he nods and gives my hand a squeeze.

"Hope everything is okay," I whisper.

"Me too, baby. We'll find out soon enough. In the meantime, let's try and enjoy the rest of our evening."

I nod and look around at the rest of the table as Ryan's father pours wine. After a few moments to gather their thoughts, everyone takes turns saying a few words to us. While I can feel a little bit of weight on Ryan's shoulders at not knowing what happened with Josh's girlfriend, with each person's words, I start to understand what I've been missing all these years.

Love.

The unconditional kind that only my mother and Ryan have ever given me. The unquestioning kind. The unbreakable bond of a family who has stuck together through unspeakable horrors and situations.

I never dared dream that one day I would be a part of this. That this would all, that it could ever, be mine.

✗✗✗✗

"I'm so happy I've gotten to spend the last few days with you," Renza says. She smiles, but it feels fake. I shake my head slightly. It's probably me reading too much into things.

I smile and squeeze her arm. "Me too!"

She takes a deep breath before looking at me. The apprehension I thought I saw is gone, replaced only with happiness and excitement. "Planning your wedding with you for real instead of just a whole fantasy. Actually picking out your wedding dress! It's so exciting!"

I search her eyes for any type of sadness or anything, but don't see it. I relax a little. "I know. It's surreal, honestly."

Renza and I are sitting in the backseat of one of Ryan's SUVs. Two of the mafia's guards are sitting in the front seat.

"I can't believe he allowed you out without him, though," she says softly. "With everything going on. And your dad knowing where you are now."

"That's why we have two escorts." I gesture to the two guards.

"You actually have four guards, Ms. Massena. There are two in the SUV behind us. Your fiancé's orders," Rico, Ryan's right hand-man says.

I smile as the driver pulls up to a boutique in downtown Chicago. I didn't know about the other two guards. Ryan was incredibly respectful of my request to pick out my wedding dress without him. I don't want him to see it. I want him to be surprised when he sees it on me for the first time.

With the threat of my father knowing where I am now, though, he hated the idea of not being near me. So he made sure that Rico is with me.

80

And since I know Rico, I'm comfortable with him. I trust him to protect me like Ryan would.

Renza and I wait for Rico to open the door for us. We get out when he tells us we can. He escorts us into the boutique, the other guards following closely behind. I nearly beam when I see Nicole and Taylor waiting inside for us.

Nicole squeals and hugs me tightly. "Tana is sorry she can't be here, but I'm so excited I get to be!"

"I'm really glad you were able to be, Nikki." I have no idea why, but having her here instead of just Renza puts me at ease. Though, I don't know why I'm nervous at all.

"Me too! You can help me talk sense into her when she comes out in a gorgeous wedding dress but finds everything she possibly can wrong with it." Renza bounces happily.

"That's why we have Taylor. A guy's opinion!" Nicole smiles adoringly at Taylor.

"Oh no. No. No. No. I'm here for one reason and one reason only. And that's so Arianna feels safe. Everything else is all on you guys." He smiles at me as I hug him.

"Thank you for coming. Even though I have all of these guards that Ryan sent."

"You're family, sweetheart. I'll do whatever I can. You know that."

"I know. That's why I asked you to be here." I may feel perfectly safe with Ryan's men, but Taylor gives me the extra that I need to be truly relaxed.

"Ms. Massena? I'm Sarah. I'll be helping you out today." I turn to the model tall and stunning red-haired woman behind me and shake the hand she's offered.

"Mr. Crane informed me that the boutique is to be closed while Ms. Massena is here. And that whatever she wants, she gets," Rico says.

"Yes, sir. I'll lock the door now." She quickly locks the door and turns back to me. "I've already pulled a few dresses that I think you'll like based on our conversation on the phone. If you'll all follow me, I'll show you to the waiting area. And then, Arianna, you and I will go to the dressing room."

"Oh. Um..." I look at Taylor, slightly panicked. The idea of being anywhere without him scares me. I'm not stupid. I know the danger I'm in.

He smiles reassuringly. "I go where you tell me, Arianna."

"Will you stay close? You and Rico? Like right by the dressing room?"

"You're the boss," Rico says.

I smile. We all follow Sarah. I haven't heard from my dad. I have no reason to be as on edge and scared as I am, but I can't help it. Without Ryan, I find myself completely freaking out.

When we get to the dressing room, Taylor takes my hand. "Hey, hold up a second." I turn and look up at him. "I can tell you're scared, Arianna. You look like you're about ready to dart at the slightest sound. But you're safe. I promise I won't let anything happen to you. Just go in there and enjoy this whole thing. Okay? I won't leave your side."

"And I won't either," Rico says.

"Promise?" I know it's childish, but I hold up my right pinkie finger. Rico smiles and Taylor laughs. They both hold up their right pinkie fingers and shake mine.

"Promise." Taylor squeezes my pinky.

"Promise." Rico smiles and winks.

I smile again, feeling better, as I step into the dressing room.

✗✗✗

Hours later, after trying on many different dresses and finding none that I like, I sit down on the floor in front of Renza and Nicole near tears.

"I've tried on every dress in this boutique, and I look terrible in all of them."

"Oh, honey. You don't. I promise. Some dresses were really pretty," Nicole says with a positive smile.

"Just because they weren't what you were looking for doesn't mean anything. It just means they haven't pulled the right dress for you." Renza gives me a soft smile.

"Exactly," Nicole says.

"Am I being too picky? Maybe I should start completely over." I look sadly around the store.

"It's your wedding dress! Of course you're not being too picky." Nicole chuckles a little, and it's a strange comfort to me.

"You want to look perfect on your wedding day. You have a vision of what you want. And that's a good thing. You need to love what you choose. And after getting to know you, I think I may have found the perfect dress. Come. Try it on." Sarah gestures to the dressing room. I sniffle and stand up. I trudge back to the dressing room and Sarah closes the door. "I know it's not in the exact parameters you gave me, but this dress is beautiful. I really think you'll love it."

I take a deep breath and try it on. I turn to the mirror as Sarah buttons the buttons. I gasp. "Oh my God." I run my fingers along the satin fabric. Tears sting my eyes. "It's so... pretty."

Sarah beams at me in the mirror. "It's almost a perfect fit. Not a lot of alterations except to the length." She cinches in the waist. "What do you think? Would you like to show your friends and family?"

I can only nod as I stare at my reflection. Sarah leads me out of the dressing room.

"Wow. Arianna. You're stunning," Taylor says.

I smile up at him as he falls into step at my side. I take my place in the center of the room. Sarah fusses with the dress and Nicole and Renza stare at me with open mouths. They both wipe away a tear.

"I love it." Nicole looks me up and down. "The train with lace and tiny jewels…"

"It's perfect." Renza looks down at her hands.

I nod and bite my lip. "It's the one."

"The one… The one?" Nicole looks hopefully at me. I nod.

"Arianna, you look amazing. Truly gorgeous." Renza is quiet. Her smile is soft.

Sarah adjusts the train so it can be fully seen. "What do you think, sweetie?"

"It's the one. I don't want to take it off. I love everything about it."

She smiles. "I had a feeling. Let's get your measurements so we can take care of the alterations quickly."

A little while later, we're leaving the boutique. Nicole left as I was getting measured so she could grab Tait from daycare. We ran later than we all thought. The daycare in Chase's building is closing soon. I can't stop smiling.

After finding the dress, I feel like a real bride.

Ryan's bride.

At that moment, fate decides to rear his ugly head. The driver of the SUV that Renza and I are in reaches for the door to open it for us.

"What the hell?" Taylor reaches for me. He catches my hair and yanks me back to him before I can get in the SUV.

I scream. "Ow! Taylor!" I rub my head where he pulled.

Rico grabs Renza by the arm and yanks her back to him. Taylor throws me on the ground and covers me with his body. I hear an explosion and scream again, covering my ears and head.

Taylor quickly stands up and pulls me up with him. My heart is racing. I'm terrified. I'm shaking. I can hardly breathe.

"Check my truck! Now!" Taylor commands.

I'm still screaming as I cover my ears. I'm crying and nearly choking as I try to catch my breath. The guards are scrambling around us. Taylor has his gun in one hand and pulls me into his chest with the other.

"Shh... It's okay, sweetheart. I've got you," Taylor says in my ear. It's only then I realize he's shielding me with his body. He has me pressed against the wall of the building with his body as he scans the entire perimeter.

"It's clear! Get her out of here!" a guard yells. I've stopped screaming, but I'm crying and shaking uncontrollably. I'm still gasping for breath. I don't know what I have a grip on, but I refuse to let go of it.

Taylor pulls me to his truck and helps me in. "Backseat, Arianna. Quickly. Get on the floor."

"R-renza." I grip Taylor harder as I suck in air.

"She's right here, sweetheart." He helps Renza into his truck and quickly but gently takes my hand off him. "On the floor. Both of you." We wrap our arms around each other and do as we're told. "Rico! With me! Everyone else, on my ass. Move out!" Before I know what's happening, Taylor is peeling away from the curb and speeding away. "Rico. Call Ryan. Tell him what happened. I need my team out there."

Taylor's phone is on speaker, and soon, someone picks up.

"What's up, Lieutenant?" a deep voice asks.

"Dane, get Zekeih and Mark to Vwidon Bridal Boutique. They went after Arianna. I have an SUV blown to hell, and a dead guard."

I squeak and shake harder, gripping Renza tighter.

"Shit. Is she okay?" Dane asks.

"She's fine," Taylor growls. "I want you, Jesse, and Reed at Ryan's penthouse."

"Yes, sir." Dane hangs up.

I start sobbing, unable to hold back any longer. The tears that had been falling are like nothing compared to the vicious waterfall ripping me to shreds now.

I'll never be able to be happy.

He'll never let me go.

Chapter Nine

☒ Ryan ☒

I stand on my balcony overlooking the city deep in thought. A war has been raging inside me for years regarding Arianna's father. I wanted to take him out the night Arianna's mother was killed. That phone call I got from Arianna that night, her uncontrollable sobbing at what she saw, ripped me apart.

Her parents were just divorced. Arianna's father had beat the shit out of her mother more than once, but it was when he tried to hit Arianna that her mother had left. I had only just started sort of dating her mother. We weren't exclusive. I hadn't slept with her, but I liked her. She was nice. She was interesting to talk to.

After I had intervened in Arianna's situation at school with her teacher, I took Arianna home. I gave her my phone number and told her that she could call me anytime if she needed help. Day or night. I was not at all expecting the phone call I got from her.

She called me from under a bridge near a river crying. Screaming. All I could get from her was a location. I sped to it. As soon as she saw my car, she dived into it. She was only wearing panties and was trying to cover herself the best she could. She was covered in dirt and cuts and scrapes.

She was shivering and crying. I had nothing to cover her with except the shirt I was wearing. I didn't hesitate to put it on her and take her to my house.

I calmed her down enough to get her to tell me what happened. She was getting ready for bed when someone broke into her house. She heard her mother screaming. She didn't think. She called 9-1-1 and ran to help her.

She didn't expect to see her own father pinning her mother to a wall with a knife to her throat. She watched her father slit her mother's throat all the while screaming how he would never allow her to take Arianna away from him.

She never said a word to anyone from 9-1-1, but they heard. They sent squads. Arianna ran, hid, and called me. She watched her father leave before the police arrived.

And it was then that my own war started. It would have been so easy for me to walk into his house and take him and everyone else out.

The problem was Arianna. If I didn't intervene, it would have gone to court. She was too afraid to testify against her father. Since she was the only witness, he was never tried or charged. I knew if I took him out, she would be thrown into the foster system. I refused to allow that to happen. She had no family. All she had was her father.

I banked on that single statement he made. That he wouldn't allow Arianna to be taken away from him. I followed my instincts and hoped like hell they were right. I didn't think he'd hurt her. I knew he'd be a dick, but I also didn't think he'd ever touch her. I didn't know until later that the reason her mother left was because he'd gone after Arianna. Arianna never told me that until much later.

To me, for whatever reason, she seemed incredibly important to him. I was right. Even though I told her to immediately contact me if he did anything to hurt her, she never called for that reason. It was always because he was being an asshole to her. After she told me the reason her mother left, I always wondered if the reason he never hit Arianna had something to do with me. I always questioned if he knew about me. I still, to this day, have no idea. He never led on that he did.

Little did I know that while he may not have known about Arianna's relationship with me, it still all came back to me and my family.

That the reason she was so important is so he could marry her off and combine two mafias to take me out.

Looking back, I should have just kept her with me and taken out her dad. I could've paid people off within the system to leave her alone and not put her in the care of the State. I don't even know right now why I didn't. I guess it had something to do with me wanting to do right by her. I didn't know that doing right by her then would've been doing everything opposite of what I had done. It's something I'll probably kick myself about for the rest of my life. I don't make mistakes. I fucked up royally this time.

I hear a noise behind me, throwing me back to reality. I quickly turn, reaching for the gun on my hip.

"Sorry, man. I didn't mean to sneak up on you. I said your name." Robby holds his hands out weakly in surrender.

I take a deep breath to steady myself as I turn back to the city. "Rule number one. Never, ever come up behind a mafia boss who everyone is out to get. You could've been shot. Only reason you're still standing is because I realized quickly who you are."

"Yes, sir. I apologize." He stands hesitantly by the sliding glass door leading to the balcony and doesn't move. I turn back to him and lean against the railing, folding my arms over my chest. He obviously has something on his mind.

"It's fine, Robby. I'm sorry I didn't hear you announce yourself. I was pretty lost in thought. Had you actually been someone who wanted to take me out, you wouldn't have had a hard time doing it."

"I doubt that. I think your instincts would've kicked in. They pretty much did." He shrugs and looks out at the city as he leans against the doorframe.

"Something on your mind?"

He looks at me and sighs as he walks the rest of the way onto the balcony. He plops into a chair. "What does it take to join a mafia?" He looks up at me, dead serious.

I blink, thrown slightly off by the question. "Uh... Well, it's not like a gang. You don't just get initiated and you're one of the boys." I sit across from him. "Care to tell me why you're asking?"

He looks down, and then takes a big, deep breath. "To protect Arianna."

I lean back in the chair and fold my arms over my chest again. His answer has me more than a little on edge. "Why?"

He looks me square in the eyes. "Because I think something is going on. I know the issue with her dad, but there are things that just don't make sense to me. Renza is hot and cold towards her. Like she's jealous one second. Next, she's the most supportive woman in the world. I... I've just been seeing things happening that I don't understand. I want to be close in case she needs me. Arianna is the only family I have. She's like my little sister. "

I watch him. The kid has good instincts. Josh noticed a few things about Renza at the reception before he took off and approached me with his concerns. I've seen more than a few things that I don't like about her myself since that talk. It's one of the reasons I sent Arianna out with four guards, including Rico, my second in command.

"How long have you been noticing these things?"

"Since right before graduation."

I nod. He's confirming suspicions he doesn't even know I have. "Mafias aren't what you think. Don't model this idea of what you think they are based on what you've observed with mine. You'd be wrong. Mine is far different."

"Okay. Explain it. I'm really serious about this."

I sigh. "Okay. You want the brutal truth?"

"Yes, sir."

"Mafias are focused on one thing. Money. Territory to gain that money. Shakedowns to get that money. Crimes committed, like drug deals, arms deals, all for money. They use guys like you for the small time shit. The deals and the transports all fall on you. You get caught, they don't give a shit about you. It's the product. They'll act like they're on your side. Get you out of trouble. And then make a deal with you. Get their money, their product, back, you're okay. But if you don't..." I shrug.

"They kill. Dispose of my body where no one will ever find it."

"And that isn't all. You stay on their good side, do what they say, they'll reward you. Handsomely. But you belong to them. Unless you're higher up in their ranks, Renza belongs to them, too."

He doesn't flinch. I'm thrown even further. Despite my feelings about Renza, she's his girlfriend. I had expected some kind of a reaction.

Maybe he's not as in love with her as I thought. That's a good thing. It means he might be willing to be my eyes and ears when it comes to her.

I continue to watch him carefully. "Typically, if you're around, and you have a claim staked on Renza, they'll leave her alone. But if you aren't around, someone else will take her, claim or not. You're not a higher up. She'll probably get passed around. In the mafia, women are nothing more than playthings. Property. A way to release sexual tension in whatever way is deemed fit. But, again, money. As soon as they get sick of her, they'll get rid of her. She's not important to them. Just a quick fuck or a way to get their product."

He continues to look at me. "With all due respect, it's not Renza I'm truly worried about. It's Arianna."

"I know, Robby. But you asked. I'm giving you the full answer." I watch him closely as he just nods. "That could mean killing her. Honestly, that would be the most kind thing they could do. What would probably happen, since Renza is both young and attractive, is she'd be sold into sex trafficking. She'd become a slave for someone who would sell her to someone else until she's considered used up. Then she'd get sold off as a regular slave. Cleaning house for someone. Doing whatever he wants her to do until she either kills herself, is killed, or dies by other means, whatever that may be. Again. It's all about the money they would make from selling her."

He never breaks eye contact, even though I know he wants to, and I'm impressed. "So, what about you? How's yours so different? I can tell it is. I know Arianna knows a lot more about it than I do, and she trusts you."

I have to smile slightly. "My goals are different. I don't care about money. I have enough coming in from all of my legal business ventures all over the world. That restaurant we were at the other night? I own it. I have a stake in both Jason's and Chase's companies. I own a tech company. I own a clothing company. I have a stake in Nicole's bakery. I own a lot of legal businesses or have a stake in them. I don't need the money. What drives me is people. People close to me."

He nods, listening intently. "Family."

"I don't like the idea of gangs and mafias and the fucking cartel coming in and taking over. Wreaking havoc. I want this world to be a safe place, at least as much as I can make it, for my family. My future children. Grandchildren. My family's kids and future family. I work closely with law enforcement. They aren't chasing me all over the fucking world. They come to me for help when they can't solve the problem. That's why I'm different."

I watch him for a few moments, his eyes still never leaving mine, and make my decision. There's something about him that reminds me of myself. A strong sense of protection. Family is important to him. He'd do anything to protect family. It's an innate sense that not everyone possesses. Those that do, though, are easily spotted.

It also goes in his favor that Arianna trusts him, and I've already vetted him to make sure he's safe enough to be around my girl.

"That's not to say I'm not ruthless when I need to be. If I allow what you have yet to ask me, Robby, then that needs to be you. You need to follow orders. You can't hesitate when I tell you to do something. You need to trust me; trust that what I'm doing is for the best for *everyone* involved. If I tell you to shoot, you do it. If I tell you to walk away, you do it. I won't ask you to do anything. I'll tell you. And if you don't, you're done. I don't give second chances."

He nods. "Yes, sir."

"You betray me, I will shoot you and not think twice. I won't have a rough night of sleep. I won't ever think of it again."

"Yes, sir."

"Trust is imperative with me. It's an absolute top priority. No one works with me if I don't trust them. And if I lose trust in them, it's over for them. Understand me?"

"Yes, sir. I do."

"I can see a drive in you. A deeply rooted sense of the need to protect your loved ones. I see very clearly that you'll do anything in your power to keep those close to you safe. Am I wrong?"

"No, sir. Arianna is the most important person in my life. Like I said, I don't have any family other than her. My dad died in a wreck a few years ago. He was driving drunk. My mom took a bottle of pills last year and never woke up. I was eighteen, so I've been on my own since. I have no contact with anyone else in my family. Don't have a lot. A cousin and an uncle. Don't talk to them, though. Don't care to."

These are all things I already know, but him being honest about it and coming clean right away is something I appreciate in someone I'm about to let into my world. "You don't question me. I can't stress that enough. If I let you in, you need to trust me."

"Yes, sir. Without question."

"Okay. Before you make your decision, there are a couple things you need to know. I pay my guards. Very well. Everyone else works to earn their keep running or managing a business. I'll buy it. I'll help you set it up. I get a fifty percent stake. No negotiation. Except in the case of family. I obviously would never ask to own that much of a family business. I wouldn't ask to own any. I'm lucky enough that my family gives me a stake anyway. So, you have a choice."

"Own a business or be a guard."

"Or both. Decision belongs to you. But, if I need my team to come together, and I don't have enough guards, I'll pull in my owners. Either way, you do what I say."

"What if I choose to be a guard?"

"Depends what level I put you. If I have you at a top level, meaning guarding me, my wife, or any member of my family, I have guard's quarters on my property. I own three lots. The lot my house is on, and the two lots on either side of me. Both lots have another mansion. Each mansion has twelve rooms. The rooms aren't huge, but they work. I have twenty-four top guards at all times. If you're a top guard, your living quarters are paid. Your vehicle is paid. Utilities are paid," I explain. He nods, still listening intently, and I find myself beyond impressed with the kid. "You're expected to workout and train every day. The routine is intense. It was put together by Taylor himself and is designed to break you. You can't get through it, you won't make it as a top guard. Lower level guards get paid well. They're expected to find their own living quarters, pay their own bills. I provide nothing. The salary is high enough that you won't have to worry, but not as large as top guards. You're still expected to do what I say and when. Questions?"

"Uh... Actually, yes. Arianna. What happens to her? You said in other mafias, she's property."

"That brings me to the second thing you need to know. Women in my mafia are treated with respect. She isn't treated like a queen, you answer to me. Any other man touches her, he answers to me." Robby visibly relaxes. "In Arianna's case, she's an extension of me. She can give commands just like I can. And it's expected that she's listened to without question just like I am. My mafia is like a family. Someone fucks with one of my guy's girls, we all come together to take care of the problem. Your situation, though, is different. You're important to Arianna. And she's just as important to you. You're like a brother to her. Which means what, Robby?" The true test. Right here.

"It means I'm family to you. And you protect your family."

"Good. You've been paying attention. So, here's my deal. You still have a choice here. You're like a brother to my girl. You're family. You don't need to join in order to protect Arianna. I'll do it for you. Especially since she's about to be my wife. She's mine. However, you're a lot like me. I think you want to feel like you have the ability and the means to protect your family on your own."

"Yes, sir. I do."

"Take your time. Think about what you want. What you really want. And then get back to me. If you join, I'd take you on as a top guard. You'll be close to Arianna. I know she'll like that. And I have a position to fill because one of the top guards left to take care of his sister who has breast cancer. So, if this is what you want, it works out. You still have that choice, though. Top guard or owning your own business and being independent, though you still are under my command." I stand to go back inside just as my phone rings. I glance at the caller ID and see Rico's name. "Hey, Rico. How's dress shopping?"

"We have a problem!"

I stop dead in my tracks. I hear panic in Rico's voice and Taylor ordering his team to the boutique. My heart stops beating.

"What the fuck happened? Why is Taylor ordering his team to the boutique? Did he just say dead guard?" I sputter. Robby is instantly at my side. I put the phone on speaker.

"We were leaving. Ricky was opening the back door for the girls, and Taylor saw something. He pulled Arianna back. I just reacted. I grabbed Renza. Taylor threw Arianna to the ground and covered her with his body. I followed his lead. The SUV exploded. The girls are okay, but it's a fucking good thing we were on the ground!"

"What the fuck! How could you let this happen?" I'm vibrating with rage at the idea someone would even consider attacking me. But going after Arianna? I feel like I could burst into flames at any moment and burn the entire fucking world to the ground.

"It was only that SUV. The other SUV and Taylor's truck weren't touched. It was a targeted attack, Ry! Fuck!"

"Get back here. Now!" I command.

"We're on the way! At this rate of speed, we're less than five minutes out."

I hang up and clutch my phone in a white-knuckled grip, nearly crushing it as I close my eyes.

"They targeted Arianna? Who? Her father?" Robby asks.

I look at him as my phone goes off again. I look at it. "Text message."

Robby looks. "From Arianna's father? What the fuck could he possibly want? How does he even have your number?"

I open the text.

Antonio: You've been warned. She's already been claimed. Give her back to her rightful owner.

Ryan: Fuck you. Come after me. I dare you. Touch my wife, and I'll torture you until you wish you were dead.

Antonio: You haven't married her yet. And you won't. I'll kill her before I let her marry you.

Ryan: Try.

Antonio: Game on.

Robby grabs my arm before I can respond again. "He's goading you. Don't let him. Don't respond. We need a plan. Now." I look at him, fire in my eyes and see my own anger reflected back at me in his. "I'm in," he growls.

"Top guard?"

"I want to guard my sister."

I shake his hand knowing I'm going to need all the help I can get.

XXX

True to his word, Rico and Taylor along with two of the three other guards I sent, come bursting through my door less than five minutes later.

Taylor is carrying a limp Arianna in his arms. "Move! Get a cold cloth!"

94

Renza launches herself at Robby. Rico runs to the kitchen. Taylor carries Arianna to the couch. I stare in horror, my feet rooted to the ground. My racing heart can't keep up with its rapid beating. I feel like I'm going to pass out.

My girl. The love of my life.

Unconscious?

Dead?

I clutch my chest.

Taylor looks at me. "What the fuck are you doing? Get over here!"

The tone of his voice snaps me out of my panic. I run to her. "What the hell happened? Rico said they were okay!"

"She passed out in the elevator on the way up. Sit down." He nods to the couch. I sit. He gives Arianna to me as Rico runs out of the kitchen. He hands Taylor the cloth. "Hold her close. She's going to jolt awake."

"What? What are you doing?" I hold her protectively to my chest.

"Trust me."

I hold his gaze a moment, then do what he says, pulling Arianna close to my body. He drops the cloth over her entire face. It's dripping wet and freezing cold. Arianna wakes up gasping for breath. I hold her still as Taylor grabs the cloth and tosses it to Rico.

"Ryan!" She curls herself into me, burying her face in my chest, as she cries. "He'll never let me go! He'll never let me go, Ryan. Never. Never...."

"Shh... Baby, shh..." I run my fingers through her hair and rock her against me.

"He'll come after me forever!"

"Shh... Aria. Believe me when I say I won't let that happen. I won't." I rub her back.

"You can't stop him! No one can. He'll never let me go. Never!"

I tug her hair so her head isn't buried in my chest and tilt her chin up to look at me. "Aria, baby, I know you're scared. I do. But you trust me, right?" I wipe her eyes as she nods. "You trust Taylor?" I nod to him. She nods again. "You trust Robby? The rest of our family?"

She sniffles. "I do."

"Then believe me when I say this. We will get him. I will not let him hurt you. None of us will, baby."

"He was so close today. If Taylor..." She looks at Taylor and lays her head on my shoulder.

She's right. She's fucking right. I almost lost her today. Taylor meets my eyes as his phone rings. He doesn't need to tell me his team has arrived and that Renza and Arianna need time. I don't want to let her out of my arms.

Robby is in a corner with Renza, but his eyes are on Arianna. I can tell he doesn't want to let her out of his sight either. But I don't want her here for this. I also don't want Renza alone with her.

"Honey, I don't want to let you go right now. But I have to talk to my guys, and I don't want you in here having to listen to this. I want you and Renza to either go to one of our rooms or go outside to the balcony. Or take Renza to the hot tub on our bedroom balcony. Talk. Be with each other. I'll have a guard out there with you that I can fill in later."

Her grip on me tightens, It pulls directly on my heart strings. "Please don't make me leave," she whispers.

"I just don't want you to have to hear all of this."

"I don't care. I need you right now. And Renza needs him. Please don't make us leave."

I take a shaky breath as Taylor enters the room with some of his team. I can't do it. I can't make her leave when she needs me. I don't have the heart to tell her the only reason there would be a guard with her is because I have my doubts about Renza. What exactly it is, I'm not sure.

"Okay. Okay, Aria. Whatever you want." I hug her close.

Taylor raises an eyebrow. "Girls staying?"

"Neither one of them wants to be alone. And I don't have the heart to make them."

"Don't blame them. Everyone take a seat," Taylor says.

Renza sits in Robby's lap as soon as he sits in a chair. Taylor sits next to me, and everyone else finds a seat.

"What the fuck, Lieutenant? Sarge called me off a callout." Reed Daniels is part of Chicago's SWAT team.

"For good reason. Look. Reed. I know you aren't technically part of my team, but I trust you, and so does Ryan. You helped us out when Chris was after Nikki after he attacked Michelle. We need you now. I can't pull my whole team."

96

"You know I'm with you. No question. I just want to know what the hell happened."

"You aren't the only one." Jesse's eyes land uncomfortably on both Renza and Arianna. He's a member of Taylor's elite organized crime taskforce and another person who helped when Nicole was in danger.

I sigh and whisper in Arianna's ear. "Beautiful. If you need to be out here, can you sit between my legs so I can talk to them? Maybe introduce you so they know why they're here?" I hug her tighter. She nods against my neck and turns in my lap so she's settled between my legs with her back to me. I put my arms back around her and kiss the back of her head. "Good girl." I hold her tightly against me. "Everyone. This is Arianna. My fiancé."

Dane, Jesse, and Reed smile.

"Congrats, man!" Dane, another member of Taylor's task force says.

"Long story short, Arianna is the daughter of Antonio Massena. He's a mafia boss out of New York." Taylor meets the eyes of everyone in the room just as my phone chimes with a text.

I look down and close my eyes as I use Arianna's intoxicating jasmine scent to center me. "Taylor, get the door. Josh and Alex just got here."

Whatever Taylor is about to say is cut off by the sharp rap on the door. He moves quickly to answer it. "The fuck?" he sputters.

"Don't ask," Alex says.

I open my eyes and see Josh holding the hand of a beautiful girl with dark hair and wide shy eyes. She's half his size and gripping his hand so tightly, I think she might actually break it. She's holding his arm with the other and is almost completely behind him with her head buried into his back.

Josh looks around the room. I can tell he knows something happened and wants to ask, but when he meets my eyes, all I see is pain. Alex called me in the middle of the night after mine and Arianna's engagement party telling me that Josh's girlfriend had a miscarriage. I've never met Lyric Sharpe, but I'd bet my last dollar that the small girl clinging to Josh is her.

I watch as Josh turns and leans down. He whispers something in her ear as he runs his fingers through her hair. She keeps her tight grip on his hand and arm. She nods, and he leads her to the loveseat near the window. Jesse and Reed vacate it, and Josh shoots them a grateful smile as he sits down. Lyric curls up next to him. Josh grabs a fleece throw from the back of the couch and pulls it around her, then hugs her tight.

"Who's that?" Renza asks.

"Family," Alex growls at her with a vicious glare that has her trembling. Renza ducks her head but keeps her eyes glued to Lyric.

After a few moments, I take another breath. "Arianna's father promised her to the son of another mafia boss years ago." May as well just blurt it out.

"When I was a b-baby," she stutters.

I hold her tighter and kiss her neck. Given what just happened and the fact that there's new people around, I know she's both nervous and scared. And I know she needs the hug.

"Arianna has been with Ryan for awhile, but she only recently turned eighteen," Taylor explains.

"But we didn't do anything b-before!" Arianna jumps in, immediately defending us from a judgment I know won't come from anyone in this room.

"Shh... Honey, no one in this room is judging you and Ryan. I promise," Josh cuts in. I give him a grateful smile.

"Not a single one of us," Dane agrees. Arianna relaxes slightly.

"She escaped last Friday," I continue as I sway gently with her. "It was then she found out what her dad's plan was. He wants to combine his mafia with the Ambrosio mafia to take me down."

"And he needs an arranged marriage to do it." Reed shakes his head as he catches on.

"Holy shit. I'm sorry, sweetheart." Jesse reaches over and gives her knee a friendly squeeze. Arianna reaches up to wipe a tear away as she nods.

"Ryan got a text from Arianna's dad Saturday. Basically telling him to hand her over or he dies," Taylor says.

I nod. "So, I talked to Arianna. We'd been talking about marriage anyway and decided we needed to fast track it."

"We're getting married next weekend." Her voice is quiet, but she's not stuttering, so I know she's feeling more comfortable.

I smile into her hair and whisper to her. "I'm so fucking proud of you. You're handling this like a pro." She relaxes against me even more.

Taylor continues. "Today, she was at the boutique picking out a wedding dress. Both Ryan and Arianna have been on edge since their engagement."

Reed whistles. "That was pretty public. I stay away from tabloids, but even I heard about it. It was all over the news. Billboards. Crazy."

"It was intentional. We needed to show her father she's mine," I say.

"Arianna texted me this morning and asked if I would possibly be able to be there," Taylor says.

"And I was pretty happy you said yes," I say gratefully.

Taylor smiles. "Anytime... On the way out, one of Ryan's guards was opening the door to the SUV that Renza and Arianna had been in when they arrived. I was right behind Arianna. I noticed a red beam on the ground right by the guard's foot. Almost like a laser beam, but thicker. The guard opened the door and the beam disappeared. That threw me for a loop. I was on guard. I saw a spark underneath the SUV right by the door. I pulled Arianna back, and Rico pulled Renza. The SUV exploded seconds later. We lost a guard in the blast."

"I wasn't at an angle to see that. Had Taylor not been paying attention..." Rico's eyes meet mine. He quickly looks away.

"You aren't trained in bombs, Rico," I say, soothing him. "I don't blame you. It's a good thing Taylor was there. He has bomb experience. Divine intervention, I guess."

"I want everyone guarding Arianna to go through a crash course in bomb detection. I'll set it up. It won't be pretty," Taylor says. I almost chuckle at the evil glint in Taylor's eyes.

Instead, I nod and hug Arianna. "Do it. Send a guy to New York to my house to put my guys through it. As soon as possible. In the meantime, the guys here, Rico, Robby, Josh, and Alex, all go through it with you, Taylor."

"Done. I'll grab Chase to help me out."

I shake my head. "Chase?"

"He refuses to hire guards, so I put him through training to defend himself."

"I know that. You told me. But bombs?"

"Damn right. He's a target just because of how much money he makes," Taylor says. I nod because I do know that.

"Wait. Please stop. Robby? You said Robby needs to go through it," Renza says. She narrows her eyes at me suspiciously.

I look up at Robby, realizing my mistake. "Shit. I... I'm sorry, man."

Arianna says nothing, which I'm very grateful for, as Renza breaks free from Robby's grip and runs to their room. She slams the door. Robby runs his hands down his face.

"It's fine. Don't worry about it." Robby glances at the room then me uneasily. I know he doesn't want to share his concerns right now. I'm not so sure I do either.

"I knew he'd ask you to join," Arianna whispers.

"For you. He asked for you."

She smiles softly as she looks at Robby. "I know, Ryan. I understand."

"Well, I hope you understand what *I'm* about to say then. You don't leave this penthouse," Josh says.

Arianna shrugs. "Why would I be upset? The meetings I have will just have to come here."

"You're certainly taking this well," Reed chuckles. "When I told Michelle she wasn't leaving the house until we took Chris down, she told me go fuck myself. And she's twelve years older than you."

I chuckle. "Arianna grew up in a mafia family. She knows all the shit I deal with in my position. She's smart. She knows the danger she's in. We don't need to explain it. She's lived it. She knows what he's capable of."

I toss Josh my phone with the new set of texts from Antonio Massena. He catches it. Taylor sits on the arm of the couch and leans over to look.

"Fuck me. I was right. She stays here." Josh tosses me my phone. I go to catch it, but Arianna beats me to it. I can't help but smile as she reads the texts.

She sighs when she's done and holds my phone in her lap. "This is going to get bad. I wish we could just run away."

"I know, baby, but -"

100

"Why don't you just do an extended honeymoon?" Lyric cuts in softly. We all look at her. Her eyes are closed, and she snuggles closer to Josh sensing our gazes. "You'd all get away. It would look like you're traveling after being married, but it gives you time to formulate a plan of action and throw him off."

"Actually, that might not be a bad idea..." Taylor says. Lyric smiles and turns her head into Josh's chest. I smile. "You're getting married next weekend. What if we moved that up to as soon as possible and you went on your honeymoon as quickly as you can? Let him chase you. Bring him to us."

I sigh. "I don't want Arianna to be looking over her shoulder. It's not fair to her. I want her to enjoy our honeymoon."

"He might be onto something," Arianna says quietly. I look down at her. "What if we allowed the two photographers to follow us? We could have them upload some of the pictures and the location to their online blog and leak some to other media outlets, but not until we move on to the next location. When we get to Hawaii at the beginning of August, we bring them to us. It's home turf because you have a house there... It's not in his backyard... We could allow them to leak photos while we're there. He'll go there to chase us. We can set him up. A takedown of all of them at the same time. You know he'll bring everyone if he thinks he caught up to us and has a chance. He'd be thrown off, just like Josh's girlfriend said."

What the hell is happening? Is she planning a fucking mission? I shouldn't be, but I couldn't be more turned on if I tried. I can't help but smile.

Alex glances at Josh. Taylor is beaming like a fucking idiot. Taylor's team all looks as dumbfounded and as surprised as I feel.

Alex clears his throat. "Uh... That could... um... actually work."

"Like a fucking charm," Josh says with what can only be described as a proud smirk. He kisses Lyric's head.

"I think your girl just planned our fucking mission." Taylor is still grinning like asshole. "With an assist from Josh's girl."

I grin wider. "We'll hash out the details when we decide on a location to get married." I look down at Arianna as she yawns and cuddles into me.

"I hate to be the asshole here," Dane starts. He's been glancing over at Josh and Alex nervously the whole time they've been here. "But who are they?" He nods at Josh then looks back at me.

"Dane. This is Josh and Alex Lucinio. Josh is the leader of the Lucinio mafia. Alex is his brother. He helps him out. Josh is new to leading. He's doing well. Taking lessons from me. They both are family to me. They can be trusted."

Josh nods. "I'll be honest. It's hard as fuck leading anything when it involves family. I don't know how Ryan does it, but he does. I'm learning. But I will say this. Alex and I are going to be here to help out because Ryan would do the same for us. Fuck, he already has."

"I don't know Josh or Alex that well," Taylor says. "But I don't question Ryan or his judgment. If he's telling us that Josh or Alex is one of your leaders and can be trusted, that's the end of the story."

Josh clears his throat. "I'm not going to sit here and step on Ryan's toes. I'm not like that. Alex and I are here for back-up. But I'm not going to ask for permission to speak. If I see a fucking problem, and I call it out, I expect my orders to be followed just as you would his. Ryan is just as much my family as Alex. He had a hand in saving my life. I wouldn't be here without him. No way in all of fuck I'll let him down."

"Questions or problems? Speak now because I won't entertain them after today." I look around the room and nod at the chorus of no's. "Good. Thank you for coming. I appreciate all of you. We'll hash out a plan, but for now get out. All of you. I hate to be a dick, but Arianna is exhausted, and I need to figure out what's going on with Lyric." I nod to Josh and his girl.

Everyone starts gathering their things. I nudge Arianna up. I kiss her neck and send her to our room. Robby glares at his closed bedroom door. I head over to him while everyone else leaves.

"I wish I knew why I have such a bad feeling about her," he says quietly.

"Keep an eye on the situation. Something seems off, tell me." He nods as he heads for the room with a heavy sigh. After a few seconds, there's blessed peace and fucking quiet in my penthouse.

"Go take care of your girl," Josh says from the couch he made himself at home on, Lyric curled into his side.

"How's she doing? How are you doing?"

102

"It's tough. But we're handling it. I'm not leaving her alone, though."

"I wouldn't expect you to. Didn't you have something going on with one of your tech companies?"

"Nope. I do have one with my finance company, though." He smirks at me.

I laugh. "You're a bigger asshole than your brother."

He grins. "Alex is on it. I don't understand shit about what's happening. Alex is the business genius."

"You need to learn it if you expect to lead anything. Legit mafias aren't just about taking out cartels and small-time gangs."

He holds up a hand, keeping his other arm snuggly around Lyric. "I know, I know. Alex said the same thing. I'm working on it."

"Took me a while. But try. Don't pawn it off to Alex just because he's willing to help you. If I'd done that with Jason, I wouldn't be where I am."

"I know, Ry. I understand. But it's not just that. This miscarriage is hard on both of us. Fuck, it almost killed her. I refuse to be away from her right now. Alex understands. Now go take care of Arianna. I'll take care of everything else. Go be the man she needs you to be for her right now so I can be what Lyric needs me to be for her."

I smile and nod. "Thank you, Josh." I head for the room as he nods and grabs the remote.

I'd never admit it, but I'm glad that I have help. Arianna is the most important person in the world to me. It's different protecting the woman I love than it is protecting my family. My family is everything to me. But Arianna is my heart. I feel my attention is split between comforting her and making sure she's safe.

I guess I never really understood how Jason, Chase, and Taylor really felt when it was them in my situation. The closest I've ever felt to this was being there to protect them. But I knew everything I needed to do. I didn't hesitate doing any of it.

Now?

Leaving Arianna's side to do the shit I need to scares the ever living fuck out of me. I've never run away from a fight. But right now, even with all the backup I have, running is all I want to fucking do.

Chapter Ten

☓ Arianna ☓

(One Week Later)

"We've got the caterer. Nicole made the cake. The decorators are just finishing. The DJ is setting up. We have the dance floor being created." Jenny Crane is a flurry of activity as she checks things off a clipboard in her hand.

It's the day of mine and Ryan's wedding, and I'm freaking out. I want everything to be perfect. But I'm sure we're missing something. And I'm terrified my dad is going to figure out our plan and ruin everything. That we're going to be unprepared.

My rising panic causes my heart rate to quicken. I have to take deep breaths.

"Oh, sweetheart." Ryan's mom kneels in front of me and takes my hands in hers.

"What about guards?" I nearly whisper.

"Ryan is well prepared. There are many guards. There's a guard outside the door. They're around the perimeter. He even has guards near the windows of this room." She points outside. I see the arms of a couple of guards leaning against the building near the window. I smile. I hadn't noticed they were there. I can even see a few in the distance.

"Everything is going to be okay. Your wedding is going to be as beautiful as you are." She hugs me tightly. I feel my tension melting away.

"All of the guys out there are armed. Even Ryan," Renza says. I don't have to see it to know that she rolled her eyes. I can hear it in her voice. I don't understand what's wrong with her lately.

"Ryan's always armed," I remind her. Renza shrugs and continues filing her nails.

Jenny laughs. "That's true. But... so is Chase today. And Jason. They don't carry unless they're forced to."

I smile and nod. "You're right. Thank you, Mrs. Crane."

"Sweetheart. You're about to be my daughter-in-law. You can call me mom. Or Jenny if you're more comfortable." She kisses me on the head as she stands. "It's your wedding day! Trust Ryan and your family. We have it all taken care of!" She blows a kiss as she leaves the room.

"She's right, you know. I can honestly say I've never felt safer. Ryan has so many guards out there. And now that Robby is one, I don't think we have anything to worry about." She forces a smile to cover her mocking tone.

I choose to ignore it. "You're right. I just need to let go. Stop freaking out. Enjoy myself."

"That's the spirit! Now, can we get you dressed, please?" For the first time in a couple of days, I can truthfully say that she seems genuine.

I won't let her weird mood swings bother me. "I really do love that dress!"

"And it looks fantastic on you." Renza pulls me up and nearly drags me to the door where my dress is hanging. She takes it out of the garment bag and helps me get it on. I look in the mirror as she buttons the buttons and ties the back of my dress.

I blush and smile. "I truly feel like Ryan's bride."

She tilts her head in the mirror. She bites her lip. "Are you nervous? Being just eighteen and already getting married?"

I smile and shake my head. "No. Ryan is the other half of my heart. I can't breathe without him."

Renza smiles and starts putting her own dress on. "That's how I feel about M-" She cuts herself off and coughs as she shakes her head. "Sorry. I got a weird scratch in my throat."

I nod slowly. Was she not going to say Robby? "It's okay."

She smiles softly and gets a faraway look. "It's how I feel about Robby."

I watch her for a few moments. Having no reason to really suspect anything, I ignore the uneasiness I'm suddenly feeling. Again. I've been feeling like this more and more lately. I don't know why. "You two have been inseparable since middle school."

"I've never wanted anyone else." She doesn't meet my eyes.

"That's how I feel about Ryan."

She smiles as she turns so I can zip her dress. She swivels back around, and we put an arm around each other's waist, leaning on one another as we look in the mirror.

"You really make a beautiful bride."

"And you really make a beautiful maid of honor."

"I can't wait until I get married."

I smile at her and hug her. I feel like she's a little jealous that I'm getting married and she isn't. I feel terrible about it, but I don't regret marrying Ryan. "Me either!"

We break apart, grinning at each other as someone knocks on the door.

"I'll get it." Renza opens the door a crack. "Hey, Taylor."

"Hey. I don't need to come in. Just dropping these off and letting you know everything's ready when you are." He hands something to Renza.

"Taylor?" I call.

"Yeah, sweetheart?"

"I'm ready. Just need to finish a couple things."

"Okay. I'll stay by the door. I'm ready when you are. Renza, Alex is waiting out there when you're ready."

"Okay." Renza closes the door and hands me the stuff Taylor brought.

"Oh, yay!" My eyes light up. Renza looks at me, confused. I laugh. "I'm marrying into the most amazing family in the world. This is from Ryan's cousin, I think. Maybe a third cousin? I have no idea, honestly. He's from London." I pull out a real sixpence. "And this is from Jessa. To match our decor." I clasp a bracelet with tiny silver seashells around my ankle.

"Okay. That's gorgeous. What's that for?" She's pointing to a blue tie.

"Um… I have the sixpence. I have something borrowed. That would be something blue, but I have no idea what it's for."

"There's a note."

I take the note she hands me and read it. I laugh as I hand it to Renza.

It goes on your leg. In place of a garter. Wrap it around your thigh and tie it tight enough to not fall off, but not tight enough that I look like an idiot trying to get it off with my teeth.

Love, Ryan

Renza reads it while I hike my dress up and follow his directions as I tie it on.

She bursts out laughing. "Oh my God, Air. Your first time is going to be something else with him."

I turn crimson. "Renza! How do you know I haven't lost my virginity to him yet?"

She laughs. "Are you kidding? We tell each other everything. You've told me how dominating he is, which is so hot, by the way You've told me everything you've done with him."

"Okay. Yeah. You're right."

"I can't wait until tomorrow when you tell me everything he does to you tonight."

"Renza!"

She laughs and pulls me towards the door. She hands me off to Taylor and nearly skips towards the entrance of the beach house we're in to meet Alex.

"You ready?" he asks, offering me his arm. I take it gratefully.

"I definitely am."

"She seems excited." He nods towards Renza.

I bite my lip and slow down. He looks down at me as he follows my lead. "Can I be honest?"

"Honey, you know the answer to that. You can always be honest."

"I just…" I drop my voice to a whisper. "I feel like something is just so off with Renza. I don't know how to explain it. She just… she acts like her normal self one second. Then the next she's… jealous?" I shake my head. "I don't know what to make of it."

"Is it something that's been bothering you? Doesn't seem right?"

"It's just not her. It's not who she is. And it just started. When we were in high school, before graduation, I really didn't feel any of this with her. She was my best friend. She still is… Well, I don't know." I shake my head. "She doesn't feel like my best friend anymore. And I don't know why."

"Have you mentioned it to Ryan?"

"Not really. I've been trying to figure it out myself. I don't know how to bring up what I don't understand. I was hoping that you could…" I look up at him. "Help me make sense of it?"

"Okay. Well, this is something that's brought some concern to you. It doesn't feel right. You don't need to really understand the reasons why. It doesn't need to make sense."

"Really? It's just that simple?" I look up at him.

"I think you need to mention it to Ryan, sweetheart. I've felt it, too. I think we all have."

I take a deep breath and nod. "I just wanted a second opinion. I've been stressed. I didn't know if I was reading too much into it."

"Instincts, Arianna. You need to trust them. They're everything. It's what we all rely on. If it doesn't feel right to you, it probably isn't."

I squeeze his arm. "Thank you, Taylor."

"I'm here for you. Anytime."

We finish our walk to the door and meet Alex and Renza. Renza is leaning against the wall boredly picking at her nails. She yawns.

When she sees me, she smiles. "Arianna! Ready to get married?"

I smile, fighting everything in me that says to confront her. This is my wedding. No one is going to ruin it. "It's finally time. I'm so happy!"

"Wow. You're gorgeous, Arianna. Really." Alex hugs me.

I deflate slightly, letting a little more tension release. I'm surrounded by a family that won't let anyone come between me and Ryan saying our vows. Alex hugs me a little tighter, sensing I need it. I'm beginning to really love that this family is so incredibly intuitive.

I breathe out a deep sigh. "Thank you," I whisper.

After a few moments, Alex lets me go. "Care to share what all that is about? Are you nervous?"

I look around and see that Taylor has led Renza away from me and Alex. "I just feel like something is wrong with her," I say quietly. "I was just talking to Taylor about it. It just feels… off. Not right."

Alex looks over my head and nods. He leans against the wall and folds his arms over his chest. "My experience with things that don't feel right is that they typically aren't right. No matter how much you try and argue with yourself about it. No matter how much you try and talk yourself into it being right. If you feel like it's wrong, then you need to listen to yourself. Jessa wouldn't be alive right now if any of us had ignored our instincts. Truthfully, Jessa probably never would've been put into the situation she was if we'd followed our instincts."

"Instincts." I smile softly as I look down. "That's what Taylor said."

"Bree. Nikki. They may not have been in the situation they'd been thrown in had instincts been followed. The night Chase was shot, his instincts told him that he should have been with Breetana."

I look up. "But he didn't follow them."

Alex shakes his head. "No. He didn't. I wasn't there. But hearing about it after the fact?" He shrugs. "You should always listen to yourself, Arianna. Always."

"Taylor said I should talk to Ryan. I didn't want to bring it up right now. At least not until I was sure something was wrong."

"Sometimes, waiting to see if something is wrong before acting can be the thing that gets you killed. In this case, you never really know. Maybe what you're feeling is the missing piece to how Ryan feels about something."

"Has he… mentioned anything to you?"

"About Renza? No. But I don't think you're the only one who questions what's going on. Talk to Ryan, Arianna." He pushes himself off the wall. "After your wedding. Enjoy this. All of us have your back. At least for today and tonight you have nothing to worry about. That's on all of us. Okay?"

"Okay."

He smiles and leads me back to Taylor and Renza. When we reach them, he holds out his arm for Renza. "Ready, Ms. Gregorson?"

Renza laughs as she takes his arm. "Ready as I'll ever be, Mr. Lucinio."

Alex pushes open the door, leading us all out.

"Ready for this? You're about to become a mafia Queen," Taylor teases.

I smile softly. "No. I'm about to marry the love of my life. No title or drama or anything else will ever come close to or overcome that."

"That's a pretty good way to look at it."

I smile up at him as we stop just out of sight of Ryan and the guests. I turn to adjust Taylor's tie. "You really look great in a suit. I think I've only ever seen you in jeans besides your wedding."

"I don't usually wear them. I wear jeans and a dressier shirt. Suits aren't my thing. If I need to put tactical gear on, I won't get hurt with all the rougher material against my skin." He smiles as he glances over my head. Renza and Alex begin their walk. "Last chance to run."

I shake my head and giggle. "I'm not running. I love him."

"Are you sure? I'll find a place to stash you for a few days." His grin is teasing.

I swat his chest and giggle. "I'm ready for my life to begin. No more running. No more being afraid of my father. Only me and Ryan."

Taylor bends to kiss me on the cheek. He peaks around the corner and straightens up to his full over six foot height. "It's truly an honor to be the one you chose to give you away."

"I was going to choose Robby, but for some reason, this feels right. I love Robby. It's not that I don't. I guess I just feel closer to you. Even though it's really not been that long that we've known each other."

"Well, it's an honor, sweetheart." He smiles widely.

I take a deep breath as he leads me to the top of the aisle where I see the beautiful face of my future. I feel my face flush when my eyes meet Ryan's. He's my entire world. Starting my life with him today feels like something I've been preparing for since I was born. Like everything I've done up to this point in my life was for him. For this moment.

It's funny because I've felt like this about several moments with him. Every first I've had with him. Every moment we've been together. To me, it feels like all of my life has been lived just for each and every moment I have with him. My heart. My soul. My life. It all belongs to him.

Chapter Eleven

✗ Ryan ✗

Seeing Arianna standing at the end of the aisle completely takes my breath away. No one has ever taken my breath away like she does. No one has ever made feel like she does. I've never wanted anyone the way I want her. Never wanted to spend my life with anyone but her.

She's everything to me. She's my entire world. As she walks down the aisle towards me, I can't stop myself from thinking, like I do every damn day, how lucky I am to have her. How lucky I am that she loves me as much as I do her.

When she reaches me, I smile and reach up to wipe away a tear from her eye, then my own. I never cry.

"You're so beautiful, Aria," I whisper

"So are you." I smile as she reaches up to smooth down my tie.

"I know you're a big shot, but hurt this sweet girl, they'll never find your body," Taylor teases with a wink.

I laugh out loud as I shake his hand. "Yes, sir!"

Taylor claps me on the back and takes his seat. I take one of Arianna's hands in one of mine and push her hair out of her face with the other.

"Ready to do this?"

She nods. "Ready." She leans into my touch and smiles up at me.

Neither one of us turn towards the officiant as he begins to speak. "Everyone. On behalf of our beautiful bride and handsome groom, thank you for coming."

Our guests hoot and holler. My eyes don't leave Arianna's. We both stand holding each other's hands and staring deeply into each other's eyes. My thumbs rub soft circles over the tops of her hands. Her sweet and soft smile warms me more than the hot sun streaming down on us.

"Weddings are a time for two people to become one. To share one life. To share one heart. To be each other's comfort in time of need. Strength in times of weakness..."

The officiant's voice fades into the far distance until all that exists is Arianna. Her dark hair being blown ever so lightly in the gentle breeze. Her lips ever so slightly parted. Her sexy, dark brown eyes shining with unshed tears of love and happiness. The feel of her barely bronzed silky skin beneath my fingertips.

"If anyone has a good reason as to why these two lovely young people should not be wed, please stand and come forward at this time." The officiant's eyes glance over the room.

No one stands.

No one would dare.

"Wonderful. Who has the rings?" he asks.

"Right here." Jason, who had been standing with me at the altar while we waited for my beautiful girl to make her grand entrance, steps up next to me. He hands me Arianna's ring and Arianna mine.

The officiant smiles. "Arianna. Repeat after me, please. I, Arianna Maria Massena, take you, Ryan Nathanial Crane, to be by husband by law and by heart."

Tears fill her eyes. She blinks them away as she looks up at me. "I, Arianna Maria Massena, take you, Ryan Nathanial Crane, to be by husband by law and by heart."

"I promise to love you and honor you with all of myself through all that life brings our way."

"I promise to love you and honor you with all of myself through all that life brings our way." Arianna's eyes shine with love as she says each word and slides my ring onto my finger.

"Ryan. Please repeat after me. I, Ryan Nathaniel Crane, take you, Arianna Maria Massena, to be my wife by law and by heart."

I smile down at my girl. "I, Ryan Nathaniel Crane, take you, Arianna Maria Massena, to be my wife by law and by heart."

"I promise to love you and honor you with everything in me and protect you with everything I am."

"I promise to love you and honor you with everything in me and protect you with everything I am." I slip her ring on her finger.

The officiant closes the book he's holding. "Arianna. Do you swear to love Ryan? To be his partner in life? The other half of his heart?"

She looks up at me and smiles, squeezing my hand. "I do. I swear I do."

My heart nearly beats out of my chest at her words. Her proclamation.

"Ryan. Do you swear to love Arianna? To be her protector in life and in love? To be the other half of her heart?"

"I swear. With everything I am."

"Then in front of your family and friends, and by the power given to me by this beautiful island of Antigua, I now pronounce you husband and wife... You may kiss your bride."

It's the moment I've been waiting for the entire day. I waste no time. I wrap my arms around Arianna's slim waist and lift her off the ground. I kiss her long and hard. She squeals as everyone claps and whistles. I shift her in my arms so I'm carrying her bridal style down the aisle as the officiant announces us as Mr. and Mrs. Crane.

"I love you." She kisses me again as we walk. "I love you, too."

✗✗✗

The reception drags on. People wish us well. Dinner. Dancing. The cake Nicole made is beautiful and tastes even better.

But there is only one thing on my mind. And given the way Arianna is looking at me, I know she's thinking the same thing. Ever since the first time we touched each other, we haven't been able to keep our hands off one another. Whether it's her mouth or hands around my dick, or my fingers or tongue buried in her, we've needed to feel each other. Like some obsessive craving.

"I feel like we've been out here for hours."

"Me, too." She grazes her finger along my thigh and squeezes.

We haven't stopped touching each other or looking at each other the entire night. My cock has been in a semi state of arousal ever since I saw her walking down the aisle towards me.

"We need to get out of here, Arianna. I don't think I can wait any longer."

"For what?" I look at her and pull her hand so it's on my dick. Her eyes widen, and she giggles. "Good thing this table is hiding us."

I swallow. Hard. I'd never do anything she isn't ready for, but I need her. I know she wants me just as much. "Please say we can get out of here."

"Okay." She smiles softly.

I breathe a sigh of relief and pull her up. I lead her behind me as I stride out of the room. I meet Taylor's eyes. He nods and smiles. I turn and pick Arianna up. She kisses me. Our lips don't leave each other, even after we get to our bedroom in the suite. She nearly tears my tux off. I force myself to slow things down. I grab her hands as she starts undoing my belt.

"Hang on. Hang on, baby."

She looks innocently up at me, a little confused. "Did I do something w-wrong?"

I nearly lose control again. "Aria. No, honey." I lean down and kiss her as gently as I can manage. "I want this to be special." I smooth her hair down and run my thumb over her lip. "Just tell me to stop if I'm going too far. Or being too rough."

She reaches up and cups my cheek. "I trust you."

She turns her back to me. I start undoing the buttons of her dress with painstaking care. After I undo the last one, I run my fingers up her arms to her shoulders and remove the thin straps. Her dress falls to the floor. I grab her hips and turn her towards me. I pick her up and lay her on the bed.

She smiles as I lean down to kiss her. I trail my kisses down her jaw to her neck, down her collarbone to her perfectly mountainous breasts. I take one in my hand, pinching her nipple and rolling it between my fingers while I take the other in my mouth. I nibble on her nipple.

"Mmm... Oh my God..." Her head rolls back as she closes her eyes and grips my shoulders.

"Feel good?"

"Yes..." I switch to her other nipple, and she arches into me. After a few moments, I run my tongue down her stomach to her pantyline. "Oh... Ryan. Ryan..." I sit up on my knees and put her legs on my shoulders as I remove her panties and toss them. I kiss up her leg to her smooth as fuck pussy and lick. "Oh! Fuck!" I smile and nip her as I pull away. I kiss up her other leg and do the same thing. "Ryan!"

"Like that?"

"God, yes... Yes!"

I grab her hips and pull her close to my mouth. "You, sweet girl, taste like honey." I dive into her with my tongue.

"Oh!" She grips the sheets as she arches into my mouth.

"Mmm... Fucking honey."

"Ryan! I'm gonna come and you've barely touched me. Oh my God!"

"Oh, sweetheart. You're gonna be coming for me a lot tonight. By the time I'm done with you, you won't be able to walk." I suck on her clit and lightly bite it. "Come for me, beautiful." I know how close she is.

She quakes and screams my name as she comes. "Ryan!"

I lick up all of her sweetness before letting go of her and allowing her to relax as I remove the rest of my clothing.

I once again position myself between her legs. Only this time, I'm leaning over her, kissing up her leg and licking it. She moans. I kiss her clit.

"Oh, Ryan..."

I kiss up her stomach to her breasts; up her neck to her lips. "Grab the headboard." She does as I say. "Good girl." I shift and find the tie I dropped on the nightstand when I took the rest of my clothes off.

She raises an eyebrow. "What are you doing?" she asks curiously.

I grin. "Trust me." I wrap the tie around her wrists, securing her hands to the headboard. I position myself over her, my cock against her wanting center, and kiss her again as she moans. "Ready?" I ask against her lips. She nods shyly. "If it hurts, tell me. I'll stop."

"I'm ready. I promise."

I'm hoping the fact that I already made her come once has loosened her up for me. She may have gotten my fingers and tongue a lot, but that's nowhere near what she's about to feel. I push my tip inside her.

She gasps and moans with wide, adorable eyes. When she relaxes, I push in a little more and let her get used to me again before I give her more.

"Oh… Ry…an… Ry…," she moans. Her pussy gripping my dick tightens. Her thighs tremble. I feel her stomach tightening and coiling as hard as the rest of her body.

"Ssh…" I kiss her softly and lightly massage her hips until her pussy unclenches and starts pulsing.

She's breathing deeply and whimpering. I look at her out of concern, but she smiles softly. "I'm okay…," she whispers.

I let out a breath and push deeper as I gently start rubbing her clit. Her eyes flutter closed. Her pussy, while still gripping me like a vice, allows me to sink in deeper until she's taking all of me like a good girl. "Still okay?"

She nods. A tear slips from the corner of her eye. I don't move, letting her stretch around my size. I keep my thumb pressed against her clit.

"You're so big," she whispers.

"I know, baby. I'm sorry." I lean down to kiss her tear away.

She laughs. "You're sorry you're so big?"

I smile, but I'm truly concerned. "Well, not until now. I don't mean to hurt you."

"You aren't. You're being so gentle and sweet. I'd hug you, but..." She bites her lip and tugs against my tie.

I kiss her, my smile becoming a little more lighthearted. "You won't be getting out of that."

She kisses me as she wraps her legs around my waist. "Is this okay?"

"Perfect, baby." My dick twitches when she moves slightly against me. "Ready?"

"Keep being gentle?"

"Always." I start slow, moving inside her at the pace she sets. "Fuck, you're so tight."

"I think you're just so big you think I'm tight."

I laugh and kiss her as I continue to move inside her and out. "No. I'm big. I'm almost ten inches. But you're incredibly tight."

"Ten inches?" She blinks in disbelief. I just grin and wink, making her giggle as I thrust deeply and gently. She lets her head fall back when I quicken my pace slightly as she gets wetter. "Mmm... So good, Ryan."

"I've waited so long for you. I'm going to savor every second of this." I give myself to her, slightly deeper. She moves against me, matching my every thrust. I lean down to her nipples and take turns sucking and nibbling on each one of them.

"Oh..." she moans. Her hips jerk against me.

Her pussy is unlike anything I've ever felt. I grip her hip and pull her up into me so I sink even deeper. "Fuck... baby, yes." I lick my way up to her neck and kiss it.

"Ryan..." She tugs against the tie securing her wrists, not knowing how fucking much it turns me on. Seeing her fight against them makes me even harder.

"You look so sexy gripping that tie, baby...," I whisper. I watch her hands tremble just as hard as the rest of her. Her pussy clenches around me so fucking tightly, but she still meets me thrust for thrust. "Pull harder," I rumble against her neck right before I start gently sucking on it.

She tugs harder as she pants and moans. I roll my hips against her, making her arch up into me. Her pussy is so wet that it makes the filthiest noises. I groan and nip her neck before kissing it to soothe the pain.

"Ah! Ryan! Please..."

I smile against her neck as I continue thrusting. "Please what, baby?"

She blushes a beautiful shade of crimson. She always gets so shy when I make her tell me what she needs from me. And when she does, it makes me impossibly harder for her.

"Please make me come," she practically whispers. I want her to scream it, but I'll work on that with her. She's still very shy.

"Come for me, honey," I whisper against her lips.

She jerks into me when I reach down and start to rub her clit. It's all it takes for her to come undone underneath me. I grab her hips as she's coming and flip her on top of me as she's coming.

"Ah! Oh my God. Ryan!"

"Not even close to done with you," I growl against her lips right before I take them with my own.

Her wrists are still tied to the headboard as she straddles me. Her orgasm still isn't through as I start thrusting up into her a little harder than before. My head drops against the pillow on a groan as my eyes roll back in my head.

"Oh! Ryan!"

I grip her ass and move her up and down my cock. She sinks herself onto me and takes all of me. "Good girl. Goddamn, you're so good. You feel so fucking perfect, Ari. Just for me. All mine."

"Mmm…!" she moans as her head drops to my neck. Her thighs quiver. Her pussy tightens even more than it already was.

I know I'm hitting her g-spot with every stroke because her moans grow louder and louder, and she slams herself down hard on my cock, taking me as deeply as she can with each thrust.

"Fuck, Aria! I'm so close." I squeeze her ass and hold her still as I thrust into her a few times.

She throws her head back and screams. "Ah! Ryan!"

My dick thickens inside her, making her feel even tighter. Her pussy pulses erratically around and clenches uncontrollably. My dick is soaked with her essence. I can feel her dripping down my balls. They tighten in response.

Jolt after jolt of pleasure surge down my spine. "Come, baby," I command. "Fuck, come for me, now." As soon as I feel her start coming around my cock, I'm done.

"Oh God! Oh God, Ryan. Ryan! Ah!" she screams.

"Aria!" I fill her pussy with jet after jet of come. My body arches off the bed as I moan and pump her full of me. She collapses on top of me as we both come.

We both shake and shiver against each other as we catch our breath. I hold her close to me as we pant. It takes her a full minute to stop pulsing around my cock. I refuse to pull out until she does because her pulsations around my dick cause me to come again.

"Fuck, Aria. Oh my fuck." I reach over my head and untie her. I take her hands and kiss each of her wrists.

She wraps her arms around me, still trembling as my come drips out of her all over me and the bed. "I'm not moving. I'm not getting off of you," she whispers against my neck as she hugs me as tightly as her pussy is squeezing me.

I chuckle. "Are you okay?"

"Yes. I'm absolutely perfect."

"You *are* perfect. So fucking perfect." I wrap her in my arms and hold her close.

"Give me a few minutes, and I'll be ready to go again."

My eyes widen, and my head snaps to hers. "What? Aria, aren't you sore? I -"

Her eyes meet mine. They're on fire. My softening cock is hard as steel in less than a second when I see her desire. "I want you. I crave you, Ryan. I've wanted this for just as long as you. Maybe longer."

"Fuck me, you have no idea how sexy an insatiable sexual appetite on a woman is." I flip her underneath me and plunge into her again.

I make unending love to her, my wife, until the sun comes up, and we're both too exhausted to do anything but fall asleep wrapped in each other's arms.

Chapter Twelve

⚔ Arianna ⚔

I laugh and squeal as Ryan splashes through the water soaking us both in the surprisingly warm spray. I try to run away, but he catches me around the waist and spins me in a circle.

"I think not. You're about to get soaked!" He laughs.

"Don't you dare!"

He flings me into the water as I scream. He dives in after me. When we resurface, I wrap my arms around his neck and legs around his waist.

"Dangerous position." He leans in to kiss me.

"Is it? It doesn't seem dangerous." I give him a playful smirk.

I feel him hard against me. I know what he wants. He growls possessively and dominantly as he reaches between us and pulls his cock out of his swim trunks. I have no time to react before he pushes the bottom of my bikini aside and plunges in.

"Oh God..." My eyes roll back in my head as his dick sinks into me.

He kisses me long and hard as he glides inside me and out with a cocky smirk. "I'm sorry. You were saying?"

"I was saying it doesn't -" He pushes my hips down against him and slides so deeply inside me that I feel like he's in my stomach. "Fuck!"

"Should we try that again?"

I tighten my legs around his waist. "I changed my mind." I kiss him just as long and hard as he did. I love playful Ryan as much as I love every other part of him.

"Yeah?" he says against my lips.

"Mmhmm..." I grip his shoulders tighter as I feel the now very familiar twinge between my legs. The ache that only he brings. He thrusts harder and faster, playing me like a violin.

"And what's the right answer?"

I smile against his lips as I meet his thrusts. "This is a very dangerous position."

"Good girl. That's what I wanted to hear."

I tighten around him and whimper as my pussy begs for release. "Please let me come."

He smiles and kisses me deeply as he thrusts a few more times. "Come for me, beautiful," he whispers huskily against my lips.

The waves lap against us in time to the orgasm that hits me as I come. He follows behind me and holds me close to him as I collapse in his arms.

He kisses me again as he pulls out of me, adjusts his shorts and my bottoms, and carries me out of the water, my legs still wrapped around him.

"I love you," I say as I nuzzle his neck.

"I love you, too."

I tilt my head and bite my lip. "Do I say that too much?" He smiles as he lets me down on the warm, pink sand of the private beach in front of our suite in Antigua. He spanks me, then rubs my ass. I jump. "Ryan!" I giggle as I smile wide.

"I'll never get sick of you telling me you love me." He looks deep into my eyes, and the love I see shining at me from them is enough to light the universe brighter than the sun has any hope of doing.

I blush. "Good. Because I really love saying it."

"And I really love hearing it." He bends to kiss me again.

"Ry!" Ryan groans against my lips as he slowly pulls away at Chase's voice. He pulls me close to his chest as he looks up at Chase jogging to us. "Don't shoot the messenger, but Taylor just got some information you might need."

"Might?"

"Yes. Might. We don't know what it means."

Ryan growls low in his chest and looks down at me. "I'm sorry. I know it's supposed to be just us today."

"It's okay. I understand."

He kisses me. "How did I get so lucky? Most women would be pissed if their brand new husband got pulled away for work while they were on their honeymoon."

"Most women didn't marry one of the most powerful men in the world. And most women don't have a mafia after her and a husband who has the power to take that other mafia completely out."

"Hmm... Yeah. You're pretty damn lucky." He grins and kisses me once more as he hugs me before he starts to walk with Chase across the beach. "You staying here?"

"Maybe for a few minutes. I'll see you back in the room. I have to get ready for dinner, but I'd like to dry off a little."

He smiles and winks at me. I melt. My husband is perfect. Strong. Protective. Powerful. Sweet. Gentle. Commanding. Dominant. Sexy as hell. He's the perfect package. And if I do say so myself, he has the perfect package.

I laugh to myself as I drop in the warm sand. I close my eyes and let the sun warm the chill of not having Ryan's arms around me and hands all over me.

After a few minutes, a shadow blocks out my sun. I'm instantly chilled. I sigh. "Ugh. I guess my sun time is over."

I sit up, open my eyes, and instantaneously stop breathing when I see a pair of tactical boots standing next to me. Ryan's guards don't wear tactical boots unless they're on a mission. No one in our family who is here enjoying the vacation would be wearing tactical boots. My eyes slowly travel up until they meet the owner of the boots.

"Arianna. Please don't run," his deep voice says to me as he slowly kneels down. He holds out his hands. "I'm not going to hurt you. You know that. You trust me."

I blink and shake my head. "Luke? How? How did you...?"

"It's a long, long story that I think I need to tell you and Ryan together. But you're in serious danger, Arianna. We need to get you the fuck out of here."

I shiver. He reaches for the towel behind me and wraps it around my shoulders. "I just... How are you here?" I ask in a daze.

"I promise I'll tell you, but we need to get you out of here. You aren't safe." He looks around. "Where are Ryan's guards?"

"All over. Hidden." I don't need to see them. I know they're close. Ryan wouldn't let them be far away.

I look up at the tall, muscular man next to me as he stands. He's always reminded me of Scott Eastwood. Taller. Definitely more defined. But he has the dangerous glint in his eyes that Scott Eastwood seems to have women falling over themselves for.

He reaches a hand down to me. "We need to talk to Ryan. There's a lot of shit going on that he needs to know if he has any hope of protecting you."

I shiver again and take his hand. He glances over his shoulder again as he pulls me up. I'm instantly uneasy. I look around myself, staying close to Luke. Despite the fact that he's one of my father's guards, something about him has always made me feel safe and secure. I've never doubted that I can trust him.

"Why do you keep looking over your shoulder?"

"Because I followed some of your dad's guards here. But I haven't been able to find the two that I followed. I lost them at the edge of the bank of trees. They vanished." He keeps hold of my hand and stays behind me as he guides me towards the suite. "If you can get me to any of Ryan's guards to give me back-up, Arianna, I'd be appreciative."

"O-okay." My heart is beginning to race as I look around, trying to stay calm. I spot Chase near the building, but it seems so far away. I point. "There's Chase. He's one of Ryan's brothers."

"Too far away. I can see one of your dad's guards at the tree line. Find me someone else."

"H-he's here?" I gasp and choke back a sob as I immediately look at the tree line.

"I'll protect you, Arianna. You know I will. But I need help."

I take a deep breath and force myself to focus. I see someone walking quickly towards us. My heart stops beating until I realize who he is. One of our guards. Thank God. Thank God for Rico.

"Mrs. Crane?" he asks when he nearly reaches us. His hand is on his gun as he watches Luke. "What's going on?"

I glance back at Luke. I thought we had sped off the beach, but we're still on it. "I…" I can't think. I can barely breathe. My attention is almost solely on the fat guy standing at the tree line leveling something shiny at me.

"I'll explain when you get her to safety. One of her dad's guards is out there."

My eyes widen. "Gun!" I scream. A shot rings out.

I almost instantaneously have a mouthful of sand. The weight on top of me holding me down is making breathing impossible. Not like I'd be able to anyway. My lungs feel as if they've collapsed. My heart is no longer pumping. The blood in my veins is completely frozen. I'd scream, but I'm pretty sure I'm dead. No one can hear a ghost.

The yells around me and the sudden flurry of activity is like a blur. I don't know what's happening. Even if I did, I'm so scared I wouldn't be able to keep up.

Just as quickly as I'm thrown down, I'm hauled back up into a solid body. A hand clasps over my mouth. The other is around my waist like a vice. I flail and try with everything I am to get away, but the grip only gets stronger. I can't see anything through the gritty sand in my eyes. Crying hurts, but I need to get away.

"Shh… Arianna, it's me! It's Josh! Stop fighting! We need to move." The commanding voice stops me cold. He removes his hand. I cough and sputter, spitting out sand as he tugs me with him.

I fall in the sand with a whimper. "I… Josh, I can't see."

"What? What the fuck happened?"

"Sand."

"Fuck." I feel him lift me off the ground and carry me. My towel is long gone. I shiver as I wrap my arms around his neck. "I don't know where your top went, sweetheart, but press against me because you're exposed."

"What?" I shriek and press against his chest.

He tightens his grip. "There's two guards flanking me. You're safe, Arianna."

"I trust you." And I do. As soon as I met him there was something about him that immediately made me know I can trust him. I felt it with all of Ryan's brothers, but it was different with him. Stronger.

My eyes burn, but I try to keep them closed, willing my tears to do their job and flush out my eyes. I grip Josh just as tightly as I'm pressed against him, trusting him to get me to Ryan.

"Find Alex!" Josh barks. "You! Grab Ryan."

"What the fuck?" I hear Chase.

"I don't know everything. I heard a gunshot, her screaming, saw someone laying on top of her with his gun pointed to the woods, and Rico pressing her head into the sand pointing his gun at the woods. Where's Ryan?"

"In Taylor's suite."

"Go. Go get him."

"I'll get you into their room," someone else says.

"Jason?" I ask, panicking slightly that I can't see everyone around me. I grip Josh tighter.

"Sand in her eyes. She can't see you," Josh explains.

"It's Jason, Air. We're getting you to your room."

I can't hold back. I start sobbing into Josh's shoulder. "The sand hurts so bad! I was trying to be strong, but it hurts!"

"Shh... I know, sweetheart. Almost there," Josh says soothingly.

I sniffle and cry because I can't help it. I try to focus on anything except the pain, but I can't. It burns. It stings. It's like everything I imagine venom coursing through my veins would feel like. Except it's gritty. My tears do nothing to resolve how dry the sand makes them.

"Can I help?" a soft voice asks.

"Yeah, baby. Follow us," Josh says.

"Take her to the kitchenette. There's a sink to flush out her eyes," Jason commands before I have a chance to ask who the voice belongs to.

A few moments later, Josh lets me down and holds me near the sink. "You need to bend, okay? We're going to flush out your eyes."

I nod as he guides me down. My eyes are squeezed shut. My boobs touch the cold metal of the sink's edge. "Ah!" I jump instinctively back.

"Arianna, stop!" Josh commands.

126

"Here. This will help," the soft voice says. "It's Lyric, Arianna. I put a towel down to help with the cold metal.

I nod. "Th-thank you. I take a deep breath and follow Josh's command to bend over the sink as he runs the water.

"Good girl. I know it hurts, but you need to open your eyes. Okay?"

I nod and shiver against the metal. "O-okay." I struggle to open them. I only get them a little ways before the pain is excruciating.

Before I can react and close them, Josh's large hand is against my eyes with water. I fight to keep my eyes open. He tugs my hair a little, pulling my head back as Lyric rubs my back soothingly. He splashes a continuous stream of water into my eyes, flushing the sand out of them.

"Arianna? Jesus Christ! What the hell happened?"

Ryan.

I cry with a wave of relief at hearing my husband's voice. Josh continues tugging my hair and keeping a steady stream of water flowing into my eyes. I don't need to see Ryan to know he's right next to me. His hand is soothingly rubbing my back with Lyric's.

"I heard a gunshot and her screaming from the beach. I ran down there and saw someone on top of her with Rico holding her head down in the sand. Both of them were pointing their guns at the treeline towards that wooded area," Josh explains.

"What? Who the fuck was on top of her?" Ryan's voice exudes all the danger and protectiveness he has for me.

"I don't know. Not one of your guards."

"Luke," I splutter as water gets into my nose and mouth. I cough. Josh pulls me up gently and hands me a hand towel as he looks in my eyes, making sure they're flushed out.

"Luke? Ambrosio?" Ryan asks, confused. "Why the hell is Luke Ambrosio here?"

I stand up straighter and start drying off my face when Josh nods. I blink a few times before taking the towel away. Josh puts another towel around my chest. I hold it there, flushing bright red that both he and Lyric saw me exposed like that.

"Feel better?" Josh asks.

"Yeah... I... Have to get something else on." I nearly flee.

Ryan follows. "Baby, what the fuck happened out there? I was away from you for less than five minutes, and I didn't hear a gunshot."

I walk into the room, thankful I can see again, and strip off my wet bikini bottoms. He does the same. "I don't know, Ryan. I was laying there enjoying the sun. And then everything started to go crazy. I thought a cloud passed over the sun. So, I thought that was it. I started to get up, thinking that the rainstorm they were talking about was coming in. But it wasn't that. It was Luke. He was kneeling next to me. At first, I freaked out. I had no idea why one of my father's guards was here. But I trust him."

"I don't know what to make of him. Taylor thinks he's a cop. That's what I got called away for, but I never got to look at what he had because Chase came flying into the room saying we needed to get out here. I come in and see you topless bent over the sink crying with Lyric and Josh. I'm hearing shit about a gunshot. Fuck, Aria, I thought you got shot."

His arms wrap around me as I'm pulling a t-shirt over my head. He crushes me so hard to his chest that, for just a moment, I feel like he might actually break me. I wiggle just enough to be able to put my arms around his solid frame. I breathe out a shuddering breath.

"I'm okay. There was a shot. But I was pushed down so fast that I didn't know what happened or where it came from. Luke was saying that he followed two of my dad's guards here, but lost them. I asked how he knew I was here, but he said he needed to talk to you." I breathe him in as he sways with me. His skin smells of salt and sand, but also the spicy intoxicating scent that is uniquely Ryan Crane. If I didn't know better, I'd say he doesn't wear cologne. That the scent I've come to love is simply him.

"Where is Luke now?"

"I don't know, Ry. He told me I needed to get him to one of the guards. I saw Chase. Rico came out of nowhere. I was just about to tell him what was going on when I saw someone in the tree line with something shiny. It took me a second to see that it was a gun. He was so far away. Next thing I know, there's a gunshot. I'm in the sand. Seconds after that, I'm being hauled to my feet, but I couldn't see. I didn't know it was Josh until he said so. I don't really know anything after that. I told Josh I couldn't see. He picked me up and carried me here. He was barking orders at people to find Alex and you. Chase went to find you. Jason took us here."

He continues to sway with me. "I need to find Rico."

"I'm sure he'll be coming here with Luke."

He pulls back only enough to look down at me. "Are you okay? Really?"

"My eyes hurt a little bit. But I'm okay."

He looks deep in my eyes. "They're red. But they look okay. I think Josh got all of the sand out."

"I don't feel sand in there anymore. They just feel like they're scratched. Sort of the way they feel after you've been crying. Dry and itchy."

He hugs me to his chest again. "I love you so fucking much, baby."

"I love you, too." I sweetly kiss his chest. I stand on my tiptoes to kiss his throat and jaw. He leans down and kisses me deeply and hard, dominating all of me as his tongue twines with mine in our own familiar dance. When he finally pulls away, we're both breathless.

"I need to find out what's going on." He helps me into my shirt before he starts getting dressed himself.

"I think we need to start packing."

"I'll have the staff do it. You need to be out there with me." He slips a pair of jeans on and a black t-shirt. I find a pair of jean shorts.

"You... want me out there with you?"

"Yes, baby. You're part of this. You're my wife. And I know you well enough by now to know that getting you to stay away from all of this is something I have no hope in making happen."

"That's..." I smile as I look up at him. "...probably accurate."

He smiles back. "Truth is, you have rapport with him. Taylor says he has information on him, and I don't know how forthcoming he's going to be when he's confronted with it. I don't know what it is."

"I don't either, but Taylor told me once that I need to trust my instincts. Well, my instincts are telling me that Luke is one of the good guys. I trust him."

"I know, baby. It sounds like I need to thank him for saving your life." He reaches out a hand to me as he glances at the door. "Sounds like we have company, judging by all the voices I'm suddenly hearing. You ready for this?"

I nod and take his hand. He leads me out to our suite's front room. He was right. There are a lot of people suddenly in the room. A lot of confused people.

I meet Luke's eyes.

Ryan is right.

It's time for answers.

Chapter Thirteen

☒ Ryan ☒

I watch as Luke sits down. Nick stands close to the couch Arianna has curled up on. I'm standing in the middle of the room trying to think through everything rationally. There are so many different scenarios running through my head, and none of them make a fuck of sense.

Chase and Jason are both pacing on opposite sides of the room. Taylor, Alex, and Rico have formed a semi-circle around Luke. Taylor is holding a manilla envelope in his hand, and it hits me that I still haven't seen it. I hold out my hand. He hands it to me without question.

I glance back at Arianna, my entire world. Her eyes haven't left Luke's. I trust her instincts and choke down every instinct in myself that tells me something about him showing up is fucked up. Josh watches me with curiosity, no doubt wondering what I'm going to do, as he sits down next to Arianna. Close. Protectively. I silently thank him for not having to give the command; for him just doing what I want without words.

It may not make sense in most people's worlds to trust someone like him after everything my family has been through with him; after everything he put Jessa through. In my world, I have to form alliances with people. And I have to trust them implicitly, just like they do me. I see how he is with Jessa and the rest of my family. I've watched the way he is with his girl. I know the amends he's trying to make for all of his past mistakes and fuck-ups.

But most importantly, he has to fit in with my family and love and protect them as fiercely as I would. Of all of the people I surround myself with, of all the relationships I've formed, Josh might just be the most unquestionably loyal and protective of them all. The most like me.

Not to say all of my brothers aren't loyal and protective. They all are. I know I can count on them for everything. But I'd always thought when it came to people in my life most like me it was Alex. Josh proves me wrong more and more every day.

"I suppose you're all looking for an explanation," Luke begins.

"Fuck right," Josh growls low.

I glare at Luke and open the envelope in my hand. I flip through the pages and look back up at him in disbelief. "You're fucking ATF?" He has the decency to look a little fearful. Fucking good. He glances at Arianna, and I nearly lose control. "Don't look at her. I'm the one you need to worry about."

"Look, I know how this looks," he begins. He looks up at me. "But I can explain."

"You better start," Alex says. "Ryan Crane isn't a very patient man."

Luke closes his eyes and scrubs his hands down his face. "Two years ago we got some intel that Stephen Ambrosio was involved with the weapons trade." He looks up at me again. "I was put undercover in his mafia. We changed my name. Gave me a fucked up criminal background. Made me sound like a badass. My story was that I was his long lost son."

"I figured that part out myself," Taylor says. "What we want to know is how the fuck you ended up here."

Luke glances up at Taylor and the rest of the room before settling back on me again. "About a year ago, I overheard a conversation I wasn't supposed to. Ambrosio was discussing the upcoming marriage of his son to complete a merger. He was talking to someone on the phone. I don't know who, but it wasn't the person he was merging with. I could tell because he kept saying Antonio Massena; the Massena Mafia."

I look down at the paper in my hand. The one that threw me and didn't make sense. "Massena. Your last name. Massena." I look back at him, demanding an explanation through the fire in my eyes.

"W-what?" Arianna whispers from behind me. She leans forward, but I see Josh block her from getting up with his arm across her torso and a shake of his head. She obeys and curls back into the couch watching us.

Luke's eyes flick to hers. He takes a deep breath. "I kept the call from my C.O. I knew if I told him what was happening, he'd pull me. I didn't know a lot about my dad. My mom kept it from me. Just said he wasn't a part of our life. I never pushed it. But... I guess curiosity got me. So, I researched. I needed DNA. I talked Ambrosio into putting me in with Massena as a spy. Make sure his merger was legit. That he didn't have plans to fuck it up somehow. Betray us. I was careful how I brought it up. I didn't let on that I had been eavesdropping on him. I said Chad brought it up, and I was curious. Chad Stephen's son."

I look down at the paper again. "DNA came back a match."

"Antonio Massena is my father. Which means the girl he wanted to marry off like a piece of fucking property is my sister. Arianna."

Arianna nearly chokes. I don't know what to think. "So, you go undercover into the Ambrosio Mafia on a weapons trade assignment." I rub my forehead. "You end up double undercover in the Massena Mafia and find out he's your father and Arianna is your sister."

"That explains so much...," Arianna whispers.

Luke looks at her. "I couldn't tell you. But as soon as I found out, my mission changed. I was still reporting the information I had to my C.O. regarding the Ambrosio mafia, but everything else was on my own. The more I saw how you were treated, the more I realized I needed to get you the fuck out. I spent as much time there as I could. After a little while, he trusted me enough and started having me follow you."

"W-why?" she asks. "I n-never gave him the i-inclination that I was doing a-anything."

"You didn't. But Chad did. Chad told him that you were constantly leaving school with this older guy. Described him as dark and always drove different cars."

"Fucking hell," I growl under my breath.

"I covered for you a lot. I didn't know who it was at first, but I ran a license plate. When I figured out it was Ryan Crane, I knew you'd be

133

okay as long as you were with him as often as possible. I observed. I didn't know a lot about Ryan. Just that he runs a legit mafia. I went right to the chief of the NYPD. Asked him what he knew about Ryan and his mafia. That's when I found out who you are and what you really do." He looks back at me. "Not everything, but I talked to some of my contacts. Some have worked with you and told me you're one of the good guys. They didn't tell me much else. Just that. But it was enough for me to trust that when it came to her…" He nods to Arianna. "She'd be safe."

"So, how did you get here?" Josh commands.

"I showed up at Massena's on Arianna's birthday. I didn't know at the time she had planned to leave, but I knew that was the day they planned to force her to marry. My plan was to contact you," he says as he looks at me. "I needed you to help me get her out. But she wasn't there when I got there. Massena was bleeding from the neck. Chad had been bitten. Arianna was gone. I tried tracking her. But her phone was off. I didn't know where she was until it came out in the papers that you were engaged. I was going to call my C.O. to get me out right then. She was with you. I figured I'd contact her later down the road. I didn't need to be in anymore. We had all we needed."

Alex reaches out a hand for the papers I have. "Let me see." I hand them to him. He looks through them and shakes his head. "This just says you did a DNA test on Massena, and that he's your father. How do you know you're any relation to Arianna? And before you say anything, I'm not fucking stupid. It may seem like it's common sense, but for all we know, Massena isn't really her father."

Luke nods. "I have more documentation not in that file. I don't know how the fuck you got all of that, but it doesn't matter."

"Nick will get it. You move, I shoot," Josh says.

"We all shoot," Jason says from the wall he's leaning on. For the thousandth time today, I'm grateful for all of them.

Luke just nods and keeps his hands where everyone can see them. "Just paperwork. Right pocket on my thigh. I already gave your guards my guns and knives."

Nick pushes him forward a little bit. He holds the collar of Luke's t-shirt from behind him as he pats the right pocket. Nick was a cop with the NYPD for a little while. He knows how to keep a suspect under his complete control. Nick pulls out the envelope and hands it to me.

I take it, keeping my eyes on him as I open it and read. "So, she's really your sister." I can hear Arianna breathe a sigh of relief. The same relief I feel.

"I stayed in while I looked for her. Like I said, I was about to pull myself when it came out you were engaged. But Massena and Ambrosio cooked up this plan. If they couldn't do what they needed to do with Arianna…" He swallows and looks down.

"He'd kill me." It's a whisper from behind me that is so heartbreaking I do something I've never in my life done. I turn my back to someone I'm not totally sure is an enemy or an ally. But I trust my family.

I drop to my knees in front of Arianna and take her hands in mine. "Baby, that's never going to happen. Never."

She smiles weakly. "I know."

I lean in and kiss her deeply, willing her to feel the trust in me I know she has. She closes her eyes and melts against me. The tension and fear she holds in her body slowly releases as my tongue teases hers.

Luke continues as I pull away. "I dropped everything. Called my C.O. I told him to get me out. I had a family emergency. I flew to Chicago. Contacted every contact I knew in Chicago. I finally got some information from a contact saying that he got your flight information, but doesn't think he's the only one who got it. And he wasn't. Massena got it as well. I found out where you were going. When you'd be here. I had a couple contacts watching Messena. I had some illegal bugs set up in his house. My contacts heard him say he was sending a couple guards here."

"We have a leak," Chase says. "No one knew our flight plan. I handed it in myself directly to your FAA contact."

I stand and turn. My eyes flick to Rico.

He nods. "On it." He heads for the door, his phone already to his ear.

I turn back to Luke. "Why didn't you contact me? Why go through Arianna? I could have had extra security on and been waiting. She wouldn't have had a gunshot fired at her today."

"I agree. If I could have contacted you, I would have. But it's not like your number is listed. I didn't know how to get in touch with you, Ryan. And Arianna has to have a different phone because I tried contacting her. Several times. All I get is voicemail."

I look at him a few moments, unable to argue because he's right. I cross my arms over my chest. "Did you leave Massena's Mafia?"

"Yes. He probably knows who I am by now."

"So, he's just as much after you as he is her."

"Probably. But I can take care of myself. My only concern is Arianna. And my mother, but I have a tail on her. She doesn't know that."

I raise an eyebrow. "Do you think he'll go after your mother?"

"I don't really know. But I'd rather have a tail on her to be safe."

I look up as Rico comes back in. He hangs up his phone. "We need to move. Massena just got on a plane."

"Did you take care of our other problem?" I ask.

"Yes, sir. He's being dealt with as we speak. But he's the least of our worries. Massena is on his way here. We need to get out and fast."

I nod. "Everyone move." I reach for Arianna and pull her up. I stop in front of Luke as I'm leading her to our bedroom. "Thank you." I extend my hand to shake.

He shakes it and nods. "I'd do anything for her." He watches us as I turn back towards the bedroom. Arianna stops and tugs me back.

"I think he should be with us."

I turn back to her. "What?"

"He's family." She looks me directly in my eyes. Unflinching. Unblinking. Determined. I hold her gaze for a second before nodding and turning to Rico. "He'll be joining us. Make the arrangements."

I have to smile as I walk to the bedroom and start packing our things.

Family.

Arianna knows me well enough to know I'd never turn my back on family.

XXX

I watch as Arianna tiredly climbs the stairs to our jet. Taylor is behind her, making sure she doesn't fall. She looks so exhausted I worry she actually might.

Jason and Nick both lean against my rented SUV next to me. They stand just like I do. Feet slightly apart. Arms folded across their chest.

136

Anyone near us could tell instantly we're brothers just by our looks, even though Nick is adopted. If they look close they'd see we have the same stance. Same mannerisms. Despite him being adopted, he looks like us. The three of us are a force to be reckoned with.

"How's Arianna holding up?" Nick asks as we all watch the plane.

"As soon as we're in the air, I'm taking her to bed. She's dead on her feet. She's stressed the fuck out. Hearing everything that happened with Luke and then finding out he might be her brother..."

Nick looks at me with a raised eyebrow. "Might? I thought he had papers."

"When have you ever known me to trust anyone I don't know?"

He laughs. "You're right. Never. Get in there with your girl." He turns to the SUV Luke is in and lets him out.

"Still don't trust me?" Luke asks, a small smirk in his features.

I tear my eyes away from the plane and meet his. "Not a fucking chance in hell. But she does. And I trust her. So, I'll double check your story. But until it checks out, you're being watched. I don't want you alone with any member of my family. Got it?"

"I got it. I understand. Man of your position... Can't be too careful. But I am who I say I am."

"I know who you are. Whether you're related to my girl or not remains to be seen. When Taylor gets the test results back, we'll talk." I gesture to the plane as Taylor appears at the top. "There's our cue."

I follow Luke up the stairs to my plane as Nick and Jason make their way to Jason's. I watch as Luke gets settled and Taylor positions himself, as I do, facing Luke. Arianna is already asleep on Chase's shoulder. I smile.

"I think she's a little shaken up. She didn't want to sit alone," Breetana says.

"She asked if I'd sit next to her until you got here," Chase says. "Wanna switch?"

"No. She's okay. As soon as we're in the air, I'll just take her to bed. It's a long flight anyway. Let her be. She needs the rest."

"We just released the photos, Mr. Crane," Marianne says to me.

"Hopefully, it'll help you gain the upper hand and throw those two off your trail." Dave leans back in his chair after putting away his phone.

I nod. "If Luke is correct, then we shouldn't have any more tails. At least not right now since he's headed to Antigua."

"Hey, Ryan. I was thinking about your leak. We need another contact in the FAA, right?" Robby asks.

"I took care of that," Rico says.

"I know, but I think we should make sure that it's a person he can't get to. You have the ability to go higher up then he does. Can't you go to a top guy? He'd never be able to get to a top guy."

"Kid has good instincts," Taylor says.

I nod. "Rico, make it happen. I thought who we had was high enough, but go higher."

He nods. "On it."

As soon as we take off, and I feel we've leveled out, I take off my seatbelt and lean down to remove Arianna's. I lift her in my arms. She blinks and curls into me, wrapping her arms around my shoulders as she closes her eyes again.

I turn to everyone. "It's a long flight. The seats recline all the way back. It's not a five star hotel, but it's comfortable. The flight attendant will be around with pillows and blankets. Let her know if you need anything." I carry Arianna to the bedroom, pull back the covers, and carefully set her down on the bed, trying not to wake her. She stirs and opens her eyes. "Sorry, baby. I was hoping not to wake you."

"It's okay," she whispers sleepily.

"Do you want a t-shirt to sleep in? Or do you want to stay in your clothes?"

She clears her throat. "How long is the flight?"

"Eighteen hours. We'll be making a stop at an Air Force base to refuel, so it adds a little extra time."

"T-shirt, please."

I smile and hand her a t-shirt from my well-stocked dresser. She undresses and puts it on as I strip down to my boxer briefs. She crawls under the covers and curls up next to me with her back to me. I wrap my arms around her and bury my face in her hair.

"I love you," I say as I kiss her neck.

"I love you."

"I'm sorry about Luke and being so cautious about him. I know you have a lot of questions for him. I know you trust him. But I have to be sure."

"I know, Ryan. I do have a lot of questions, and I do trust him. But above all else, I trust you. I don't think he'd hurt me. I think he's telling the truth, but I trust you."

I kiss the back of her neck. "Thank you."

"I'll always trust you. You never have to worry about that. I know you do what you do because you love me and our family."

I smile and kiss the back of her neck again and hold her close to me as she falls asleep once again. I haven't told her where we're going. I want it to be a surprise. After making her leave Antiqua early and knowing how stressed out she is knowing her father is after her, she deserves this. She deserves everything. I hope to hell our plan works and the photographers can keep her father one step behind us. I want Arianna to enjoy herself and not have to worry about him trailing us.

I wrap Arianna tighter in my embrace as the weightlessness of the plane gliding through the air finally lulls me to sleep.

Chapter Fourteen

✗ Arianna ✗

I wake up to a jolt.

Like I'm dropping from the sky.

Ryan's arms are wrapped around me. He groans. The jolt happens again, and a small scream escapes my throat. Ryan's arms tighten around me.

"Shh... It's okay, baby. It's just turbulence. Probably just hit an air pocket. Go back to sleep." Another jolt happens. It's far worse than the first. The plane seems like it's falling out of the sky. My nails dig into Ryan's forearm. "Aria, I promise we're fine. If anything bad was happening, someone would come back here and tell me."

Another jolt happens. I start crying as I turn around and bury my face in his chest. "It feels like we're being shot at."

Ryan chuckles. "Sweetheart, we're *not* being shot at. It's just turbulence. It happens. And the pilots we have are the best of the best. They're retired Air Force combat pilots."

I can't help but laugh. "You really don't half ass anything, do you?"

"Nope. All of my bases are always covered. Always."

I look up at him as he holds me tightly. He kisses me. I give myself completely to him as he trails kisses down my neck.

His hand sneaks under my shirt. I shiver as his fingers find their way to my nipples. He runs his thumb across them and takes one between his fingers. He pinches it. I gasp. He rubs it back and forth, making it immediately harden for him.

"I could take your mind off the flight."

I smile shyly. "You could."

He grins cockily and kisses me as he moves to the other nipple. "We could waste some time before we land."

I give him a teasing smile. "Are you a member of the Mile High Club?"

He laughs as he runs his tongue along my lower lip. "Sweetheart, I'm not only a card carrying member, I'm President."

I laugh at his teasing, then gasp as he pulls me close to him. His incredibly hard cock is proudly standing at attention against my stomach. "I'm not sure how to take that. How many other women have you had in this bed to make you President of the Mile High Club?"

I bite my lip and attempt to look upset, but I can tell there's a teasing glint in my eye. I know my husband's reputation. It's been plastered all over sleazy tabloids around the world for years.

Ryan catches the glint in my eye. "Hundreds. Thousands even."

I playfully smack his chest. "Gross!"

He laughs and pins me underneath him. "God, you're beautiful."

"And you're incredibly hot. It's unfair, really."

He laughs and crushes his lips to mine. Very suddenly our playful banter turns into a very hot and heavenly make-out session.

He presses himself against me. I moan into his mouth and wrap my legs around his waist. I drop my head back to give him more access as he trails kisses down my throat. I spear my fingers in his hair and arch into him.

"I'm so happy that we don't have to stop at this anymore. I crave you, Ryan. You're like a drug. I'm addicted."

"I feel the same way. I could be inside you all day and still not get enough."

He pushes himself up to his knees, straddling me, and holds out his hands. I take them. He pulls me up. He takes the hem of the shirt and pulls it off of me as the plane jolts again.

I close my eyes and take a deep breath. "I hate that."

Ryan kisses me as he pushes me back onto the bed with his body. "I guarantee you'll like it when I'm inside you." He rolls off of me and strips off his underwear. I reach for my own but he growls, grabs my arm, and pulls me on top of him so I'm straddling him. He spanks me.

"Oh! Ryan..." White hot electricity shoots right to my core.

"Haven't you learned not to do anything unless I tell you to?" He gives me a playful smirk.

"Have you ever thought that maybe I like when you spank me?"

"Is that so?" He acts like he has no idea, but I know him better than that. He runs his hands up my legs to my panties. "I'll have to think of another form of punishment when you break a rule." He grins and pushes my panties aside. I bite my lip and pout. "Something... a bit more..." He plunges his middle finger inside me.

I gasp. "Holy God."

He thrusts his finger inside me deliciously slowly but hard. I close my eyes and give into his tantalizing thrusts. "Enjoyable for the both of us." He removes his finger. I whimper. I watch as he puts it in his mouth and sucks.

I blush. "How do I taste?"

"Like honey." His hard length beneath me is driving me insane. I move against him, needing release. He smiles as he puts his thumbs inside the waistband of my panties. "You know what I love so much about these lace panties you like to wear?"

"They're see through?" My eyes widen as he smiles wickedly and rips each side of my panties. He throws them on the floor somewhere. "Ryan!"

"They're easy to rip off you."

"Pretty sure this is like the fifth pair you've ripped off. The way you're going, you're going to have to buy me new panties every week."

His smile goes from wicked to wolfish as he reaches down between us and grabs himself. He positions himself at my entrance and guides me down slowly onto him. "Worth every dollar to feel you tight and wet around me."

I close my eyes and moan. "Mmm... You don't need to rip them off to feel me like this."

"It's so much more fun, though." He gives me another of his signature cocky smiles. I close my eyes as he starts moving himself inside of me and guiding my body the way he wants. I love when he guides my movements. "Congratulations."

"Oh...," I moan. "On what?"

"Becoming an official member of the Mile High Club."

He lifts me up and drops me on top of him. His massive dick slides deeper inside me than I've ever felt. I love him like this. I love being connected so intimately; so deeply. I love how much he cares about my pleasure while he chases his own.

"Since you're the President, what does that make me?"

"That makes you the First Lady."

I laugh as he quickens his pace. He continues alternating between moving me against him and dropping me on top of him. The ferocity of his pace; the intensity of the sensations he gives me sends me straight over the edge.

"Ryan! I -"

"You know what you have to do if you want to come." He thrusts harder as my thighs shake.

"Please! Please let me come!" My pussy clenches hard around him as I try to hold back. I'm being as quiet as possible because we're not the only ones on this plane.

He groans. "Fuck, Aria. Come, sexy girl."

"Oh! Ry -" I can't finish the sentence. I completely come undone. I pulse around him, clenching tight. I keep riding him through my release.

The plane hits another air pocket, and Ryan slips deeper inside me as his own release hits. I gasp as my eyes roll back. I come a second time. He continues thrusting until both of us are done pulsating. I collapse on top of him, panting. He hugs me as tightly as he can while we catch our breaths.

"Holy fuck, baby."

"Am I the best of all your Mile High Club conquests?" I smile into his chest as he laughs.

"By far!" He grabs my hips and flips me onto my side. He assaults me with kisses along my chest, lips, neck, and jawline. "Breakfast?"

I giggle "Only if Quesadillas are on the menu."

"Quesadillas are always on the menu for you, baby."

XXX

Hours later, the plane is getting ready to land. Ryan is holding my hand. We hit a storm on the way into wherever we are going, and the past hour has been spent fighting turbulence. The plane feels like it's being thrown all around.

Both me and Breetana are fighting nausea. As the plane jerks yet again, I nearly lose it. Breetana isn't so lucky. She barely gets the sick bag to her mouth in time.

"Eeew! You're going to make me throw up just seeing you throw up," Nicole whines.

"I'm so sorry," Breetana says into the bag as she loses it again.

"It's okay, honey. I don't think any of us are doing so well." Chase rubs her back.

I bury my head in Ryan's shoulder. "I hope Jessa, Jason, and Nick are okay."

"I'm sure they're fine, sweetheart. Jason's pilots are combat pilots just like mine."

A few torturous minutes later, we're finally on the ground.

"Thank the fucking Lord." Taylor puts his hand to his mouth and dry-heaves. He closes his eyes a second as it passes.

"Shit. You're telling me." Chase hugs a very green looking Breetana.

"I don't think I've ever been so sick in my life," Renza grumbles.

"You'll feel better tomorrow after we sleep this off." Robby makes no motion to comfort her. I'd question what I'm missing, but I'm too sick to care.

"Where are we anyway?" I ask quietly. Everyone looks at each other, then Ryan. "Am I... the only one who doesn't know?"

Ryan smiles. "Remember when we went to Taylor's and Nikki's wedding, and you and I were joking around about me flying you anywhere you wanted to go?"

I look at him a second, completely bewildered. "Yeah?"

"Do you remember what you said? Where you wanted to go?"

My heart starts racing. Could he really have remembered? "Australia?"

"Do you remember what you told me you wanted to see?"

Tears sting my eyes. This can't be happening. He can't be any more perfect. "Kangaroos?"

He smiles and stands up. He holds out a hand. I take it. "Welcome to Kangaroo Island... Australia."

I squeal and throw my arms around him as he pulls me to my feet. "Are you kidding?"

"Nope. You're about to step foot on Kangaroo Island."

"I can't believe it!" My excitement gets the better of me. I nearly run to the door, but stop myself and wait impatiently as the flight attendant opens it.

Ryan turns to the photographers. "Please tell me you got that."

Marianne smiles. "All of it, Mr. Crane."

Dave nods. "We'll pick the best ones and add them to the scrapbook."

"Good. One more thing. I know I promised separate bedrooms, but the resort we rented out is a room down. A water pipe burst. Everyone else is already bunking with someone else. You guys think you'll be okay together for this leg of the trip?" Ryan asks slightly hesitantly.

I look over at Ryan and Dave and Marianne. I know he saw the chemistry between them that I did. And I know he's playing matchmaker. Big bad mafia boss forcing love. I stifle a laugh.

Dave looks down at Marianne. "Uh... I... If you're okay."

Marianne's face turns red. "Oh! Um... I... Sure. If... it's okay with you, too."

Dave smiles so widely I feel he may break. "Yeah! For sure! I mean... um.... Yes."

"Yeah, they have a thing for each other." Renza hugs me as she walks to my side.

"I know. And so does Ryan. That was intentional."

"Genius is what that was."

We both laugh as Ryan winks at us while everyone grabs their things.

145

After we arrive at the resort and get settled, I stand next to the floor to ceiling window of our bedroom in our suite staring at the unsettled ocean. Ryan comes up behind me and slips his arms around me. He kisses the back of my neck.

I smile. "Looks scary out there."

"It's kind of beautiful, though. Despite the chaos."

"I don't think anything about Australia is ugly." I turn to him. He leans down to kiss me. "Thank you. For taking me here."

"This was number one on your bucket list. I wanted to make sure we got to spend as much time here as you want." Ryan's brows crease as my face falls as a thought hits me. "What?"

"My bucket list. I... I didn't take anything from my dad's house. Including my wish box."

"Your... what?"

"My wish box." I close my eyes a moment before opening them again. "It's a box that has everything I wish in it. There's a kangaroo for wanting to see a kangaroo and visit Australia. I had a key chain of the Eiffel Tower for wanting to visit Paris. There's a postcard of Buckingham Palace for wanting to visit London. I made a wedding invitation with our names on it to signify my desire to marry you." I grow slightly more panicked as my eyes widen. "Ryan. Everything is in there. All of the places on our itinerary are in that box."

"Hey. Shh... It's okay. Nothing is going to get in the way of our trip. Nothing."

"What if he shows up?"

"Then we'll deal with it. But nothing is going to stop our happiness. Nothing." He leads me to the bed, and we crawl under the covers. "Get some rest. Tomorrow is the beginning of a really great week. Don't think about him."

Ryan wraps me in his arms. I try to relax. It isn't easy. I have an uneasy feeling that my father will figure out the game. That he'll outsmart us. That he'll see through the plan.

I snuggle into Ryan. The storm raging inside me is just as vicious as the one outside. For the first time ever, Ryan's strong embrace does nothing to calm it.

Chapter Fifteen

⚔ Ryan ⚔

(Two Weeks Later)

Watching Arianna's excitement the entire day has been one of the highlights of my life. Taking in a traditional Australian lunch, then taking her on this nature walk has been the best part of this trip so far for no other reason than the pure joy she's exuded.

"Ready?" My hands are covering her eyes. She's practically jumping up and down.

"Yes! Yes! Yes!"

"I want an award for being the best husband ever. Huge engraved golden trophy." I remove my hand and hold Arianna close to me, her back against my chest.

"Oh my God... He's so beautiful." She's nearly whispering so she doesn't scare him away.

Dave and Marianne are both snapping pictures. The kangaroo watches Arianna and slowly hops towards her. I start to pull her away, sensing danger. She untangles herself from my embrace and kneels down in front of the kangaroo.

"Uh... Baby, what are you doing?"

"Shh... Be quiet." She holds out her hand to the kangaroo.

I don't know whether to be pissed off or turned on that she just shushed me. "Baby, I really don't think this is a good idea."

The kangaroo hops closer to her. Arianna can touch him now. "Quiet, Ryan. You'll upset him." She speaks soothingly as she focuses all of her attention on the kangaroo. He steps slightly closer to her. She slowly and very gently strokes the kangaroo's chest.

I swallow. "Holy shit." The kangaroo puts his head down, I inhale sharply. I try to keep my voice calm and soothing like she did, but I fail miserably. "Honey, please get away from him. He looks pissed."

She smiles brilliantly. "Pissed? You're not pissed are you, sweet angel? No. You're so cute, though. Beautiful, aren't you?" She continues to talk to him soothingly as she pets his head. I can't believe how calm he is. And how he's taken to her.

A sudden rustling causes me to look up. The kangaroo jolts and turns towards the noise. Another kangaroo appears. I fight to grab Arianna and run. "Aria..."

"Shh..." The kangaroo turns back to Arianna and nuzzles her cheek before he turns and hops away. Arianna stands with the biggest smile on her face that I have ever seen. "She's a she! Not a he! She has a baby!"

I slip my arms around her and pull her close to me. "Please never do that to me again."

She laughs and looks up at me. "Is my big bad husband afraid of kangaroos?"

I give her my best wounded expression. "Me? I fear nothing. How do you not know that?"

She laughs as she grabs my hand and pulls me down the wilderness trail. "I need to see a koala."

"They said to keep your eyes out for them as we enter the tree bank. Look up in the trees for them," I say. Arianna keeps a firm grip on my hand as she concentrates on the trees. I stop and pull her to me so I can kiss her. "You being all carefree is one of the most beautiful things in the world."

"Even more beautiful than a kangaroo?"

"Yes. How the hell did you get her to do that? Come to you like that?"

149

She shrugs. "I don't know. I felt a connection with her."

I shake my head and smile like a lovesick fool. "You're amazing." I lean down to kiss her again. When I pull back I see a glimpse of the ocean beyond the tree bank. "You know, if you're up for a little hike, I heard there are sea lions that hang out on the beach somewhere around here. Wanna cut through the trees? Maybe we'll see a koala along the way."

Her eyes widen. "Really?" She glances over her shoulder towards the trees and bites her lip before looking back up at me. "We won't get in trouble?"

I smile mischievously and shrug. "Do you really care? Or do you really want to see a koala?"

I know I've won the battle of good versus evil raging inside her as soon as she gives me a devilish smile. "I really want to see a koala."

I grin and lead her into the trees "I thought you might say that."

We walk for a few minutes in comfortable silence. Our eyes are peeled for koala sightings. She's concentrating hard on the trees as we walk and doesn't notice when I stop. I smile as she runs out of arm length. Our hands are still tightly entwined, so she can't go far before I am pulling her back.

"I'm telling you. Best husband award. Gold trophy." I point above us. Her eyes follow my finger, and she lights up in delight.

"Oh my God, Ryan. So, so beautiful." She wraps her arms around me and stares up at the sleeping koala. "Definitely a gorgeous creature." She looks up at me and kisses my arm. "You know, koalas have claws. I'm sure they could do more damage than a kangaroo can."

I laugh. "Maybe. But kangaroos have the ability to kick me in the nuts. Hard. I do intend to have kids with you someday."

She laughs and the koala looks down at us. "Awe... That might be our cue to move on." She looks back at Dave and Marianne. "Please say you got him sleeping. That was so cute."

Dave smiles. "We got him, Mrs. Crane."

She smiles. "Mrs. Crane. I love everything about the way that sounds."

"Good. Get used to hearing it." I bend to kiss her neck, and we start walking once more. "So. Dave. Marianne. How have the last few nights gone? With you rooming together?" I hear Arianna snicker as Dave and Marianne both clear their throats.

Marianne stammers, "Um..."

"Oh. Well..." Dave rubs the back of his neck.

"It's fine."

"Yeah. We're... fine, Mr. Crane."

"You both know I know you have a thing for each other, right?" I say with a knowing grin.

Marianne coughs."What? No! We don't -"

"No! We just work together," Dave says vigorously. I don't have to turn around to see them both turning different shades of red.

"Babe, I think the next hotel was saying they didn't have enough room to accommodate all of us." Arianna looks up at me and winks.

"What?" Dave asks.

I nod. "Yeah. I got a call saying we'll have to double up again." I put my arm around Arianna.

"It's... okay. I really wouldn't mind," Marianne says shyly.

I smile. "I thought so."

Arianna laughs. "Seriously, though. We do need to know your preferred sleeping arrangements for the rest of the trip. We do have two separate rooms for you, but if you prefer..." Arianna trails off and glances over her shoulder at Dave and Marianna.

I laugh. "Baby, I think we know their preference. Stop torturing them."

"Fine. Fine." She leans against me as we reach the beach and her eyes widen. "Holy crap. There really are sea lions here."

I laugh. "Did you doubt me?"

She shakes her head. "I did not. I doubted the island," she says matter of factly and without missing a beat.

I shake my head at her. "I love you."

"And I love you." She leans against my chest as she watches the sea lions frolic.

One catches my eye. "Hey. Look at that one. Looks like we caught his interest."

She looks over and smiles brightly at the sea lion watching us. He sticks his tongue out. "Definitely a show off."

"Looks pretty young. I wonder where the parents are."

At that moment, one of the sea lions seemingly answers my question by making a very loud and irritating noise. Arianna covers her ears as her eyes widen in surprise. The baby sea lion bounds off towards his family.

"Okay. We can be done with them now. Cute, but annoyingly loud."

I laugh. "I *could not* have said it better myself."

My phone goes off. Arianna sighs as we turn back to the trees. "At the risk of sounding annoying myself, you promised no phones today."

"I know, baby. But I gave orders not to disturb us. It wouldn't be going off if it weren't important." I take out my phone and see a text from Taylor.

Taylor: Luke has information. When you get back, we need to talk.

I sigh as Arianna bends to rub her legs. I stop to check out the view with a soft smile. My wife is stunningly beautiful.

I begged her this morning to wear the shorts she has on right now. Short jean cutoffs with a tight as fuck tank top that shows off every single one of her perfect curves. I bought the outfit on a whim for her, knowing getting her to wear it would be a fight to the death. I finally got her to at least try it on. When I saw her in it, it nearly brought me to my knees.

"Are you staring at my ass?"

I blink and smile, realizing she caught me watching her. "In my defense, you have a very sexy ass. It's hard not to look."

"That's because you're obsessed with it." She smiles as she wiggles her ass.

I laugh and grab her around the waist as I spank her. I squeeze both of her cheeks. She giggles as I kiss her. "Ready to head back?"

"Actually, yes. My legs are starting to burn. Apparently walking fifty miles hurts." She grins up at me.

"Okay, first, we're like two miles from the parking lot. Second, your legs hurt because the entire walk was uphill until we got to the point where we veered off. Third, what kind of husband would I be if I didn't help you out in your time of need?" I turn my back to her and kneel down.

"You can't carry me on your back all the way to the Jeep!"

"I can and I will. Jump up."

"Um... Okay..." Arianna hesitantly climbs on my back. I stand. She wraps her legs around my waist and her arms around my shoulders. "Aren't I too heavy?"

"Aria, are you joking? What the hell do you even weigh? A hundred pounds?"

"Um... One eighteen. I have a big butt and boobs for my size."

I laugh as I start walking, holding her legs tightly and close to my body. "You really don't. Everything about you is perfect."

✗✗✗

Later, after Arianna and I get back to the resort, I settle on a couch. Arianna props her legs up on my lap so I can rub them as I promised I would. We wait as everyone else joins us.

"Mmm... Right there. It's so cramped," she whimpers. I lean in to kiss her.

"Sorry to interrupt." Taylor and Nicole walk in and grab a chair. I ignore them and kiss Arianna anyway.

"How was the walk?" Nikki asks.

"Oh God, it was so good, Nikki. We saw kangaroos, a koala, and sea lions!" Arianna excitedly says.

"And she scared the ever living shit out of me when she pet the fucking kangaroo."

"You pet a kangaroo? Like a real one?" Chase asks when he walks in with Breetana.

Arianna smirks. "Yes! Ryan was terrified."

"I was not terrified."

"How did you pet a kangaroo?" Breetana asks.

"She just came up to me."

"Huh. I suppose she saw you're a kind soul." Taylor winks. Chase and Breetana find a seat. Chase pulls Breetana into his lap.

I laugh. "There are pictures. Just in case none of you believe it."

"And I'm sure Ryan looks terrified in all of them," Arianna teases.

"Stop. I was not terrified." I laugh again because I definitely was.

"Pictures of what?" Jason plops down next to me and Jessa sits next to him, curling into his side.

"Air pet a kangaroo." Chase nods to Arianna.

"No shit?" Robby asks.

Renza's eyes sparkle. "That's amazing!"

"And Ry was scared out of his mind." Taylor smirks.

"Fuck you all. I was not scared."

"You were a little scared." Arianna holds up her thumb and finger with a small gap between.

I wink at her. "Keep it up and I'll stop rubbing that cramp."

"Nooo! I'll stop. I promise."

I smile and kiss her. "That's what I thought."

"I want pictures or it didn't happen," Nick says as he plops down in a chair next to us.

I laugh. "Dave and Marianne got a lot of them."

"Arianna says Ryan looks terrified in all of them, but she can't tell you that because he'll stop rubbing her leg." Taylor winks at Arianna. She smiles as she acts like she's zipping her lip and throwing a key.

"We got you, Arianna. Don't worry!" Chase winks.

She laughs. I growl and stop rubbing. "Noooo! They did it. Not me!" She looks up at me with owl eyes.

I laugh and continue rubbing as Luke sits next to Nick. "Where's Alex, Josh, and Lyric?"

"Right here. Sorry. We were dealing with a little business back home." Alex sits down on the chair across from Luke.

Josh props himself on an oversized chair next to us and pulls Lyric into his lap. "Our mother seems to think that the house is too big for her. She wants to downsize. We think it's the perfect size, and her issue is that she doesn't like the neighborhood."

"Senior living, you know." Alex shakes his head.

"No one likes senior living," Lyric says teasingly to Alex. Alex rolls his eyes with a grin.

I look around the room. "Looks like we have everyone. So? Luke? What do you got?"

"Me first," Taylor cuts in. "I got DNA results. Dane called with them about an hour ago." He glances between Arianna and Luke. "You two are definitely related."

Luke shrugs. "Told you."

I glare. "You know as well as I do that you'd have done the same damn thing."

"You're probably right. Can it be my turn now?" he grins cockily.

I glare at him more dangerously, but Arianna puts a hand on my arm to stop me from saying anything. I sigh. Fucker is way too much of an asshole like I am. Why the hell do I surround myself with people like me? "What do you got, Luke?"

He looks at Arianna. "I'm sorry, Arianna, but I think he knows where you are."

"W-what?" She looks at me. I see the tears fill her eyes, and my heart shatters. "How do you know?"

"Because I saw two of his guards here. I immediately called Nick."

"I sent out a couple guards to deal with it," Nick says.

"Massena's guards have been taken care of," Robby confirms.

I take a couple of moments to compose myself. "We had planned to leave tomorrow morning anyway. Is there any reason why that can't still be the case?"

"He could be on his way here now, honestly. I don't have contact with him, so I can't be sure, but if he has guards here, they're probably scoping everything out ahead of him."

"He'll have people scouting ahead." Arianna sniffles sadly. "Our entire itinerary is places I wanted to go. It's all in my wish box".

I kiss her neck. "Don't worry, baby. We have one hell of a team. Nothing is going to happen to you. If he has guards scouting, though, I want them captured and brought to me. I want as much information as I can get on Massena and Ambrosio."

"I can identify them," Luke says confidently.

Arianna nods but says nothing. I continue absentmindedly rubbing her leg as the conversation around me continues.

Arianna's plan had us taking Massena and Chad down in Hawaii, but the more I think about it the more I want it to be done in New York. Home turf. Hawaii is too neutral of a playground.

I don't like that.

At all.

No. This ends in New York.

Home.

Chapter Sixteen

⚔ Arianna ⚔

I smile softly as I quietly walk down the beach towards Luke. He seems to be really upset about something. The vicious way he's throwing the rocks gives him away.

He growls and throws another rock out into the water. We haven't left Australia yet. There was an issue with the plane that needed to be addressed. Something about a small crack near the cockpit. Probably wouldn't have been a big deal, but Ryan is just as cautious as his pilots.

Besides, I'm enjoying the solitude the sunrise brings. It's mostly up in the sky, but there's still a little pink tinting the water.

I glance up towards the hotel and see many of Ryan's guards in plain view watching me. I really don't need to see them. I can feel them there. I've never felt more safe.

Luke tosses another rock, skipping it across the smooth surface.

I smile. "If you throw that any harder, you may actually hit the rock bank out there."

He spins around at my voice. "What, uh, are you doing here?"

"I would think the reason is the same as you. Enjoying the peace a sunrise brings."

He looks behind me as I walk closer. "Where's your dick of a husband? I would have thought he wouldn't let you out alone." I smile softly as I look down at the sand beneath my bare feet. "I'm sor-"

"It's okay. I know Ryan can be a lot. He can be intimidating. He can be an asshole. But everything he does is for someone else."

He chuckles. "I'm having a hard time believing I'm willingly working with a mafia boss."

I hug myself as I nod. "Ryan is more than that."

He looks down at me. "Tell me."

I take a breath and look up at him. "Well, you've heard a little bit. You've done your own research. Ryan owns legit businesses all around the world. He turned his mafia legit a long time ago. His goal isn't money. He has enough of that. You've never seen him in the news in trouble with the law. Everything he has ever been arrested for happened before he was twenty. After that, there are so many news articles about him becoming legit. Him turning things around. Things he's done to help poor communities all around the world." I smile and look back over the water. "About five years ago, there was a big story that came out about him helping out in Africa. The work he's been doing is more than what so many others could ever say. He's personally turned an entire community around just by building a business nearby and giving them jobs. He supported the community through the whole transition. He helped build homes. He got his brother involved."

"Give a man a fish, he eats for a day."

I nod and look back at him. "Teach a man to fish…"

"He eats for a lifetime," Luke finishes.

"And that's not all he does."

He laughs. "There's more? I think you gave me enough to think about."

I smile as we turn to head back to the hotel. "Ryan spends a lot of time helping clean up cities. He has contacts in Law Enforcement all over the world. You work for the ATF, right?"

"Uh... Yeah, but I took leave until this was over. Why?"

"Ryan doesn't keep anything from me. Including his contacts. You should talk to Shane Nelson."

His eyes widen at me saying his boss's name. I bite back the smile threatening to steal my lips. "What? Why?"

I shrug. "Because he's Ryan's ATF contact. Do you know him?" I smile sweetly, already knowing the answer.

I can see him swallow. "He's my... my..." He shakes his head. "My boss, Arianna. Shane's my boss."

I smile again and nod as we both enter the hotel. We walk in silence to his room. I pat his arm when he stops and continue down the hall to mine and Ryan's suite.

An hour later, we're all packed and ready to go. I won't lie and say I've become more and more nervous, scared my father will show up before we're able to get on the plane. I'm sure it shows because Ryan refuses to leave my side.

When it's finally time to leave, his large hand engulfs mine as he leads me to Luke's room. Luke opens the door seconds after Ryan knocks. Ryan squeezes my hand as he looks at Luke. "So? You two talked?"

"A little." Luke's eyes flick to mine, then back to Ryan's. I smile at how unsure he is.

"She doesn't keep anything from me, Luke," Ryan says, reading him and the question he wants to ask but doesn't. "Just like I don't from her. I know what she told you. And I know how hesitant you are. But just like I told her. Do the research. Form your own opinion."

He says nothing. Just nods and turns for his bag, following us out to the vehicles. He climbs in the back of the vehicle Ryan is driving and takes out his phone. Nick climbs in beside Ryan.

"What are the chances you have a map of all of Crane's territory in New York?" he asks, looking up at Nick.

Nick chuckles. "A hundred percent. I'll email it to you."

Luke looks at him incredulously. "Seriously? You just happen to have a map you can email?"

"You think his family doesn't keep track of him? I have a map of all of his territory in every single city he's in. He's my brother. Of course I'm going to back him up as much as I can with any and all information I can get."

Luke gives him his email, and Nick gets to work sending him each and every map of all of Ryan's territory in every single city he's in. By the time we are in the air, Luke is buried in nearly a hundred maps, and Nick is still sending them. I have to laugh as I cuddle into Ryan.

"How the fuck many cities are you in, man?" Luke asks.

"Pretty close to two hundred."

He looks at him and blinks before he turns to me. "How long did it take you to get through all of this?"

"Nearly a week." I smile as I stand up and walk to the back of the plane. I return a couple of minutes later and hand him my laptop. "It'll go faster if you're using this instead of your phone."

"Thanks." He gets to work on the laptop.

Over the course of the incredibly long flight, I watch as his confusion about Ryan and just what he does evaporates. It's obvious Ryan's goal is to change the world. The violence and crime in his territories has drastically declined and stayed that way. Luke, being a cop, has to understand crime waves. There's no way he can't see that what's happened in these areas is unnatural. Astounding.

After a few hours of him having his head buried in research, he looks up at Ryan. The confidence he lost when he showed up here returns. It exudes from him just as it has every single day since I've known him. He's no longer unsure.

"My goal when I came into this was to protect my little sister. While that has not changed, it has broadened. I intend to gain your trust. Work with you. Prove to you that I'm on your team. Who the hell wouldn't want to be on your team? You've managed to do more for this world than I've managed to do in one State since I started my career in Law Enforcement."

Ryan smiles. "There's a lot that goes into being a part of this, Luke. Commitment. One fuck of a sense of justice. But most of all you have to be willing to toe the line between good and evil to protect the ones you love. Family is everything to me. There's no line I won't cross to defend my family."

"I have never in my life believed in someone and someone's goal as much as I believe in yours. I don't know how the fuck you've done it, but I want to be a part of it. All I've ever wanted is to help people. Defend my loved ones. I can't do all I want having to abide by policies and laws that even have my partners scratching their heads. Now is my chance to reach that goal. I won't let you down."

I know Ryan can see the incredible determination in Luke's eyes that I do. I can feel the trust between them growing and being reciprocated by both of them. I couldn't be happier at being right about the relationship budding between them and the rest of this family.

Out of the corner of my eye, though, I see Renza glaring at Robby as he scrolls through his phone. Robby seems indifferent. I watch them for a moment before glancing at Ryan. He's working on something on his phone. I question if I should bother him, but I haven't told him my concerns yet. There just hasn't seemed to be any time.

I bite my lip and glance at Taylor. He nods towards Ryan as if he knows exactly what I'm thinking. I take a deep breath and put my hand lightly on Ryan's arm. "Can we talk?" I whisper.

He doesn't take his eyes off his phone as he nods. "Yeah, baby. I have to send this out."

I smile and lean into him. Watching. "Who is it to?"

He smiles and turns his phone towards me. "There was an issue with one of our accounts. Nothing major. Just a deposit from one of our companies in L.A. was stopped. I needed to send this to approve it. The company is new. The bank didn't recognize it."

I kiss his shoulder. "So…, it's a safety net? So nothing gets put in there that shouldn't be?"

"Exactly." He pushes send and looks at me as he puts his phone away. "What's on your mind, beautiful?"

I blush. I love when he calls me beautiful. "Um… maybe we could go to the bedroom?" I glance nervously at Renza and swallow as she glares at her phone. Robby still hasn't made a single move to talk to her or hug her or anything.

Ryan follows my eyes as he stands. He reaches out a hand to help me up, then leads me to the bedroom. He sits on the bed and pulls me gently onto his lap. I settle into him and hug him close, breathing in his calming scent.

He kisses my neck as he hugs me tightly. "What's going on, Ari?"

"I… just…" I shake my head and sigh. "There's just something… wrong… with Renza. I don't understand what. I can't make sense of why I feel like I do, but… her actions just don't make sense. They aren't her." I bury my face further into his shoulder.

"What kinds of things are you observing to make you feel the way you do?"

"Well…, she's hot and cold. One second she seems like she's happy for me. The next she's acting like she's jealous. At the wedding, when we were getting ready. One second she was bored out of her mind and seemed like she could care less. Next, she's envisioning her wedding to Robby. Telling me how in love she is. And out there? I don't understand what's happening, but Robby is totally ignoring her. And she's glaring at everything and everyone."

I can hear Ryan swallow. I look up at him. His eyes are stormy. "There are a lot of things going on with her that I'm questioning myself, honey. I can honestly say that you aren't the only one, though. The best thing to do right now is be observant with her. If you see something or hear something that sounds off to you, say something to me."

I nod. "Taylor and Alex said that I should trust my instincts."

"They aren't wrong. And I know that they also question her. Some of her actions are throwing us. Robby's also questioning her. He's been suspicious of her for a while. But the truth is, none of us really know what's happening. To us, she's kind of just portraying jealousy."

"That's what I thought," I say quietly.

My heart hurts thinking my best friend is really jealous of me during the happiest and highest point in my life. I'd never feel that way about her and Robby if it were her that had gotten married, and not me.

"Aria, the truth is, we don't know what to make of her. I've kept quiet about it because I don't want to believe the things I'm thinking. I can't understand how someone who's been in your corner for so long can become jealous like this."

I look down with a sad, soft whine. "Do you think that's all it is? Jealousy?"

"Do you?"

I shrug. "I just don't know. But I've never felt like this towards her. I've never felt so…" I look up at him again as he gently rubs my thigh with his thumb. "Suspicious? Untrusting?"

He leans in and kisses me. "You aren't the only one there either, baby. My advice is the same I gave Robby when he came to me saying he didn't know what to make of her recent actions either. Observe. Report to me."

My eyes widen as my suspicions are confirmed. "Robby is suspicious?"

Ryan nods. "But I don't want anyone acting differently around her. We can't observe and gather information if she's suspicious of us being suspicious of her and watching her."

I lean my head on his shoulder. "I'm just going back and forth on her. I'm so confused."

He kisses me again, nipping my lip as he pulls away. "We all are." Ryan nudges me up. I stand. He follows, looking at me hungrily. "How about I make you forget for a little while?"

I watch him just as ravishingly as he slowly begins undoing his belt. My hands automatically find their way under his shirt and to his abs as I look up at him. The heat in his eyes lights me on fire as I start tracing the sharp ridges of his abs.

Moments later, Ryan is deep inside me, plunging in over and over. Each thrust puts Renza further from my mind. Each kiss and nip pushes her confusing behavior away to be thought of another day.

Not now.

Not with Ryan on top of me. Inside me. All over me.

I hold on for dear life as Ryan takes me to heights only he can. And when the ecstasy pushes me over the edge, I push him on his back and ride the ride all over again.

As I drop myself on him again and again, I feel all of my concerns; my worries vanish into the air we're gliding through until I feel nothing but Ryan. When he fills me a second time, I collapse in a heap on top of him, letting him carry me to that place of calm and serenity that belongs to only us.

And just like that, all that matters is him. His arms around me. His protective aura shielding me.

Just me and Ryan.

Chapter Seventeen

⚔ Ryan ⚔

I sit on the end of the bed and remove my shirt. Arianna is standing at the window of our penthouse bedroom in London taking in the view. We can see the entire downtown area. All of the city lights are twinkling below us.

I stand and join her at the window. I slip my arms around her waist and pull her close to me. I know she's lost in her head, barely even seeing what's around her. I've come to know her expressions well.

The one she wears now is blank. Like she's aware of her surroundings, but she's too deep in her own thoughts to really see them. I'd distracted her for a while on the plane, but as soon as we stepped off, she ended up right back in her own head.

I bend to kiss the side of her neck, just where it meets her shoulder. She shivers. I switch to the other side. I kiss her in the same place as my hands travel up to her supple breasts. I run my hands across her nipples.

She sighs. "You always know when I'm in my own head. Don't you?"

"I know you, baby. I'd say get out of your head and concentrate on the view, but I know you won't until you talk it out." I wrap my arms across her chest and kiss her cheek as she continues to look out the window. "So? Tell me. What's going on in that beautiful mind of yours?"

She's quiet for a few moments before she takes a deep breath. "It really is a gorgeous view, isn't it?"

I smile and look out the window at the city of London at our feet. "I think this is the best view in the city."

She turns to me and smiles. "You're saying that because I'm in your view."

"Is there something wrong with enjoying how beautiful you are with the backdrop of London behind you?"

She shakes her head. I smile as I lean down to kiss her. It isn't long before our tongues are fighting for the dominance she knows damn well belongs to me. My fingers tangle in her hair and hers bunch the fabric of my jeans in her fists.

She moans into my mouth. "Ryan..."

Her whispered plea is all my body needs. I strip her shirt off her and toss it as I back her against the glass of the floor to ceiling window. She gasps as the cold glass meets her warm skin. I kiss down her jaw, her neck, her shoulder, her collarbone. My hands trail down her ribcage as I kneel in front of her.

"You're so beautiful, Aria."

She runs her fingers through my hair as I unhook her bra. She spills out for me. I lick one of her nipples, then the other. She tugs my hair a little.

"So are you."

I smile as I kiss down her stomach to the waistband of her jeans, kneeling along the way until I'm on my knees in front of her. I drop my hands to her feet and run them up her legs. When I reach her upper thighs, I move to the inside of her legs.

"Mmm...," she breathes.

I guide her thighs apart and run my hand slowly back and forth across her pussy. She moans in pleasure as she closes her eyes and drops her head back against the glass.

"Do you like that?" I grin because I know she does.

"Yes..." She moves against my hand. I rub a little harder. "Ooh..." She squeezes her legs around my hand.

I pull her roughly off the window and spank her. "What am I going to do with you?" I rumble against her stomach as I kiss it. "Did I say you could close your legs?"

"Oh! No. You didn't." She looks down at me, a soft blush on her beautiful face. I smile against her stomach and nip her as I squeeze her pussy. "Why does that feel so good?"

I laugh as I unbutton her jeans. "It seems a little pain turns you on, huh?" I look up at her.

Her eyes are on fire. I roughly pull her jeans and panties down. I really didn't need to ask. I know what turns her on. I know what she needs, and when she needs it. Her nails rake across my back. She doesn't want me to be gentle tonight.

I pin her against the glass and lick from her hot center to her beautiful bundle of nerves.

"Mmm... Ryan!" She arches into me. Still keeping her pinned with one arm across her stomach, I dive into her deeply with two fingers. "Ah!"

With my tongue on her clit, I give her both the pressure and the rough pace that she needs. She struggles against my arm and digs her nails into my shoulders. When I feel she's getting close, I suck on her clit.

"What do you say?"

"Please, Ryan. Please! Please make me come."

"Good girl." I nip, lick, and suck on her clit. "Come for me, baby." I thrust my fingers deep and hard inside her, spreading my fingers wide.

"Ah!" she screams as she comes.

I stand and hold her against the glass as I drop my jeans. I grab her ass and lift her up. She wraps her legs around my waist and her arms around my neck as I plunge inside her, slamming her against the glass.

"Oh fuck...." Her pussy tightens around me with a vice-like grip that has me groaning and instantly about to come.

"Ah! Ow... Ow... Stop... Just… stay like this… for a minute." She's gasping for breath as she buries her face in my neck.

"Shit. Baby, I'm sorry. I got carried away." I feel her tears against my neck. "Fuck, honey. I'm really sorry." I pull back slightly and brush her hair away from her face as I kiss her cheek. "Are you okay?"

"I will be. Just give me a minute? Let me get used to you. I'm sorry."

"For what? You don't need to be. It's my fault. Sometimes I forget how small and tight you are, and that it takes you a second to stretch around me."

She smiles. "I wanted it rough. I got rough."

"There's rough, and there's too rough. I lost control and made it too rough for you."

She kisses me. Long and deeply. After a few moments, she shifts and starts to move against me. I gently thrust inside her, slowly, as our tongues dance "Mmm... So good."

Reading her body, I start giving her a little harder thrusts. My nails dig into her ass cheeks. She softly bites my lower lip. "Feel good still?"

"So good..." She pushes herself against me harder. I give her a little more and thrust deeper and faster. "Mmm... Perfect. Just like that."

She's taking me a lot rougher than I thought she'd be able to. It's taking all of my control not to drive myself into her as hard as I can. I know she's not ready for that yet, so I force myself to hold back. "Goddamn, Aria. You're so tight. So wet."

"For you."

"Only for me."

"Ryan, I... Oh! Mmm..." She tightens and clenches uncontrollably around me as I slam into her heat. Her thighs start trembling. Her pussy pulses uncontrollably.

"Not yet. Wait for it." I drive into her as deeply as I can again and again. My dick gets impossibly harder; thicker. She bites down on my shoulder, not hard, but hard enough to leave her mark. I fucking love when she marks me. I love when her nails scratch me; her teeth scrape along my skin.

"Ryan, oh God. Oh my God!" Her pussy clenches tightly around me. I know she's about to lose it. I give her a couple more hard, deep thrusts. When I'm as deep as I can go, I reach between us and start rubbing her clit. "Ryan! Ah!"

"Fuck. Come, Aria. Give me what I want."

"Ryan!" She screams and throws her head back as she starts pulsing and clenching hard around me, milking my dick.

I come inside her harder than I've ever come in my life. I bury my head in her hair and kiss her neck as my hips jerk against hers and my dick throbs inside her. "Aria. Fuck, baby. You feel so fucking good."

"Mmm..." She holds onto me tightly. After a few minutes I pull out and carry her to the bed. I set her down. She practically collapses.

I kiss her and smile against her lips. "I'll be right back."

"Where are you going?"

"You'll see." I kiss her again and walk to the bathroom. I fill up the Jacuzzi tub, then walk back out to the bedroom. Arianna is rubbing the inside of her leg. I raise an eyebrow. "Cramp?"

"Yeah. I was fine. Then I tried to get up. My legs were just shaky. So, I sat back down. Now, I have a cramp." I smile and pick her up bridal style. "Woah! Ryan!" I kiss her and carry her into the bathroom. She gasps when she sees the tub. "Are those rose petals? Where did you get rose petals?"

I give her a mischievous grin. "I have my sources."

I set her down next to the tub. She smiles up at me. She's the only woman in the world who's ever been able to make me lose control and feel like I'm the world's luckiest man. The way she looks at me both breaks me apart and builds me up at the same time. The longer I'm with her, the more I realize I can't live without her.

"Join me?"

"That was the plan, beautiful girl."

She smiles brightly as she steps into the tub. "Oh God. It's so warm."

"Too warm?"

She shakes her head. "Perfect. It's perfect."

I step in after her and sink into the water. It's gloriously hot. I grab her hips and pull her to me. I drop my hand between her legs and start rubbing her groin muscle.

"Mmm… I think I need to drink more water."

"Actually, I think this cramp was my fault. During sex, the harder it is, the more you hold on. And since I had you against a window, your legs were wrapped pretty tightly around me."

She shifts so she's sitting in my lap. I continue rubbing her groin muscle as she lays her head on my shoulder. "Do you trust Luke?"

I chuckle. "Coming out swinging, huh?"

She kisses my shoulder. "It's been on my mind. That's all."

"Well, let me ask you. Do you trust him?"

It takes her a minute to answer, but I say nothing as she works through it. Instead, I continue to rub her muscles. "I trust him."

"Why?"

"Because of his actions when I met him. I think he knew then that we were related. I guess I'm not sure when he did that test. And also because he covered for me when my dad had him follow me. When you were in Chicago, he found reasons to be there everyday so I wasn't alone. And he saved my life in Australia."

I nod, playing devil's advocate. "But he wasn't there the day you left. When you needed help."

"I thought about that. He said he was there, but it was just after I left. I bet if I'd waited until he got there, he would've blown his cover to help me."

I make a mental note to ask him about that day. Get more information about what happened. More than just what he told me. "You know it takes a lot for me to trust anyone, Aria."

She shrugs. "You trusted Chase pretty quickly."

Leave it to her to call me out. "That's different."

"How?" Dammit. She's not going to drop it. "He's one of the people who has access to your buildings. The high security clearance that so few have."

"Because he proved himself, baby. He proved that he was trustworthy and loyal. That he'd do whatever it took for family."

"Hasn't Luke done that? He's betrayed my father. Well, our father, since he's his father, too. He's reported his guards to you. Or Nick, I guess. He saved my life."

"He's on his way. He's got a long way to go. There's just something about him that… I don't know. He's not too forthcoming about his history. I don't like that. But to answer your question, I'm starting to."

She kisses my neck and burrows into my arms. "I guess that's okay. For now."

I kiss her forehead. I haven't made a decision about Luke. Mainly because I haven't really talked to him since the day I met him. I haven't had the time.

I know I need to, though. He wants to be a part of this. Wants me to let him in. I need to see if he follows orders. If he sees more of

Massena's scouts and kills them instead of bringing them to me, we'll have issues.

I know he wants to be in Arianna's life, though. I'd never keep her from her family if she chooses to associate with them. So, it looks like I'm going to have to try and get along with him. The only way to do that is to talk to him. Despite all of my issues with who he is and where he has come from. I don't like secrets.

✗✗✗

(One Week Later)

"Oh my God. Ryan, you don't understand how happy I am."

I laugh as I hug her and kiss her on top of the head. "I know how much of a history buff you are. So... Welcome to a place few have seen."

"Isn't it on the tour list of tours people can take?"

"It is. But getting a private tour like this is pretty unheard of. No one gets to actually touch stuff."

"How did you do it?"

I grin sardonically and point to myself. "Billionaire."

She laughs. "Okay! Point taken." We're standing in Winston Churchill's war room. I'm pretty sure Arianna is in her literal Heaven. "Did you know that the people who worked down here during the war were required to spend time in front of sun lamps?"

"Really? Why?"

"Because they weren't allowed to leave for long periods of time. So, in order to combat depression, that was the solution. It's been said that a woman once nearly went blind because she forgot to wear the required goggles."

I laugh. "What other interesting facts do you know?"

"So many!" She runs her finger across one of the maps pinned to a bulletin board.

"Lay 'em on me." She looks over her shoulder at me. I smile. I can feel my eyes shine with pride.

She smiles back at me. "Okay. Churchill was the only one allowed to deviate from the script for the radio show. Everyone else? They got in loads of trouble. Their speeches were immediately cut off by security."

"Makes sense. Churchill was the leader. He made the rules."

She turns to me and smiles wider. "I bet I could be a tour guide for this place. Did you know there's a room that was designed specifically for confrontation? It was called the Cabinet Room. Churchill was known for pushing his military leaders way past their comfort zones. The room was designed so everyone was face to face as they discussed things related to the war."

"Sounds like my kind of guy."

She laughs as she hugs me. "Thank you for taking me here."

"Not our only stop today. Lunch, then somewhere else."

"You really enjoy surprising me, don't you?"

"It's all because of the look you give me. And the thanks I usually get later." I shoot her a sexy wink.

She laughs and swats me. "I love you."

"I love you, too."

"Okay, Mr. Crane. Where to next?"

"Nice try, Mrs. Crane. My lips are sealed."

She laughs as we walk out of the War Room. I entwine our fingers together thinking how truly lucky I am that she chose to be with me. It's like my entire life was spent preparing for this moment with her. This life.

✕✕✕

Later, after lunch, I have Ariana blindfolded and am leading her through the streets of London. "You sure you can't see anything?"

"Positive." She nods. Her smile could light up the world.

"Good. Stop right here." She stops, and I pull her closer to me. I lean down to kiss her because I can't resist. "Remember when I said I wanted a trophy for being the best husband ever?"

She laughs. "It's sitting on the mantel at home as we speak!" She sounds so confident that I question if she actually did it. I reach up to untie the blindfold. As I drop it from her eyes, her mouth falls open. "Oh. My.

God." She runs up the stairs. She's always wanted to visit the Museum of Natural History, but I didn't expect that reaction.

"The hell? Aria!" I run after her. "Fuck. I didn't think you'd be that excited."

"Are you kidding? Every person who likes history dreams of being able to come here!" She bursts through the doors.

I follow her laughing, but it dies in my throat when we enter. I blink as the doors close behind me. My mouth falls open, though I can't do shit about it. "Holy shit. What is that?"

"Gaia."

"What?"

Arianna looks up at me. "It's called Gaia."

"Why is it not just called Earth? It's a giant Earth."

"Because that would take away from the artistic creativity of naming something." She giggles. "But in this case, it actually literally translates to Earth. In Greek mythology, Gaia was the Goddess who presided over the Earth." I look down at her. She's looking at me with so much love and admiration that it makes me even more crazy for her. She blushes. "What?"

I shake my head and smile as I take her hand in mine and lean down to kiss her. "You're amazing. So smart. It's like you know something about everything."

She beams with pride, and her cheeks heat up a little at my praise and compliments. "Thank you."

"I might be the luckiest man in the entire world."

We turn and begin walking through the museum. Rather, I keep up as she drags me ecstatically up and down the rows upon rows of displays.

"Why do you say that?" she asks randomly after a few minutes. "That you're the luckiest man in the world?"

"Because I married someone who is incredible in every sense of the word. You're beautiful. You're smart. And for some reason, you being a part of planning my missions is a huge fucking turn on, Aria."

She laughs. "Most people would call me crazy. Marrying a guy older than me who's the leader of such a huge mafia. Being smart, planning missions, knowing all about your kills and everything else and not batting an eye." She turns to me. "Not much about that is normal."

I laugh and lean down to kiss her again. We don't release each other's hand. "You forgot beautiful."

"A travesty," she says mockingly.

I smile. "You're a triple threat. Gorgeous, smart, and deadly." She laughs as she leans into me. I kiss the top of her head before turning to look at the two things in front of us. I tilt my head, completely baffled at what they are. "Miniature… aliens?"

We both laugh. Arianna kisses my arm. "Maybe. But according to scientists? Cockroaches that survived a nuclear war."

"Gross." I can deal with just about anything. But fucking cockroaches? No. I push her further along.

"Blood doesn't bother you, but cockroaches do?"

"Yep. And I'm man enough to admit it."

"I'm finding out so many new things about you. Kangaroos scare you. Cockroaches gross you out."

We both laugh again as she teases me. "What about you, Girl Wonder? Fearless around me. Planning my missions. Screams and falls apart at the sight of a tiny spider."

"Hey, spiders are scary. For such small creatures, they can cause a lot of damage. And they're, in your words, gross." She shivers.

I put an arm around her. "What else?"

She looks up at me a little shyly. "What else scares me?"

I nod. "That I don't know. I can see how much stronger and braver you've become over the years. And over the past few weeks, how your confidence has grown. But what do you really fear?"

She thinks for a moment. "Well, my dad. But you know that. Losing you. But you also know that. Other than those two things? Probably fire."

I look down at her. "I'm going to kill your fucking father for instilling fear in the first place. You're never going to lose me. But fire... Really?"

"Mmhmm. I freeze up. Become practically catatonic. I don't know why. I'm okay around campfires and stuff, but I can't light a grill. I can't light a fire. And if I'm actually around one, like a house fire or something, I can't move."

I suddenly think back a little. "You were spending the night at Renza's. You were texting me. The next thing I know, you were calling, but you didn't say anything when I answered."

She nods. "I hit the call button when we realized there was a fire. I didn't mean to. I think now it was just a natural reaction. I sensed danger. I called you instinctively. Her door started glowing. We had the window open because it was warm that night. The fire was drawn to it. It took only seconds before it was licking up her door."

"You never told me that. All I heard was Renza screaming that you had to move. Scared the ever living hell out of me. I was in the middle of a mission. I dropped everything and drove straight to her house."

She looks up at me and smiles softly. "You never hung up. I didn't say anything to you at all. You never hung up."

"I heard sirens, and thought the worst. I don't think I've ever gotten anywhere so fast. You can't imagine the relief that washed over me when I got there and saw you and Renza hugging each other outside."

"When I saw you, I knew everything was going to be okay. I had no idea how you'd shown up, but I knew then that I was in love with you. When you hugged me the way you did and took us all to your house, and then didn't let me go the entire night... I was so scared. You took me with you to Jason's even though you had business to take care of."

"I wasn't going to leave you alone when you needed me. I think I was falling in love with you at that time, but I didn't know what the hell it was. I'd never felt that way for anyone."

"When did you know? For sure?"

"Remember when I told you I had to go to Italy with Alex?"

She thinks for a moment as we continue walking through the museum. "When Alex was having an issue with an employee at a company his family owns? Josh had just taken over the mafia side I think."

"Yeah. It wasn't just one employee. We found out it was an entire department. Led by one guy. But it was a huge problem. I helped him restructure the entire company. We ended up taking that guy completely out because he was involved with this small-time Italian mafia. The rest of the group ended up in jail. Usually on a mission like that... one that took as long as that one did?" I glance down at her. I know she knows the way I was before her, but I still hate what I'm about to say. "I would've been finding some female companionship."

She grimaces. "I think I read about more than I care to admit, and I want all of them dead."

I laugh and hug her closer to my side. "No one compares, Ari. Not even close. Anyway, in Italy, all I could think of was you. You'd been pretty much the only woman on my mind for quite awhile. I tried calling my usual escort service, but I couldn't bring myself to do anything with her but have a drink. After I sent her away, I kept kicking myself day after day that I was thinking about you in that way at all, given your age. Every time I saw you after that, I just wanted more time with you. And after I took you home, I yelled at myself about how inappropriate all of my thoughts about you were."

"So, wait." She stops walking and looks up at me. "You haven't been with anyone else? Since realizing you were in love with me? That was like... two years ago when you went to Italy." She bites her lower lip.

I run my thumb across it and lean down to kiss her. She runs her tongue along my lower lip before I pull away. I have immediate goosebumps. I smile and nip her lip, making her giggle, before I take her hand and start walking again. We're nearly back where we started.

"I've always had a fascination with dinosaurs." I stop to admire a rather large fossil model of one.

She smiles and squeezes my hand. "You totally changed the subject." She says it as softly as her smile is when she looks up at me. Her eyes, though, burn into mine with such intensity and love that I nearly drown.

I don't need a mirror to know that same fire is reflected in mine. "I haven't wanted anyone like I want you, Ari. You told me the other day that you crave me. That you can't get enough. I feel the same way, and I've never felt it for anyone else. The moment it hit me, realizing how far I had fallen for you, I tried to forget it. I'd met a lot of women, but I couldn't take it further than dinner and drinks." I caress her cheek. She leans into my touch. "None of them came close to you. I didn't want them to. I gave up fighting it."

"Ryan..."

I turn and start walking towards the exit. I don't think my heart can possibly grow any larger with the love I have for her. This forbidden yet perfect relationship with this beautiful, smart, and slightly dangerous woman.

174

"Instead, I decided that I was going to wait until you were eighteen. And then I was going to talk to you about everything. If you rejected me, it would've sucked, but I figured I'd survive. Now? No fucking way I would've. I need you."

She laughs and hugs my arm. "You may be the sweetest man I've ever met. And I'm so incredibly happy you're mine."

I smile and stop at the door. I kiss her forehead. "Anything else you want to educate me about before we take off, Girl Wonder?"

She laughs as she shakes her head. We turn to the door. "Nope. Take me back to the penthouse, Batman!"

"Shh!" I look around like I'm a covert spy, then lean down to whisper in her ear. "Can't let people in on my secret identity."

We both laugh as I help her into the car. A few moments later, we're headed back to the penthouse.

No phone calls. No texts.

Just a day of peace and quiet with my beautiful wife.

Normal. Just like she's always wanted. And I'm truly honored that I get to be the man to give that to her.

Chapter Eighteen

⚔ Arianna ⚔

(One Week Later)

I love spending time with Ryan. Ever since meeting him, it's been one of my favorite things to do. But, over the course of the past few weeks, I have grown to love spending time with our family nearly, if not *just*, as much. I've grown used to having everyone around for dinner nearly every night.

"And then in walks this cocky son of a bitch giving my Sergeant orders like he's a member of his mafia. Here I am sitting behind my desk thinking to myself that I'm a fucking Lieutenant, and this dude from the mafia is running my entire operation!" Taylor laughs as he gestures to Ryan.

Ryan smiles. "In my defense, you were dragging your feet thinking you know everything there is to know. Meanwhile, I have all of this intel and can take them all down myself, but I'm trying to do the right thing."

Taylor shakes his head. "The entire time, Dane is looking at me like he knows I have absolutely no control over the entire thing."

"He was right. I knew I liked him the first time I saw him!" Ryan says.

Everyone laughs. I love the stories they all tell. Like they've all been this family since they were kids. Even though everyone on this balcony has been brought together as a family by Ryan. This incredible, perfect man who I get the distinct pleasure and honor to call mine.

I curl up next to Ryan as we all eat and enjoy the warm, summer evening in London.

"Before I forget, I actually got something for all of you, but I left it in the car. I meant to get it earlier, but Arianna distracted me." Ryan winks at me. I feel myself turn numerous different shades of red. He grins cockily and kisses me as he gets up. "Be back!"

"That man is going to be my downfall." I smile as everyone laughs.

We've been here for two magical weeks so far. With everything everyone wants to do, we've extended our stay, especially since we didn't get to spend as much time in Australia as we wanted to. Lyric is from the UK. Her family is spread all over London. She doesn't want anything to do with being here, but Josh has talked her into doing a few fun things. Like going on the Harry Potter tour thing. All of the guys were beyond excited to go. Us girls loved watching them all geek out.

My phone vibrates. I pick it up thinking it's Renza. She and Robby went to a fancy dinner downtown. She's been surprisingly chipper. More like her old self. I've been enjoying it.

I'm slightly disappointed to see an email instead of a text, but as soon as I see it's from Juilliard, the disappointment is completely forgotten. Just less than a month before I start my Freshman year there. I'm growing more excited by the day.

That excitement, however, vanishes quickly as I read the content of the email. My face falls further and further. By the time I'm done, tears are streaming down my face.

"Air? Hey, what's going on?" Taylor asks, concerned.

I shake my head. "He... He d-didn't..." I stand and run from the balcony into the penthouse. I'm not watching where I'm going, though, and I trip. I catch myself and simply sit on the floor.

Taylor and Luke both kneel down next to me. Luke squeezes my leg. "He didn't what?"

I can't even speak. I dropped my phone somewhere, so I can't show them the email.

I should've known.

I hadn't thought about it. I should've.

This is all my fault.

"Arianna?" Nicole sits on the floor next to me. She puts her arms around me.

"Sweetheart, what happened?" Taylor asks me.

I look up. Everyone is gathered around me. Jason kneels down and picks up my phone near where I tripped.

"I can't go to Juilliard. I messed up." I burst into tears, and Luke pulls me close to him as Lyric appears out of nowhere and hugs me from the other side. Taylor squeezes my leg.

"Honey, that creates more questions than it answers," Chase says softly.

I hear Ryan walk through the door, but I can't physically pull myself up. I feel like my entire life force has been drained out of me.

"What the fuck?" Ryan asks immediately when seeing the scene.

"Honey, does this have to do with the email open on your phone?" Josh asks from where he's leaning close to Jason looking at my phone.

"What email?" Ryan drops to his knees and pulls me into his arms. "Baby, what happened?"

"We've been trying to get that out of her. Jas just found this email," Jessa says as Jason holds out my phone for her to read it.

"She just got up and ran in here." Breetana bites her lip and looks down sadly.

"She tripped. Took a hard spill," Alex says. I start shaking and crying harder.

"Stop. Everyone stop. You're overwhelming her," Lyric says as she rubs my back.

"Someone tell me what the hell email we're talking about," Ryan commands.

"It's from Juilliard," Josh says. "It says that her enrollment has been rescinded due to non-payment. Half of her tuition was due July first."

"Two weeks ago," Jason finishes.

"M-my dad s-said he'd t-take care of i-it," I sob.

"It says her spot will be given to someone else," Nick growls. I cry even harder.

Ryan runs his hand down my back and through my hair. "Baby, why didn't you say something?"

"I didn't th-think about it. After I left ev-erything ha-happened so fast. It's m-my fault."

"Hold on a sec. The email says that if she calls by the end of this week, which is tomorrow, and pays the total balance plus a late fee, she could be reinstated," Alex says.

"Could be?" Ryan growls low in his throat.

"It's up to the admissions director and the Dean, but I know the person who sent this email. Let me give Jillian a call. I'll see what I can do," Josh finishes. I try to catch my breath.

"Josh is right," Alex says. "She has pull. She can talk to who needs to be talked to, and by the time we call her again tomorrow, she'll have an answer. Maybe even by the time we go to bed, given the time difference." He looks at his watch.

"You'd think with everything that's happened, she'd get an extension," Nick says as he stands over us.

"She'll get admitted if I have any say." Ryan tenses.

I hug him tighter. "Juilliard is a-all I've ever wa-wanted." My stupid stutter makes me cry harder. "I d-don't have th-the money to p-pay it all on my o-own. He c-cut me o-off."

"Honey, you married into a family that is very well to do," Jessa says quietly as she kneels next to me on the floor by Luke and Lyric.

"You don't need to worry about money." Chase shakes his head with a soft smile.

Ryan pulls back slightly and cups my chin between two of his fingers. He tilts my head up and kisses me. I close my eyes, focusing completely on him.

Luke squeezes my arm. "I may not be a billionaire, but it doesn't matter. I'd scrape every last dollar I had to send you to Juilliard."

Ryan pulls back slowly and looks in my eyes. "I'll set up a couple of accounts, beautiful. One for school. Tuition, books; whatever you need. And another for you to do whatever you want."

"Ryan..." I don't know whether to kiss him or cry harder at his generosity. I sniffle and shake my head. "You don't have to. I'll get a job."

179

Ryan shakes his head. "Arianna, come on. Did you forget how much I'm worth? I think I can afford it. You're my wife. Your financial worth is just as much as mine now."

"And if he couldn't, I can," Chase cuts in. "So can Jason. And Alex. Josh. Nick."

"If none of these guys could, I'd find a way." Taylor squeezes my leg.

"Even I'd help," Lyric says with a quiet smile.

Nick tangles his fingers in my hair and tugs gently. I look up at him. "All of us together? We can make anything fucking happen, Arianna. You're going to Juilliard."

I laugh a little as Ryan pulls me up. "Baby, look around you. Every single person in this room would move mountains for anyone else in this room."

"It's what family does, Air," Nick says.

"And that's what we are." Nicole smiles as Taylor helps her up.

"Nick said it best." Breetana leans against Chase.

"Yep.," Nick agrees. "Together, we can do anything."

"I may be new to this, and I may not be fully accepted by everyone yet, but I'm with them. Together? Not a fucking thing can stop us," Luke says.

Josh reaches over and gives my shoulder a squeeze. "Relax tonight. Have Ryan run you a bath. Take a time out. I'll call Jillian right now. I'll text you as soon as I'm done. We should have a meeting time with the Dean and admissions director scheduled by the end of the day. Okay?"

"Trust in your family, Air. Your husband. We won't let you down." Jason hugs me.

"Bath?" Ryan whispers in my ear. I nod. He leads me to the bedroom and closes the door, trusting everyone to leave when they're ready. "Go get ready. I'll meet you in the bathroom."

"Stay with me? Join me?"

"Not joining you wasn't an option, baby." He leans down to kiss me, then heads into the bathroom. I undress as he starts the water.

I've never felt this family dynamic. It's overwhelming. But the more I'm a part of it, the more I realize one thing. I not only married a wonderful man who respects me and loves me with everything he is, just like I do him, but I've also married into a family that is exactly the same way.

No matter what happens, I'll always have Ryan. All of them. I can't ask for more than that. I wouldn't even want to.

✗✗✗

I take a deep breath and knock softly at my brother's door. I smile when he answers it and steps back to let me in. This is my first time being alone with him. Really alone. More than just the beach in Australia. I can't say I'm not excited, but I'm mostly nervous. Not because I don't feel safe, but because I get to spend real time with my brother. A brother I didn't even know I had until a couple weeks ago.

Luke smiles. "I gotta go. Arianna is here. We're spending a little time together seeing the sights." He nods. "Yes, sir." He's about to hang up but stops. "Yeah?" He pauses then nods. "Understood." He hangs up and turns his attention to me. "Just talking to Shane. He was telling me that Ryan is a good guy, but if I betray him, he'll kill me and my body will never be found."

I can't help but laugh. "That's rather accurate. My husband has a scary side. One he's kept away from me, but I know it exists. Anyway, are you ready? I'm really excited!"

"Definitely ready. You look great. Like you're ready to take on the entire city."

I look down at my jeans and London tourist-looking tank top and bite my lip as I blush. "Are you sure? I thought this tank top was so cute when I bought it, but after I got it on, I sort of feel like I'm…" I flutter my hand at my chest. "Too big for it." I look at it sadly.

Luke laughs. "It's fine. Really. You honestly look amazing. But, if you get uncomfortable, I'll take a jacket or another shirt for you to put over it."

I look up at him shyly. "Really?"

"Of course, Arianna."

"I'm trying to be... I don't know. More... sexy? And confident. And Ryan seems to really like the change."

181

He smiles. "You want me to be honest?" I glance up at him and nod. "Okay. Speaking as a red-blooded man but also platonically because ew, you're my sister, you're sexy, Arianna. No man in his right mind would think for a second that you aren't. But it isn't the outfit that makes you gorgeous. It's you. Sure, the outfit is a nice bonus. But I think you like them and how they make you feel. And I think Ryan likes them because he's picking up on how different you feel in them. More confident. And to him, that is sexy."

I feel myself turn red with embarrassment. I clear my throat. "You look great, too."

He chuckles. "Nice change of subject."

I smile. "Thank you."

He offers his arm as he grabs another light jacket. "Buckingham Palace awaits."

"Yay!" I bounce happily and smile brightly as I take his arm, and we leave the room.

✗✗✗

I stare in awe at Buckingham Palace. Probably unblinking. A tear shines in my eye as I take in its majestic beauty.

"You look so excited," Luke says quietly next to me as he watches me.

"Buckingham Palace. The Royal Family is the epitome of poise and grace. And that?" I gesture to the Palace. "That is the symbol of elegance."

"I bet there's a lot that those Palace walls hide."

"Probably. Did you know there are seven-hundred-seventy-five rooms in the Palace?"

He whistles. "That's a lot of rooms."

"Guess how many doors and windows it has."

He laughs. "Okay. Uh... Windows. Has to be maybe eight hundred. And doors? A thousand."

I shake my head. "Windows. Seven-hundred-sixty. Doors. One-thousand-five-hundred-fourteen.

He looks down at me. His eyes shine with both surprise and pride. "How the hell do you just know that?"

I smile up at him and decide to paraphrase Ryan's own words. "I know a little bit of everything."

He laughs. "I don't doubt that!"

We head back to the car laughing and talking as we head to the next location on my list. Seeing all these sights is fun, but getting to know him is the best part of my day.

I've had facts for every single location we've visited both today and on every outing we've been to with the family. I used to be shy about sharing them. I didn't want anyone to think of me as too cocky or too... superior. But lately, being around this family, my family, I'm learning that being myself is... actually okay.

XXX

Much later in the day, we both sit down on the grass in front of the Tower of London. I sigh. "My feet are killing me. And I have so many cramps. My cramps have cramps. I'm not used to the cramping. I've even been drinking tons of fluid. Ryan made me drink pickle juice the other day." I make a face.

"We've definitely done a lot of walking today."

I smile. "Did you enjoy it? All of the sights?"

"I did, but mostly all the facts you spouted off."

I laugh. "What was your favorite?"

"Honestly?" He nods towards the tower. "Right here. The Tower of London."

"Mine was the Palace. But this is a close second."

He lays back in the grass. "Tell me a fact the tour guides didn't tell us."

I smile. "Okay. Um... Well, they talked about the moat and it being filled with flowers for all the lives lost in the war, but not why it was drained in the first place."

"I was wondering that. Why is it empty? I thought moats were supposed to keep people out."

"Well, those who lived here before the Duke of Wellington never drained it or cleaned it. It was so full of bacteria and disease that those who lived inside the castle were getting sick. So, Wellington drained it. It's been empty ever since." I look up at the darkening sky.

Luke chuckles as my stomach growls. "Getting hungry?"

"Famished." I look at him as he sits up. "But I'm going to have to starve to death. I can't walk."

He laughs. "I'll do the big brother piggyback thing." He stands and helps me to my feet.

I wince in pain. "Ow. I think I have a blister. All the blisters."

"I may have a few myself." He kneels down and waits for me to climb up. I do. I wrap my legs around his waist and arms around his shoulders. Once I'm settled, he stands.

I chuckle. "I may be a little spoiled. Everyone has been really nice and helpful since Ryan started bringing me around."

He shakes his head. "I don't think you're spoiled at all. I think you're getting everything you deserve." He starts walking back to the car when I feel him tense.

I'm immediately on guard. Instinctually, I know something is off. "What's wrong?"

"Why do you think anything's wrong?"

"You tensed."

"Thought I saw something."

At that moment, two guys Luke and I both recognize right away turn the corner.

"No." My voice is little more than a whisper. Luke lets me down slowly and keeps me behind him.

"Well, well, well. Look who we have here." I shiver at the tone of John's voice. Sinister.

"If it ain't Traitor Luke and his sexy little plaything." Jarrod's is even more menacing.

Both are intimidating in their own right. They could be in Hells Angels if they wanted to be. They look greasy. Dirty. Terrifying. Leave it to my dad to send the two guards who leered at me all the time. The two who watched me with ogling eyes.

"Don't talk about her like that," Luke growls in warning. "Women deserve respect. They aren't sex objects."

184

"Man, I'm gonna have fun with her on the way home." John smirks at me

"After me. I've wanted her a lot longer." Jarrod winks. I choke back the bile.

John tilts his head. "Would you like that, little kitty? Both of us taking turns?"

"Or maybe together. Always wanted a threesome. Kind of thought I'd get two women, but hey. I'll take what I can get." Jarrod grins.

I stand closer to Luke trying to hide. I'm trembling, but I won't let them see it. I won't give them that power.

Luke chuckles darkly. "I'm going to enjoy this." He cracks his knuckles and stretches his neck. "You want her? You get to go through me first. And I'm not in a very good mood seeing you two." They both laugh, and I involuntarily cower behind his back. I know he can feel me shaking. "Showing up here. That was mistake number one. Making her shake? Oof. Mistake number two. But forgetting your weapons? Biggest mistake of all."

Jarrod glares. "We definitely don't need guns to take you down. What the fuck are you? Six feet two, and half my size?"

Luke reaches behind his back and pulls out a couple pairs of handcuffs from his belt. He hands them to me. "Take these, and go stand over there by that tree. Okay, honey?" He keeps his eyes on my dad's thugs.

My heart drops into my toe. My vision blurs. My head spins. "What if there's more?"

He shakes his head. I question why he doesn't take the gun at his hip and shoot. "I doubt there's more. If you feel safe staying close, then stay close. But you have to give me a little room to work, sweetheart. I promise this won't take long."

"Okay…" I hesitantly take the cuffs and take a few steps back. I move to the side within his line of vision.

He gives me a wink, and a bright smile. "Smart girl."

He holds up his hands and gives Jarrod and John a come hither signal, and a huge smile. All at once I realize that he's thoroughly enjoying the challenge he's about to face. I have every confidence in the confidence he has in himself being able to take them on.

John cracks his neck. "Two on one. I like the odds."

They both advance on Luke. Jarrod swings first. Luke dodges and quickly jabs him in the face. He staggers backwards. Luke kicks him in the kneecap as hard as he can. He topples to the ground in pain.

John spears Luke out of nowhere. It takes him by surprise. They both topple to the ground. His hands are immediately around Luke's neck.

"Fuck!" Luke yells. He grapples with him.

"Luke!" I scream, finally finding my voice. I start running towards him to help, but out of the corner of my eye, I see Jarrod stagger to his feet.

"Not such a tough guy now, are you?" John growls at Luke.

"Get... off...!" Luke punches him in the throat as Jarrod limps towards him. I know I have to do something.

"You're fucking dead." Jarrod is getting closer, despite his obvious injury.

"No! Get away from him!" I have to help.

I fly towards Jarrod and kick him in the kneecap Luke had moments earlier. Jarrod screams as he falls to the ground once more.

I jump on John's back and wrap my arms around his neck. I'm not letting him pin Luke to the ground and choke the life out of him.

"Fuck! Get off me, you little bitch!" It doesn't take much for John to throw me off him.

I hit the ground with a whimper. "Ow…" I shake it off just as Luke gets to his feet. He jumps up and has John face down on the ground within seconds.

He looks at me as I crawl towards him. "You okay? Are you hurt?" He looks me up and down as I shake my head. I hand him a pair of cuffs. John is bucking beneath him. "I need your help, Air. Can you do it?"

I take a deep breath. "Yes."

"I need your knee right here between his shoulder blades. If he moves, drop your knee down and put some weight on him until he stops flailing. Understand?"

"Get off!" John screams.

I do exactly what he tells me to. He crawls to John's side. "Press down. I need his hands."

I press down. John screams. "Fuck! Get off me, bitch!"

I watch as Luke bends his wrist so it snaps as he puts cuffs on. I look at him wide-eyed, but don't question him. John screams in pain.

"I told you. Respect her." Luke and I watch Jarrod attempting to crawl away. "Stay just like that with your knee where it is. He gives you shit, drop your knee."

I nod. "Okay."

He jumps up and stalks towards Jarrod. "Now where do you think you're going?"

Jarrod puts up a hand. "Stay away. Just get the fuck away. I'm sorry, okay? Just following orders!"

"Hmm.... Yeah. Don't care. You don't fuck around with a man's family." He shoves his knee into his back and cuffs him before he looks back at me. He grins proudly, and a sense of accomplishment washes over me. "Hey, sweetheart, can you get him up or you need my help?" He stands and drags Jarrod up with him. Jarrod howls in pain.

"Got it!" I think of all the defensive training Ryan and Taylor have been doing with me lately and smile. Luke grins again while he watches me. I force John to his feet using his broken wrist for leverage. He cries as I walk him over to Luke, controlling him with his broken wrist.

"Ryan teach you how to do that?"

"Taylor, actually." I smile proudly.

"Man. I don't think I could be a more proud big brother if I tried."

I smile. "What do we do with them?"

"We'll get them in the car. Then, I'll give your husband a call." He smiles down at me. I'm struggling with my blisters, but I'm trying not to cry. I force myself to hold it together because I know Luke needs me. "I'm proud of you. You don't know how much."

"For what? I just did what anyone would have."

"No. What you did was brave as hell, Air. Not many would've jumped in like you did. I would've been okay but worse for the wear."

"I don't know that I would've been able to do it if you weren't family, honestly. I was really scared." We reach the vehicle.

"When I get out of here, I'm killing both of you. Right after I fuck you so hard, you can't see straight, Arianna." John sneers.

Something inside me snaps. Completely. Every fiber of my being quivers and shakes. "Shut up!" I scream as I slam John into the car with so much force that I hear a sickening crunch. He screams in pain.

Luke looks at me with both shock and awe. "Shit. You broke his fucking nose."

I grin like an idiot as Luke shoves him in the car, followed by Jarrod. I truly feel like I'm coming into my own. All I want is to be able to feel like I'm protecting my family. That I'm capable of defending them.

Because they're my life.

Chapter Nineteen

✗ Ryan ✗

"I can't believe you let her go with him alone." Taylor is pacing back and forth in front of me. I chuckle. "He hasn't been with us long enough to come close to gaining our trust." He checks his watch for the thousandth time.

I casually put a hand in front of my mouth to hide the laugh. "You may be more protective of Arianna than me."

He stops in front of me and glares. "You realize they're an hour late?"

"Did you not get the group text Arianna sent to us? She said the tour ran a little late. They're behind."

Taylor takes out his phone. He scrolls through, reads the text, then grunts as he puts his phone away. My phone starts ringing.

"Is that 'Crazy' by Aerosmith?" he asks, blinking at my phone incredulously.

"Arianna's ringtone. She had my phone the other day and assigned a specialized ringtone to everyone."

"Yeah? What's mine?"

I smirk and laugh. "No idea. Call me and find out." I answer my phone. "Hey, baby. Are you on your way back?"

"Uh... Yes."

I raise an eyebrow. Something's off. "What does that mean?"

"Well, it's a long story, but to make it short, Luke took out a couple of my dad's guards."

I glare at Taylor. He looks at me perplexed. I choke back a growl even though I'm pissed. I'm angry the guards went after her. I'm angry I wasn't there. And I'm even more angry that my explicit orders were disobeyed.

"Baby, I'm glad you're okay, but I gave explicit orders. I wanted them alive."

"Oh! I'm sorry, I didn't mean took them out as in kill them! I meant took them out as in, they're both in the back of the car, and we're on our way to you. They're alive."

I let out a breath. My fucking emotions are all over the place and mirrored on Taylor's face. "Honestly, are you okay? Where are the guards I sent with you?"

"Guards you sent with me?"

I glare at my phone. "Yes, Arianna. I had two guards downstairs waiting for you. Where are they?"

"There weren't any guards downstairs waiting for us. It's just been me and Luke all day. You didn't tell me you had guards waiting for us."

My heart somersaults. "Son of a bitch. How far away are you?"

"Um... I'm not totally sure. Hang on. I'll put you on speaker." I hear shuffling as she puts me on speaker. "He wants to know how far out we are."

"Four minutes out, Ryan. I have them both cuffed in the car."

"Taylor and I will meet you downstairs. Where's the guards I sent with her?"

"Dude, I wish I knew. When Arianna got to my room, I was getting off the phone with Shane. We left. I figured you had them hidden, and they were following us. No one was down there when we got down there."

I look at Taylor again as I growl. "I want you to bring Arianna up to our suite. Order dinner. The rest of the family will meet you both up here. Arianna isn't to be left alone. Understand?"

190

"Got it."

I signal for Taylor to follow as we head downstairs. "All of my brothers have keycards. All of them. No one should be knocking. Anyone knocks, figure out who they are. If no one knows them, I want them held for me."

"Understood. We're a block out," Luke says. I nod and hang up.

"What the fuck happened?" Taylor asks.

"Two of Massena's guards. Luke is bringing both of them here."

"What about the guards you sent? Why was Luke the one to take Massena's guards out? His focus should have been on Arianna."

"No clue. They both said they weren't downstairs when they left. Luke thought they were just hidden and tailing them. And I don't know why I don't suspect foul play on his end, but I don't." I take my phone and call one of the guards that should've been with her. He doesn't answer. "What the hell?" I dial the other one. He doesn't answer either.

"I don't like this. At all."

"I know. Something doesn't feel right. Stay vigilant. Call Josh and Alex."

"Always."

We both take out our guns as we make our way to the doors. Taylor calls Josh and Alex as he watches for anything out of the ordinary.

The benefit to being as powerful and having as much money as I do is that I can rent out entire resorts or hotels and pay off the entire staff to stay quiet. If they aren't, they face consequences. I usually don't have a problem. We stay just inside the doors until we see Luke pull in.

"Leave them in the car until Arianna is safely inside," I command.

"Dude. You don't need to tell me. Alex and Josh are on the way down."

Moments later, Josh and Alex appear, guns out just as we have. The four of us move as one out to the car. I open Arianna's door.

"Don't be mad. I broke one of their noses."

I shake my head and blink. "You... what?" I stare at her in a state of pure amusement and confusion.

Luke chuckles. "John was talking about how he was going to fuck her until she couldn't see straight, then kill her. So she slammed him into the roof of the car. Broke his nose." Luke is radiating with pride as Arianna smiles up at me.

I lean in to kiss her. "You'll have to tell me that story. But later. Right now, go with Luke. Stay in the suite." She smiles as Luke rounds the car.

"Stay in front of Luke, sweetheart. Let him act as a shield," Alex says.

"Isn't the threat neutralized?" She looks up at me as she gets out of the car.

"Not taking any chances, beautiful. Go with Luke," I say. Luke leads Arianna away.

"Where the fuck are the guards? I don't like this," Taylor says.

"I know. One step at a time. Arianna is safe with Luke. He'll have Jason or Nick with him to help. I'll talk to Luke later about what happened and get Arianna's take when we go to bed after everyone leaves. Right now, we focus on them."

Taylor nods and opens the back door to the car. He pulls one of them out.

The guy howls in pain. "Watch it! Shit! He fucked up my knee."

Taylor laughs. "Please ask me if I care. You went after my little sister. The only reason you aren't dead is because I have orders."

I lean in, pull out the guy with the broken nose, and grin. "I'm going to have a lot of fun with you. Unless you tell me what I want. I'm kind of hoping you don't."

"Fuck you," he spits out.

The four of us laugh.

"They never learn, do they?" Josh asks.

"Nope. You'd be amazed at the amount of guys I deal with who know nothing of what I'm capable of." My eyes darken. We push the two guards ahead of us into the building, keeping our eyes open for an attack. I glance at the front counter at the young woman staring wide-eyed at me. "Bren, right? Get someone to park that car."

She nods. "Yes. Yes, sir. Right away." Alex shoots her a wink. She melts.

I chuckle as we step into the elevator. "Good thing you're a flirt. I think you calmed her down."

Alex shrugs and gives me a cocky as fuck grin. "Women have types. Obviously I'm hers. Why not have a little fun?"

We all laugh as the elevator door opens. We shove both guys forward. Taylor takes out his key card and opens the door.

"You're bringing us to a fucking hotel room to question us?" the one with the fucked up knee asks.

"You're stupider than I thought," the other idiot says.

"The phrase you're looking for is more stupid. Not stupider," Josh corrects.

Alex smirks. "Looks like you aren't as smart as you thought."

Taylor and I shove both of them on the ground.

"Damn! Oh damn." I look down at the one with the broken nose. Both of them try to catch their breath though the pain of their current injuries.

I look down at my phone at the text that comes in and smile. "Arianna says the one with the fucked up knee is Jarrod. The one she broke the nose of is John. I do like not having to waste time on names."

Taylor steps down on the back of Jarrod's knee as he cracks his knuckles.

Jarrod screams in pain. "Get off! Fuck, dude. Get off! I'll talk! Get off!"

"Well, well. I think we found our weak link," Josh says, grinning down at him.

"It's always the big guy, isn't it?" I smile sardonically.

"Shut up, Jarrod! What the hell?" John yells, glaring at his buddy.

"Just get off!" Jarrod whimpers.

Taylor steps off and kneels next to Jarrod. "Keep in mind it's not likely I ask a question I don't know the answer to. So, tell me. Did you report to Massena?"

"Yes. Yes. Right before we confronted Arianna at the Tower of London. He's on his way." Jarrod starts crying. I can't help but laugh. "It hurts! It hurts so fucking bad." He starts taking deep breaths.

"What about the guards supposed to be with Arianna?" Alex asks.

"We killed them. We s-saw them waiting and took them out. Never saw us coming." He cries harder. "It hurts! Get me a doctor!"

I shake my head. "No. Where are my guards?"

"I told you we killed them!"

"Where did you put them?" Josh demands.

He continues crying and starts hyperventilating. "In... the... trunk... of our car. It's... at... the Tower." I watch Jarrod's breathing slow.

Alex's mouth drops. "Did he just pass out? He did not just pass out."

Taylor stands and hauls Jarrod up. He drops him in a chair. His bone is protruding from his knee. He's gushing blood. "Guess we get to focus on this douche."

I smile as I kneel next to John. "Let's see." I look at both of John's wrists. I can tell immediately which one is broken. "Who's Massena bringing with him?"

John glares. "You can kill me."

Josh laughs. "Well, fuck. Don't tempt him now."

John smiles. "I'm not like him. I ain't singing like a canary like him."

Taylor laughs. "I think you'll be telling us what we want."

"Pretty confident about it, actually." Alex stands. "That wrist doesn't look good."

"How's that nose look?" I ask.

"Not pretty, bro. Definitely busted." Taylor smiles at me, an evil glint in his eye. I've let him be in interrogations with me, but I've never let him participate. I'll let him have a little fun, but I won't let him cross lines.

John glares at us. "Fuck you all. I won't be saying shit. But when I get out of here, Arianna is first on my list. I plan on enjoying her."

I can feel the shift in the room. Alex, Josh, and Taylor look just as vicious as I feel. Taylor snaps and slams John's head into the ground. John screams in pain. Alex steps on his broken wrist, still cuffed behind his back. It's so swollen, the cuff is digging into his skin.

As Alex steps down, John screams again. "Stop! Ah! Stop! Fuck! Fuck!" Alex lets up.

"How about we try that again, huh?" Josh says as he kneels and grabs his other wrist.

"Who's Massena bringing with him?" I ask again.

"Fucking kill me," John whimpers. Josh bends his wrist. Slowly. Until he's groaning.

"Last chance. Who?" I ask again. He grits his teeth and fights the pain. I chuckle. The darkness in me that I rarely ever let out is bubbling to the surface. "I knew I'd have fun with you." I nod to Josh. He snaps his wrist. John screams and cries, writhing in pain.

"Damn. He's a fighter, isn't he?" Alex says with a dangerous grin.

"Definitely a fighter," Josh agrees.

I look down at him. "We'll keep breaking bones. I don't mind at all."

"Knee next?" Alex moves to John's legs. He kneels and puts both of his knees on one leg to keep him still. Josh follows. He grabs John's leg. "You want to break it? Or you want to keep him still?"

"Break." Josh's voice is dangerous. I can't help but feel a little proud.

Taylor tilts his head and grabs John's hair. He forces him to look up at him. "You know what's about to happen. I'm tired of playing fucking games."

"I'll ask again," I begin.

"Fuck. You."

I nod at Josh. He bends John's leg up. "Who's he going to have with him?" I ask.

"How many times do you want me to say it?" John growls.

I nod and look up at Josh. "Josh." I hear Jarrod groan. I glance at him. Josh twists until John's knee pops.

John screams. "Shit! Shit! Holy fuck! Fuck!" He doesn't cry, just screams.

Jarrod throws up.

"Who's he bringing?" I ask again as John groans and grits his teeth. It's not going to be much longer before he passes out. I look up at Alex and Josh again. Josh slams his knee to the ground. John screams in pain, then screams louder when Josh kneels on his now broken knee. Alex grabs his other leg and bends it up. "You're getting pretty damn close to passing out, John. I know the pain is excruciating."

"Fuck... you..."

I grin. "Man. I almost admire you." His breathing grows ragged. "Listen, John. I'll level with you. If you don't give me the information I'm asking for, I'm going after Jarrod the moment you pass out. We both know he's your weak link." John groans and whimpers. "Who's he bringing?"

"Go... to... hell."

I laugh low in my throat. "Been there once. Satan himself kicked me out. I liked it so much he feared I'd take over."

I nod to Alex. He twists slowly. As soon as John can't take it and starts screaming, Alex snaps his other knee. John inhales sharply before he passes out.

"Damn," Alex says disappointedly.

"Looks like Jarrod's awake," Taylor says, nodding towards Jarrod, who's covered in his own puke.

We all stand and advance on Jarrod.

His eyes widen in fear.

"Tell me who Massena's bringing with him and when he's landing, and I won't break every bone in your body." There's nothing I wouldn't do for my family. For Arianna. Including becoming the dangerous mafia boss everyone fears.

"He's flying in from New York. He'll have Stephen Ambrosio and Chad Ambrosio with him. He always travels with six guards."

"Seven hour flight. When did he leave?" Taylor asks.

"We called him around six. Just after Arianna finished her Tower tour."

"It would take about an hour to get to the airport and take off." Alex says.

I nod. "We leave tonight."

Taylor looks at me. I can see the sadness in his eyes that he tries to hide. "Arianna's going to be pissed. You know that, right? She was looking forward to that private tour you booked for all of us at Buckingham."

I've never been good with knowing my girl is upset or disappointed. Taylor hates making people sad. "I'll make it up to her. We'll have to do it when this is over."

"Look. Dude. Please get me a doctor. Please," Jarrod begs. "I've told you everything."

I grin sardonically.

Alex laughs. "You actually think we're going to let you go?"

"Taylor. Time to go." I meet Taylor's eyes. I can see the war waging inside him. It was the same one I saw when we took out the gang fucking with Nicole. He wants to stay and finish this, but he knows the rules. He knows I won't let him.

After a few moments, Taylor takes a deep breath and leaves the room. Jarrod has given up all hope and accepted his fate. He closes his eyes. I watch Taylor close the door knowing just how difficult it is for him to leave this part to me. His protectiveness of his family is no different than mine.

Josh puts a hand on my shoulder. "Don't worry. He'll get over it."

"I know. Let's just finish this." I tear my eyes away from the door and take out my gun. I shoot Jarrod between the eyes at the same time Alex shoots John in the back of the head.

"I'll call our cleanup crew," Josh says.

I look down at my shirt. It's splattered with blood. Alex's is as well. "We can't walk back in my suite like this. I don't want Arianna to see this part of shit. Even though she knows."

"I get it. We'll head to my suite and clean up. You can use one of my shirts." I glance at him and raise an eyebrow. He's a big guy, but I have a couple inches on him and a lot more muscle. No way one of his dress shirts is going to fit me. Alex rolls his eyes. "I brought t-shirts, too, you dick."

We all laugh as we head out of the room. Josh makes a call to their cleanup crew as we enter Alex's suite to clean up. Josh heads up to my room. He lucked out. Managed to stay clean.

Just once I'd like to be able to stay in one city the length of time we planned. We planned three weeks here. Arianna deserves it. I wanted her to be able to relax before she started college. Enjoy being free of her father and married to me.

Unfortunately, Arianna was right. Her father will never let her go. So long as he's still alive.

I truly want to wait here and take care of him tonight. But I never do anything on a whim. Without a plan. I always do surveillance. I always gather as much information as possible. Doing things on a whim isn't an option in my book. Doing things on a whim with no information or plan is a great way to get killed.

Especially since I'm positive there's more going on here. More that I simply am *not* understanding. I don't like not knowing. I sure as fuck don't like not understanding. But what I hate the most is knowing there's more that I'm missing. I don't like missing anything.

My job is to protect my family; my wife. I can't do that if I allow someone to get a step ahead of me. No. I'll let him chase us. It gives me time to figure out the entire story here.

And then I'll let him walk into the trap I set for him. I'll let him think he's one-upped me, but he won't get close to Arianna.

Ever again.

Chapter Twenty

⚔ Arianna ⚔

I've been in the bedroom on the plane ever since we got up in the air. Ryan is talking to everyone about plans for the rest of the trip. I simply can't stand to hear anymore. I'm tired of plans. They always get ruined.

I sniffle and wipe away my tears. I hate my father. He'll never leave me alone. I'll never be free of him. I look at the door as someone knocks, but I say nothing.

"Air? It's me, sweetheart. Okay if I come in?" Taylor asks.

I sniffle again. "I don't care."

Taylor slowly opens the door and closes it behind him. He sits next to me on the edge of the bed. "Ryan kind of has the feeling you might be a little upset with him. Renza told everyone they should leave you alone because you need time to process everything, and you do it better on your own."

I shake my head and glare at the wall. "That's never been true. I don't know where she got that or why she would say it. I do better talking things out. Even if I'm angry." I look up at him. "So, you're the only one brave enough to come back here to face my wrath."

He watches me for a moment before smiling softly. "Ryan wanted to, sweetheart. I begged him to let me."

I furrow my eyebrows. "Why?"

"Because unlike Renza, I know you well enough to know you need to talk this out. And I know how to get you to do it."

I chuckle and glare back at the wall. "And you think Renza doesn't? Or Ryan?"

"No, honey. I know Ryan does. He does it with me all the time. I don't know about Renza, but I'm starting to think she doesn't know you that well at all." He takes a deep breath. "Maybe I need to talk it out a little bit, too." Taylor looks at the wall a moment before looking down at his feet.

I wait a few moments before speaking. "I'm upset. But not at Ryan. Or anyone on this plane. Well, I might be with Renza, but I'm really upset with my dad. And Chad. For consistently finding ways to ruin my life. I hate him. I hate both of them. I've never hated anyone in my life, but I hate them both. So much. I feel like it's just eating at me. I can't control it. All I want to do is lash out and be the one to pull the trigger."

"I understand. I felt the same way about Chris when he was fucking with Nikki and the bakery. I wanted to be in there when Ryan took care of them. I forced myself out. I wanted to be in that room tonight with them and your dad's guards when they finished them. I was pissed Ryan kicked me out. I still am." Taylor looks at me.

"You know he was protecting you."

"Yeah. I know. But some sick part of me doesn't want him to anymore. I'm tired of walking away instead of finishing the job."

I purse my lips, thinking. "You're talking about fighting two sides of yourself. One side knows following Ryan's orders is the right thing to do to keep you both safe and out of trouble. The other side simply doesn't care. You just want to protect the family like he does. You resent him forcing you to walk away."

He smiles, but I can see the battle raging behind his eyes. It's the same as my own. "Knew you'd understand. You feel the same way."

I'm surprised he can tell. "I'm just so angry. I'm hurt. I know Ryan will deal with it. I know you all will. But I don't like just sitting back waiting for it all to happen. I feel like all of this is happening because of me, and I'm both not allowed and not able to do anything to help." I look down at my hands. "I feel helpless. Just like high school."

I feel the tears start again. I try to hide my face, but Taylor pulls me to him. I bury my head in his chest as the dam gives way. I had been thinking about something else. Something I hadn't told anyone.

"You just made me realize something, Arianna. We're helping any way we can. Me with the research. Questioning the guards. Being a part of keeping you and the rest of the family safe." He hugs me and sways with me a little as his words sink in. "And you by staying strong and making suggestions on how this should all go down. You being there for Ryan when he needs you to be. Coming through for him when no one else can reach him. You're doing that for not just him but all of us." He hugs me a little tighter as my tears begin to subside.

"I feel like I'm falling apart."

"You have me. You have Ry. You have everyone else to keep you from that. We all play a part, Air. I guess it took me coming in here to talk to you before I realized it myself."

I nod into his chest, but I don't let go of him. I need to get this out. I can't tell anyone else. Taylor is the only one who would possibly understand. I take a deep breath.

"There's one more thing... Something I haven't been able to tell anyone, but I've thought about..." I close my eyes and blurt the words out. "I'm postponing my admission to Juilliard. Until next semester."

Taylor stiffens. I feel him breathe in deeply. "Why?"

"My father. He'll do anything he can to ruin it for me. I can't concentrate on school when I'm constantly worried about what his next move is."

"Hmm... Can I ask you something?"

"You know you can."

"Is there a reason you don't think we'll have him dealt with by then?"

I'm silent for a moment. I don't know how to word my thoughts. Finally, I quit trying and just blurt it out. "Because no matter how hard I try, I can't imagine a life without my father in it. Even though I know Ryan, all of you, of us, will do everything in our power to make it happen."

"I understand, sweetheart." He pushes me back a little so he can look at me. "I know it's hard to imagine, but I promise you won't have to postpone Juilliard. Ryan won't let that happen. None of us will, Arianna. Trust me. Trust us."

"I'm trying. But having a family I can rely on is still so new to me. I get inside my own head and overthink everything. For so long, all I had was Ryan, Renza, and Robby. And not even they had the ability to make everything perfect. I'm just so scared that it won't matter how hard I trust... something awful is going to happen."

"Air. Tell me the truth. Whenever you've been totally up front and honest with Ryan, with me, has the problem you had gone away? Been solved?"

I'm silent as I think. The guy who shoved me into my locker and grabbed my chest as he tried to kiss me had been arrested, thanks to Taylor and Ryan. Other than Chad, all of my other bullies had stopped as soon as they saw what happened to him.

"Um... Yes. Actually."

"Then, get out of your head. You forced me out of mine. So, let me force you out of yours. We all have a role. And we'll all play them. Force yourself to follow your instincts. Listen to your heart. You're head will only fuck with you."

I laugh for the first time all night. "Very Taylor of you."

"I try." He kisses me on the forehead. "Ready to go out there? Let the family vibe calm you down?"

"I hope no one hates me for disappearing."

"Not a single person out there blames you for needing time alone. No matter the reason. To process, or to just escape. You're human, and we all love you regardless."

XXX

I lean into Ryan and look up at the massive yacht in front of us. My stomach does a flip, I take a deep breath. I've been fighting nausea ever since we got off the plane. I'm pretty sure it has everything to do with the fact that I hadn't eaten in nearly twenty-four hours.

"Still sick?" Ryan asks quietly.

"Yes. I think it's because I haven't eaten. I'm just too nervous my dad is going to jump out and take me away."

Ryan gently turns me to face him, then puts his arms around my waist so he can pull me close. "Never ever happening. I won't let it. Neither will anyone here." He bends to capture my lips with his own. I melt a little as Robby and Renza walk up to us.

"Hell of a yacht you got here, boss," Robby says in awe.

"It's gorgeous," Renza breaths in awe. "I've never seen anything like this."

"There's a room for everyone," Ryan says. "As soon as we board, I'll show you around."

"Do you seriously have a helicopter on your yacht?" Nicole asks as she leans against me staring at the one-hundred-million dollar yacht in front of us.

"I own two yachts. Both built by Blohm and Voss. Both custom designed. Both have helipads in case of emergency. Or in case I want to take it out and fly." He smirks.

Jason laughs as he appears next to us. "We both took lessons when we were younger. Most of the time when someone wants to rebel, they get a motorcycle. Ryan bought a helicopter, two sports cars, a yacht, and a mansion in Hawaii."

"Blew my entire inheritance, but I regret nothing. Jason, on the other hand, invested it and built his own empire from the ground up."

"And you took over for your father," Dave says.

Ryan laughs. "Turned his beloved mafia legit within a couple years. He didn't talk to me for a couple of years after that. Maybe longer."

"I don't think it was that long. He realized pretty fucking quick you were right. That you were more successful than even him," Nick says.

Jessa smiles. "And you all are so close now."

"We got over it." Ryan kisses me on top of the head. "Looks like they're ready to board. The staff's quarters are all on the lower level. Every other room except mine and Arianna's is fair game to the rest of you. Drop your stuff when we board. We'll do the tour and pick rooms, and then you all can grab your stuff and unpack."

We all board the yacht and follow Ryan to the back of the ship.

"A pool. Of course you have a fucking pool." Luke shakes his head in disbelief.

I laugh. "What good is a luxury yacht without a pool?"

Nicole beams. "Taylor and I don't need a room. We're never leaving those chairs."

We all laugh.

"Sorry, beautiful, but no way in hell we're sleeping on those," Taylor says with a grin.

Ryan takes my hand in his and leads us all inside. We're surrounded by luxury and soft, velvety white seating. "This is the sitting room. There's enough room for all of us."

Chase's mouth drops. "Okay, this is bigger than mine. I need an upgrade."

"I love our yacht. Don't get rid of it. It's so cozy!" Breetana says looking up at him. Chase leans down and kisses her.

I smile widely as I lean into Ryan and look up at him. "Relationship goals."

He raises an eyebrow. "Really? You're modeling us after them?" His voice is light and teasing as he laughs and leans down to kiss my neck and whisper in my ear. "I cannot wait until you see our bedroom." He entwines his fingers with mine once more and leads us all through the yacht until we get to the dining area. Ryan nods to the table. "Obviously, that ain't fitting everyone, so we won't have any formal dinners onboard, but when we do eat onboard, feel free to sit here if you choose." We follow Ryan to the side of the ship near the dining area. "The staff serves breakfast here. With all of us, I've ordered each morning to be served buffet style."

Jessa blinks and smiles widely. "Okay, Jas, you know I don't care about money, but we need this sitting area for the mornings on our yacht." She gawks at the cozy white seating.

Jason laughs. "You want it, it's yours. I'll upgrade as soon as we're settled for the night."

She looks up at him. "Really?"

He grins. "Haven't you figured out by now that all you need to do is say the words?"

I look up at Ryan as Jason kisses Jessa. He smiles. "New relationship goals?"

"Yes."

He chuckles as he leads us to a hallway. "Bedrooms. Pick one. Each has a private bathroom. Don't fight over them, or I let Arianna choose for you."

I laugh, feeling happier and happier as the day turns to night. I smile as everyone starts grabbing their things and moving them into their chosen rooms.

"I love how everyone is happy. And I love how Marianne and Dave are finally not hiding how they feel."

"Thanks in large part to your amazing husband." He gives me a cocky wink.

I laugh as he slips his arm around my shoulders and leads me to the last bedroom. "I'll have to remember to thank him," I tease.

"I know him pretty well. He'll take kisses as a thank you and you naked underneath him."

I laugh. "Lucky for him, I like being naked underneath him."

"He's very lucky then. Because you, beautiful girl, are incredibly sexy." He reaches around me and opens the door when we reach our bedroom.

It's spacious for being on a ship. It's not much smaller than a master bedroom. It matches Ryan's pristine theme. The bed is covered in a white bedspread. The dresser and nightstands are wooden. The walls are white, but there's incredible artwork all over the place that gives the room color and character. The windows and doors are all accentuated with a deep rose oak wood. There's a giant TV mounted to the wall. The room is very Ryan, and I love it so much that I'm speechless.

"Wow. It's incredible." My eyes sting with tears as they fall on the pink and white flowers in an enormous vase. They sting a little more when they fall on another vase filled with white and purple flowers. "Carnations. And lilies."

Ryan closes the door behind us and slips his arms around my waist, pulling my back close to his chest as he hugs me tightly.

"I wanted to do something to cheer you up. I know the last few weeks have been hard."

"It really has been hard."

"I'm sorry he keeps ruining it for you. I'll make it up to you, though, baby. I'll still get a private tour of Buckingham Palace. I know you were really looking forward to that."

I smile softly and untangle his arms from my waist as I walk to our private bathroom. "Wow. You could sleep in that shower."

"I have no intention of sleeping when I have you in that shower."

I laugh a little as I turn and walk to the bed. I sit down on the edge. Ryan sits next to me. He says nothing, knowing I need the words to come out on their own.

"I... was... thinking. Maybe I should take a semester off. Or maybe the year." Even after talking to Taylor about it on the plane, I still feel like it's the right thing to do.

"From school?" Ryan asks softly. I nod and look down. He stands and walks to the dresser. He pulls out a t-shirt for me and hands it to me. We both get ready for bed. When we're under the covers, he pulls me close. "I ordered a couple of sandwiches for dinner tonight. I thought maybe you'd just like to unwind. Just us."

"That's exactly what I want. What I need."

"They'll be here in a few minutes, I'm sure. In the meantime..." He kisses my forehead, cheek, then my lips. He's so gentle and sweet with me that I melt into his embrace. Just like I always do. "I'll support you in whatever you think you need. But you worked hard to get into Juilliard, baby. Your tuition issue was taken care of. I don't want you to not go because of your dad. And I get the feeling this is coming from someplace of fear."

"I'm just... scared. I keep going back and forth between being okay and strong. Fearless, even. But then I freak out a little and get in my own head. I get scared all over again. I told Taylor that it has a lot to do with not being used to having this entire family willing to fight for me. To protect me against him. All I've ever had is you and Robby and Renza. Having a whole family is both amazing and scary."

"You're waiting for someone to betray you."

I burrow into his arms. My mind automatically falls on Renza. I shake it to banish the thoughts. "Kind of. Yeah."

He hugs me as tightly as he can. "You trust me."

"Of course I do. You know I do."

"And I trust our family."

I kiss his chest and smile. "You're saying that by trusting you, I should trust them by proxy."

"That's my girl."

A knock sounds at the door. Ryan quickly kisses me and then walks to it. I sit up and reach for the remote. I find a movie as he climbs back into bed with our dinner on a tray.

"My plan. Dinner and a movie. Shower. You. By tomorrow, we should be in Athens. Right?" I look up at him. He's grinning. I really love his smile.

"By the time we wake up. We'll be heading into town to visit a flea market. I want to visit the street market. They have incredible Greek cheeses and this amazing oil I want to get for a new recipe I want to make for dinner."

I smile, allowing being with him to center me again. To make me whole. "Yum. I already know it's going to be amazing. And after tonight's shower…, I can't think of anything better than being underneath you."

He nearly chokes. "You're every man's dream. You know that, right?"

I laugh as we eat our sandwiches. When we're finished, I settle between his legs, and his magic fingers take away all of my stress. With each kink he massages out, I feel more and more of my fear slip away. By the time he's done, and he has his arms around me as we finish the movie, I've made my decision.

From now on, my father doesn't get to control my life. I won't let him control me and my emotions. And I refuse to allow him make me doubt the only family I've ever known.

This family. My family.

I snuggle into my husband with a content smile.

Our family.

Chapter Twenty One

✗ Ryan ✗

"You know I make you beg for stuff because you begging is one of the sexist things in the world."

Arianna grins wickedly as she stalks towards me and straddles me. My hands automatically find her perfect ass. I give her a light squeeze. She pushes herself down on me and rubs against my cock.

"Mmm... Aria. Not here. Too many people can see."

"Since when are you modest?" She rubs against me again and again until my cock is begging for her. But we're in the middle of the common area of my yacht. "I don't see anyone." She rubs her bikini clad pussy against me one more time for good measure.

I close my eyes and moan as I reach between us and grab her. "Is it just that you can't resist me, or is it the excitement of someone possibly walking in and catching us?" I run my hand along the outside of her bikini bottoms.

"Maybe a little of both." She runs her hands up my abs.

"Are we really doing this here?"

She bites her lip and nods. I smile and move the bikini bottoms to the side. I dip my middle finger inside her. She sighs and closes her eyes as she moves against it. She leans down and kisses me as I take my finger out after thrusting a few times to make her wet for me. I reach down and slip my shorts down enough so that my cock is free.

"People are going to be up soon. I truly don't care who sees, but I don't want you to be embarrassed," I rumble.

"Then, we'll be fast, and I'll be a good girl and be quiet." She smiles again as she kisses me. I groan because her saying she'll be a good girl makes my dick harder than fucking steel.

I slip her bottoms to the side again and guide her on top of me. "You can't possibly be more perfect."

"Mmm... Ryan," she whispers as she grips my shoulders and buries her face in my neck. After she adjusts to me, I start thrusting inside her. She meets my thrusts as she moves her body against me. "You feel so good." She kisses my neck. A throaty moan escapes her lips.

I bury my face in her hair and kiss her neck and shoulder. Her pussy feels so tight around me. So warm and wet for me. "So do you. So wet and tight around me. Always."

I keep one hand on her ass and wrap the other around her waist as our hot breath hits one another's necks. I intensify my thrusts and push into her harder and deeper.

Like the good girl she is, she starts dropping herself on me as our pace quickens even more. "Oh, God... Yes..."

I grip her hips and move her back and forth over me. Her pussy clenches tight as she quietly moans and softly sighs. Her fingernails dig into my shoulders and lightly scrape across them. I grip her ass and bounce her even harder on top of me.

"Oh, fuck yes...," I rumble against her neck. "Such a good girl for me."

"Mmm... Ryan..."

It only takes a few moments before Arianna's thighs start trembling. I feel her body beginning to vibrate around me as her pussy gets tighter and pulses for me. I know she's about to have an intense orgasm, and I can't wait to feel her walls collapse around me.

She tightens her grip around my shoulders. "Ryan... Please... Make me come for you..." Her whispered plea in my ear is all I need. My dick throbs inside her as it thickens. My entire body jerks at the jolt that shoots down my spine. I push her down hard on top of me and hold her quivering body still.

"Come for me, baby," I whisper dominantly against her neck.

"Mmm…!" Her hips move on their own as her walls do exactly as I wanted them to. They collapse around my cock squeezing me as her release hits.

I hold her as tightly as I can and kiss against her neck as my own body trembles. I come hard, filling her pussy with jets of me.

"Fuck…," I moan. "Fuck, Aria. Good girl." I hug her even closer to me as we finish together.

Not that I'm complaining, but Arianna has seemingly needed quick sex a lot lately. With everything else that's been happening with her, specifically the nausea and cramping she's been getting, I've begun questioning if maybe there's more to it than just her craving her husband. I haven't said anything about it yet, but I've been observing things. If I'm right, she doesn't know how happy she's going to make me.

After a few moments, she smiles down at me. "So…, can we go to the Acropolis?"

I laugh. "Now we get to the truth. It's not that you crave me. You were seducing me so I'd say yes!" I look up at her as she continues straddling me, me still deep inside her. She kisses me as I hear a door open. I quickly pull out and pack myself away, making sure her bikini is in place.

Luke comes around the corner and stops. "If you two are having sex in that chair, and I just walked in on it, I'm going to throw up."

Arianna stands up, and Luke eyes both of us warily. "Nope! Discussing an aerial tour of Athens."

My eyes widen. "What? No. Aria, you said you wanted to see the Acropolis. Not an aerial tour of the city!" She looks at me with incredibly sexy, pleading eyes. I smile and shake my head. "You're going to pay for that."

She winks at me. I laugh. I'd give her anything she asked. The sexy begging and sex I get are both very much appreciated bonuses.

I stand up and head to the bedroom to change for the day I planned at the market.

"I'll admit, Athens is beautiful," I say as I look around at the colorful homes.

Renza spins in a circle. "I love how the old architecture meets new architecture."

"I just want to take all of these flowers home!" Nicole reaches up and touches some flowers hanging around a lamp.

"They really are pretty!" Breetana agrees as she smiles at her sister.

Arianna slips her hand in mine and forces me to slow my walk. I look down at her as we fall behind the crowd. She looks tired. "Are you okay?"

"Just... kind of nauseous."

I raise an eyebrow and stop as everyone else continues walking ahead. "Honey, how long have you been feeling like this?" I whisper. She shrugs and looks down. "Aria. Look at me, baby." I squeeze her hand. She looks up at me. She's so incredibly beautiful. If my hunch is right, the same one I had this morning when she was riding me, I can't wait until she has that gorgeous glow. I smile and lean down to kiss her. "You were nauseous when we got off the plane last night. Have you been feeling that way awhile?"

"No... It just started."

"Okay. You've been getting a lot of cramps this past week. Australia, I'm pretty sure was the hike, but when we were in London, you had a pretty bad cramp. We hadn't even left the Penthouse yet that day. You had one on the plane. And after sex in the chair this morning, you got a cramp you were complaining about when I came in to change."

"I... guess. I don't know what it means."

"I don't remember you getting any before we got married, baby. And I've had you in some pretty... um... interestingly flexible positions. Cramps are indicative of many things, but given everything else?" I shrug and let her come to the same conclusion I have.

She looks at our family, who have stopped to wait for us at the end of the pathway. She looks back up at me. "That's not possible. I just got over my period last week. You know that."

"I know. But you also said it was really light."

"But I still had it. Periods don't happen with pregnant women."

"You know as well as I do that isn't always true. Pregnant women have mistaken spotting for their period for decades. You and I have sat watching the TV show you like about women who didn't know they were pregnant until they gave birth."

Arianna closes her eyes and takes a deep breath. "I can't be pregnant." She opens her eyes. My heart shatters when I see the tears. "What about Juilliard? What about us? And traveling?" She turns and takes a few steps away from me before turning back to me. "Am I being selfish? I'm being selfish!" She covers her face with her hands and crouches on the ground as she bursts into tears.

I crouch in front of her and take her hands in mine as I pull them away from her face. "Hey, hey, honey. Listen to me. We don't know for sure, right? We need to get you tested. That's step one. I don't know if it will show. It's only been about five or six weeks since we had sex the first time. After that, we'll figure it out. We can talk to Juilliard about holding your position. We'll figure it out, okay? You and me. Together."

She nods and hugs me. I stand and pull her up with me. She burrows into my chest. "I was afraid you'd be upset."

I hug her tighter. "No. No way. I already told you that I never wanted kids until I met you. I thought it would be a little while, especially with you being on the pill, but it's okay. If it happens now, it happens now. I'm not going anywhere."

"I'm so sorry."

"For what? Getting pregnant? Honey, it takes two people to make that happen. I'm not upset. I love you. I'm not going anywhere. And get out of your head. I know you're thinking this is going to ruin your life, and you won't be able to go to Juilliard, but I promise you that will not happen. I promise." She nods into my chest. I glance up at our family again. Jason meets my eyes. I give him a quick nod. "Ready to hit the flea market and market?"

"I'm ready." She nods. I take her hand, and we start walking. "Do you think maybe we could keep this quiet? Until we know for sure?"

"Of course. I'd rather know for sure before saying anything anyway."

We reach the family. The old Greek neighborhood we had been walking through is like a pathway that opens into the flea market.

"Holy shit." Arianna smiles brightly at the throngs of people and shops in front of us.

Taylor hugs Nicole close. "Incredible, huh?"

Nick's eyes widen. He's immediately far more on guard and tense as he looks around. "Way bigger than I thought."

"Hey, Arianna. You can see Acropolis from here." Jason points. I'm not even sure Arianna hears him, but I know she's already eyed the temple because she can't keep her eyes off it.

Nicole bounces on her heels. "Arianna, I see really cute handcrafted stuff at a vendor. Come check it out with me! Breetana wants to go see the one with the dresses. Please, please, please?"

Arianna smiles and Nicole pulls her away from me and grabs Lyric's hand. Jessa and Breetana head for dresses and Taylor and Chase follow. Luke, Nick, and Alex head for a food vendor. Robby and Renza follow Dave and Marianne. Josh trails behind them. I can feel the suspicion radiating off him, but I trust him to work through it and tell me if he needs me to follow up on something. I glance around and see all of my guards stationed exactly where I want them, even the ones camouflaged in the crowd. Eventually, it's just me and Jason.

"I want to hit that market and find those cheeses and oil I want," I say, glancing over at him.

"Well, let's go find them."

We head towards the market. I let out a long sigh before reaching up to scrub my hands down my face.

"Stress finally getting to my invincible brother?"

"I'm not stressed about Arianna's dick father."

"You're stressed about something." My brother and I are as close as twins, even though I'm almost two years older than him. We've always been able to read each other. We know each other just as well as we know ourselves.

When Nick was adopted into the family, everyone referred to us as the Crane Triplets. We all share similar looks, but, most importantly, we're all close. We have a bond. An unbreakable one. We all can read each other as well as any twin could read their other twin.

"I'm not supposed to say anything, but I do need to stop in that shop right there."

Jason looks towards where I'm pointing. "Yeah. Me too. I think Jessa's pregnant."

I stop and shake my head. "Wait. What?"

He stops and looks back at me, smiling. "We weren't going to say anything, but she stopped taking the pill a little while ago. And... we're thinking she's about five to six weeks or so. Pretty early. I'm not even sure tests will pick up on it that early."

"You... that puts you about where Arianna and I got married."

We both walk into the store and head for the pregnancy tests. We find a variety of tests for Jason. I take a deep breath and pick out the same tests we had just grabbed him.

"Uh.... thanks, Ry, but I think the six I have are enough."

"I know. These... are for Arianna." I bite my lip. Jason's mouth falls open. I glare. "Not a fucking word. I mean it. Not until we know for sure. I promised I wouldn't say anything."

He pretends to zip his lip and throw the key. I laugh. He grins like an idiot. "How far do you think she is?"

"Same as Jessa. What I don't get, though. I took her to a doctor, a very discreet doctor, before I left for Chicago to get her birth control. We talked about it and decided it was for the best right now. She gave Arianna a six month supply because of our trip to make sure she had enough to cover us for the duration."

We pay for our stuff and head to the market as we talk. "Birth control isn't a hundred percent."

"I know. I know. But she had to have gotten pregnant on our wedding night. Our first night together. She's taken the pills religiously starting nearly a month before we got married. They would've had plenty of time to work into her system. How does she get pregnant right away?"

Jason thinks a moment as I pay for the cheese. "You're not thinking that she switched them for sugar pills or something. Because not only do I not think she'd do that, but I don't think she wanted to get pregnant right now. She really wants to go to Juilliard."

"I don't think she did, Jas. But I do think they were switched out."

Jason blinks a couple times. "Shit. That would make sense. A lot of sense. Her father wants that alliance. I bet all my wealth that both he and Ambrosio wanted an heir."

"To seal the deal." I pay for my oil, and we start heading back to the family.

"Are you going to tell her?"

"Not until I know for sure. I'm going to have Taylor send the pills for testing after she takes this test."

"What if it's negative?"

"Then she can continue taking them. I won't say anything, but I'm still getting them tested. It just doesn't feel right. None of any of this feels fucking right."

Arianna meets my eyes. She smiles softly. She looks exhausted. It's not lost on Jason. He nudges me. "I think we need to get Jessa and Arianna back. They both look like they need a nap."

"I think you may be right."

At that moment, Luke walks up to us. I watch Nick, Alex, and Josh flank Arianna, Nicole, and Lyric, and lead them towards us.

"Son of a bitch. How the fuck are they here so quickly?" Jason asks.

"They're scouting ahead using Arianna's list from her wish box," Luke growls.

Alex, Nick, and Josh reach us. Arianna steps into my arms. Josh pulls Lyric close. Taylor hugs Nicole. The rest of the family surrounds us. Renza steps to my side, shaking. I put my arm over her shoulder and pull her to my side as I hold Arianna to my chest. I don't know if it's real or an act, but I can act even better.

"Where's Robby?" I ask.

"I sent him to observe until Josh and I get back to him," Alex says. I nod. That would explain Renza being scared. Even if she is stupidly jealous, being alone and defenseless in this situation would be scary for anyone.

Nick looks at me. "What's the plan?"

I shake my head. "I don't need them. I have the information I need right now."

"I want everyone back on the yacht. We can secure it better. We have two other yachts with guards. The yacht is better for observation," Taylor says.

I nod. "I'm with you, Taylor. Alex, find out if they've reported yet, then kill them."

"On it. Let's go, Josh."

Josh turns to Lyric. "Stick close to Ryan, baby." He leans down and kisses her before guiding him to me. She hugs herself, but does exactly as he says. Taylor, following my lead, sticks close to Renza as I pull Lyric into me and Arianna.

We all hurry back to the yacht and wait for Alex, Robby, and Josh to return. Arianna has gone quiet. She's barely said a word since we boarded.

"Aria, come here. Let's go to the bedroom. Talk it out." I help her off the couch and lead her to our room. She sits down on the bed. I sit next to her.

She sniffles. "We're leaving again. Aren't we?"

"No. We aren't."

She looks at me. "How can we not? He found us. Again."

"It's different this time, baby. We aren't in a hotel in the middle of the city. We can go back and forth between here and Italy for the next month if we want to. He can't get on the yacht. I have far more people here than he has in his entire mafia and Ambrosio's combined. All we have to do is disappear for a day or so in the sea and come right back."

I can see the immediate change in her mood as she kisses me. "You're so smart."

"I have my moments."

"I don't mean to sound like a whiny brat, but I'm so sick of him ruining everything for us."

I shake my head. "Baby, that's not what you're being at all. You're allowed to be upset that he's ruining what should be the happiest moments of our lives."

She smiles and kisses me again. I know those few words were what she needed to feel okay about her feelings. She grabs the bag of pregnancy tests from the chair I dropped it in and nearly skips to the bathroom.

I take a deep breath. After a few moments, I'm up and pacing. Arianna comes out of the bathroom. I look at her hopefully.

"Well?"

She shrugs. "Not sure. It said to leave it on a flat service for three to five minutes." She steps into my arms. I hug her. "I took all six of them."

216

I chuckle. "Why?"

"I figured you can't get a false negative or positive on all six of them."

"Smart girl." I hold her until the five minutes are up.

"Ready?" she asks, looking up at me.

"Are you?"

"As I'll ever be."

I grin and kiss her before leading her into the bathroom. She has each test in a neat line on the counter. My eyes widen as I look at them. "Shit."

"Oh my God... Ryan. We're... you're..."

"You're going to be a mother, beautiful."

She beams. "You're going to make an amazing father."

I turn to her, hearing the crack in her voice. "You okay?"

She searches my eyes for several moments before taking a deep, steadying breath. "You aren't going to leave me?"

I shake my head. "Never."

"Then, I'm okay. We can do this." She nods. I pull her close, then lift her off her feet. She squeals. "We're going to be parents!"

I carry her out of the bathroom and bury my face in her hair as I kiss her neck. "You don't know how happy you've made me. How happy you *make* me." I kiss her neck again and again. She hugs me just as tightly as I hug her.

I don't know how long we stay like this, but I don't care. She's carrying my baby.

This perfect woman is carrying a baby I never thought I'd have.

"I love you, Arianna. So much."

"I love you, too. More than I could ever put into words."

Chapter Twenty Two

✕ Arianna ✕

(Two Weeks Later)

"Holy shit. How do you always end up with Park Place and Boardwalk every single time we play?" Lyric asks in disbelief and awe.

I laugh as I pay Nicole, our banker, for the Park Place I just landed on. "Because I have mastered the game of Monopoly. I've become one with the board." I close my eyes and act like I'm meditating over the board.

Nicole and Breetana burst out laughing. I giggle as Jessa and Lyric join in.

"Oh! I'll be right back," Lyric says. "I just need the bathroom, and I'm going to grab a hoodie."

"Can you have Jas get me one?" Jessa asks. "It just got chilly in here."

"Yep!" Lyric bounds out of the room. I'm so happy to see she's started to open up to us. It took her a while, but I think being around the family has really helped her to keep her from sinking into a darkness she'd never be able to come out of.

We pause the game. I stretch and Breetana shakes her head after a few moments. "Renza is sure missing out on our game nights."

I bite my lip and look down at the board. I've honestly felt like her and I are drifting apart. Not just that she's jealous, but that we're barely even friends at all. After Jessa and I announced our pregnancies a couple of weeks ago, Renza has hidden in her room. She's barely said three words to me. It went from her being totally normal around me again to… whatever this is.

"I'm not really sure what's going on with her," I say quietly. "I always thought we'd support each other through marriage and pregnancies. But she… she's just drifting away from me. And it's been happening a while. She's making me so nervous."

"It may be that she's having a hard time adjusting to all of the changes." Nicole smiles softly at me and gently rubs my back.

I shrug. "I'm really not sure it's just that."

"I think we're all a little suspicious of her," Breetana says.

I look up as Lyric slips back into the room. She hands Jessa a hoodie as she sits back down. "Well, that was completely disgusting."

I tilt my head. "What?"

"I just heard Renza. I don't know if she was on the phone or video chat or something, but she was talking super weird."

Jessa furrows her brows. "We… were… just talking about her, actually… What happened? What did you hear?"

"I have no idea. I was going to talk to Josh about it, but it sounded like she was talking to someone about how she's bored out of her mind and wants to go home. Then, I heard a male voice say something like about soon. And then something about her being his good girl and showing him some pussy. From there, it just got gross."

"So, she's talking to someone not on this yacht…?" Nicole asks.

"And since I know that voice wasn't Robby's…," Lyric trails off. "Fuck, I hate cheaters," she sighs.

"Like that's not fucking suspicious at all, though," Breetana says.

Before anyone has a chance to say anything more, someone knocks on the door. I jump a little at the urgency.

"Coming!" Jessa gets up and walks to the door.

As soon as she opens it, Ryan's eyes meet mine. My heart sinks. Something is wrong.

"What happened?" I ask quietly.

"Luke's mom is in trouble. She's on a date with your father. We have a rescue mission going on, but Luke is pretty fucked up."

I nod, knowing exactly what Ryan is asking. I've gotten very good at being my brother's anchor. Much like I'm Ryan's. I love that I can help Luke when he needs it. He's already done so much for me in the short time we've known each other. I stand up and smile softly to my girls. My sisters.

"Go. We'll pick up where we left off tomorrow or something," Jessa says, smiling.

Nicole smiles reassuringly. "Game isn't going anywhere."

Lyric smiles. "Besides, I need to talk to Josh." She wrinkles her nose. "Maybe he'll be able to get rid of that vile image from my mind, too."

"Thanks," I say to her and the rest of the girls.

Lyric squeezes my hand as she passes me, hurrying down the corridor. I hurry after Ryan to my brother's room. Ryan opens the door as soon as we get there. I rush to Luke. Ryan closes the door gently and sits next to Luke on the bed as I drop to my knees in front of him. Luke looks broken. Shattered. His body is wracked with uncontrollable, gut-wrenching sobs.

I take his hands in mine. "Luke?"

He looks at me. The pain and fear on his face is like a million tiny needles straight to my heart. "He has her, Air. He..."

He can't finish as sobs take over once more. I stand, then sit on one of his legs. His arms are immediately around my waist; his face buried in my hair. He squeezes me so tightly, subconsciously being careful of my stomach, that I nearly break into pieces.

But I refuse to. He needs someone there for him for once. Someone he knows he can count on and be real in front of. I'll be that person. Ryan will be. Hell. We all will be. We're his family now. And we'll save his mom.

I look at Ryan. He can see the pain in my eyes. I know he can. He stands. "I'll figure out where we are on the rescue mission."

"Thank you." I love how he knows what I need him to do before I tell him. I love how intuitive he is.

220

Ryan leaves the room just as Robby is about to knock. Robby comes in as Ryan leaves. He sits on the bed next to us. He rubs Luke's back as I hug him. I let him hug me as tightly as he needs to being the anchor he needs.

"What if... he...?" Luke begins but trails off.

I shake my head. "No. Don't think that. Let our family do what they do. They'll get your mom. She'll be safe." I reassure him the best I can.

"She's.... she's all I've ever had. If he... I don't know what I'll do. I don't... think I... I won't come back from that. I'll cross lines, Arianna." He looks at me. "I won't come back from that."

I run my fingers through his hair. "You know how Ryan won't let Taylor or Chase or even Jason be involved in really bad stuff? Like in London, remember when Taylor came up to the room before Ryan and Alex and Josh?" I don't stop soothingly running my fingers through his. He nods and buries his face in my hair again.

Robby hugs him from the side. The two have become so close lately.

"That's because Ryan won't let them be involved in the truly horrible things he has to do. I know he wants to keep me away from all of the kills, but I'm not stupid. I know what he does." I rest my head on his head. "He'll do the same for you, you know. He won't let you cross those lines. No matter how badly you want to, he won't let you." I tug his hair a little so he looks up at me. "And neither will I. Neither will this family. We'll all understand how badly you want to. We'll understand exactly why. But we won't let you cross into a territory you can't come back from, Luke."

"Hell, forget Ryan. I won't," Robby says. "I know you'd be able to handle it. You're the strongest man I know. But I'd never let you cross lines that would have a permanent effect on your life."

"Thanks for trying to save me, Robby, but I think I can handle it," Luke chuckles.

Robby smiles. "Probably. But I'd still go all protective and refuse to let you cross all those lines."

Luke smiles softly. "You're... probably one of the only people in my life I'd allow to stop me from doing anything." He gives us both a weak, half smile before he settles himself in my hair once more. "No one except my mom has ever been able to do this. To calm me down like this. But you and Robby... You're both like this calming force in a raging hurricane."

I smile. "I always will be. I'm not going anywhere."

Robby reaches up and tugs the short hair at the back of Luke's neck. Almost lovingly. I say nothing as I watch. "So will I. You don't ever need to worry about me going anywhere. You're stuck with me, man."

"None of us are going anywhere, Luke."

He smiles into my neck and looks at Robby. "Thank you."

"Anytime, Luke." Robby smiles as his face flushes slightly. I tilt my head curiously as he looks down to hide it. I briefly think of what Lyric said about hearing Renza, but not only will he find out soon enough, but I'm not sure he'd really care.

I can almost feel something… different in the air between the two of them. There's like this low hum of electricity flowing. I force myself to shake the thought from my head. Whatever I'm feeling between them has to be my pregnancy hormones. The romantic in me. The need for both of them to be happy.

Before I can question it, a knock sounds on the door, and Ryan pokes his head in. I look over my shoulder. He tilts his head to the side before walking away.

"Looks like they have information," I say quietly.

Luke takes a deep breath and lets me go. I stand and offer him a hand. He takes it gratefully. Robby and I lead him out to the common room. Renza is, surprisingly, sitting with everyone else.

"Uh... Ry?" Luke says softly, his voice only being heard by us. Ryan looks at Luke. "If I'm overstepping, I don't mean to." He takes a deep breath and looks back at Ryan as his trembling hand squeezes mine. "I feel kind of stupid and like a little fucking kid for asking, but Arianna is all that's keeping me from losing my mind."

"You need her with you, keep her with you. I doubt I'd be able to tear her away from you if I wanted to. Which I don't. She'll never leave your side if that's where you need her to be."

Luke nearly collapses next to Robby, pulling me on his lap. Robby has settled as close to his side as I think he can manage. Renza glares and scoffs, but I ignore her. A fight with her can wait for another day.

222

Ryan clears his throat, and everyone sits down to listen to him. "As you all know, Luke's mother is in the hands of the enemy. We aren't allowing that. Nick just got the call that his contacts were able to secure her. She's with them and Luke's boss at NYPD's headquarters."

"My pilot said my plane is an hour out. He'll meet her at JFK," Chase says.

Ryan nods. "We have a choice to make. As a family." Ryan looks down at us. I feel Luke hold his breath as he squeezes me tighter. "Honey, I know we have Paris and Rome left on the list, but I think we need to get out of here and regroup. Hawaii wasn't on your wishlist. I have a house in Maui."

I don't hesitate for a second. "Ry, I trust you. You're right. Paris and Rome aren't going anywhere. Just like Buckingham Palace isn't. We need to go somewhere to regroup."

Luke exhales and closes his eyes. "I don't care where we are. I just want my mother safe with us."

Robby squeezes Luke's thigh. I see Ryan raise an eyebrow as his eyes flick to mine, but he says nothing. Robby looks up at Ryan. "I don't know if my opinion matters much, but I think we need to be where we can formulate a fucking plan to take him down. I'm done with this. Arianna should be able to enjoy this and her pregnancy without this shit to stress her out. So should Jessa. And Luke shouldn't have to be worrying about his mother. We need to take Massena and Ambrosio out. Now."

"I'm with him," Jessa agrees. "I'm feeling the stress. I know Arianna is, and poor Luke..."

Taylor nods. "I think we're all in agreement here."

"I know Dave and I aren't really part of this...," Marianne begins shyly.

I shake my head as I meet her eyes. "You're here. You're part of it."

"We protect our own. Arianna's right," Ryan says. "You're part of it. Of us."

"Then my vote is Hawaii," Dave says.

"Let's get the fuck out of here, then. Tonight," Josh says. Ryan looks at me and Luke.

Luke looks up at him, shakily. "It's a long flight from here to Hawaii."

Ryan nods. "Almost two days. We'll need to refuel. We can fly your mom to Chicago. She can stay with my parents and Chase's and Taylor's mom. My second in command is with them. It's a precaution we took when all this shit started."

I look at Luke. "We can schedule her flight to land with ours in Hawaii."

"I'll take care of it as soon as we're in the air," Chase says.

Luke deflates a little. Ryan notices and sits on his other side. He notices Luke's hands are shaking. I hug him as tightly as I can. Robby sits a little closer and starts rubbing his thigh once more. My eyes widen and snap to Ryan's when I feel Luke get hard beneath me.

Ryan's eyes flick to mine in warning before focusing back on Luke. I keep my mouth shut. Ryan pats Luke's shoulder. "Luke. Trust us. She's safe now."

"I don't want Shane to leave her side," Luke nearly whispers.

Taylor nods. "He won't. I'll call him now."

Luke looks at everyone else. "I don't want her traveling by herself."

"She won't be," Lyric says. "We'll make sure of it."

"Luke. She'll be okay. She's okay now. She'll call you as soon as she's on the plane." I look at Chase as Luke's grip tightens. I wince a little and take a deep breath. "Right, Chase?"

"Absolutely. I'll make sure of it."

"Everyone pack up. We leave in an hour," Ryan commands. Everyone hurries to their rooms. Ryan stands with me and Luke. Luke refuses to let me go. Robby refuses to leave his side. "Aria, I'll take care of both of our stuff. I don't think Luke should be alone."

I shake my head. "I don't think he can handle being alone."

Luke shakes his head. "I can't. You and Robby are the only things holding me together." He looks at Ryan and shakes his head again. "I'm sorry, man. I... I'm sorry."

Ryan hugs him. "Don't." He looks at Robby. "I'll have someone help Renza with your stuff." Ryan leans down and kisses me before he heads to our room. Robby can do nothing more than nod. I lead Luke to his room. Robby quickly helps him pack his things.

Within the hour, we're all heading to the airport. Robby is reluctantly riding in another vehicle with Renza and Josh. The Captain of the yacht is under strict orders to sail to Italy where Ryan's yacht will be shipped to Hawaii. Alex is in the front seat of our vehicle with Ryan. Luke has me tucked under his arm.

"I'm sorry I'm acting like this," Luke says quietly.

"Don't be," Alex says.

Ryan takes a breath. "I'd be the same fucking way if it were my mother."

"Fuck. Me, too," Alex agrees.

"If Arianna is what keeps you from losing control, I'm fine with it."

"Speaking of Arianna," Alex starts as he looks back at me. "What the fuck is up with Renza now? I know we talked about it, but ever since you guys announced you're pregnant she's been acting more strange than before. And Josh told us earlier that Lyric heard some shit that didn't make sense to any of us. Is she cheating on Robby?"

I shrug. "I wish I knew. She won't talk to me. Robby seems super suspicious of her. He said she barely talks to him, but she's on her phone all the time. She seems really jealous of me, but I don't know. It just feels like more than that. Especially with what Lyric said she heard."

"I hate to say this because I know she's your best friend, but I think we need to keep an eye on her. I know you were hesitant about some things before with her. Didn't know what to make of it, but I know you wanted to give her the benefit of the doubt." Alex says.

"She's not really acting like a best friend." Luke squeezes my arm gently.

Ryan glances in the mirror at us. "It's something Arianna discussed with me a little while ago. We've been keeping an eye on her because we all seem to have some suspicions about her."

I don't say anything. Instead I bury my face in Luke's chest. He hugs me tighter. "We'll figure it out," he says.

No one really breathes freely until we're in the air and Luke has talked to his mother. After everyone is settled, Ryan and I head to the bedroom. I barely get his t-shirt on before I'm collapsing on the bed, exhausted.

Ryan crawls in next to me and wraps me in his arms. "You've been incredible today making sure your brother has what he needs. Fuck, making sure we all do. What do you need? What can I do for you?"

I start crying. Ryan hugs me tighter. "I'm an e-emotional wr-wreck..."

"You're stressed, beautiful. That on top of being pregnant has to be tough." He kisses me and rests his hand on my stomach. I love when he sleeps with his hand on my stomach.

After a few minutes of letting all of my emotions out through my tears as Ryan hugs me close and allows me to cry, I wipe my eyes and turn in his arms so my back is to him. "I love this position," I whisper.

He kisses the back of my neck and pulls me closer, his arm across my stomach. "When we get to Hawaii, I want you and Jessa looked at. I'll fly in a doctor from New York so you two don't have to transfer care."

"You can do that?"

"Honey, haven't you learned by now that I can do whatever I want?" I laugh the first real laugh I have in what feels like years and hold his arms tighter to my body. "Tell me what you need, Ari."

"Just you. Like this."

He nods and kisses my shoulder.

Safely wrapped in his arms, I'm asleep within seconds.

Chapter Twenty Three

✗ Ryan ✗

I can tell Luke is getting closer and closer to hysteria. He's talked to my mom. He's talked to Shane. He knows she's okay. But I know that until he sees her, until he has his arms around her, he's not going to be okay.

Fuck. I wouldn't be either.

"You've been spending more time with Luke than your own husband, Arianna. Anyone would start to wonder what's happening." Renza isn't wrong. Other than when I forced her to go to bed last night, Arianna hasn't left Luke's side. She's currently in his lap. I truly believe if she weren't, he may have jumped from the plane and swam to Hawaii by now.

I watch Arianna tense. Her grip on the laptop open in her lap tightens. Luke and Josh are both enraptured in her song writing process. It's obvious the distraction is helping Luke.

Robby is on the other side of Luke. It's not lost on me that Robby hasn't left his side either. The two of them have become incredibly close. I see them huddled off to the side together a lot talking, laughing, and joking. It's pretty obvious to me that Luke has a real thing for Robby.

Seeing Arianna's reaction to Robby lightly rubbing Luke's thigh sealed the suspicion. I know Luke got hard.

Judging by how Robby has a pillow over his lap right now, I'm pretty sure the reaction for him is just as strong. Considering that up until right this moment I thought Robby was as straight as can be, his reaction is a little surprising.

Truthfully, though, I'm as much of a romantic as Nicole and Arianna are. I didn't know it until Arianna came into my life, but I want everyone to be as happy as we are. It's fairly obvious to me that Luke and Robby could very well be each other's soulmate.

Robby shakes his head with a sigh. "Luke is her brother, Renz. She's supporting him."

Renza shrugs and gives Arianna a condescending look that makes my blood boil. "I'm just saying... it doesn't look very innocent."

Lyric, who is sitting next to me, crosses her arms over her chest and shoots a withering glare at Renza. "If her husband doesn't have an issue with it and understands what Luke needs, why can't you? Maybe you need to stop paying so much damn attention to her and focus more on what a bitch you're being to someone who's supposed to be your best friend."

Renza's mouth drops, and her eyes turn to Robby. "Are you gonna let her talk to me like that? Say something!"

Robby raises an eyebrow. "You want me to defend you against the things she said, and in the process anger the Mafia King she's practically married to all because she told you the truth? Fuck no. You're fucking crazy."

Josh chuckles. I bite back the laugh as Josh pats Robby on the head and winks. "Good boy."

Robby grins. "Ruff!"

It's the bark that causes us all to lose it and crack up. Renza pouts and lets out a huff as Arianna goes back to her process giggling and not acknowledging Renza at all. Her tenacity and strength to simply let it go is one of the most amazing things about my wife.

I look up as the flight attendant bends down next to my ear. "We're beginning our descent, Mr. Crane. Your vehicles are all at the airport ready and waiting. Your brother just landed. Mr. Shaw's plane was early. Mr. Massena's mother is already at your house."

I nod as she stands and heads to her seat to prepare for landing. "We're starting our descent," I say. "Everyone buckle up. Luke, make sure Arianna is in a seat."

Luke nods, and Josh stands. Arianna takes his seat as he joins me. He sits across from Lyric. I watch as Arianna leans her head against the seat and grips Luke's hand tighter as she closes her eyes. Luke glances at me.

I smile. "She doesn't do well with takeoffs and landings." I mimic putting my arm around Lyric. Luke smiles as he puts his arm around Arianna.

"Thank you," Luke mouths.

When the plane lands, Luke has his seatbelt off and is practically running for the door. As soon as it's open, he's flying down the stairs before any of us have a chance to stop him.

"Luke!" Chase calls after him. He ignores him as we all start getting off the plane. It's obvious he has one thing on his mind, and that's his mother. He searches every vehicle waiting for us on the private air strip before I have a chance to tell him where she is.

"Fuck!" He looks at me as I walk up behind him. "Where the fuck is she? Why isn't she here?"

We can all see he's losing the last shred of control he's managed to hold onto. I touch his arm, trying to get him to calm down enough to listen. He shoves me off with enough force that I actually take a step back out of surprise. His cheeks are wet from tears. He shoves me back again.

"Luke. She's fine. Calm down," I command.

"No! You said she'd be here! Where the fuck is she? Did the plane crash? Did he get to her? Fucking tell me!"

Taylor walks over to help calm him down. He touches his shoulder, but Luke shoves him off just as he did me. "Luke. Stop it. She's fine, man."

I see Arianna walking towards us, but Chase and Jason stop her.

"Don't. Let them calm him down," Jason says.

"He's upset. You might get hurt if he shoves one of them off. They could stumble into you by accident." Chase pulls her back.

Arianna shakes her head. "No. Let me go. He needs me." Arianna hurries over. Luke shoves me back again. Arianna wraps herself around him not even bothering to touch his arm or anything to let him know she's near.. Luke takes a few deep shaky breaths as Arianna hugs him tightly.

Taylor's mouth drops in amazement. "The fuck?"

I smile as Luke holds onto Arianna and looks back up at me. There's still a war happening on his face. "Rico and Shane are with her," I say. "As are my parents and Taylor and Chase's mother. She's already home. That's what I was trying to tell you."

He nods. Arianna takes his hand and pulls him with her to our SUV. Taylor and I follow behind. Robby shoots me a look from the SUV behind ours as he helps Renza in. The concern pouring off him as he watches Arianna climb in behind Luke is enough to knock the wind out of me. I give him a small smile and nod. He takes a deep breath and disappears in the vehicle.

"Okay." Taylor shakes his head. "We'll talk about whatever that was later." He gestures to Robby. "What the hell just happened? How does she calm him down that fast?"

I smile at my girl. "Told you. They have a bond."

"Un-fucking-real." Taylor heads for his vehicle as he shakes his head.

I smile as we all pile into the vehicles. Luke's eyes are darting around like he's looking for some kind of a missile to blow us off the map. I know it's because he wants to make sure his mother is safe, but I'm just as on guard as him. I trust no shadow right now. No glint of light in the distance. Nothing.

"Almost there," Arianna whispers.

"Shit, I feel like I'm losing my mind," Luke whispers back.

"Man, I'm with you," Alex says. "No way I'd be as calm as you if it were my mother. I probably would've knocked Ryan out by now. Twice."

I laugh. "Yeah, right. You couldn't take me ten years ago. You can't take me now."

"Sixteen. And I was only sixteen at that time. I was young and dumb."

"Sixteen years since you started becoming a pain in my ass?"

"Me? You started a war with us."

I give him a cocky grin. "Bullshit. I've never started a war in my damn life. Your douchedick dad started that shit."

"Douche-dick?" Luke asks with a quiet smile.

Alex smiles. "If you had met my dad, you'd understand."

I shake my head. "There are no other words. Good thing he's dead."

"After what he did to Jessa? You better fucking believe he'd be dead if he wasn't already," Alex growls.

"What happened to Jessa?" Luke asks, obviously needing the distraction.

Arianna gives a small sad sigh. "Alex's dad convinced his twin brother to stalk Jessa. There was some kind of mind controlling serum involved. Long story short, Josh, put her in the hospital a few years ago. But Jess thought he was Alex."

"Shit. That's fucked up," Luke breathes.

"Yeah, my dad pretty much had Josh completely brainwashed. We found out he was drugging him with some serum to make him easier to control. He was so fucked up with jealousy over me that had been fed to him from our father, he didn't know what the hell was right and wrong anymore. Fuck, he didn't even know who he really was anymore. By the time it was over, and he'd come out of it and realized all of the shit that was happening, he became one dangerous motherfucker."

"Helped us take down their father. Burned their house to the ground," I say with a grin.

"Josh took over the mafia like he was always meant to do," Alex says.

"And Alex and I have been helping him out every step of the way. He turned it legit like I did. The Lucinio Mafia is thriving. They're just as big as I am now. And getting bigger by the day." I can't hide my pride.

Luke looks up at both of us shaking his head incredulously. "And there's no... animosity or power struggle between the two of you?"

I shake my head. "Nope. When it comes down to it, it's about family. For both of us. Not money."

Alex shrugs. "It's about making this world a better place for our family. Ryan and I have been as close as brothers for a long time. He's become just as close to Josh. Really it's just two families that have come together to take down some really bad guys."

I nod. "We work with law enforcement. Take some people out. They turn their heads because they know we have the power to do what they can't. So long as they help us out and keep it quiet."

Luke nods. "Shane mentioned it's pretty nice and fucking easy when you clean up after yourself."

Alex laughs. "They get big busts. It all looks legit. We get to help out by making the people they can't make shit stick to disappear."

I can hear Arianna's breathing start to slowly even out. I realize she's fast asleep.

Luke chuckles. "That didn't take long. Arianna's out."

I nod. "She hasn't been sleeping well. She's really worried about Renza."

"Yeah, I don't trust that girl." Alex glances back at Arianna.

I give a troubled smile. "This is new. When Arianna was having trouble in school with the bullies, Renza was right there with her. It was Renza who finally called me."

"Robby told me she's been on her phone a lot. And that she's been sleeping with it. Like she's trying to hide it." Luke looks down at Arianna and shifts her so she's more comfortable against him.

"Yeah, he mentioned that to me, too, when I went to the bedroom to grab a blanket for Arianna on the plane." I glance in the mirror at the vehicle behind us. I can't see who it is exactly, but judging from where the glow is coming from, I'd say Renza is once again on her phone.

"We need to watch her. There's been something about this entire thing that doesn't make sense to me at all. And with Arianna coming to me a little while ago concerned about her behavior, it sort of just sealed it for me." Alex turns and glances back. I'm sure he sees the same thing I do as he turns back around and shakes his head.

"Me, too," Luke agrees.

I'm with them. But I'm curious what they think. If they're following the same path that I am. "What are you thinking? What makes it fucked up to you?"

"How do the scouts know where Arianna is going to be? Athens is a pretty big place. Lots to do. Same with London," Alex says.

"Exactly. How did they know we'd be at the Tower of London?" Luke asks.

I shrug, acting like I really don't know. "Her wishlist."

"I've seen her wishlist. London, all she had was Buckingham Palace. Greece? Just the Acropolis or whatever that temple is. How did they know we were at the market?" Luke asks.

Alex nods. "How did they know what time you'd be at the Tower?"

I nod, pleased they are on the same path as me. "Think I have a leak?"

Alex shakes his head. "Not with the guards."

I meet Luke's eyes in the mirror. "Is she still sleeping?"

Luke looks down at Arianna and gives her shoulder a little squeeze. She doesn't move. "She's out."

"You'll have to wait a few extra seconds when we get to the house before you dart for your mother. I don't want her woken up."

"It's fine. I don't either. She's been my fucking angel through this. Time for me to be hers. I won't jump out of the car until you have her."

I nod. Time to come clean. Tell them what I've been questioning for so long. Why I've been so intent on observing Renza. Having people with her at all times. "You both think Renza is the leak."

Alex doesn't hesitate. "Fuck yes."

Luke shrugs. "I honestly don't know. Something is going on. I hate how she's treating my sister, but I'll reserve judgment until I have the evidence."

"Dude. You're just like Taylor. You're so good, it makes me sick." Alex turns and winks at Luke before he smiles and laughs.

Luke chuckles and smiles as I turn into the long driveway. I take a deep breath. "You both have asked me several times why Josh seems to always be around Renza. Since she's annoying and bitchy and we all know he can't stand her. And also since Lyric is here, why he's not stuck to her side like glue. The reason is because he and I have had suspicions about Renza for a long while. Josh mentioned his concerns shortly before Robby approached me. He made the decision to keep an eye on her, and Lyric completely agreed with him. Lyric is quiet, and Renza ignores her most of the time, so we've even had her watching her. Then Robby mentioned a few things before the wedding. Things that had me questioning a lot of things about her even more than I already was. A few weeks ago, Arianna came to me with some concerns of her own. That sealed it for me."

"So you agree with me. Renza is the leak," Alex says.

I shake my head. "I don't know. I don't have any solid proof. Josh hasn't caught her doing anything. Robby hasn't either. I haven't. Arianna hasn't. Lyric caught that conversation, but she didn't hear much of it. I do believe that something is going on. And if I had to just go off instinct? Then yes. I think Renza is the leak. Why? Don't know. But she needs to be watched. Arianna is not to be alone with her. Renza is not to be alone at all."

"She's been alone, though," Luke points out. "A lot. She shuts herself in the room."

"I know. But we have to change that. Robby is with her as much as he can stand, but it's pretty obvious to me that being around her is making him physically ill. Whenever I see him in the morning he looks like shit. I'm getting to the point of having cameras installed to watch her just so he doesn't have to."

I watch as Luke bites his lip and focuses on what's coming into view ahead of us as I drive through the gate. My house is the most modern, sprawled out mansion on the entire island. It sits on the cliffs overlooking the Pacific Ocean and is so hidden from the road that if a person didn't know where they were going, they'd never know it was here.

Luke's eyes widen. "Shit."

"Crane just loves to show off," Alex teases.

I laugh quietly. "Fuck you. You own six houses."

Luke nearly chokes. "Six? Fuck. I thought Ryan lived lavishly."

Alex shrugs and grins widely. "He does. Just not as lavishly as me."

I laugh quietly again as I park. "You... are an asshole."

"You should see what Josh has. He makes mine look tiny." Alex laughs as we both get out of the SUV. I open the back door and gently extract Arianna. As soon as I have her, I step back.

Luke bolts. He almost sprints to the house. I can't help but smile as I watch because before he can reach the door, someone opens it. Shane stands in the doorway. Luke's mother is behind him. Shane smiles and moves aside. Instantly, Luke's world is righted.

"Mom." Luke stops. Sonya Redstone runs and leaps in his arms.

"Luke! My baby! My baby..." She sobs into his neck.

"Are you okay, mom?" he asks her.

234

"I really don't understand what's going on. Shane tried to explain, but..." She reaches up and palms his cheek as Luke sets her on the ground. "I know you've always tried to make sure I'm safe and protect me, but I need an explanation, Luke."

"Yeah, I'd like one, too," Shane says, leaning against the doorframe and crossing his arms over his chest.

I walk up to his side with Arianna in my arms. "Take them to your room. Upstairs. Second door on your left. They'll be on either side of you so they're close. We're in the master bedroom at the end of the hall."

He nods. "Thanks, Ryan."

"You're welcome." I nod to his mother and take Arianna inside and upstairs to our bedroom.

Luke was right. Arianna is out like a light. I gently lay her down and get one of my t-shirts for her to sleep in. I carefully get her out of her other clothes and in the t-shirt before I tuck her in. I kiss her forehead and smile at the adorable moan she makes in her sleep.

A few minutes later, I'm sitting downstairs in my living room. Alex plops down on the couch next to me. I glance over at him. "Everyone settled?"

"Taylor and Nicole are upstairs. So is Chase and Breetana. Luke, Shane and his mom are up there. Your parents are in their normal room. Dave and Marianne are next to them. Me, Josh and Lyric, Nick, and Rico are all in the rooms near Renza and Robby. Robby is in there with her."

I nod and scrub my hands down my face as my brothers start trickling into the room. When they're all seated, I look around at them and take a deep breath. "Look. I'll level with all of you. We have a problem. I can't sit here and tell you with certainty that it's Renza, but things don't add up." I say the words quietly glancing towards the hallway Renza and Robby are in.

"We have Robby in there with her right now trying to find out anything he can," Alex says. "In the meantime, just observe."

"And she stays the fuck away from Arianna," I say dangerously.

"At the risk of sounding ignorant," Chase begins. "What the fuck is happening? I thought we thought she was just jealous."

Jason leans back in the chair and crosses his arms. "How long have you thought Renza is leaking information?"

Leave it to Jason of all people to completely call me out. I smile tiredly. "I can't be sure, Jas. I'm just suspicious."

Josh looks around and stands. "It makes sense. I've been suspicious of her since before the wedding. Her behavior says one thing while her words say something completely different. It's why I make sure to stay close whenever we are out as a group. It's why I asked Lyric to help me observe her."

Alex pats my shoulder. "Go be with your girl. I think you both need sleep. You can trust us. We have a plan to stay up in shifts. Renza will be watched all night."

"Robby is in there. He'll know if anything happens," Nick says.

"I don't like being kept in the dark. Knowing things is my job. I don't like not knowing something that could affect my wife." I drop my head in my hands and rub my eyes.

I refuse to cry in front of any of them. I'd never tell them that being so fucking suspicious and not being able to prove any of it is taking it's toll. I've spent more sleepless nights choking back tears than I care to admit, even to myself.

"Ry, don't. Rely on your family. That's what we're here for," Taylor says as he stands.

"I know." I stand with him wanting nothing more than Arianna to be tucked safely in my arms. "I know. Just..." I look around the room.

"We know, Ry. Anything raises a red flag, you'll be the first to know," Josh assures me. "Go to bed. You need it."

I don't waste time as I head up to the bedroom taking the stairs two at a time. The overwhelming urgency to have Arianna close overpowers everything else. I've never allowed anything to get in the way of protecting my family, but the words of both my father and Taylor slam into me as I crawl into bed with my wife.

I need to rely on my family. For the first time in my life, I don't think I'm strong enough to handle the looming battle on my own.

Chapter Twenty Four

☒ Arianna ☒

Coming out of sleep lately is like coming out of some strange alternate universe. My dreams are so vivid that I almost feel like I've lived them. It takes me several moments to acclimate myself to my actual surroundings as the dream fades away.

After a few moments, I'm back in my own little Heaven with Ryan pressed against my back. One of his arms is acting as a pillow. The other is holding me tightly, his arm protectively across my stomach. His head is buried in my hair. I can feel all of his perfect ridges against me. It makes me smile. Just his touch makes my entire body want him. Crave him. I feel like I'm on fire with need.

I begin to turn towards him but stop. The all too familiar nausea sets in. I suddenly fear any movement at all. I take a deep breath, but that's all it takes. I run to the bathroom stripping off Ryan's t-shirt along the way, and slide across the floor to the toilet.

"No, no, no…," I whimper.

Very suddenly, I'm throwing up. I hate throwing up. Throwing up makes me cry. Crying makes me throw up more. This morning sickness is a bitch. A fucking hideous asshole.

I hear Ryan enter the bathroom. I can see him walking towards me, but I put up a hand. "Don't. Please don't come closer."

"Baby, let me at least hold your hair back. I hate seeing you like this."

"Please, Ryan. Don't. I'm begging you." I can't let him near me. There's something he doesn't know. Something I haven't told him because I don't want to hurt him.

"Aria, I'm not letting you go through this alone. Why you fight me every fucking morning when you know I'm going to do it anyway is something I'll never understand."

He kneels down next to me and pulls my hair back as he rubs my back. My stomach turns. I start throwing up all over again. Tears stream down my face. I hate what I'm about to say, but I can't handle it anymore. I've fought it for too long.

"Ryan, please go. It's your cologne!"

"What?"

"The scent of your cologne in the morning makes me sick!"

He slowly lets go of my hair and stands up, backing away. I hate myself. He doesn't say anything as he leaves the bathroom.

After a few minutes of composing myself, cleaning off the subtle scent of Ryan on my skin from his t-shirt, and brushing my teeth, I attempt to steal myself for my husband as I leave the bathroom. Ryan is sitting on the edge of the bed. He looks heartbroken.

I nearly break down in tears. "I'm so sorry, Ryan. I didn't want to tell you. I didn't want to hurt you. I've been fighting through it. And it's only in the morning! It doesn't happen anytime else." My lip quivers as he looks up at me.

"Is this why you force me to be near Taylor in the morning? His cologne overpowers mine?"

I nod and wipe a tear away. "I'm so sorry. Please don't hate me. I love being surrounded by you and your scent usually. It's just in the morning."

He nods and looks down at his hands a moment before he looks back up at me. His eyes linger on my chest. I look down completely forgetting I'm wearing nothing but panties.

"You're lucky I love you. Because it's taking all of my willpower not to pin you against that wall while I fuck you."

His words send white hot heat to every part of my body. For just a second, I wonder if I can fight the nausea and jump him like I want to.

I start walking towards him. He watches my every movement with an intense hungry look reserved just for me. The closer I get to him, the more I want him, but the nausea overpowers the desire. Eventually, it wins out, and I stop, giving him a sad look.

"I'm so sorry."

"It's okay, sweet girl. I've heard stuff like this can happen. Get dressed. Meet me downstairs. I'm going to take the first soapless shower of my life. And then you and I are going to figure out what kind of cologne I can wear."

I've already moved away from him and to my suitcase that I haven't unpacked yet. Ryan heads for the bathroom. "After breakfast."

"Of course after breakfast, baby. I wouldn't dream of depriving a pregnant woman of her bacon and cream cheese bagel craving."

My mouth waters at the thought. I moan. Ryan laughs as he closes the door. I quickly get dressed.

I walk down the stairs with my hand on my stomach, feeling for any kind of a bump. I know it's too soon, but I really want to feel something. Anything. Other than a little firmness in my stomach, though, I feel nothing.

I walk into the kitchen, slightly disappointed. Taylor is sitting at the counter watching me. "You told him yet?"

"I didn't have a choice." I sit next to him and frown into the cup of milk he hands to me. "He came in to hold my hair back like the perfect husband he is, and I lost it all over again. It was worse than ever. So I blurted it out, then threw up more because I knew how much it hurt him."

"Yeah, guys don't like being told that their scent repulses their wife," he teases as he gently elbows me.

I laugh as I take a sip of my milk. "I also don't think they like hearing their brother's scent calms their wife's stomach down instantaneously."

Taylor laughs. "Probably not. Where is he? We need to figure some shit out."

"Taking a soapless shower."

"What? Why? I thought it was just his cologne."

I shrug sadly. "I don't know what it is. It's just his scent in the morning. So, he's taking a soapless shower. Then, we're going to figure out what he can wear and shower with that doesn't make me sick."

"Damn. I'm glad I didn't make Nikki sick when she was pregnant."

"In all fairness, she was long past morning sickness when you met."

"I suppose that's true."

Taylor and I both look towards the stairs as Ryan comes down. He looks amazing in his jeans and long sleeve, pale blue shirt. He takes a couple steps towards me.

"Well?" he asks hopefully. I take a couple of sniffs.

Taylor gets up and heads for the coffee pot to refill his cup. He laughs. "Man, it has to suck knowing you make your wife sick." He shoots Ryan a teasing grin.

Ryan glares. "How the fuck do you know, but I didn't?"

I bite my lip. "I sort of had to tell him and Nikki something."

"I had a feeling and forced it out of her when I noticed she'd stand near me and deeply inhale whenever you were anywhere near her. She made me and Nikki take a blood vow of secrecy." Taylor winks at me, and I laugh.

"You know, I told Alex he was a pain in my ass yesterday. I was wrong. It's you. You're the pain in my ass." Ryan tries to glare, but I can see the corners of his eyes crinkle.

"You love me. When are we meeting with everyone to figure this bullshit out?" Taylor asks.

"I need to make Arianna her bagel and Jessa her sausage skillet. Then I'll be out."

"I'll get everyone gathered."

"Thanks."

"I think you should just make a giant skillet for everyone." I look up at him.

"You do, do you?" He leans down to kiss me, putting both hands on the counter behind me.

I smile widely when he pulls away because for the first time in days, his scent doesn't send me to the bathroom. Or to Taylor. "I do. I love watching you cook."

"Well, I'd hate to deprive my beautiful wife of anything that makes her happy." He kisses me once more before heading to the fridge to gather what he needs for breakfast.

"Do you have a helicopter here?" Watching the contours of the muscles in his back and arms as he begins scrambling eggs forces me to cross my legs and squeeze them tightly.

He turns, seeing my movement, and smiles before he goes back to cooking. "No. The one on the yacht is the chopper I kept here. My other one is home in Manhattan." He pours the eggs into an oven pan and some into a fry pan. He quickly starts chopping things while both bacon and sausage fry in other pans.

My husband is a beast in the kitchen. Huge turn on. Crossing my legs is doing nothing to help me out. I really do crave him. I clear my throat and sneak my hand between my legs over my jeans. I'm not completely crazy, but I need extra pressure, or I'm going to jump him right here.

"I was just wondering. I really want to see some volcanoes." I squirm against my hand as I rub my legs together. Ryan throws the vegetables into the eggs and puts them in the oven. He throws the rest into the fry pan and puts my bagel into the microwave.

He glances at me and shakes his head with a grin. "I can rent one if you want. The yacht should be back in a few days. Chopper is with it."

I remove my hand but leave my legs crossed as he takes the bagel out. I let out a little moan as he puts cream cheese on my bagel. Then bacon. He cuts it in half and walks over to me, setting the plate in front of me. He slips his arms around me from behind.

He drops one hand between my legs. I gasp. He kisses my neck and licks up to my ear so he can whisper in it. "I don't think there's anything sexier than you touching yourself in this kitchen while you watch me cook."

"I just can't control myself around you. It's embarrassing." My pouting turns quickly to surprise as Ryan pops the button on my jeans and slips his hand down my panties. "Ryan! No. What if someone walks in?" I keep my voice low as he slips two fingers inside me. I lean against him. His other arm across my chest holds me tight to him.

"You want me to stop?"

"Oh my God, no."

"Then be quiet and let me work. Not a sound, or I stop. You know the rule."

I nod as his incredible fingers relieve all of the tension between my legs. He expertly brings me closer and closer to my peak. "Mmm... Ryan. Oh my God," I moan almost silently.

He kisses my head and cheek. I turn my head to him. He kisses my lips. He dips his tongue in my mouth, swallowing my moan as he sets his thumb against my bud with the perfect amount of pressure. My hips jerk. I grind against his fingers and thumb.

"Come for me, my girl."

"Ryan..." I collapse against him as I pulse and clench around his fingers. He sends me careening over the edge in seconds, his fingers slowly continuing to glide inside and out of me until my orgasm ends. He pulls away from my lips as he slowly removes his fingers. He puts both of them in his mouth and sucks them clean.

"Most delicious breakfast ever." He winks at me as he walks back to his culinary masterpiece.

"Shit," I whisper, biting my lip. I button my jeans and smile as I start eating my bagel.

"Breakfast. Meeting. And then you and I are finding a cologne that doesn't make you sick."

XXX

Later that night, everyone is gathered in the family room talking, laughing and joking. I'm sitting next to Ryan and notice Renza is nowhere in sight. As everyone jokes and laughs, I decide it's time to sit down and have a conversation with her. She's my best friend after all. We've been through so much together.

I kiss Ryan on the cheek and stand up. He gives me a light tap on the ass. I grin at him as I head to Renza and Robby's room. Outside, I take a deep breath and quietly open the door. Renza is sprawled on the bed naked. Her laptop is open in front of her. I put my hand over my mouth and close the door so that it's only open a crack, but so I can still hear and see her.

"This is what you like?" She slides her hand down her body and starts fingering herself.

"You know what I like. Fuck, you're so sexy," a deep unknown male voice says.

Renza giggles. I quietly close the door. I turn, my hand still over my mouth, and run directly into a solid brick wall. Strong arms encircle my waist to keep from falling.

"Holy shit. You okay? What happened?" Luke asks quietly. I burst into tears, staying as quiet as I can and bury my face in Luke's chest. "Arianna, look at me. What happened?"

I drag him into the nearest room and shut the door. "She's... Renza... She's in there..."

"Sweetheart, I know. But what happened? Tell me what's going on. Do I need to get Ryan?"

"She's fingering herself."

Luke chokes as I try to get the words out. "Air, I -"

"On the computer with someone."

"What?"

I take a deep, steadying breath, swallowing the shock. "She's on the computer with someone. A guy. She started fingering herself. The guy was telling her he liked it. He sounded older. I didn't recognize the voice." I nearly throw up again and rush to the bathroom. Luke follows and holds back my hair as I lose the entire contents of my stomach.

"Fuck, sweetheart. Do you need Ryan?" I nod my head as I heave. "Okay. I'll text him. I don't want to leave you." He continues to hold my hair as he texts Ryan. I'm trying to take deep breaths. "He's on his way, honey."

I start dry heaving into the toilet. Luke rubs my back. Out of the corner of my eye I see Ryan come into the bathroom and close the door.

"What happened?" Ryan kneels next to me and rubs my back as Luke keeps my hair out of my face. I'm still trying to take deep breaths to stop the heaving. I'm trying to make sense of what I saw, but I can't.

"She walked in on Renza having some kind of virtual sex with someone on her laptop. Says it sounded like an older guy. She couldn't recognize the voice," Luke explains. I silently thank him.

"Fuck. Robby suspected. So did Lyric. Go get him." Ryan kisses my shoulder. I lean into him. He pulls me into his lap and wraps his arms around me. "Shh..."

"What is going on?" I whisper into his neck. I really don't understand.

"Honey, I wish like fuck I could answer that for you. But I really don't know. I'll figure it out. I promise."

Robby and Luke come back to the bathroom. Luke closes the door. I look up at Robby and nearly start crying again.

"Air, are you okay? What happened?" he asks, kneeling next to me.

"Renza... She... I saw her..." I can't find the words to finish, so I turn to Ryan and rest my head on his shoulder.

"She saw Renza video chatting with someone," Luke says.

"Who?" Robby asks as he rubs my knee.

"I don't know." I slouch miserably.

"It wasn't innocent. She was touching herself," Ryan says.

"And was naked." Luke makes a quiet gagging noise.

Robby scrubs his hand down his face. "Fuck me. I knew it. I've been trying to catch her. She's been distant. I've caught her a few times on her phone. She hides it as soon as she notices."

"Baby, did she see you?" Ryan asks. I shake my head. "Good. Don't say anything. Act like you saw nothing."

I look up at him. "Okay."

He looks down at me. "We think Renza may be talking to your father. It explains how he keeps showing up wherever we seem to go."

Robby sighs. "Or Chad. Which is who *I* think she's talking to. Especially after what you just saw."

Luke kneels down. "We need Robby to confirm it, but he hasn't been able to get her phone."

Robby squeezes my knee. "I don't want to raise her suspicions before we figure out what the hell she's doing."

I shake my head. "It wasn't Chad. I know his voice. This voice was older. I know my dad's voice, too. It wasn't him."

We all look at each other. I can feel the uneasiness growing in the room, but what I don't like is that I can feel it the most in Ryan. Ryan has always been the strong one. The most sure of everything. I trust him. We all do. But I don't know what will happen if the man we all look to for guidance is unsure and uneasy.

I take a few moments to steady myself as Ryan buries his face in my hair, lightly kissing my neck. I've come to learn that Ryan's way of calming himself and centering himself in situations he feels he can't control is by focusing on me. He's always been the strong one for me. All of us. I'll be damned if I fall apart on him when he needs me to be his rock like he does now..

Chapter Twenty Five

✕ Ryan ✕

(Two Days Later)

It's been a couple of days since Arianna saw Renza. I can see how hard it is for her to deal with the betrayal. Whenever Renza comes into a room, Arianna leaves it. I had to talk to her about it after the third time. Renza was starting to pick up on it. I know she hates being anywhere near her after finding out the truth, but she can't let on that she knows anything. She has made the effort to stay in the room if Renza enters for just enough time to make it believable before she leaves and finds something else to do.

I reach over and make sure Arianna is strapped into her seat in the helicopter I rented for the volcano tour I'm taking her on. She smiles at me a little nervously.

"It's just like Greece, beautiful."

"But it's not your helicopter."

"Doesn't need to be. Flies the same." I tighten her seatbelt and run my hand across her stomach. "You both are gonna be just fine."

"It's not that I don't trust you. I just know you make sure your helicopters, planes, and vehicles are all serviced and good to go."

"And you're afraid this company doesn't?"

She bites her lip and looks out the window. "Maybe we should just wait until your helicopter is back."

"Honey, I trust this company. I've used them more times than I can tell you. I bought my chopper from this company. I promise you'll be safe, but I'll never make you do something you don't want to."

She takes a deep breath and smiles as she takes my hand. I bring it to my lips to kiss it. "I trust you."

"Good. I need both hands to take off, but then I'm all yours."

She lets go of my hand but puts hers on my thigh. I flip a few switches, and the helicopter blades whir to life. Moments later, we're in the air. I feel Arianna relax as she takes in the island from above.

"Wow. It's breathtaking."

"Only going to get better. Remember a couple years ago when that big volcano was erupting?"

Her eyes widen. "Oh my God. It wouldn't stop. I felt so bad for everyone."

"I know. I remember watching the news for hours on end with you about it. You wouldn't let me change the channel."

"Because we were watching history unfold."

I smile. "Remember what you told me?"

"That I wanted to see it." She smiles as I take her hand and effortlessly steer the helicopter through the air.

"I know it's active and stuff, but they actually say it's technically still erupting."

Her eyes widen even more. "Seriously?"

"Yep. You can still see the magma and everything." I kiss her palm. She smiles and chuckles. "What?"

"Nothing." She shakes her head and blushes.

I laugh. "What? Tell me."

"It's just... it's lava."

"What?" I tilt my head, slightly confused.

Arianna looks at me and smiles softly. "Magma is what it is when it's underground. When it reaches the surface, it becomes lava."

I look at her and shake my head as I chuckle. "You're so smart, baby. Why? What's the difference between the two?" She loves when she gets to explain things. It makes her feel special.

Her smile gets wider. "Well, magma comes from an Italian word that means a thick, pasty substance. That's how molten rock is when it's within the Earth. Lava, which is another Italian word, means to slide. That's what molten rock does once it reaches the surface. Even though it's still within the chamber, it's still sliding around like it would when it erupts."

"School wasn't hard at all for you, was it?"

"No. Not really, but you knew that. That's why I started taking so many advanced classes and college prep classes. And even they weren't really a challenge."

"I've always thought you were smart. I couldn't believe some of the homework you brought home."

She smiles and squeezes my hand. "When you brought me to your house the night my father killed my mom, that was it for me. I've never felt more at home. I felt like that's where I belonged."

"That's where you do belong."

"It's not really the house, Ry. It's you. You're home for me. Wherever you are is where I belong. I didn't really know then that I was in love with you. I knew the night of the fire at Renza's. But if I'm being honest? I was probably in love with you that night."

I smile and hit the hover button. I unbuckle my seatbelt and lean over to kiss her before I unbuckle her seatbelt and pull her into my lap.

"Ryan! What are you doing?"

I kiss her neck as I hold her close. We both look out the window. "This is Lehua Island. It's an inactive volcano that's become part of the ocean."

"Oh, wow. I've heard of it but never actually seen it."

"There's a couple of them. There's another one around here that sailboats actually use as sort of a safe harbor. I don't really know why, though. The Coast Guard actually warns against using it for that." I keep her in my lap and flip hover off.

"I should go back to my seat," she says nervously.

"Aria. Trust me. Take the controls."

"Are you crazy? No way!"

I chuckle and take her hands. I put them on the controls and put my hands over hers. "I won't let go."

She shakily grips the controls. After a few moments, she's smiling. "Holy God. Am I actually flying this?"

"Sort of." I gently move the controls to the right to fly around the island. "On the other side of the island is the other one I was talking about."

We round the island and Arianna gasps when she sees the giant volcano. "It's beautiful."

"This one is called the Molokini Crater. And if you look up on the cliff there, you'll see our house."

"Wow. This is amazing. You know a lot about all of this."

I smile. "I studied up. Have to keep up with you somehow."

Arianna laughs as we continue to fly. After a few minutes, I let go of her hands.

"No! What are you doing?"

"I'm right here, baby. You got this." I drop one hand to her waist and rest the other on her stomach. "What do you think we're having? A boy or a girl?"

"A girl. I can feel it. What about you?"

"Definitely a boy. We don't have girls in my family."

She laughs. "Well, our baby will be the first."

"You're so sure, huh? Have you thought of names?"

"Bella Marie."

"Like Isabella?"

She shakes her head. "Nope. Just Bella."

"Well, it's a gorgeous name. Too bad we'll be having a boy. Christopher Ethan."

"I love that you're paying homage to Jason by using his middle name and to your father by using his name. But she's definitely a girl."

I laugh. She's incredibly fucking smart. I love that I didn't need to tell her where I got the name. She just knew. I kiss her shoulder. She shivers.

"You're doing great, baby, but I need you to buckle back in. We're coming up on the active volcanoes. It can get a little shaky sometimes. I might have to maneuver us away quickly."

"O-okay."

"Don't worry. You're safe. Both of you." I rub her stomach as she moves back to her seat and buckles in. I take her hand and entwine my fingers with hers again.

"Oh, wow. There's no lava in this one. Is this one inactive? Is that water?"

"It baffles scientists. It's an active volcano, but there's heated water pooling at the bottom. The temperature is actually as hot as the temperature lava would be if it were there in place of the water. That water should evaporate."

"I don't even know what to say. Seeing that is just so... cool."

I smile. "I need my hand back for the next part. It's gonna be a little rough." I kiss her hand as she takes a deep breath. She holds onto her seat as I navigate. "This is Kilauea."

She smiles so widely, I fear her face may actually break. "Oh my God! Ryan! Really? This is the one that erupted?"

"Yep. Let me get a little closer." The controls shake a little as I drop us lower so she can get a better look.

"I hate to say this, but it's beautiful. It really is. How can something so beautiful be so destructive?"

"It really is an incredible creation." The helicopter starts shaking a little more as the wind from the volcano's atmosphere hits it. Arianna gasps. I pull up steadily. "Seen enough? Ready to head home?"

"Mmhmm." We fly in silence for a little while as we head back to the helicopter airfield. "Thank you for doing this, Ryan. I've always wanted to do this. Volcanoes are just incredible."

"Breetana said the same thing when I took her and Chase up."

"Doesn't Chase have his own helicopter?"

"He does, but they wanted a tour. They were going to hire someone. I just took them up myself instead."

"You're amazing."

I laugh as I start to land. Arianna is beaming with happiness. It's all I want. Just that beautiful smile back on her face.

Taylor, Robby, and Rico are following me as I drop guards at specific places around my property.

"You're absolutely positive she was talking to Chad." I look down at Robby.

"Yes, sir. A hundred percent. She fell asleep with her phone, but I was able to get it away from her this time without waking her up. No way he isn't coming here," Robby says.

Taylor scoffs. "No way he isn't already here."

I shake my head. "It doesn't make sense. Arianna said the voice wasn't Chad's. So what the fuck is she doing talking to him?"

"I don't know, boss. But that's who she was texting. It didn't look sexual in the slightest, though. Just a bunch of bullshit regular friendly conversation and those numbers."

I growl low. The numbers he's talking about are coordinates. How the fuck she knew any of the coordinates to where we were or the coordinates of where we are now baffles the fuck out of me.

"Did you figure out where those coordinates she sent tonight are?" Taylor asks Robby.

"It pinpoints our exact location. The house," Robby says.

I shake my head again. "She can't know that."

"She can if she's getting fed information from a track on her phone," Taylor says. "GPS is a wonderful thing for those in law enforcement."

I look at him incredulously. "Who the fuck would she be getting information from that has a track on her phone?"

He shrugs. "Don't know. But it's about the only thing that makes sense to me. If it were Arianna, I'd say she knows how to find the coordinates of where she is herself. She's fucking smart. I know she could figure it out. But this isn't Arianna. She has to be being fed the information."

Robby shakes his head. "No. Renza isn't on the same level as Arianna when it comes to that. She failed a lot of her classes. I don't, to this day, know how she graduated. The only ones she did well in were the ones she didn't have to work. There's no way she could go out there and figure out the coordinates. Not on her own."

"Exactly. Someone is feeding her the information," Taylor says. "Someone has to be tracking her phone. And if it's Massena or Ambrosio, she'd have no reason to give them coordinates. They have them."

I stop. "You think there's someone else involved?" It's like a sucker punch to my throat. It's what I've been thinking for a long time, but hearing it validated by someone else right now is both vindicating and scary as all hell.

Taylor turns and looks at me. "It just seems to be the only thing that makes sense to me, Ryan. You can't honestly tell me you think a small mafia like Ambrosio's can combine with another small one like Massena's and have any hope of taking you out. They have to know how big you are. There has to be a bigger force at play. Someone is manipulating this."

"Wait. I just got a text from Renza." We all stop as Robby reads the text out loud. "She just says she's coming out." Robby shakes his head. "What the hell? What the fuck is she talking about?"

"I…" I look back up at my house. Something isn't sitting right with me. Nothing has for a long time, but something about all of this has all of my instincts in overdrive.

"No way. How did they get through?" Robby asks. "There's too many guards. A fucking fence all over the property.

It hits me so hard I actually get dizzy. "I don't think they did."

Robby swallows hard. "Renza."

Rico grabs my arm and points. "Is that...?"

The bile rises in my stomach. "Shit."

"Smoke?" Robby chokes out. But I can barely hear him over the blood rushing to my ears. We all start sprinting towards the house.

"All the girls are still in there!" Taylor yells.

"I know!" I can't breathe. My entire family is in that house. My wife and baby.

The house is almost fully engulfed by the time we get there. I don't know how the fuck that's possible, but I'm witnessing it with my own fucking eyes.

When we reach it, I see everyone is in the driveway in front of the house. Taylor runs to Nicole.

"Where the fuck is Arianna?" Robby yells over the roar of the flames.

"I don't see her!" Rico yells just as loudly.

I don't hesitate. I run towards the flames. "Aria! Arianna!"

"Stop! Ryan! Fucking stop!" I hear Jason, but I don't listen. I have to get to her.

"Ryan!" Chase yells.

"Holy shit! Stop!" Taylor commands.

Strong hands grab me and drag me back just as I'm nearing the door. "Get off!" I fight whoever it is off only to be grabbed by someone else. Then more hands are on me dragging me back. "Get off! Get the fuck off me!"

"Stop it! You can't fucking go in there!" Taylor says, yanking me back again.

"You'd do the same thing if it were Nicole! She fucking freezes around fire, Taylor!"

"Son of a bitch," Jason grunts as he helps the others in keeping me from running into the flames. I fight them as hard as I can, but I can't break free.

"Let me go! I have to save her!" At that moment, a part of my house explodes with such force, it throws all four of us back. Someone is screaming. It takes me a second to realize it's me. "Arianna!" I get up and run towards the house again just as Luke appears in the door carrying Arianna. "Fuck! Thank fuck." I rush to him and help him get away from the flames.

Luke drops to his knees in front of me when we reach everyone else. He sets Arianna on the ground. He starts coughing as he begins compressions on Arianna. "She's... not breathing." Luke starts coughing harder, then collapses on the ground.

"I got him!" Nick says, appearing from nowhere like a fucking saint. "Alex! Call 911 back! Make sure they have an ambulance coming! Josh! Get over here and start CPR on Arianna."

Josh reluctantly leaves Lyric's side. Alex pulls her into him. Josh pushes me aside as he kneels next to me and starts compressions on Arianna. "Tilt her head back, plug her nose, and give her two breaths when I tell you to," he commands. I nod. "Now!"

I do as I'm directed. Josh starts compressions again. I hear sirens in the distance. Everything is going in slow motion. Josh's voice seems so far away. The breaths I give Arianna seem to take an insane amount of time.

Time.

That's all I need. Just more time.

Time with my wife. My family. Time to meet my baby. Our baby.

When the paramedics arrive, Josh pulls me off Arianna. He forces me to look at him. "She's in good hands. She'll be okay."

The paramedics hook up an oxygen mask to her. They hook something up to her chest. Everything around me stops. All I care about is her.

"She's pregnant! What are you doing?" I yell. Arianna chooses that moment to wake up. She coughs and sputters. "Oh God. Thank God!" I crawl to her and pull her into my arms. She's crying. "I'm here, baby. I'm right here. I've got you." I rock with her in my arms. "I've got you."

Our entire family is gathered around as the firefighters put out the flames. Luke has also woken up and is being tended to by the paramedics. I hold Arianna tightly.

My mission was to take out Arianna's father, Chad, and Stephen Ambrosio. Renza-fucking-Gregorson and her mystery virtual fuck buddy have just been added to the list.

Chapter Twenty Six

✕ Arianna ✕

Beeping. I hear beeping. I heard it the last time I woke up, too. I hated it, so I went back to sleep. Ryan's arms are wrapped tightly around me. I try to snuggle into him, but the beeping is so aggravating. I try to get up, but Ryan pulls me into him.

I open my eyes. "Ryan, let me go. I have to stop the beeping."

Ryan bolts upright. "Baby?" He cups my face in his large hands and looks at me, eyes filled with tears. My eyes widen as everything comes back to me in a rush of flashing memories, like a movie.

"Oh, God. Renza." My hands fly to my stomach. "Our baby! Is our baby okay? Ryan!"

"Shh... Baby, you have to calm down. Your heart rate is off the fucking charts."

"Ryan, what happened? What happened to our baby? Please tell me I didn't lose her. Please!" What was steady beeping has now become erratic. Tears are streaming down my face. "Oh God! Our baby!"

Ryan pulls me close. "Shh... Honey, baby is fine. Just fine. You're okay. You're both okay, sweetheart." Doctors and nurses burst into the room to check on me as Ryan holds me tightly.

"Please don't let me go. Please!"

"I won't. Baby, I won't. Just calm down for me, okay?" he whispers soothingly. I nod into his chest, breathing him in.

"What happened?" one of the nurses asks. A big, tall guy.

"Her heart rate is elevated," another nurse says, an older grandmotherly lady. Everyone sounds panicked. I hold onto Ryan with all of my strength as I tremble.

The doctor moves towards Ryan. "Sir, you'll have to step back."

"No!" I scream and cry. I cling tighter to Ryan, even though I'm not sure where the strength to do that comes from.

"Not happening," Ryan growls. "Where's her doctor?"

"Please don't make us call security. We need to check her. We can't do that with you there," the male nurse says.

Ryan doesn't move. "The only person touching her is her doctor. Where is Doctor Chantau?"

"We're more than capable -" the doctor begins.

"What the fuck did I just say?" Ryan snaps as I cling to him. He holds me tighter.

I jump and bury my face in the safety of Ryan's chest when an older doctor comes sprinting into the room. "Mr. Crane! I'm here. I was taking a nap in the on-call room since I haven't slept. I got the page and ran here."

Ryan keeps me tightly to him. "It's okay. Just check her. Please."

"Everyone out," Ryan's doctor commands.

"But -" The older female nurse begins.

"Now! If I need you, I'll call!" I feel the doctor sit behind me and put a hand on my back. "Arianna, I'm Doctor Chantau. I need to check you out, honey."

"Please don't make Ryan leave," I beg.

"He's not going anywhere, sweetheart. But you have to turn to me, so I can get a look at you."

I shakily turn towards him, but I don't let go of Ryan. I keep his shirt in a death grip. I feel my hands shaking. I'm so scared, I don't even make an attempt at hiding it.

Ryan takes both of my hands in his and pries them off him. "Aria, you have to let him look at you. I'm not going anywhere. I'm right here. I know you're scared, but I'm not going anywhere." Ryan keeps his arms around my waist and me close to him as Dr. Chantau examines me.

"You're doing great, Arianna. Baby is healthy. You're healthy. Your blood work looks great. I want your blood pressure to come down, but we can work on that while not in the hospital."

"Both of them are good to go?" Ryan asks.

The doctor nods. "I'll get the discharge papers. We can be in the air within an hour."

"Great. Get it done."

I look up at Ryan. "A-are you sure it's a good idea for me to leave so s-soon?"

Ryan cups my face in his hands. "If Dr. Chantau didn't think it was a good idea, he wouldn't let you go. And I trust him. That's why I hired him for you and Jessa. He did a great job with Nicole."

"What do you mean? Does he live in Chicago?"

"He lived in Minnesota. When we evacuated Breetana and Nicole, we needed a doctor to travel with us. He was available and willing. He was there when Chase got shot. He stayed in Chicago and became our family doctor. He's discreet. You know we need that. And he's damn good at what he does."

"But we live in Manhattan."

"He'll be in Manhattan through both yours and Jessa's pregnancy. If he chooses to stay, I'll get him set up in New York. Either way, he's trustworthy."

I settle myself in his arms. "I just need another minute before I get up to get ready. I'm having trouble processing everything. I don't understand how Renza could do what she did."

"Take all the time you need. When you're ready, I need to know what happened."

I nod as he holds me tightly, but I can't process that my best friend tried to kill me.

Later, on the plane, I step out of the bedroom and make my way to Ryan. He pulls me into his lap and nuzzles my neck, resting a hand on my stomach.

"How's my girl, and my guy? Feel better after that shower?"

I can't help but chuckle. "Both of your girls are just fine."

He keeps his hand firmly on my stomach and the other around my waist as he kisses me. "I'm telling you. You're carrying a boy. No one in my family has had a girl."

"He's right, you know," Jason says. "I had to do a family tree my senior year of high school. We went back a hundred and thirty years."

Ryan smiles. "All boys."

"You and Jessa are both carrying boys," Jason concludes.

I shake my head. "Jessa may be. But I'm carrying a girl." Everyone laughs. I curl into Ryan's arms. "I'm ready. But I think everyone should know."

He kisses my cheek. "I agree. That's why I have Jason and Jessa flying with us."

I take a deep breath. Time to get this over with. "I was in our bedroom asleep. I woke up to someone sitting on the bed. I thought it was you coming back, but when I turned, I saw Renza. I sat up really fast. I asked what she was doing. She told me she had hated me for years. That she hated how I had everything. A nice house. Powerful family. But mostly that I had you." I look up at Ryan. "She said that Chad was helping her. That he was going to marry me and get an heir for his family. Then…" I force myself to stay strong and continue, but everything I'm about to say makes me sick. I close my eyes and choke down the sob. Ryan's fingers run through my hair.

"They were going to kill you." Ryan hugs me closer. I nod. A tear escapes as I open my eyes. Ryan's grip tightens.

Taylor kneels in front of me and Ryan and squeezes my leg. "Hey. Not happening, sweetheart."

Chase looks over at me. "No fucking way."

Ryan gets a slightly confused look on his handsome face. "She was jealous for that long and was, what? Sticking by you while destroying your life?"

"She and Chad started all of the rumors. The days Chad got to me? She distracted Robby long enough so that he could get to me. Otherwise,

Robby would have been there. And that guy who shoved me against my locker and grabbed me? She told him where I would be."

Robby growls dangerously. "I swear to fucking God, Air. If I had known I would've stopped her. I would've been there for you."

I look at him. "You were. If it weren't for you, it would've been worse. Ryan could only do so much. You got me through the rest of school."

Jason rubs his eyebrow. "Why did she call Ryan that day?"

"Because she wanted to keep looking like the good guy," Lyric answers.

"She wanted me to think she had my best interest at heart. But she was jealous of my relationship with Robby. That he was and still is always there for me. She hated that he joined this mafia, this family, for me. To protect me." I look at Robby. "All she wanted…," I shrug, "…was to make me pay for hurting her by outshining her. By being spoiled and having everything." I lean my head on Ryan's shoulder.

Ryan rubs his temple. "What happened after she explained?"

"I smelled smoke. She had opened a window in the room. Just like…" I shiver.

"Just... like the fire... at her house," Ryan says as if it's dawning on him. I'm sure I don't need to tell him what happened, but everyone else needs to know.

"She started the fire at her house when I was sixteen. She knew I would freeze up. I didn't know. I blocked a lot of what happened that night out because I was so scared, but I remembered everything as soon as I smelled the smoke. That night she was screaming that we had to move, but she didn't help me. She jumped out the window. Her parents couldn't get to me. The second floor was completely ablaze. A firefighter saved me because her parents were screaming that I was still in the house."

Chase nods. "That's exactly how it was this time. Luke was in his bedroom. The rest of us were downstairs."

"Nikki and Bree couldn't sleep. I took Nikki downstairs to make her tea. Chase and Bree were down there already," Taylor says as he squeezes my knee.

"Luke and I smelled smoke about the same time," Shane continues, filling in the parts of the story I don't know. "He made me get his mom out while he went for Arianna."

"The flames were fucking intense. I wrapped my face in a towel and leaped through, but the bedroom door was locked," Luke says.

"I saw the flames licking the door," I say quietly. "Just like that night. And I froze. Renza went out the window. I couldn't move. I couldn't follow. I heard Luke trying to get in, but I couldn't help him. I passed out from fear."

"When I got in, I saw Arianna on the floor. The flames took over the room fast. I couldn't get out the window. It was covered with flames. There was an opening at the door I thought I could get her through. I picked her up and just ran."

"Alex and I couldn't get to her. I pushed Lyric into Shane when he took off with Luke's mom. Then, we both ran up the stairs and started beating the flames back, but we couldn't get through them," Josh says.

"The more we beat back, the hotter everything got. But we saw Luke running through the hall screaming that he has her. We trusted that and went for your parents. They had just smelled the smoke and were getting out. It woke them up," Alex finishes.

Robby swallows, his eyes swimming with an emotion I don't recognize. "What about the explosion? Right before you got out."

Luke scrubs his hands over his face. "When we got to the door I saw a duffel bag. It was on fire, but inside, I saw a canister. Like for a soda stream or something. I kicked the duffel bag as far as I could. It blew up in the air. I covered both of us as best I could, but I was growing pretty weak. I couldn't stop coughing. Turns out, there was more than one canister. I kicked it into the kitchen. I think it took out the fuel line or something because the secondary explosion knocked me on my ass."

"It knocked us all on our asses," Ryan says.

"I got up as quickly as I could. By that time, even though she was passed out, we both inhaled a shit ton of smoke. It really hurt to breathe. I couldn't see. But the door wasn't far, so I fought like hell to get out."

Ryan hugs me tightly. "I'll never be able to thank you for that."

Luke shrugs, like it's not a big deal. "She's family. I'd do anything for family. For anyone in this plane."

Taylor stands. "As soon as we get off this plane in New York, I think everyone should stay together."

"I agree," Alex says. "Everyone together. Just like what we did with Jessa."

Ryan nods. "And Breetana and Nikki."

"Ryan's house is bigger," Jessa says quietly. "He has guards right there. We wouldn't have to move anyone."

"His house is also Fort fucking Knox," Taylor says. "No one is getting in there."

Marianne clears her throat. "Um... I... Should we just go home?" Dave takes Marianne's hand. I can see how scared she is.

I shake my head, making the decision for everyone. "You both have been here since the beginning of this. You aren't targets, but we said we're sticking together."

"And I told you both on the yacht that we protect our own," Ryan agrees. "I meant that."

Chase smiles. "I don't think any of us consider you guys anything but one of us at this point."

Luke leans back against the couch near me. "Man, I'm with you on that one. You two are fucking troopers for not having run away by now."

Marianne smiles a very watery smile. Like she's barely holding it together. I don't blame her. I'm barely holding it together myself.

"Feels like we're descending. Come Jessa and Arianna," Ethan stands and holds his hand out for both me and Jessa. "You both need to be buckled in."

I smile at Ryan. "Now I know where you get it."

"He's a good man. Protective of family." Ryan smiles.

"Just like you," I whisper.

He kisses me before I stand. We take our seats and buckle in. He slips his arm around my shoulders and pulls me into him. I relax. The landing happens quickly. I hate landing and taking off. They're both the worst.

A few minutes later, Ryan and I are walking hand in hand to the SUVs. Ryan lifts my hand to his lips and kisses my palm. "Just need to talk to Jas quickly before we take off. I'll meet you at the SUV."

"Okay." I smile up at him. He winks and heads over to his brother as I continue towards the SUV.

"Gun! Arianna, get down!" Alex yells.

"What?" I turn towards Alex, confused as I start to duck.

Alex, Josh, and Rico are both running towards me. Jason is pulling Jessa down with him.

Chaos ensues as a barrage of gunfire suddenly rings out. I look for Ryan. He's running towards me, but it's Rico who reaches me first. I'm crouched on the ground near the SUV covering my ears when he gets to me. He spins me around, his body pressing me against the tire of the SUV. I start screaming as his heavy body covers mine and pushes me harder against the vehicle.

Alex grabs me and pulls me behind the vehicle as Ryan reaches us. Rico falls to the ground.

I scream. "Rico! No! Get Rico! Alex! Help him! You have to help him!"

His strong arms hold me tightly to his chest. "Shh... Arianna. I'm sorry, but he's gone."

"No! Why? Why is this happening?" I scream and cry as he moves with me.

"We need to get in the SUV. Understand? We're moving." Josh covers us as Alex pulls me and Lyric with him. I numbly move as I cry. He nearly shoves us into the SUV.

"On the floor, girls! Alex, don't fucking leave their side!" Ryan commands. Alex jumps in the back as Ryan gets in the driver's side and Josh jumps in the passenger seat.

Lyric and I cower and cry hugging each other as Ryan peels out. "Rico... Why? This is all my fault. He's dead because of me." The thought sends me into harder sobs.

"Arianna, stop it," Ryan growls. "He's dead because your father is fucking crazy."

"He died protecting me!" I scream.

"Ssh..., Arianna...," Lyric whispers in my ear. She sounds calm, but I know she's not. She's trembling just as much as I am.

Alex runs his fingers through both mine and Lyric's hair. "We can't help our parents, honey. You blaming yourself for his death would be like me blaming myself for what happened to Jessa. And that wasn't my fault, was it?" I shake my head, still trembling.. "Damn right it wasn't."

"It's okay," Lyric whispers over and over. I'm not sure if she's doing it more for her or me, but it seems to work for us both.

I hate my father more than I can express. I just want this to end.

As soon as we get home and I step out of the car, I'm clinging to Ryan. Josh is carrying Lyric. I can't imagine she's used to seeing anything like what has been happening since she's been around with us for this whole thing. I see Luke running for me, but I'm too weak and scared to meet him halfway.

"Thank God." Luke wraps me in his arms and breathes out a sigh of relief. "Thank God you're okay."

"Get him inside!" I turn at the sound of Doctor Chantau's voice.

"Shit! Holy shit, he's alive!" Alex runs to help the doctor and Nick, who is propping Rico up.

"Rico?" I break free of Ryan's and Luke's grips and run to Rico. I don't need to see them to know they've followed. "Rico! Oh my God, I'm so sorry. I'm so sorry!" I reach up to touch Rico's face. My hands are shaking. I can't stop myself from crying hysterically.

"I'm... I'm okay, sweetheart."

I look at Ryan and Luke, then the doctor. Rico's voice is weak at best. He looks like he's about to lose consciousness.

Doctor Chantau keeps his voice low as he speaks to Ryan, but I can hear him. "It looks like both hits he took went through. I don't think any internal damage was done, but he's lost a lot of blood. We need to get him inside now. I have to look closer and stop his bleeding."

Ryan nods. "Take him to the first room on the right by the stairs. I'll get your equipment for you."

The doctor nods. Nick and Alex move quickly. Josh, with Lyric in his arms, stays back with us. Ryan barks out orders to the guards to grab equipment.

My head starts spinning so fast that I can't keep up. It's like all of the emotions I've ever felt in my entire life suddenly dumps from my body.

I collapse into Ryan and just cry.

Chapter Twenty Seven

✖ Ryan ✖

"This ends. It has to. Now." Luke glares out the window, frustrated.

"No. Think like a damn cop." Taylor is just as frustrated.

"We go flying in there unprepared, shit will go south. You know better than that." Shane sits down and rubs his head.

I watch as Luke glares at both Shane and Taylor. He knows they're a hundred percent right. He shakes his head. "I fucking hate both of you."

Shane smirks. "No you don't."

Luke scoffs. "Dick."

"Top priority should be Rico right now anyway." We all look at Dave, astonished that he spoke up. "I... mean. Family is top priority. Shouldn't we make sure he's stable before we're talking about anything else right now?"

We all look at him a moment longer before Robby clears his throat. "He's right. With Arianna and Luke both having been in the hospital for a day, and then our entire day lost to flying, they have two days planning on us."

"Ryan will never go for jumping in head first," my dad says next to me.

Chase nods towards Robby. "And he's right. We need a plan."

Taylor nods in agreement. "We need observation."

Jason shakes his head as he stands. "We need a break. We need to take five fucking seconds to calm down." He points to me. "Especially you."

I don't say anything as everyone scatters.

Except Luke.

"How's Rico?" he asks.

"Doc has him. Kicked me out of the room." I smile a little at the door slamming in my face when I tried to follow him in. Not many people stand up to me. Not many are capable. I admire the hell out of Doctor Chantau for being brave enough to do it. "But he checked in before they left. He's doing surgery on him. Took him to the hospital."

Luke leans back tiredly in his chair. "Arianna okay?"

"No. She's pissed off. So am I. We need time to cool down. She's relaxing in the bath. She needs it."

"Thinking Rico was dead. That had to scare the shit out of her."

"I know. She was pretty upset thinking we left him there on the tarmac. She cried for an hour in my arms before she got angry at all of this. She screamed and yelled about how much she hates her dad and everything he's done. How she wants him dead for trying to kill us all. I couldn't agree more with her. We both just need time to calm down. We're both fucking pissed at everything. If I walk up there right now, none of you are getting sleep." I give him a teasing smirk.

He looks like he's about to be sick. "Fuck you. I don't want to know what the hell you do to my sister behind closed doors. God, you suck."

I chuckle and lean back against the couch. "So? Talk to me."

"About what?"

"Let's start with what has you so testy? Not thinking things through."

"I haven't been testy."

"It's not just the fire. There's something else."

He looks at his hands. "No there isn't."

"Hmm… Well, when you decide you want to tell me, I'm here." I start to stand, knowing he'll stop me, and tell me what I already suspect.

"Fine. You really want to know?"

I lean back again. "Wouldn't have asked if I didn't."

He sighs. "This has been on my mind for a long time. So, don't do the protective big brother bullshit and try to talk me out of it."

I grin. "I'm not making any promises. If it's stupid, you're going to hear about it."

He glares at me before staring hard at the wall in front of us. "I'm quitting the ATF. I love the job, but I never felt like I was actually making a difference. That's why I joined. I wanted to do some good. Yeah, I got some guns off the street. Even some drugs. But it seems like the more I fucking do, the more there fucking is. Like I'm doing nothing."

I quietly listen. I know where he's going with this. It's been obvious with how deep in thought he's been; how much research he's been doing into me. Ever since he realized what exactly it is I do and how much I've done, he's been spending a lot of time thinking.

I watch him as he works through everything in his head. I've learned over the years the best thing to do with any of my brothers is to let them work through it on their own. Be that guiding force they need when and if they need it. It doesn't seem to be much different with Luke.

"I've always had this idea that being a cop would allow me to help people. Make a difference. But honestly? It doesn't feel like that at all. In the NYPD, I dealt with the same people every day. I'd help a woman whose boyfriend beat her up and think it was all good. Then, I'd be back the next day because she didn't want to press charges, and he'd beat her up again. And in the ATF? We'd take out a gang only to have to take out higher ups. And then even more higher ups." He takes a deep breath and shakes his head. "And here you fucking are. You go into a section of the city and crime is down immediately." He looks at me. "That's what I want, Ryan. To feel like I'm making a difference and actually being able to see the fucking results."

He closes his eyes and leans his head back against the chair. Being a cop is exhausting. I saw the toll it took on Nick. I see what it does to Taylor. Working day in and day out with the same people. Going on the same calls in the same neighborhoods. Taking out gangs and small mafias only to have other ones or larger ones pop up.

I give him a small smile. "Are you asking me if I'll let you in?" I already know the answer.

"I'm not asking. I'm saying I want in."

I take a deep breath and let it out slowly. "It's not all glitz and glamor. Cleaning up neighborhoods? That takes a lot of work. And not all of it is legal. I break the law, pay people off to stay quiet, befriend people in high places to keep me out of trouble..."

"I know, Ryan. I get it. Okay? I'm not a fucking kid."

"Never said you were. I just want you to understand what you'd be getting into. Maybe you should think about it more."

"I don't need to. I have. A lot. I want in. I want to be a part of something that matters. I want to be able to protect my family. I want to be able to bring my mom with me if I think I need to. I want to be able to send her protection if I can't be there and trust that she'll be safe with who I send. I understand fully what I'll be getting into."

"Luke, if I ask you to shoot someone, I need to know the goodness in you won't cause hesitation. Because you hesitating means someone dies. You have to trust me. Implicitly. Even if you initially disagree. I have a reason for everything. A plan. A back-up plan. And a back-up plan to my back-up plan."

"I know. I understand. I've seen you in action. Everything you do is to protect good people from bad ones. To protect your family. I want that opportunity. That's all I've ever wanted."

I watch him for a few minutes. What he doesn't know is that I've already made the decision to take him on. I don't know when exactly my hesitation to trust him stopped, but I do know that when I saw him carrying Arianna out of the house, that was it. It's what sealed the deal. Any lingering trust issues I may have had, reservations about him that may have existed, vanished in that moment.

"I need someone I can trust to run this operation in my absence."

"I'll learn. And if I haven't earned your trust, I will."

"Someone who knows my operations inside and out."

"Just give me the chance."

"Someone who does mundane bullshit just as well as the major bullshit."

"I'll do it. I trust you. I believe in what you're doing. And I love this family. I've never felt like I belonged anywhere, Ryan. I feel like I

267

have a place now. A purpose. Give me the opportunity. That's all I'm asking. I'll start out at the bottom and work my way up. I just want to be a part of it."

I sit forward and rest my elbows on my knees. "I'm not asking you these questions and telling you this because I want you at the bottom, Luke. I'm talking to you about it because Rico needs to step back. With his injuries he'll never be a hundred percent. The hit he took to his shoulder shattered bone. Before the doc took him, we talked. He asked to step back. He'll still be a part of the family. And he'll still be a higher up guard." Luke looks at me as he sits up and rests his elbows on his knees as I'm doing. "But I *need* a second in command. I can't do what I do without one, and I don't trust just anyone to do that. I have to know that you'll do anything for this family, and that you won't hesitate when I tell you to do something." I stand and pat him on the shoulder. "If this is what you want, that's your position." I start to walk across the living room to the stairs.

"I'll do it."

I nod but don't turn. "Good. Get your shit upstairs. Your room is next to ours. Arianna wants you close. Then gather the guys. We need a plan."

After dropping Luke off in his room, I stand outside the door to my room and try to steady myself.

I can't blame her for thinking I left Rico to die. That's what fucking cuts me. If I were her, I'd think the same damn thing. I hadn't even thought to tell her someone grabbed him. Hell, I'd seen the blood. Josh, Lyric, Alex, and I all thought he was dead. But it never crossed my mind to tell her I would never leave him. I'm so used to the way I do things. I'm used to my team doing what I need them to without me telling them to. It's easy to forget that Arianna has no idea. She's never seen this side of shit.

Fuck me.

I lean my head against the wall. This whole thing is so fucked up, and I feel like shit that she had go through that emotional dump that she did.

Stealing myself, I breathe in deeply. Letting it out slowly, I open the door.

Arianna is propped up against the headboard of the bed with her laptop in her lap. She's wearing one of my t-shirts. I can't help but breathe a sigh of relief.

268

She looks up at me and smiles. "Come see."

She beckons me over to the bed. I crawl in next to her and grab her laptop, setting it aside as I cover her mouth with mine. I wrap my arms around her and pull her close to me as I dip my tongue in her mouth. Like she usually does, she wraps herself around me. I'm grateful as hell.

After a deep and passionate kiss, I gently pull away and brush her hair off her face as I tangle my fingers in her still slightly damp hair.

"I'm sorry, baby."

"So am I." Her voice is soft. Her lip quivers. "I thought you left him. I can't believe I thought that.."

"You had every reason to. I never thought to say I'd never do that." I run my hand down her arm, leaving a trail of goosebumps in my wake.

She smiles softly and leans in to kiss my cheek. "You never should have had to. I should've known better."

I frown and squeeze her hand. "You couldn't have been expected to know. With everything going on, there's no way you even would have thought about it."

She settles into the crook of my arm. I kiss her head as she wraps her arms around me. I pull her in tightly.

"I'm scared, Ryan. Getting shot at? Being on the run? And being pregnant on top of it? I know what you do. But actually being in the middle of it... I know he didn't die, but I thought he had. I thought someone died right in front of me. I know I'm lucky in the fact that even my father kept that away from me. I mean, not really counting my mom in that..." She reaches up and wipes a tear away.

I catch her hand and kiss her tears away instead. "I love you, Aria. This is all something I never wanted you to see. I thought I could keep all of this away from you. I never thought we'd be walking into an ambush when we stepped off the plane. I never thought he'd ever take shots at you, even with what happened in Australia. I thought he was taking shots at Luke or Rico. I underestimated him, and I let you walk into this unprepared. I'll never let that happen again."

She bites her lip and is quiet for a long while. She traces random patterns on my abs. Finally, she looks up at me. "What's my role within the mafia now? What's expected of me? As your wife?"

269

It's my turn to fall quiet. It takes a few moments to really organize my thoughts because I know she knows the answer. She just wants confirmation. She needs to feel some semblance of the power and control over herself and her life that's been stripped from her.

"Well, in this mafia, you're considered a leader now. You're not expected to go on missions, and fuck if you think I'd let you anyway, but you are considered a leader. Guards will look to you for direction. They'll follow your orders. I'm an incredibly important figure in major cities and countries throughout the world. I don't necessarily care for the adoration I get, but it's part of it. It comes along with what I do. As my wife, you're part of that now, too."

Now the really hard part. The part that I hate, but that she really does need to know. I bury my face in her hair a moment as I take a deep breath. Fuck me. I love that subtle jasmine scent. I will never get sick of it.

"You're... uh... considered incredibly important now. Your last name will get you places you never dreamed. But with that comes consequences. It means you can't go anywhere alone. You'll have guards and security with you all the time, even if I'm with you. You're a target. Our child is a target." I put my hand on her stomach. "It means even when you're in class at Juilliard, guards will be there. I'd prefer you have a driver. That you don't drive anywhere without me or a guard in your vehicle." I begin absentmindedly rubbing my hand across her stomach. "And lastly, it means you, like my mother is to my father, are my partner in all of this. You're by my side through everything. Much like you are now except on a much more formal level. Public events, you're expected on my arm. If I have to go, you're expected to be able to keep everything here running smoothly if you're not with or can't come with me."

She nods and kisses my chest. "I think I knew all of that."

I smile because I know she knew all of it. "If you question something, baby, ask me. If you don't know what's expected of you, ask. I know being in this position in this type of operation is a new thing and a hell of a shock. It can't be easy. But I'm here for you. All of us are here for you."

She smiles up at me and kisses me. Everything is suddenly right again as she melts against me. The moment doesn't last long. My phone vibrates in my pocket. I sigh as I take it out.

Luke: Guys are ready.

Ryan: Give me a few. Explaining shit to Arianna.
Luke: Take your time.

I put my phone back in my pocket and kiss Arianna. "Show me what you wanted to show me later and throw a pair of shorts or something on. We need to make a plan, and you have a decision to make."

She grins brightly at me as we make our way down the stairs hand in hand. I reach a chair and pull Arianna into my lap.

Taylor smiles. "Are you two good now?"

"We're better than good." She kisses me in front of everyone.

I feel myself getting hard underneath her. Why the hell do I do this to myself? Having her close to me makes my body react in ways it never has to another woman. But having her in my lap? That's pure fucking torture.

I hold her still, resting one hand on her stomach and wrapping the other one around her as we settle. "We need a plan. First step is surveillance. I already sent a team in to do that."

"His house?" Taylor questions.

I nod. "Both houses. His and Ambrosio's. That's where Chad is."

Robby scrubs his hands down his face. "So, who are the main targets now? Originally, we were just going after Ambrosio and Massena."

"And the guards standing in the way. No prisoners." I'm done fucking around. I'm as good as I am because I'm not afraid to eliminate the bad guys.

Luke sits down on the arm of the chair next to Robby. "I think our targets have expanded. Chad and Renza. We need to deal with them."

"They tried to kill Arianna," Jason agrees.

"They tried to kill all of us," Chase corrects.

"It was just Renza that started the fire," Arianna says quietly.

"She's tried to kill Arianna twice. She's done. She's on our list. And Chad helped her plan. He's done, too," I say dangerously. Arianna stiffens a moment before nodding and sighing. "I'm sorry, baby, but I'm not giving them the opportunity to come after you again. We need to take all of them out."

"I know. I understand. I'm just sorry it's come to this." She squeezes my arm. I kiss her neck.

Josh looks at Arianna tenderly. It's a look he has reserved for very few people. I'm sort of honored that my girl is one of them. "She isn't a

271

friend to you. I know you feel bad, but look at what she's done to you. To us."

"She tried to kill your whole family, honey," Lyric says.

"Our," Arianna corrects without hesitation. Lyric smiles shyly and a little tearfully.

Josh leans down, kissing her head with a grin. "I told you so," he says quietly, but still loud enough for a few of us to hear. The rest of us grin from ear to ear. Lyric is definitely a part of our family.

"And I know. I do. Part of me still can't believe it, but I know." Arianna reaches up to wipe a tear away.

I hug her tighter. "We hit both houses at the same time. I'll lead one team. Luke, as my new second in command, will be with me. Josh and Alex will be hitting the other."

Everyone looks at Luke in surprise.... except Arianna.

Hmm.

"No shit?" Taylor asks.

My dad beams. "Congrats, young man. A great decision."

"Wait... you mean...?" Shane asks.

Luke nods. "I need more fulfillment in life. We talked about this, Shane."

"This is what you want?"

"Absolutely."

"Fuck, I'm proud, man. I had a feeling. Resignation effective immediately?"

"Yes, sir." Luke meets Arianna's eyes. Almost like he's looking for approval.

Arianna smiles. "I'm glad you finally talked to him. I'm happy you're finally at a place in your life you can be proud of."

Luke smiles like an idiot. I shake my head. "You knew he wanted this?"

She settles into my arms, her head on my shoulder. "I've known for a while. But that conversation with you wasn't my place."

"If you said no, though, she was my backup plan," Luke teases.

Everyone laughs. I shake my head again and hold up a hand to silence everyone. "Okay, enough. Two teams. Josh. You'll take Alex and your team. You're going after Massena."

"Got it," Alex says.

272

"I'll get our team together now," Josh says as he takes out his phone. He kisses Lyric again and makes his way to the kitchen.

I nod to Nick. "With our entire family here, I want you here with Chase. That being said, Arianna." I look down at her. "Make your decision. You have Chase and Nick. The sheer number of people in this house requires more than just the two of them. Obviously, I'll put guards on the perimeter, but I want three people in this house, and I need one more person to help lead and command my team since Luke is technically training. Jason or Taylor are both capable of coming with me when I raid Ambrosio's house. The question is which of those two do you want here?" I already know her answer. I don't have to ask, but I do it anyway.

Taylor meets her eyes. I smile into Arianna's hair to hide it. Taylor laughs. "You really have to ask? You know who she's going to choose."

Jason laughs. "We all know she and Taylor have a bond. No way she's choosing me if you give him as an option."

Arianna smiles softly. "Sorry, Jason."

"No need, sweetheart. I don't mind. And I absolutely don't mind kicking a little ass. Sons of bitches are all going down for what they did to my family."

"So, Taylor is staying?" I ask.

"If that's okay," she says as she looks at me.

"I wouldn't have given him as an option if it wasn't okay." I kiss her neck again. She shivers and wiggles against me. I can't take much more. "Robby, you'll be with me and Jason. This is your first mission, too. I don't want you or Luke to be overwhelmed."

His eyes look like they catch fire as he looks up at Luke, but he tries to hide it. "I'm good with that."

"I knew you would be. We have a plan then?" I know there are important things happening that need discussion, but I'm about done. I can't help how much my body craves my wife.

And I can't help how hers craves mine. She's crossed her legs and squeezed them together at least six times since she's been on my lap. I'm keenly aware of every movement. If I'm not inside her soon, I'm pretty sure my dick will fall off.

Josh comes back into the room hanging up his phone. "We have a plan. I'm also giving Lyric a gun to back them up. She's trained, and we can't be too careful."

"Works for me," I agree.

Nick looks down at both of us and grins. "You better get her upstairs. I don't think either one of you are going to make it any longer."

Arianna turns red with embarrassment as I pick her up.

Luke makes a mock gagging noise. "Fucking Christ, I hate all of you."

I laugh as I carry Arianna upstairs. It doesn't take long before I'm on top of her and her legs are wrapped around my waist. Just the way I like it. I sink myself into her, burying myself inside her to the hilt.

"Mmm... Fuck, I wasn't lasting another second. I needed to be inside you."

"I know. Oh God, I needed this. How fucked up is it that I wanted you so badly in the middle of a planning session?"

"I felt the same way, beautiful."

I start thrusting hard, deep, and fast inside her. Her wet, tight little pussy wrapped around my cock is something I'll forever crave. Her sensual breaths; the way she closes her eyes and whispers my name as she meets me thrust for thrust. I bury my face in her hair and gently bite her neck as I cup her breast.

"Ryan..."

I run my hand down to her hip and pull her up into me. She gasps with the new sensation as I hit every spot that makes her shudder with each deep thrust.

I quicken my pace, thrusting faster and harder. I kiss her neck down to her tits. I take each one in my mouth in turn, lavishing them before licking, sucking, kissing back up to her sexy, kissable lips.

We ravish each other. I flip us over and grip her hips as she rides me. I let her fuck me as hard as she wants to before I flip her back over and take back control.

"Ah! Ryan!" she screams as I pin her and pound her pussy.

Her thighs start trembling. Her pussy clenches even more deliciously around me. She throws her head back on the pillows and tightens her legs around me. Her nails dig into my shoulders.

"Come for me, Aria," I whisper in her ear.

"Oh... Ryan... I love you." She lets go, and the pulsing of her orgasm rips my own from me.

"Mmm... I love you, too, Aria."

It takes me a few moments before I pull out and move to her side. She burrows into my side and wraps herself around me like she does every night.

I relish in it. I've gotten pretty damn used to being what my wife craves, so I can only hope her sex drive stays this way; that she keeps needing me as much as I do her.

I chuckle as her breathing evens out. She doesn't sleep unless my arms are around her. If I move or she rolls over in her sleep, and my arms somehow end up not around her, she sleeps like shit.

Tonight, I refuse to let her get a bad night's sleep. She'll need all of her strength to get through the next couple of days.

XXX

(Five Days Later)

I hold up a hand. "Alright. Quiet. I know there's a bunch of excitement going on, as always, but we have work to do." Everyone quiets down and gathers around me, Jason, and Luke. "There are eight guards in the house. Surveillance has them all on the lower level. They're watching, so anything changes, I'll know. Team One will be with me. Team Two will be with Luke and Jason. We have two kill teams. My team will take Chad. We're Team One A. Chad's is the first room on the left upstairs."

"Team Two A is the second kill team," Luke says. "You'll be led by me. We're going after Stephen Ambrosio."

"Jason doesn't take the fucking shot. He's just helping Luke in leading you. I find out he took the shot, you all will face consequences." I glare at them. They all look down at the ground. "Robby is with me. Chad is the only one we're taking out of here alive. I know Arianna has questions. So do I. Mainly where the fuck Renza is. Surveillance doesn't have her here or at Massena's. She's not with her parents. She's vanished. Everyone else doesn't survive this mission. I don't need to question anyone other than Chad. Shoot everyone else on the spot."

"Any questions?" Jason asks.

"What if Chad doesn't know where Renza is?" one of my guards asks. "Wouldn't we want to ask Ambrosio? Since Arianna said the voice was older."

I nod. "Good question. The answer is no. I don't need him. We've already verified that he isn't the one she was talking to. We recovered her laptop from the fire. Robby was able to track the IP address. It went to a location that was in constant movement. We think it was on a plane. I don't pretend to know shit about technology. Also, we verified that at the time she was video chatting, Ambrosio was here."

"Any other questions?" Luke asks. Everyone shakes their heads.

"Then we move out," Jason commands. "Team One will be going in the front. Team Two will be going in the back. As soon as we get in, we combine. Take out the threats. Both Kill Teams will be breaking off and going upstairs. Ambrosio is the master bedroom at the back of the house. I know Ryan said I don't take a shot. If I can help it, I won't. If I have to, I won't hesitate."

I shake my head. I've always been able to count on Jason to undermine my rules. No point in arguing with him, though. He's one of the few I won't win against. "Cleanup crew. Take the basement. You're Team Three today. Let's get this done." We all move into position, and I keep a close eye on my watch.

"Why 2:37?" Robby nearly whispers the words as we crouch down into position.

I grin and look over at him, pleased he asked about the entrance time. I keep my voice just as low. "Would you expect an attack at 2:37? Or would you think it would happen at, say, 3:00AM?"

He chuckles. "Fair point." He focuses his attention on the house.

I smile. "We kick the door open together."

"Got it."

I check my watch again. "Ready?"

"Yes, sir." He looks at my wrist and tilts his head. "Are you nervous?"

I stare at him blankly for a moment before looking down at my hands where his eyes are focused. I'm subconsciously rubbing the worn, brown leather band on my wrist that I got from my grandfather years ago. He wore it for good luck. Ever since I started wearing it, I've only taken it off once, and that was to get it repaired. I rub it before every mission I'm on. It's so normal for me now that I don't notice it.

I nod. "I'm good. It's just something I got years ago from my grandfather. Good luck to me." I give him a confident grin. He smiles back. The nerves he seemed to portray at me being seemingly nervous completely dissipates. I give him another nod as I focus my attention on the door. "Teams. Three... Two... One... Go!"

Robby and I lunge for the door, our team behind us. We both kick hard. The frame splinters. Pieces of wood fly everywhere as the door crashes to the ground. We make our way quickly to the staircase where Jason and Luke meet us.

Before any of Ambrosio's guards can figure out what's happening, they're all lying on the ground. My team is trained to aim for the head. Less chance of survival. Each shot taken by my team is silenced by the silencers we all have on our guns. Not a single one of Ambrosio's guards survives the assault. It's over in mere seconds.

"Kill teams, on us," Luke commands.

We make our way up the stairs. I look at Robby. "Gun up. Surveillance says Chad sleeps with a gun under his pillow. We go in. We stay low," I whisper. Robby nods. "We won't let him get a shot off. I want him alive, but if it's us or him? You *do not* hesitate. Understand?"

"I won't. Who grabs him?"

"You got cuffs?"

"Zip ties."

"Detain him." I glance down the hall at Jason and Luke. They meet my eyes. I nod. We crash through the doors at the same time.

Chad comes up with his gun. Robby shoots, hitting the gun and knocking it out of his hand. "Holy fuck!" Chad screams as he looks at Robby in disbelief. Seeing that he's outnumbered and outgunned, he holds up his hands. His eyes meet Robby's. "Don't kill me, man."

"You're in luck. We aren't here to kill you," Robby growls low.

I chuckle. "You didn't think you'd get away with trying to kill my family, did you?" I keep my gun trained on him, as does everyone on my team.

Chad's eyes go wide. "I had nothing to do with that! That was all Renza! I wasn't there!"

I look at Robby. Robby takes out his zip ties. We all hold our guns on Chad while Robby secures his wrist… tightly. Tight enough to cut into his wrists and almost immediately draw blood. Chad winces.

"Take him to the SUV," I say as Robby hauls Chad up and roughly pushes him forward.

"Can I at least get a pair of boxers on?" Chad asks.

"Fuck you, Chad. After everything you've done, be lucky I don't shoot your tiny little dick off."

I bite my lip to hold back the laugh as he leaves the room with him. Kid isn't wrong. I'm not sure Chad even has a dick. I sure as fuck didn't see anything more than a button. Everyone else follows Robby, but I turn back to the room, scanning it.

"Everyone's taken care of. What are you looking for?" Jason asks.

"I gave Arianna a bracelet for her sixteenth birthday. It was customized and means a lot to her. It fell off during the fight with Chad the morning she left."

"You think it's in here?"

"I have a feeling. I at least have to look."

"Just get her a new one."

"Jas, it's sentimental to her. What the fuck would Jess do to you if she lost that necklace you got her and you just bought her a new one instead of attempting to look?" I start going through drawers as Jason opens the closet.

He grabs a shoebox from the top shelf and opens it. "Looks like her wishbox."

"Take it with."

The two of us work through the room. My heart sinks a bit further and further the longer we look and don't find her bracelet.

"I'm not seeing it, Ry. And we really should get the fuck out."

I sigh and rub my temple. "Yeah. You're right."

We head out. As soon as we reach the SUV, my frustration turns to pure rage. I tamp it down as I climb behind the steering wheel. My wife and family's attempted murderer is bawling his eyes out. I don't care what he says about not being involved. We all know he had something to do with it. We know he was talking to Renza.

"Shut the fuck up, Chad, or I'll let Robby follow through on his threat to shoot your pin-sized dick off."

"Where are you taking me?" Chad asks fearfully.

I give him an evil grin as I pull away from the curb. "To meet your maker." I wink. He stops crying immediately and bites his lip as he looks out the window.

Robby laughs. "You're really not going to like it." He smiles at him. Chad whimpers. I bite back my own laugh. He really isn't going to like it.

XXX

I pull into the rendezvous point for Massena's attack. Alex and Josh are both putting their gear away. I park and step out. Robby and Luke both follow. Josh turns as he starts taking off his vest.

"How did it go?" I ask, leaning against my SUV. Luke walks over to Alex and helps him finish putting away his gear. Robby leans next to me.

Josh pulls his vest over his head. "Cried like a little bitch. Begged for mercy." He tosses his vest to Alex. Alex catches it and puts it with his.

"Did you get anything out of him? Who the fuck he's working for?"

"He wasn't too forthcoming. But we did find out that he is working for someone. Says it's someone who has the ability to decimate you and us both."

I smirk. "This coming from the guy who thought that combining with a small-time mafia of about eighteen would be able to take out someone with thousands of people working for him?"

"That's what I said. I wouldn't discount this, though. He knew who we are. Called us by name. Nothing about this feels right to me. It feels almost like we're being manipulated somehow."

Alex and Luke finish and turn to us. Alex crosses his arms over his chest. "There's someone pulling the strings. Someone who has a lot of resources at his disposal. If you want my guess? I'm thinking along the lines of law enforcement."

Robby shakes his head. "What? There's no way."

"The only people who have the ability to do some of the things happening is law enforcement," Alex says.

I scrub my hands over my face. "It would make sense."

"Think about it. Taylor even told us," Alex starts. "They have a way to tap in and get exact coordinates using the GPS on phones."

Robby shakes his head. "I have the ability to tap into any phone here and get coordinates on any of you."

I look down at him a little astounded. "You can do that?"

He laughs. "Are you kidding? Any hacker can do that. GPS isn't that hard to get into and get coordinates. This... doesn't feel like law enforcement to me. Especially since you work so closely with them. Why the fuck would they want to mess up a good relationship with a man they have no hope to ever bring down? Why wouldn't they want to continue the relationship?"

Luke leans against the SUV on the other side of me. "It doesn't feel like law enforcement. When we tracked GPS, we got an area the person could be in. We deduced from that information where that person was. This feels too advanced."

"When I had Jessa tracked, that's how it was," Josh says. "I saw him do it. An area around her house. We figured out it was the house. When he got the area around her work, we figured out the workplace."

Robby looks at him with a raised eyebrow. "You didn't have a very good hacker. There are layers to GPS. It uses satellites. You can get exact coordinates if you know what you're doing."

I hold up a hand. "Stop. All of you. Josh. When you tracked Jessa, you didn't get exact coordinates? I'm not a computer genius. Explain it."

"My guy just pulled it and told me where to go. But the one time I saw it, it was just this red circle on a map. I'm not a computer genius either, man."

"We're getting off track," Alex says. "We need to figure out how Renza got coordinates. If it's not law enforcement, then who? Because all I'm thinking is the military and the CIA."

I look down at Robby. "You good with this shit?"

"Top of my class in school. Recruited by MIT. Didn't want to go. I didn't know until a couple months ago what I wanted to do with my life." Robby looks at Alex. "I respect the fuck out of you, but this isn't law enforcement."

Alex smiles. "I don't take offense at a guess being wrong. If you know something I don't, enlighten me. We have a hacker on our team.

He's fucking good, but I don't know near the shit that he can do. I've never sat down and watched him. We tell him to do something, he does it and tells us the results. The one Josh had is no longer with us. He disappeared a couple years ago when the cops were coming down on him for hacking into a bank and skimming money off the top of a lot of companies. So, I don't know what he was capable of either."

Josh laughs. "I'm pretty convinced he took that money and is living lavishly in China. Fucker was obsessed with Beijing."

Robby smiles, then shakes his head. "Look. We know Massena and Ambrosio had nothing to do with the tracking. We know Ambrosio and Massena are working with someone. No amount of questioning or torture is going to get it out of them. We already know all of that. They're smart enough to know they're going to die. Why give us information that could help us thwart their end goal?"

I nod again with a small smile and look into the vehicle. "Chad is who we need to go through. Problem is, I doubt he knows who exactly it is. I think he knows enough to give us something to go on, but I doubt very seriously anyone told him the entire plan. He doesn't seem mature enough to take on a mafia, let alone lead one."

"What are you thinking?" Josh asks.

"Robby will take him to the basement in my house. I'll let Arianna question him. Josh will be down there for back-up. Alex and I are going to get in contact with Lucinio Mafia's hacker. Find out everything we can about GPS and tracking and coordinates."

"I can -" Robby begins.

I stop him with a firm shake of the head and hand on his arm. "You need to listen to the questioning. Josh and Arianna know nothing about tech stuff. That's what they need you for. I don't know what he knows, but I do know that he has to know something. And I know that whatever it is, it's going to be connected to something tech related. You'll need to figure it out. I don't even know where the fuck to start with that."

"Why do you want Arianna questioning him?" Alex asks.

"Because Arianna has a way of getting information out of people that Ryan doesn't," Josh says for me.

I smile, pleased he's following me. "Some people respond differently to particular tactics. Arianna is Chad's age. She went to school with him. She's connected to him. He'll feel he can appeal somehow to her. That he can somehow get the upper hand on her. That he can manipulate her. We all know how smart Arianna is. She won't let that happen. She'll get what we need so I can focus on how the fuck things are happening the way they are. Any tidbit of information he shares could be the piece we need to figure this out. Because this isn't over."

I push myself off the SUV. Taking my hint, Josh, Luke, and Robby all start piling into their vehicles. Alex, however, reading me like a fucking book, stays right where he is. Watching me. Unflinching. Arms folded over his chest like a jackass.

"What is it you aren't saying?" he asks.

I laugh because I can't help it. "You've known me for too long."

"And I know you well enough to know that there's something you're holding back."

I sigh. "I'm tired, Alex. I'm tired of fighting my fucking self. Do you know how difficult it is for me not to tear Chad apart limb by limb? Just take all of this anger I have at his father and Massena out on him? All this frustration?"

"Yeah. I do. You remember how Josh and I were when we confronted our father."

I nod slowly. I do remember. They both were fighting themselves. Just like I am. I sigh. "I'm having a difficult time keeping myself from turning into the fucking ruthless mafia king that everyone thinks I am." I lean over the hood of the SUV and put my head between my arms. "That monster that doesn't give a shit about anyone as long his end goal is met."

I don't see him, but I feel Alex lean over the hood next to me. "Is that the real reason you're asking Arianna to question Chad?"

"No. I'm doing that because..." I shake my head. "Fuck."

"Because you know that she'll protect you from crossing lines that even you don't want to."

I let out a long breath and pick my head up. It feels as heavy as I do. Like I've been covered in cement and thrown over a bridge. I look over at him. "What the hell kind of man does that make me?"

"It makes you a human being and not the superhero that we all think you are. The invincible Ryan Crane... Not really Batman, after all."

I chuckle. "Asshole."

"Look. I'll level with you. You know what Arianna is capable of. You said it yourself. That girl is capable of anything. And when it comes to you?" He smiles. "You have to know she sees the stress this is taking on you. How you're beating yourself up over not knowing what the fuck is going on. We all see it. She's the one who is with you all the time, Ryan. She's the one you've confided things in that I bet none of us know. If your instincts are telling you that she can handle this, trust them. But if you're worried you're throwing her into something you shouldn't because you're struggling? Get the fuck out of your head, Ry. We all would do anything for you. Her included."

I smile as he pats me on the back. He heads for his SUV and climbs in without another word. I do the same.

He's right. I may have struggled slightly with it before, but when it comes down to it, I know anyone in my family would step up if I couldn't. I keep all of them from stepping into forbidden and dangerous territory. It's a different line for each of them.

Maybe it's their turn to keep me from crossing mine.

Chapter Twenty Eight

✕ Arianna ✕

Waiting for Ryan to get back from this entire thing is definitely taking a toll on my psych. I can't sleep. I haven't sat down since I said goodbye to him hours ago.

Chase is standing by the window. Nick is doing a check around the house. The girls are asleep. Well, maybe except Lyric. She hasn't been able to sit still either. She's been walking around the house. And Taylor is sitting on a chair watching me.

Taylor chuckles. "Sweetheart, you're making me dizzy. Sit."

"I can't, Taylor. I'm worried." I start biting my fingernails on one hand while hugging myself with the other.

"Okay." Taylor grabs my arm as I pass him and pulls me into his lap.

"Hey!"

"If you aren't going to sit, I'll just make you. Chase, can you grab her some milk, please?"

"Sure." He steps back from the window as I glare at him and walks towards the kitchen. He chuckles. "Don't bother arguing with either of us. Nicole and Breetana try all the time. Fail miserably."

Taylor hugs me, sensing I need it, and I relax almost instantly. "How is it possible for everyone to be sleeping right now?" I ask.

"I think they're just exhausted."

Chase returns with my milk. He hands it to me. I take a drink. As soon as it hits my tongue, though, I sigh in contentment. The anxiety seems to dissipate.

"I knew that would work."

"How?"

"Because it always works with you." Taylor smiles. I lean back against him. "Look, sweetheart. You know as well as I do that Ryan has done this many, many times. And he's always come home, right?"

"Right, but -"

"Stop. No more. He's good. He knows what he's doing."

Chase sits down on the couch. "Ryan has better technology then the police, Air. No one is going to move so much as a millimeter without him knowing."

Nick walks around the corner and smiles. "They're coming in right now, sweetheart."

I nearly drop my cup. Chase catches it as I leap from Taylor's lap and meet Ryan at the door. I leap in his arms as soon as he opens it.

"Shit. Baby. What's wrong?" He catches me and stumbles backwards before gaining his balance.

"I'm happy you're okay." I bury my face in his neck as I tighten my grip around his waist with my legs. Lyric does the same thing as soon as she sees Josh.

Ryan's grip on me tightens as he kisses my shoulder and neck. "Honey, I'm good. We all are. Your father won't be bothering us anymore. Neither will Ambrosio."

I look at him, eyes shining with unshed tears. He smiles and kisses me softly. "I can't believe everything you do for this family. For me." I glance down at my stomach. "For us."

He kisses me again as Robby pushes a very naked Chad in ahead of him. "Basement?"

"Yep. Sit him down in a chair. Stay down there with him. Arianna and Josh will be down there in a minute."

"Yes, sir." Robby looks pissed. Chad looks terrified. Ryan lets me down.

I look after the two of them, slightly confused. "Why is he naked?"

"That's the way he was sleeping. I left the choice to let him get dressed up to Robby."

"And he said… no?"

"Choice was his." He shrugs. I only nod. "I brought him here because I know you need some closure. I know you want to know why he did what he did to you. I also want to know where the fuck Renza is. I think he'll tell you. Regardless, we need to be done with this chapter of our lives."

"I know."

I know he's trying to avoid having to torture the information out of Chad. I know it's not something he enjoys. No matter how much he tries to say it doesn't bother him. I've always seen the toll it takes. He doesn't need to tell me how much this entire thing has bothered him. I hear him cry at night when he doesn't think I'm awake.

I steel myself and look over at Josh. He kisses Lyric and smiles at me. "I'm ready when you are, sweetheart."

"I'm ready." I smile up at Ryan as I head towards the basement. I really don't know what I'm doing, but I'll follow my instincts just like Ryan has always taught me. If this is something he feels I need to do, I'll do it. Especially if it means taking just one small burden from his shoulders.

Josh follows closely behind me. "Just tell me when you've had enough. I'll take over, and you can leave. Okay?"

"Okay."

We make our way into the basement. As soon as Robby sees me, he gives me a soft squeeze on the shoulder and goes to stand in a corner. Josh stands against a wall behind me with his arms over his chest. Chad is sitting in a hard chair with his hands behind his back.

Almost immediately, the anger I've felt at him for so long, bubbles to the surface. "Why? Why would you do this? Why did you spend so much time just making my life miserable? Because you could?"

"No." His eyes dart from Robby to Josh before landing back on me. "No, Arianna. I was under orders. My father told me that I needed to beat you down then build you back up, or his plan would never work. Arianna, I swear -"

I hold up a hand. "Stop." I close my eyes a second before I open them and glare at him fiercely. "So, it was just you were under orders? Why? What was this big plan?"

"The marriage. To combine our family. To align them against the Crane mafia. None of us knew you were with him!" Chad starts to cry. "Not until you left that morning and ran to him."

I shiver and glance back at Josh. Josh doesn't move. Just stares down at him with such a cold intensity that I can feel the temperature in the room drop a few degrees.

"How did you know she ran to him?" he asks. "When did you know? She left her phone here. You couldn't track her."

Chad looks between the three of us again. "We knew because Renza told us."

"When did you start talking to Renza?" I nearly choke on the words. I'm not sure I want to know the answer; how long the betrayal has been going on.

"Only since the beginning of senior year." His eyes dart back to Josh. I can tell he's decided that Josh is the biggest threat. He's probably right. "But she approached me! She knew about the alliance. She never told me how! She kept feeding me information. She said it would help me!"

I meet Robby's eyes. He stares at me just as confused as I feel. I look back at Chad and step back towards Josh. "Wait. Renza… knew?" I tilt my head.

"She knew! I don't know how. But she approached me. She said that she knew about it, and she could help. It was just after I started bullying you. She said she could help me because she knew your fears and schedule. She told me where you'd be and when so I could get to you."

"We know that," Josh cuts in. "What we don't know is how the fuck she knew about the alliance. I think you know more than what you're telling us."

"I don't! I swear I don't. Renza knew more things about Arianna that we were trying to figure out. Like when she ran, we had no idea where she was. We couldn't find her. I had reached out to Renza, but she didn't answer me for a few days. She texted and said that her and Robby were in Chicago. The next day, your engagement was plastered all over. So, we all sat down and made a plan."

"Stop. Go back." I close my eyes a second before looking back at him "When did Renza tell you about me and Ryan? When did you know I ran to him?"

Chad's eyes fly between me and Josh. "She told us right away. The day you left. We spent time trying to find Ryan, but we couldn't. Ryan isn't an easy person to find. It wasn't until a few days later that she told us that you were in Chicago. But she didn't tell us that until she and Robby showed up for your engagement. She told me that she knew you were there, but was told that we didn't need to know that right away."

I look back at Josh. "She... had my number. Ryan said I could give it to her. That was a couple days after I got to Chicago."

Josh nods and looks back at Chad. "Why didn't she tell you right away?"

"She said we didn't need to know!"

Josh shakes his head. "Bullshit. Why didn't she tell you?"

Chad is silent as he starts to shiver. "Because..." he closes his eyes. "Because of Ryan's security in the building they were in."

"So, she gave you coordinates that directed you to Arianna's exact location. But you couldn't get to her because of security," Josh says. "You knew where she was long before the engagement."

Chad sighs and opens his eyes, knowing he got caught in a lie. "Yes."

"Care to try again? Without the fucking lies? Because one more lie comes out of your mouth and I start breaking bones."

Chad's eyes go wide as he nods. "She... didn't know where she went until she called from Chicago. She only knew that Arianna was with Ryan. She told us where she was when she got there." Chad looks back at me. "She told us she'd be there with you. That it would be easier to get to you with her there."

"What about the explosion at the dress shop?" I ask, becoming more and more angry. I blink to stop the tears threatening to fall.

"She gave us coordinates."

"How did she get them?" Josh demands.

"All she said was that her contact gave them to her. We were able to get to the vehicle they had been in and wire it because she told us which one it was. The guards were inside with Arianna. Renza was pissed because we almost took her out."

288

"Why did my father want to kill me?"

"Because... that's..." Chad swallows hard and shakes his head. "It's what we were ordered to do. Your father told us that there was this guy from another mafia that had planned to help him. We didn't know who he was."

"Did your dad or hers have phone conversations with him? Emails?" Robby asks.

"I was never a part of them. I still don't know who he is. But..." he looks up at Josh. "I... think whoever he is is who Renza was talking to. Her contact."

"My father sent guards to Antigua. If Renza was feeding you information..., why didn't you get there until after?"

"Renza told us where you were, but she didn't tell us until after you were married. She said it was what her contact told her to do."

I shake my head even more confused. I don't realize how much I've backed away until Josh's solid chest hits my back. Josh's hands grip my hips as he moves me next to him. He steps forward a couple steps so I'm safely behind him as I try to gather my chaotic thoughts. Thoughts I'm sure Josh has already put together and come to a conclusion. I just need to think it through.

"So, she was feeding you locations. Why did you not show up in Australia for a few days? Why did it take you a couple days to show up in Greece and Hawaii?"

Chad looks up terrified. "She didn't tell us. As soon as she told us, we mobilized. We knew your exact coordinates when you were sailing, but we had no way of getting to you on the water. She said you'd be in London. We were there before you. Ready. She gave us coordinates of all of your locations that you'd be visiting in London, and when you would be there. We thought we had you, but we lost contact with the guards. Renza told us that Ryan's team caught them. She said you were going to Hawaii. We didn't know where exactly you would be until she gave us the coordinates. We mobilized. Came up with a plan."

My eyes widen as I realize the plan. "You planned to kill me in the fire."

"No, Arianna. By that time, our end goal had changed. The goal wasn't to kill you anymore. The goal was to use you as leverage to get Ryan to do what we wanted. Since we kept missing you, Renza said she

289

was going to deal with the problem herself. That she and her contact were tired of waiting on us. She was going to kidnap you in the chaos of the fire. She said she'd be able to get to a meeting point. We'd have you and could leave and prepare for an attack on Ryan when he came for you."

"But she never showed up," Josh says.

"No. No, she never showed. We waited for a while thinking maybe she got caught up in the chaos of the scene. Then all of the emergency vehicles showed. We wouldn't have been able to get to her."

"So, you left and set up an ambush at the airport. If you wanted Arianna, why the fuck fire shots at her?" Josh growls.

"We weren't firing at her! I swear! We were firing on everyone else! We didn't expect that all of you would fire back! We had to back off. We were outnumbered. We knew then that even with an alliance, there's no way we could take the Crane mafia down!"

"Well, at least you figured that part out," Robby mumbles.

"I don't understand," I say quietly. "Where is Renza?"

"I don't know, Arianna. She vanished. We thought she was killed in the fire."

"She wasn't," Robby says. "Arianna said she left through the bedroom window."

"She did. But where did she go?" I ask. "She was talking to you. You have to have some idea."

Chad looks at all of us uncomfortably. We all know he's not telling us something. Josh kneels down in front of him. "You have a choice here, Ambrosio. You can either tell us what we want to know and make your death quick and painless. Or I can send Arianna back upstairs now and get that information out of you the fun way. You think Ryan Crane has a dark side? You've never come up against me."

His words send shivers down my spine. Ironically, I don't fear him in the slightest. But it's pretty obvious by Chad's wild eyes that he does. "I might be the only person saving you right now, Chad. It's really in your best interest to not keep anything from us."

"Your end isn't going to be different. Just the way you choose for it to happen." Robby boredly looks at his fingertips. "Personally, I'd like to see the kinds of horrors Josh could rain down on you."

"Okay! Okay!" Chad gives in. "She said she'd been talking to a powerful man. Someone that makes Ryan look like nothing. That's all she told me. She wouldn't say anything else. But she did say that she was brushing up on her Italian."

Josh stands with a nod and looks back at me. "Time to go, sweetheart. I don't want you down here for this."

"I told you what you wanted to know!" Chad tries to get out of the chair he's in but manages to do nothing but fall on his face. "Help! Help!"

I look up at Josh for a moment. He doesn't break eye contact with me. "Tell Ryan we'll be up in a minute." He gently guides me to the stairs.

I nod. "Okay."

I turn and start walking up them. Chad's screams, pleas, and cries for help ring through my ears. Oddly, I feel nothing for him. No regret. No remorse for what's about to happen. All I feel is this calming sense that, for once, my husband has someone on his side who is watching his back.

I thank God for Josh. He may not know it, but I do. I can feel it. This chapter of our lives isn't over. I truly feel deep inside that it's only just beginning. And while it scares the hell out of me, I'm comforted knowing that Ryan won't be battling this unknown force alone.

Chapter Twenty Nine

⚔ Ryan ⚔

I weave through traffic on the way to Lake Shore Drive in Chicago. A very, very prestigious neighborhood. Arianna is sitting next to me tapping out an email to Jamma, the manager of Eleven, the restaurant she fell in love with and bought. It was in trouble. She couldn't bear to see it close. With a new menu and lots of new staff, Eleven is doing incredibly well.

She drops her phone into the cup holder next to her. "I always forget I get carsick when I read or type. And then I hate myself for causing myself to get carsick."

I chuckle and hold out my hand for hers. She smiles and takes it. I entwine my fingers with hers and lift her hand to my lips, giving it a kiss. "Almost there, pretty girl."

She smiles and sighs. "I've been thinking. I love the penthouse, but maybe we should start looking at getting a house? Chris is going to be walking before we know it. And I really would like a nice backyard."

I smile and glance in the rearview mirror at my sleeping six month old. I had been right. We had a boy. And so had Jessa and Jason on the same day as us. Our kids are the same age. They'll be able to grow up together. Jessa and Arianna were happy as they could possibly be about it. Lyric has turned into one hell of an aunt. I knew she would.

After we had taken down Antonio Massena and Stephen Ambrosio a little over a year ago, we'd decided New York wasn't for us. It didn't feel like home anymore, but we didn't want to leave our family. After having a family meeting, Nick, my parents, and Jason and Jessa had decided they agreed. We all made the move to Chicago. We'd all been living in penthouses while construction had been being done to our homes.

Arianna, though, has no idea. There's been a lot of construction going on near Taylor's and Chase's houses. It's becoming a gated community. What she doesn't know is that the gated community is all for our family. Me, Jason, and Chase had all come together to buy out all of the homes in the area so that we could create our own neighborhood surrounded by our family. The neighborhood spans a few square blocks.

"That's a good idea. We can start looking if you want to." I pull into a driveway.

Arianna suddenly looks suspicious. "This isn't Taylor's house. Or Chase's."

I smile and nod. "You'd be correct."

She narrows her eyes at me. "What did you do?"

I laugh. My girl knows me too well. "Remember all of that construction going on here?"

"Yes..." She looks around and gestures. "It's still going on."

"Well..." I stop in front of a newly built house right next to Taylor's and point. All of our family is standing outside in front of it.

Arianna's mouth falls open. "No. Way."

"Yes, way. We own it. All of this actually. All of this property belongs to us. Our whole family." I jump out of our SUV and open the back door to grab our son. He coos at me and reaches for me as I scoop him up in my arms. Arianna lunges for Taylor as I follow behind. Luke and I both laugh.

"Hey, sweetheart." Taylor kisses her cheek as he catches her and lifts her off the ground. She wraps her legs around his waist and arms around his neck.

"Man... I share blood with her, and I can't get a greeting like that?" Luke teases.

Arianna smiles wickedly as Taylor releases her. Taylor shakes his head. "You're in for it now."

"You asked for it." I laugh

Luke looks at her suspiciously. "What are you doing?"

Nick smiles. "I made that mistake once."

Jason looks at him and laughs. "You won't do it again."

Arianna stalks towards Luke.

Taylor watches with his arms folded over his chest; a huge smile on his face. "I'm telling you. It's our thing. I expect what she's about to do. I prepare for it."

Luke takes a step back. We all laugh as Arianna lunges into his arms. She wraps her legs around his waist. He falls on his ass. Taylor doubles over laughing. Chase literally falls to his knees. Arianna kisses Luke all over his face as he attempts to shove her off. Tait joins in the fun and tackles Luke, as well.

I laugh along with everyone else. "Honey, I think he's learned his lesson."

"You think so?" She keeps Luke pinned. "Well? Did you learn your lesson?"

"Get off me! Lesson learned! Christ!" Luke bellows with laughter as Arianna gets up. He grabs Tait and starts tickling him until Tait is squealing with laughter and begging him to stop. Arianna reaches my side again and gives Chris a kiss.

I smile down at her. "Ready to see inside, beautiful?"

"So ready."

I look up at Taylor. "Taylor, did you guys get her surprise ready?"

"Yep. It's ready. Took all damn day."

Arianna smiles so brightly that she rivals the sun. "What surprise?"

Chase laughs. "Nice try. No way after all that work we're ruining it."

I look over at Jessa. "Jess, did you and the girls get the other surprise ready?"

"Yep! We're all set!"

Arianna bounces on her heels. "Come on. What surprise?"

Breetana shakes her head. "Nope. You won't be getting that out of us!"

Arianna pouts, but I can see that playful spark in her eyes. "You all suck."

"You'll love it, sweetheart," my dad says.

"And the tour!" mom says excitedly.

"Tour?" Arianna looks up at me.

"Tour." I take Arianna's hand and lead her inside the house.

"Oh. Wow." She looks around wide-eyed at the modern interior. The fireplace. The mantel. The giant TV spanning one entire wall.

"Down this hall are bedrooms, an indoor pool, and hot tub."

"There's also an outer pool. Which is so adorable!" Eve says bouncing as she looks towards the back of the house.

Sonya nods as her and Eve walk arm in arm through the house. "I plan on being over here every day of the summer in that pool."

We all laugh as I lead Arianna down another hall. Everyone else scatters to do their own thing as I give Arianna the tour of our new home.

"Down this hall there are more bedrooms and..." I tug her around a corner. "Surprise number one."

"Oh my Gosh. Ryan, it's..." She rushes to the sleek grand piano in the middle of the room and plays a few cords. I smile as Chris coos. We both love when she plays. She looks back at both of us, tears of happiness in her eyes. "It's perfect. I love it. The acoustics are amazing in this room."

Glass makes up three of the four walls in the room. There are green plants sporadically throughout the room. It overlooks the garden, which I made sure is stocked well with carnations and lilies.

She stands up and walks back to us. She hugs me and kisses my arm. "Is your arm getting tired yet from Chris?"

"Are you joking? You want him, you'll have to fight me." I give her a smirk.

She gives me a devilish smile. "Where's the nearest bedroom?"

I laugh. "After the tour." I lean down to kiss her as she pouts. She runs her hand across my zipper. I groan, my cock hardening immediately. "You're killing me, beautiful." I kiss her again before grabbing her hand. I walk with her through the rest of the house until we reach the kitchen.

"Hmm... And we've reached Mr. Crane's favorite part of the house."

I chuckle low in my throat. "Second favorite. First is our bedroom." I lead her upstairs as she laughs. "There are a few more rooms up here, but I think you'll like this one." I open the door. "Surprise number two."

"Oh, wow. I love it. And Chris loves his little stuffed owl. He'll love the mural of that one above his bed." Her fingers run across the snow white owl with his wings spread open soaring through the clouds. "And the pretty sky-blue on the walls. So pretty!"

"The girls decorated."

"It's gorgeous." She runs her fingers along the solid oak crib and looks at me.

"Ready to see the rest?" Chris snuggles into my shoulder and yawns. He bunches my shirt in his tiny little fist. I melt.

"You're so good with him."

I smile at her and hold my hand out. She takes it. I pull her out of the room. "Ready to see the master suite, Mrs. Crane?"

"More than ever, Mr. Crane."

I open the door to our bedroom. She explores the bedroom and bathroom before she says anything. Both are spacious. Everything a master suite should be. I even put in floor to ceiling windows that overlook the lake behind our house. I treated them with reflective glass. One way. No one can see in, but we can see out.

Finally, she turns to me. "You made sure there was a Jacuzzi tub."

"I know how much you loved the one in Australia. And the one we had in our wedding suite. I wanted to make sure our new house had one since the penthouse and our house in New York don't."

Chris has fallen asleep. I melt a little more. Arianna stands on her tip toes and pulls me down to her. Her soft lips mold to mine. I can't help but once again think how lucky I am. When she pulls away, she's smiling up at me.

"What, baby?"

"I smell barbecue. Is dad barbecuing?"

I laugh. My heart actually blooms at her considering my parents hers. "I'm sure he'll tell you it's all him, but Jason is really the Grill Master."

I lead her to the balcony off our bedroom. It overlooks the garden, pool, backyard, and the lake. Our entire property is laid out at our feet.

"God. It's beautiful."

"The only thing I don't like is there's no fence around the property. But since all of us live next to each other, I think we're going to fence all of our properties off as one."

"So…, you mean there will be free reign between all of our properties?"

"I think so. That's what we've been talking about anyway. But with the kids running around, we want the lake blocked off. What do you think? Think you'd be okay with that?"

She leans into me as I put my arm around her. "I'd love it. But we have to do it quickly. Tait is two now. And Chris and Jackson are going to be running around soon, too."

"Couldn't agree more, beautiful." I kiss the top of her head. "We have a lot more to see." I lead her back downstairs and outside.

Mom makes a beeline for us. "Need grandbaby time. Give him up."

"You have both Jackson and Tait. No way." She fixes me with her mom-look, and I relent. "Fine." She beams as she takes him from me.

Arianna laughs. "You're such a softy."

"Don't know what you're talking about." I teasingly, but roughly pull her with me.

She laughs again as she falls in step next to me. "What else is left to see?"

"A couple things. Guards quarters. And I know you want Luke close."

She looks up at me as we walk. "You mean…" I smile at her and lean down to kiss her. When I pull away, I point to a small cottage. Her eyes light up. "Really? He's going to really stay here?"

"Since his mom and Shane are together now and living here, he wants to live in something more than just the penthouse we set him up in. He'll have his own house in the community, but for now, this is what he wanted."

"I'm so happy. Really. Having Luke and Taylor close means so much to me."

I smile teasingly. "Me, Chase, Robby, and Jason don't come close, huh?"

She grins up at me and playfully pushes me. "You know what I mean."

"I know, baby." We continue walking. She pauses when she sees a garden and tilts her head. I smile when I see Josh hugging Lyric and whispering something in her ear. "Lyric has become pretty close to us."

"So, you made them a memorial," she whispers. "For little Jaxon."

I nod and smile as Josh sways with Lyric. "It's a place they can go to whenever they want to visit. A little corner just for them to be with each other and feel closer to their baby. I put a stone bench in there and a swing for them."

She sniffles and wipes her eyes as we continue walking. "I really love that they have a place to feel closer. That miscarriage was so hard on them."

I hug her a little tighter. She's not wrong. Lyric almost died. Josh didn't leave her side for months afterwards. When Arianna and Jessa delivered, it was the first time I think I saw Lyric smile; the first time I saw life in her eyes. I thought it would be a lot harder on her, but she loves the kids and is great with them. Even Tait has taken to her.

I stop in front of another structure and clear my throat. "This is the garage. Well, one of them. There are going to be several more on the property. They'll hold all of the SUVs. Robby will be living upstairs from this one. He asked to have a place of his own. Even if it was small."

"I love how much family means to you."

"A strong family bond is a strong foundation. If you don't have a strong foundation, you can't be successful." He leads me to an area near the lake where there's already a fire going in the fire pit. "These are all of our sitting areas. Robby wanted to hang out here later, so he started up the fire pits."

"I want the fence to encompass all of this. I don't want the kids to be cut off from family time down here."

"You want the fence before the rock wall down there?"

"I think that would be best. We don't have to worry about the kids getting into the water that way, but they can still run around and have fun."

"Anything you want, beautiful." I take her hand, and we walk back towards the house.

"What's that?"

I follow where she's pointing. There's another huge mansion next to ours. "That's the guard's quarters."

"Wow. I think it's bigger than ours."

I laugh. "We have twenty-four guards. Each needs their own room."

"That place looks like it has more than twenty-four rooms."

"Well, it has a state of the art gym. That was Taylor's demand, so they could train the way he wants them to. It has a pool and hot tub for cooling down. Of course it has a kitchen and a large common room."

We reach our house. Conversation and warmth surround us. Arianna turns to me and slips her arms around my waist. I pull her close and tuck a strand of hair behind her ear. I lean down to kiss her.

"I love you," Arianna says with a soft smile.

"I love you, too."

We both turn towards our family and enjoy the time we have with them. I watch as Arianna gets up and starts cooing at our son as she picks him up. Luke sits down next to me and hands me a beer. I twist the cap off and take a drink.

"How'd she take me and Robby being so close?" he asks.

"Just like I said she would. She's happy about it. She likes her family close."

He smiles widely. He stands up and heads towards the grill where Jason is trying to shoo our dad away. I lean back and sip my beer. My family is enjoying themselves. Everyone's happy.

Content.

The sun catches Arianna's hair. I can feel myself softly smiling. I don't care what comes our way. I can conquer the world as long as she's standing next to me.

Tait comes running towards me. I stand and scoop him up. He squeals in delight as I run around the yard flying him like an airplane.

I don't know what's going to come our way. I can feel this isn't over, but I know we can conquer the world.

As long as we have each other.

The End

Next In The Crane Family Series

The dark and sexy Crane Family Series continues with *His Heart*.

I don't know what's worse. Not knowing who killed my parents when I was ten years old, or being a kid alone in the streets of Manhattan. Luckily, I was saved by Ethan Crane, a mafia boss who treated me like his own son.

I made it my life's mission to avenge my parent's death. With the Crane Mafia's support, I've been close many times only to be led to a dead end. Still, we've never given up.

Then I met Dani Jade. Beautiful. Fiercely independent.

I made a promise to Dani that my family and I would keep her safe from the phantoms she's running from.

Unbeknownst to us, I'm her salvation, and she might be the key to my past. Her phantoms could be my demons.

To save her and get my revenge, I'm violently shoved back into the darkness I spent so many years separating myself from.

But I'll embrace my evil if it means saving the woman who managed to chip away the ice around my heart…

~ This book is a steamy Cop/Mafia Romance that has dark and violent themes, kidnapping, MM Romance (side characters), and strong language that may not be suitable for all readers. ~

Order *His Heart* Today!

The Crane Family Series

Available Now

The Reluctant Mafia King
Sweet Lies
Billion Dollar Love Story
Be Mine
Protecting Her
Dangerously Forbidden Love
His Heart
Love In The Dark

Box Sets Available

The Crane Family Series

Other Books By Melony Ann
The Beautiful Dream Series

Available Now

Loving You
My Love, My Heart
Softening Lyric
Undercover Temptations
Captain Charming
Breaking Boundaries
Crashing Into You
Tactical Inferno
Ravishing Our Queen
Cherished By The Texan
Unveiling Our Passions

Box Sets Available

The Beautiful Dream Series: Box Set: Part 1
The Beautiful Dream Series: Box Set: Part 2

The Deimos Trilogy

Available Now

Connor's Legacy
Aryan's Alpha
Kade's Redemption

Box Sets Available

The Deimos Trilogy

The Forbidden Temptation Series

Available Now

The Detective's Forbidden Temptation
The Running Back's Forbidden Temptation

The Lucinio Family Series

Available Now

Rising From The Ashes
The Player's Rebel
Encrypting My Heart

Multi Author Series
Piper Falls: Firehouse 49

Available Now

Ignite My Fire by Melony Ann
Regain My Fire by Kindra White
Playing With My Fire by D.L. Howe
Fight My Fire by Darley Collins
Against My Fire by Anneke Boshoff
Relight My Fire by Louise Murchie
Harness My Fire by Ayana Lisbet
Quench My Fire by Havana Wilder

Let's Be Friends

Follow me on

Bookbub

Facebook

Goodreads

Instagram

Tik Tok

Visit my website
www.melonyannauthor.com

Subscribe to my newsletter and get a FREE never-seen-before NOVELLA
just for subscribers!
https://www.melonyannauthor.com/exclusive-content

Join my Facebook Reader Group!
Jason's and Melony's Sizzling Book Nook

The official Crane Family Series Playlist on YouTube
https://youtube.com/playlist?list=PLGEiD5wbQmDc78K7gNeODh-
janqmIFiie

Dedication

Our love is as dangerous as it is beautiful.

Acknowledgements

Brad - I feel like I might say it too much, but I love you. You're my rock.

Laura - Again... I feel like I say it too much, but I love you. Sometimes, I don't think I could get through the day without you.

Jay - Thank you for being around to keep me from breaking.

Dan Rengering - Thank you for being Ryan. I wouldn't have done this without you. I never would have had the confidence without you having my back and giving me the nudge I needed to do it.

Ayana - Thanks so much for being in my corner always! I love you, girly!

Anneke - You're so very much my Girl Wonder. I love you to the moon and back.

Jason - I might run out of words eventually... I probably say it a lot, but I don't think I can say it enough. Thank you for everything you do for me.

To the Bookstagram Community.

To my family.

To all of those who believe in me and support me.

To all of those who don't.

Cover by: Carter Cover Designs

Edited by: Alyssa Skaggs

Cover Model - Dan Rengering

Photographer - Jean Woodfin of JW Photography

About Melony Ann

Melony Ann began writing short stories and poetry as a child. She continued honing her craft over the years until she took the plunge and began publishing her work, despite having severe anxiety.

Melony writes contemporary romance stories that are full of suspense and a lot of steam.

When she isn't writing, she is loving her family and working to make her life something she deserves.

Melony believes that if her writing can inspire just one person, then all of her hard work is worth it.

Her hope is that her writing allows each and every one of her readers to escape for a little while. To dive into a different world one book at a time.